About the Author

Angie Lem welcomes adventurers to worlds, characters and stories that shine the light on passionate and thrilling adventures. She originates from Macedonia, is an admirer of many things and ever since, creates works from the soul that display the very love that is found inside of them. A curious imagination, Angie Lem is one for expanding perceptions, travels, exploration and existence beyond the planet, Earth. The cosmos, as we know it, is an infinite sky of many unknown elements, homes and experiences yet to be discovered. Angie Lem begins with *Xira — Dawn Of Guardian*. Adventures await in the beyond!

Xira — Dawn of Guardian

Angie Lem

Xira — Dawn of Guardian

Olympia Publishers
London

www.olympiapublishers.com
OLYMPIA PAPERBACK EDITION

A CIP catalogue record for this title is
available from the British Library.

ISBN: 978-1-80074-329-8

This is a work of fiction.
Names, characters, places and incidents originate from the writer's imagination.
Any resemblance to actual persons, living or dead, is purely coincidental.

First Published in 2022

Olympia Publishers
Tallis House
2 Tallis Street
London
EC4Y 0AB

Printed in Great Britain

A shadow cast alongside the window, with the wind howling and brushing past the moonlit street. Everything else seemed silent, yet echoes of the distant neighbourhoods in a flurry burgeoned through the air, beginning to entwine with the wind. The TV from the next room was emitting static noise as the loud thumps on the front door seemed like it would break open any moment. Xira rolled off her bed, shoving her phone in a back pocket and glanced out the bedroom window. She noticed her mail box was knocked down on the lawn with envelopes sticking out, barely encased. Meanwhile, two purple robe locust trees were swaying in rhythm, occasionally brushing the front entrance cover.

The weather didn't appear to be subsiding anytime soon, but Xira didn't feel like staying put either. Grabbing a pair of fingerless gloves from the dresser and a Scooby-Doo themed flashlight from under the bed, she scurried to the kitchen to search the drawers and cabinets for any spare batteries. After clearing out each section, she slid over the bench and continued scavenging the living room and the cabinet on the other side of the room. No matching batteries were found, so she decided she'd improvise with whatever was left in the current pair and any recovered resources. While dashing around the house in the search, she started bringing items to the hallway, preparing everything from necessities to personal belongings. The lights throughout the house were becoming dim as the weather grew more tempestuous. Packing a woodlands backpack, almost every space was filled to the brim as the side and back pockets were the remainder of vacant spaces. She hurled it over her back and briskly made her way to the front door. Looking around, many thoughts and questions surrounded her mind. Pondering the safety of a cherished home ground, she reflected upon the pleasant and welcoming experience that was had here. If only this disquiet could nurture the comfort that is sought. What will protect the home that's been here for decades? Will it be graced by another's presence once again? Her thoughts flung about in the voices of ones' wisdom once shared... *This place contains much of the past and eras carved into these walls and floors, such a departure is quite remorseful. It would be sweet to bring this arcadian warmth and infinite treasures in the pockets as well. Once was a place that gave the care and safety, with an open, welcoming heart... a rarity in all sprouted universes. Although now, it's kept as multiple plants in a garden of infinite treasures, guarded by its myrtle vines.* Like she believed; home isn't solely one place… not the walls or gates, nor the streets or path-walks… it's everywhere *you* go, it's in your heart. *An immortal element inside ethos. Not always is a departure a sombre incidence, it often contains a mysterious memorandum to unravel. Light and darkness hold hands across fields like the sunset brushes the sea, an amity that floats through space. The moment that adventure howls with the wind, the full moon lights up the great epitome of paradise.*

Xira let out a sigh, as she glared out the front window, wondering what was happening out there. *Going forward is the only way out,* she thought, *I need to know what's going on, there's no sleeping through this. No matter the distance or magnitude, there's something ominous out there.* Without a doubt, she definitely was going to miss this place, but curiosity and the hunt for answers hold the helm. Before she closed the door, she quickly pulled out a miniature owl token from her front pocket, something she'd carried that belonged to an old mentor named Serenitatem, that once lived here and given shelter to her and an old friend, Jay'eo. She placed it on the plinth next to the wall, on her way out. Closing the door, she grabbed her phone, checking for signal. None. *Right. As assumed.* The street lanterns were barely flickering and the sky became even more cloudier, covering the glowing moonlight. Trees were whistling and flailing around, while a dog's bark resonated in the distance. As the torch provided enough light to guide the way, the force of the wind was quite a concern with the already perilous surroundings. Pushing forward, Xira shielded herself as much as she could from the gust, in the midst of maintaining direction and found herself at an intersection with an abandoned car on the right. There was nobody inside, as far as the windows revealed, but Xira was eager to find anybody who could provide some information. She walked over to the front passenger window and peered inside. The only things remaining were an old magazine, a bottle of whiskey, a slightly torn shirt, a fruit bar and a large handkerchief drooping from the dashboard. She grasped on the handle and slowly opened the door while bracing it with her left foot against the wind, then searched the area around the seats for any loose change. Aside from a small pocket necklace that was found in the glove compartment, the few items scattered about were the only leftovers. The necklace looked like it was partially opened, with the slide clasp that'd been broken off, but no initials as to who this had belonged to. Inside was a piece of a photograph that showed a little girl holding an umbrella and two colourful crystal fragments resting on a burnt handwritten note, which was partly tainted due to the flame and the dusty surface. Some of it read;

"…My dear Aunt Fiona…
…Thank you for being the loveliest auntie for me…
…I know you'll keep these safe,
Therefore, I trust you to keep my privacy.
With love…"

Xira turned the note to read the name that was written on the back. *Olive.* It appeared likely that the person who was in this car before it got abandoned was the Aunt Fiona that was mentioned in the note. She looked at the girl in the photograph once more, assuming it's a younger Olive from a certain time in the past. Those crystals seemed like they meant a lot to her, although a large chunk was missing from them, supposedly an event took place which caused her to only be left with what was in here. Placing the necklace on the passenger seat, Xira leaned in to grab the handkerchief and the torn-up shirt from the driver seat. She noticed a stain that was possibly from a warm beverage that Fiona was carrying, on both the seat and near a corner on the handkerchief. *I could use this,* she thought to herself, as she tucked the handkerchief in a front pocket of her jeans. The shirt wasn't exactly intact, but she figured the material may come in handy for something else. There was a side pocket that had sufficient space, so after folding and tucking it in, she picked up the necklace and placed it next to the shirt as well. The fruit bar contained a mixture of various ingredients including the town's most renowned cereal, *Fresh Crunch*. A tasty, nutritious treat for on the way and it was safely in its wrapper as well. She recognised the engraved whiskey bottle's brand *Logi*, meaning flame, which was a favourite to one of the inhabitants that lived with her a while ago. Kip would always bring one every week from the downtown liquor store, wave it in the air as he'd walk through the door, with a huge smile and a bellowing laughter every now and then, for how much he'd enjoyed that specific whiskey. It originated from an owner in a cosy town far on out where he and his merry friends lived, where they established their whiskey brand and would produce large quantities to import to as many thirsty folk out there. It was like a tradition, albeit Xira didn't drink, it was a humble moment each time to share the giddiness of a friend. The bottle had a few droplets left, but given that she had to choose, considering the necessity, she felt that the giant glass bottle could be helpful but the lighter the baggage, the further practicality raises the efficiency altogether.

She quickly flipped through the old *Cooking & Gardening* magazine that had a couple of briefly folded pages, which had some red and black ink markings on it. Skimming through those pages, she noticed a recipe that was circled, with an arrow pointing to the note written below the page.

"Olive would love this!"

Then another arrow pointing to the depicted image of the recipe; '*Mini Huckleberry Cakes decorated with fondant tulips*'. It had appeared that Fiona was either on her way to Olive's house or a downtown grocery store, according to the findings. Xira looked closer at the dashboard, checking the fuel gauge. Almost empty. She wondered whether the abrupt desertion was because of the fuel warning or some other occurrence. Leaving the car right here was questionable, as it's much safer to remain inside rather than getting in close quarters with this weather. As the wild breeze whirled through the gaps from between the door and seat, Xira knew she had to continue onwards, whether or not Fiona was nearby. Since the car was vacant, it didn't seem like someone would approach to steal it, as there wasn't any odd reason to — besides, there's already a lot going on around for anybody to have such a devious plan. Only taking some of the items with her, she thought about the odds of Fiona and Olive reuniting, if they would meet at a crossroad. Their bond appeared to be very special and it reminded Xira of a certain someone that once along a meadow had a warm and trusting connection with her as well. She grabbed the magazine, ripping the page where Fiona had marked the recipe and took it with her. Returning the rest of the magazine on the seat, she took one more look at the fruit bar but decided she'll leave it in there, just in case…

After closing the door, the force of the weather almost felt like it was going to shift the car. Xira continued down the road from before, noticing the street lanterns were sequentially waning while the distance was mostly covered in darkness and fog alike. Her torch only revealed so much, though it didn't help that there was debris up ahead. Carefully and quickly hopping over logs, street signs, pieces of metal and such, while lunging over larger chunks, she reached another intersection where the left lead to an enormous field, the right to the other neighbourhoods and stores towards the way too, except that there was a security border blocking the way, with tall flaring LED lights from each side. A number of people were circling the area, including security in their uniforms, talking with the others in line. Although there was some outdoor cover around the gates, every inch was barricaded with metal barriers, restricting pass to the people who had to check through the border to reach the path up ahead. Other than the other towns and the Ice Sphere that were located on that side, she wondered why it was solely this path that was particularly fortified. The Ice Sphere was one of the historical landmarks that was founded by a palaeontologist and astrologist from this town, Glacial Mist, where Xira lived. For over half a decade, their identity was well hidden due to many people wanting to discuss the discovery and pry on personal matters, meanwhile they were known as "the scientist from Glacial Mist, founder of The Ice Sphere", an icy covered sphere which exerted cool sublimation that formed a thin fog below its base, which was floating in reaction to its mystical features. It would make the surroundings seem like another world entirely. Much like Xira's town, the sparkles that drifted in the air created a galactic view if you should sit directly underneath it, therefore providing a mesmerising and tranquil experience. Enjoying a crystal view of the sky whilst the shiny and glittery substance that flowed about added to the mystical space that formed a shield to the outside world, revealing the true nature of the planet's atmosphere and its wonderful characteristics. An ethereal touch in the air, which felt like the sky's clouds had descended and fused with fairy floss, truly composing a galactic and chill atmosphere, as nature's sound whistled through the cool air and unveiled an aurora with the wonderful night sky.

Some people in the line were divided to the side, looking disappointed by whatever the guards told them. There was a baby wrapped in a blanket and hugged close by the mother, letting out a soft cry as she caressed her newborn. The surroundings were as sombre and vicious as ever, it felt like the desolation that was going down wasn't letting up anytime soon. One of the men that was standing beside their companion walked up with a newspaper to a guard on the side.

"Silence… covers the page?" he exclaimed, waving the newspaper near the guard's face, "Nothing to tell anyone what in the fresh hell is going on? Mayhem! Mayhem, I tell you!"

The guard with a mere impassive expression stared nonchalantly in the man's face. No response whatsoever, just a slight gesturing shove to the side. The others in line were growing just as flustered as the man with the paper. Another guard walked up to the barriers, grasping a young man by the back of his jumper and muttered something in a raspy tone to a guard standing at the front. The boy looked baffled and was taken to a security truck with the label 'PBTU' and a logo with a symmetrical letter 'Y' mirroring the one below it in engraved plaster. Xira wondered what it meant and why they were deploying checkpoints, given that these forces haven't been around here before. They didn't appear to be so kind, let alone give any respect to citizens who were alarmed and rushing to get out. Something was going on that they didn't want to expand on, to inform the people that the matter surrounding them is responsibly administered. This kind of weather was quite an extremity for these neighbourhoods, so it seemed a larger phenomenon was involved that fostered all this havoc, despite that it's an otherworldly mystery, it's rising Xira's suspicion, that something rather ominous was marking the land.

An hour had gone by. The line was barely dispersed, as the space around was getting occupied now that more citizens arrived. A few of the previous ones had managed to get through, although it had appeared that they'd have to be carrying some form of pass to get the gates opened for them. In any case, Xira didn't have what they were looking for, but there had to be a way or another. She rested on a log by the left side of the intersection, looking at the field ahead, while staying covered from the gusts as best as possible. Comfort was sparse here, making it even more so that one of the guards standing directly under the checkpoint cover was glaring as if he was inspecting her every trace. She put her hands together, twisting them around for extra warmth. Although her gloves provided well enough, the fingertips were catching the icy-cold. Pulling her hoodie over her head, she grabbed and held up the collar of the jacket over her nose, then pulled the lapels closer together to huddle and warm up. Slight drizzles of rain began to appear on her combat boots

— she looked up as droplets fell to her face and noticed a few light flashes across the sky. Immediately, a booming crash was heard in the distance, as something plummeted down to the ground from above, far ahead in the fields by the speed of light.

The surrounding smoke travelled towards Xira's location, making the atmosphere foggier, as many heads turned simultaneously, coughing when the thick areas of the smoke got intense. Fortunately, she had her face covered, though the fog was still passing through with the gusts. Once the air had cleared, the panic of the people was pushed further in disarray, as they all flailed furiously while shouting at the guards to open the gates to their escape. Eventually, the commander of that dispatched faction stepped out from one of the larger trucks and walked towards the crowd while carrying a device that had a circular frame above the handle, making a static cyber noise. The crowd muttered in confusion, staring at the device in the commander's hand. They huddled in closer, shouting to let them all through but the guards quickly encircled the people and ordered them to form two clean lanes. It extended through the street from where Xira arrived, with families trying to stay together while they were getting frisked. More of the people were sent through and the line got shorter, although a fair number were escorted to either the trucks or the right corner of the intersection. A couple of them at a time walked through the checkpoint, as the commander slowly paced up and down the sides, hovering the device above them while they moved towards the gates. A few others had arrived, unsure of the situation before them. Some sat near the area where Xira was, along the curb and on the grass hills further down. It was past midnight, as the giant digital time above the checkpoint flashed the hour. The mellow sound of chimes and birds were heard nearby, when a vibration rasped from her back pocket. Xira's phone was ringing, but abruptly stopped when she got another notification chime. Quickly pulling her phone out, she noticed the new messages appear on her lock screen with the recent call. She opened the messages to find that they were all from her dear friend Willow, who had been searching for her. The four messages showed up like a paper scroll.

MistNet OS ◖》 *&G* ▥ *98%* ▮*12:08 AM*
(1 missed call)~ Received: 12:04am {!}(4 new messages) ~ Received: 11:45pm > 11:55pm > 12:00am > 12:06am {!}

From:WILLOW~ {1}<WILLOW>{11:45pm}

Hey! Where are you? I dropped by but nobody was home. What the heck is going outside? Please reply asap!!!

—————————————<>———————————--{2}{11:55pm}

Uhh, I'm near the fountain and there's a bit of cover here, so please contact whenever you get this. We should meet by the orchard that's up north.

—————————————<>———————————{3}{12:00am}

Ok so there are some weird guys with trucks rolling around the streets, they look suspicious… please call when you can and be careful!

—————————————---<>———————————--

{4}{12:06am}

Hey I'm getting concerned… is your phone charged? Are you somewhere safe? I'll go somewhere else with a better signal… please, call.

—————————————--<>———————————---

Just as Xira was about to call Willow back, a shout blared from far behind her. She turned to realise that it was indeed her friend running towards her, swinging a bag on one arm. It was a delight to finally be greeted with a friendly and familiar face. Willow's facial expression shifted from astonished to concerned within a second of contact. She dove in for a hug, while keeping her stance, making sure they weren't going to capsize on the ground.

"This bloody town, I swear… it feels like the start of an Armageddon," she spoke, catching her breath, "Were you at this crossroad all this time? What happened here?"

Xira uttered a quiet laugh while observing the vast field ahead, but as she was about to reply, a guard jogged up to interrupt the girls with another device.

"Are you heading this way? We'll need to do our safety procedure if you choose to cross this checkpoint, oh and you'll both need one PBTU pass each." He stated, pointing behind him.

Willow looked at the device in his hand, then exchanged a quick glance with her friend, before looking towards the gates. The guard seemed to be in a hurry, despite that he was smelling of cigarettes — even if he had recently returned to his shift, some of his comrades seemed to leave more than staying on location.

"Well actually, we were thinking of taking a different route, more to our liking," responded Willow with a slight shrug, gesturing towards Xira.

"Suit yourselves. I have to get back to my duties, as it is to check up on each possible pass holder," he replied, "though I would recommend you find a safe one, only very few provide absolute security."

"May I ask, what is—" Willow was attempting to question the situation, but the guard quickly dismissed her halfway with his blunt answer.

"I'm sorry, distributing that information is strictly forbidden for all of us stationed here and every other checkpoint." He walked off with a nod of farewell, as both of them stared him down in suspicion.

The lanes were rolling slowly with the cries of newborns and toddlers from some of the families grouped together. It was evident that this circumstance was quite overwhelming for a lot of the people here, including some of the patrolling guards. Rain poured heavily across the crowd, as Willow stuck her hand out to feel its spear-like drops, along with the guidance of the wind breezing through, whistling an enchanting melody.

"Anyway… You were saying?" she spoke, resuming their previous conversation. Xira turned her attention to a young man running up to them, holding up a bundle of papers. He sounded exhausted as he was catching his breath.

"Hey, I hope you don't mind… I wanted to ask you both something," he began, "I've only lived here for a couple of months and it's not exactly like every other neighbourhood that you'd come across, hah… So, these maps…uh—" exhaling, he handed a few over to them. Willow looked at the man with surprise as she showed him the page which had a layout of a part of the neighbourhood, where a "back exit" was etched in the corner of the map. She pointed at the markings made next to it with an underlined key word, "Revi".

"Is this what I think it is? How do you know about this?" she questioned him eagerly.

The man frowned as he looked at the page, but glanced up with a corner grin, hiding the rest of the papers inside his coat.

"Of course, yes that was uh, given to me by one of the librarians that had lived here for a long time. She was very friendly, claimed that it was a hidden or somewhat mythical tale told by previous ancestors that were here," he explained, "The information…was only passed down to a certain amount of folk who could be trusted to keep it a secret unless it was an urgent matter, as such. So, I assume this is the location she talked about? Revi? I certainly hope it's not hazardous, or uh, closed."

"What was her name?" Willow seemed to be on her toes, unsure whether to trust this person with how he seemed as if he wasn't telling them everything, "No one is supposed to know about that, not even the loyalists… who are, by the way, an overall home code for, ones who have lived here indefinitely." she waited for his reply, but he seemed speechless and rather frightened.

Xira looked at Willow and the man, analysing the subject in front of them and their responsive emotions. She laughed under her breath, but kept quiet for the moment. Knowing she couldn't trust him either, she too wanted to know the intel he had been given by this particular librarian.

"I… pardon me, like I did mention, I have only lived here awhile. Certainly, you're not new around this neighbourhood, so I'm sure we can meet halfway on this." He continued, "Between you two and me, I'm not entirely comfortable going through this exit, with all these… patrols and security alike." He seemed to be somewhat of an honest person for the most part, but Willow was still in awe about what he was told. She was still dwelling on the matter that he hadn't mentioned the librarian's name or why he was given this secured information. It wasn't a secret that there were a few ways to enter and leave the place, but Revi was one of the ancient tales of Hidden Portals where there were owls at night with glowing red eyes that would surround the grounds with thorns, leaving only the path through. Marked as a treacherous area and specifically closed from any passers-by, it was known to scare away any daredevils whom come across it. Therefore, the ancestors from that time of discovery had vowed to keep it hidden and to pass it down to no one but between their mouths and ears.

Willow locked eyes with the man once again, her feeling of discomfort colliding with warnings. Calmly putting her hand on his shoulder, holding the maps in the other, she politely but firmly questioned him again.

"What was her name?"

There was a silence, a waiting in between the large drops of rain splashing and the whistling of the wind. A frightened expression appeared across the man's face, with a worrying look in his eyes. He seemed to be caught up in a thread that he didn't intend to meet with. The thought of blackmail circled about Willow's thoughts but she was keeping her composure, gliding away from stating any accusations. The man exhaled before pointing at the maps she was holding under her bag.

"Her name was Erma. Seemed like a woman in her forties... well..." he spoke rather quietly but huddled in, "she knew of my recent arrival in Glacial Mist and wanted to uh... give me guidance of a sort, I suppose — to present me the land as she knows it, or parts of it, as shown on these papers." He opened his coat slightly to show an inside pocket with the etched maps.

"Why couldn't she give you a tourist map like many others have received before? The library always has a huge amount to give out and it has everything you need on there, including gateways," replied Willow, her suspicions growing.

"That's what she said to me... that this was the absolute layout of the land, with all its tales and secrets. I was surprised that she chose to confide in a total stranger about things nobody else should have apparently uncovered, although she did give me this red hexagonal gem to keep, for "a blessing". It's not with me right now but it was sweet of her." He explained, slowly looking down at the paper that Willow was holding, with a grin, "I know she's probably one of those librarians that love to have a warm conversation, besides having to lodge in books and monitoring cabinets. It's still baffling that she has this tale in her pocket but she's indeed full of question marks. You did say this was an ancestral protected secret. She's usually there at night, as she mentioned she prefers the late hours."

Willow handed over the rest of the papers back to the man. Understanding where he was coming from, both girls knew they needed to get more answers. They noticed the lines were receding and filling up simultaneously, keeping the guards busy as ever with minimal disputes. It was a good distraction for their conversation. Xira noticed the partially soaked papers that Willow was trying to keep dry underneath her bag before, as the man tucked them inside the other pocket of his coat.

"Whether you leave tonight or not, don't speak to anybody about any of this — Please rid of those papers." Willow declared with a serious tone.

"You got it," he replied, tucking the coat in. As he was leaving, she called out to him.

"And your name?" she quickly asked.

"Jerril Hank," he responded kindly, then continued walking off. The crackling of a megaphone could be heard close by, from one of the PBTU trucks. A tall lieutenant with a fancy hat and brooch was testing it. Xira and Willow exchanged glances as they hurried to a nearby tree, covering up from the downpour. Thinking over what Jerril had told them, they both still had their suspicions and missing answers regarding the librarian known as Erma. Xira opened up the online directory on her phone to search the name, but strangely it did not show up. Since the name wasn't a prevalent choice in this town, it was all the more alluring. It was a mutual agreement that this was a dilemma which soon needed a way out. Both girls' attention was directed towards the front space of the crowd, where the tall lieutenant was standing with the megaphone, looking around and unfurling his umbrella, which was specifically sent from their organisation that had their logo scotchgarded on the canopy. Xira quickly put her phone away, as Willow grabbed her bag in case of a sudden flee. The commander from before stood beside the lieutenant, still holding the device with the circular frame while he placed his hands behind him, awaiting the announcement.

"We have to disperse," he began, perusing the crowd, "Our next station has been assigned as of now — evacuation commences in thirty minutes. You must have your passes for we will not offer liberation to those who oppose. This is the guaranteed procedure to get you all through to a secure base, fail to comply and heed the warning of that which is termination of a second gate, therefore... either a cell or desertion..." The lieutenant made his way back to a truck, opening up a crate, which had the same logo that was seen on the trucks with the symmetrical and mirrored letter 'Y' engraved in white plaster. Xira noticed he was rummaging around the inside, what seemed to be filled with equipment from their own suppliers. The angst and pandemonium of the crowd coursed like waves of a forthcoming storm.

Willow turned to Xira, grabbing her by the arm like an idea just formed. Although it was more of a panicking reaction.

"We have to leave, they can't find us hiding here. They'll know we don't have passes and—" she was cut off by a loud crash similar to before, only betiding in the opposite direction, to the distant right. Quite alarmed, Willow looked at Xira once more with eagerness as without a thought, they began pushing through the crowd, holding hands and guiding each other towards the way to the field on the left. Discreetly enough, they made their way out and inconspicuously darted past the corner and into the shadows. While they ran, most of the field was illuminated whenever the moonlight broke through the cluster of clouds, though they made sure to stay hidden in the darker areas. Xira's torch helped light the way but the occasional flickering gave them an adrenaline rush which felt exhilarating as creating their own escape.

"Look," called out Willow, pointing ahead, "there's a couple of rocks underneath that bridge curve, we can rest there for a little bit. Good temporary cover, too."

They placed their bags in front of them as they climbed up on top of the rocks and sat beside each other. Watching the rain splash on the ground, it almost seemed like tiny pieces of rocks in formation. Herds of people passing across the bridge above were shouting and chanting simultaneously, with some of the security minding the edges as a few of them exclaimed orders over megaphones and various sirens. Xira looked ahead of the field, noticing a steep hill leading somewhere below. It'd appeared to be covered in ice on the surroundings and smoke was steaming from the surface like frost flakes. She grabbed her bag, putting her torch away and pulled out the pocket necklace, examining it again on her lap.

"So, do you want to continue our conversation? About what happened over there?" Willow asked.

Xira sighed quietly, as she observed the view and the locket again. She dangled the chain across her hand, trailing it along.

"Early wind, early storm… the rain was a peace offering," she replied calmly, "I was walking down the road, found this car… abandoned… kept going forward and lots of debris was everywhere. Then arrived at that checkpoint. Only, it wasn't as crowded yet but something felt quite peculiar about it."

A siren blared from over the bridge, as raucous footsteps followed along the concrete. More shouting combined with muffled cries collided.

"I wonder how long that checkpoint has been there. Could be hours. Do you think there's more of them near here? Did you run into anybody from the neighbourhood?" questioned Willow while retying her hair.

"I secured the house, no one else was inside. Jay'eo has his phone though, it probably requires charging but it always does. The streets were practically a ghost town, so charmingly serene." Xira leaned back on her right elbow, resting the necklace in her palm, "It was like a noir raven tune snowed the entire town."

Willow nodded in awe of how mysterious this all was and everything going on out there spiralled all of the towns in a wild vortex ride. What once was a distant echo was now a close encounter.

"The only way out is through," Xira continued, "I left the owl token that Serenitatem gave to me long ago, it should protect the grounds now that it is unoccupied. Hopefully if someone from the kin returns there, will know and understand of the message and pass it along to the others… if they're still around… at least some of them."

The pools of water that was absorbed by the grass began to create muddy piles around the gaps in between the rocky textures, followed by a cloud of thick smoke emerging from the direction which they'd arrived from, slowly making its way towards the field, accompanied by tall silhouettes and a sound of an engine. Both of them immediately grabbed their things and leaped off the rocks, bolting down the muddy grass. Splashing and sliding, they did not look back as they spotted a couple of sand barriers scattered up ahead. Without scrupling, they rolled over the ones near the bridge while swinging their bags above. Peeking from the edges, the silhouettes neared as the smoke was thinning out, revealing them up-close. They were armed, wearing large gas masks, dressed in seaweed green overalls and marching with a mini mud truck behind them.

Willow leaned close to the ground, clutching the side of the barrier. "Why are they carrying those weapons?" she whispered alarmingly.

"We'll keep watch. Just stay low." Replied Xira, on the other side.

The truck rolled to a halt, as a few of the masked jumped on the back. One of the others was unloading cases from a munitions' chest, storing the weapons they were carrying.

"FTs are in?" the driver leaned out, sounding hoarse. One who was sitting at the back banged twice on the side of the truck, as the unloader hopped on and took a seat. The engine roared as they slowly continued forward with some of the masked still walking beside the truck. Xira spied from the top of the barrier, keeping low as possible as they now had placed a vehicle light that would rotate to scan the surroundings. Carefully, the girls walked over to the other barrier to keep track of the masked. They'd created a good distance between them, allowing some reflection space before deciding on their next objective. Chatter could be overheard between the masked, but it turned more muffled the further away they went.

"That's strange… what do you think they were saying?" asked Willow quietly, alternating between looking at her friend and the truck.

"They mentioned FT's. That must be what they were carrying and as bizarre as it may sound, it seemed like they meant flamethrowers," Xira noted, "and these people weren't with the guards before, so they're just another wicked group to be vigilant towards."

Looking out into the distance, the field seemed like it vanished into the horizon, where the mountains were located. Moments later, they continued their voyage in the rainfall, as Willow yanked out a picnic blanket she had tucked in her bag, pulling it over themselves to create a decent cover for the meantime. Their next point of interest was the icy hill up ahead, suddenly emitting a fluorescent glow around the icy exterior. The smoke emerging from the surface was resembling blue frost flakes, as the area grew colder the closer they were approaching. Observing around the hill, they found what seemed to look like a chasm of a sort, just below the hill's point. As Xira leaned in to examine the frontier, a thunderous sound clapped with a purple neon light zipping across the sky, towards the direction which the truck had gone, on the left valley path. The icy smoke started to drift along the grass, gently, then swiftly surrounding them, as a spheric ball of light, with swirls of white, light blue and black orbiting the floating sphere emerged in front of them, with a twinkling glow — like communicating to let it guide them somewhere. Hovering higher, it began sailing through the wind, signalling to them with a sweet, mystical flute whistle.

They kept close on its trail, a glowing shadow painting the soaked grounds after each footstep, then absorbing into the soil as they ventured further. Arriving at a cave's entrance, the sphere dove into the darkness and for a little while there was silence.

Putting her bag down, Willow wrapped the blanket on the handles.

"Do we go in?" she whispered.

A whistling sound of a flute echoed through the cave, with a glow that sparkled for a brief second.

"That's our call," replied Xira, treading closer, "The light's inside."

Examining the sides of the cave, Xira pulled out her torch while laying her bag on the edge of the entrance. Shining around, she gestured to Willow as she followed closely, resting her bag near Xira's. She brushed on an icicle covered stalactite, as it left a frosty texture on her fingers. Walking towards what appeared as embers from a previously kindled campfire, a purple trace of neon liquid revealed a trail. They continued onwards, noting each step and direction, while the torch flickered more, each time they approached closer to the destination of the trail. The space seemed to grow darker but the sufficient glow of the torch and the neon liquid was their promising lead and guiding them truthfully. The whistling flute tune echoed again, getting slightly louder the closer they were to the origin. After making various turns and crouching through a few rocky crevices, the area grew colder, darker, yet longer as the paths seemed to resemble a slide except it was a bumpy platform extended as the path forward to the tune. Following the corner which had a couple of rocks on the way, Willow gasped as she held onto Xira, feeling in awe about what they'd just discovered.

The sphere was indeed whistling the tune as it glowed brighter to reveal a circular space which appeared to be the destination that it had been wanting them to find. Xira placed her torch in her other back pocket, just enough to keep it safe as the space was already full of the colours and light that the sphere had provided with the sparkles and glow of its mystical aura. Completely transforming the encompassed cavernous spot into an empyrean bliss, they made their way forward, as Willow gently followed behind and the orb transcended through the cave, emphasising with a beam on a carved stone that was resting on the bottom of the wall, with engraved letters that read;

"Spirit of the light, the ever-watchful guide, shall always be with you by your side, all day and all night."

As they read it in a whisper, orange glowing symbols appeared sequentially above each word of the message. A crackling was heard beyond the cave's walls, as a vicinal yawn, heralding something curious amidst, rumbled deep beneath the crumbling soil while the dust on the surface rose to float like sand underwater, as it cascaded further grounds. The sound of the wind echoed around the cave, as it flurried past the entrance. While Willow was scraping the floor, looking for the traces of neon, she subtly leaned on Xira as she turned around. The glow in the corner had lifted to the brim of the area's rocky dome, coating the walls while it descended to the stone's edges.

"What just happened? That... sphere thing... disappeared. How are we getting out of here without that trail?" she asked worryingly. Xira examined the stone, brushing across the symbols. The orange glow had smeared onto her fingers and over her gloves. Noticing the glow getting brighter on her hands, she brushed across the floor where they'd stepped a few moments ago. Intriguingly, she continued on forward while crouching, as the liquid powder substance traced the tracks from before, along with the print of the purple neon trail.

"Brilliant. This should bring us back to the entrance — follow closely and carefully," Xira informed, as they made their way. Throughout some of the turns, ledges and rocky surfaces, the space seemed to give the sinister feeling of something lurking about and all the peculiar aspects of unearthing the depths. As they approached closer to the amplified icy gusts flowing through, the trail was marking a boulder projecting from underneath that they hadn't come across on their way in. Xira grabbed her torch to examine — albeit its gleam was quite sombre, it sufficed to reveal a way through. Putting her torch back, she felt around the edges and above the openings. The trail continued over the other side of the boulder, which evidently connected to the downward path. It could just about get them through with each other's help, as it wasn't a smooth and spacious gap. Gripping on the boulder, Xira pushed with her foot on the side wall, lifting her other foot over and between the two surfaces.

"Quick boost?" she signalled to Willow while tapping her dangling foot on the boulder. After launching herself over, a brief scrape was heard, followed by a low growl.

"Everything okay over there?" asked Willow, partially leaning on the wall. For a moment there was silence and the sound of the growl nearing closer, "Xira?"

The muffled sounds of action and sporadic thuds were overheard by

Willow which led her to feel anxious and believe there was a threat on the other side. Whatever was lurking, she was desperate to get to her friend and find out what was happening. She forced herself above the boulder, barely clinging onto its sides as she propped her right foot in the corner of the gap, retaining her position and attempting to push through as much as she could, all while keeping her attention to the matter at hand. Suddenly, a fierce cry echoed through the cave, movements and footsteps accompanying as well. The silence that followed rendered like a tune of the dark cave in all its mysterious aura, as the cold breeze rushed through the cave's hall and softly touching Willow's face. Quiet steps and the whistling wind were approaching towards Willow's gaze, while she harrowingly awaited the figure emerging from the dark depths. Uncomfortably clutching with all her might, she heaved a brief sigh, trying to sustain her composure. It was rather quiet, even with the gusts.

"Need help?" a voice called out to her in a slightly low tone. Xira walked up to grab and pull her over.

"What the hell happened? You scared me, XiXo!" cried Willow, latching onto her arms in a bear-like hug. They continued down the rocky hall, tracing the trail as Xira had already illuminated the path with the unique substance. There was silence between them for a little while as they quickly made their way closer to the entrance.

"Well... what WAS that, then? I know that something strange was in here," Willow eagerly asked, staying close to her friend.

"Nothing virtuous of your gracious and attentive efforts." Xira replied solemnly, brushing along the icy walls with the tip of her fingers, the purple imprinted trail almost fusing with the floor, as they greeted the cave's opening with the weather resembling a snowy atmosphere. They grabbed their bags, to find that they'd been tampered with and there were items missing. Frantically searching through all of the pockets, almost the entirety of their bags had been emptied, with only a few of their belongings remaining. A book was left open near where they'd been, with a chemical liquid stench exuding from the papers.

"Can I use your torch for a second?" spoke Willow in a soft voice, sounding quite brittle. Xira gently glanced at her friend and back at the rainfall, as she put her bag down in front of her.

"It's broken. Lens are shattered, the damn twisty thing flew off in there... so did the centre piece and button compartment..." she told her.

"Though the batteries were wearing out too... so."

Willow knelt to take a look at the book, feeling its covers and sifting through the pages. Her eyes watering, she started to sniff, to withhold getting too upset, but it had gotten quite overwhelming. Xira caressed her friend's shoulder, as the tears on Willow's cheeks trickled down her face and gently fell on her scarf. She lifted the book for display, while Xira knelt next to her.

"This belonged to my mother," she uttered, her voice thickening, "it was her 'everything and eternity' journal, she would put all of the things that she wanted to tell me and... a motherly guide... I recall... with the guru formulae."

"All of the pages are ruined?" asked Xira, looking at the book. Willow wiped her face, slowly closing the book firmly, placing it back in her bag.

"I need more light to check each page. For now, I really don't want to think about it, ugh... how... it — I need to cool off. Can we please just go?" She answered as she stepped out into the rain, without her blanket cover this time. Xira hauled her bag over, as they walked off to the right. Some time went by and the wind seemed to lighten with a wintery feel, while the rainfall was calming and refreshing, droplets of icy cold splashing on the muddy outlines of the field, forming swampy puddles that resembled pudding. The smell of smoke wafted in their direction, indicating that something was burning nearby. As the intensity gently solidified, they spotted a lone camp ahead, with small benches surrounding a fire barrel in the middle. It had a brief cover, but no sign of containers or gear left behind.

"Strange... but hey we sure need this," Willow remarked, cautiously approaching it.

They scanned the area in case of any campers, then continued to examine the camp. After sitting down, they rubbed their hands together against the barrel to warm up, the glowing light of the fire reflecting in their irises. The air they exhaled morphed into swirls and waves of cloudy fairy floss, entwining with the smog arising into the atmosphere. Looking at her gloves, Xira noticed the orange substance had vanished, with only earthly textures of dirt, flecks and dried blood grazed within the threads and across her fingertips. She glanced down at her boots, which had also been smeared and scratched on the vamp and heel area.

Spotting a silver lighter next to the barrel, she picked it up and felt around the exterior, examining the etchings on the lid. It had no initials or brand name, just a tiny skull symbol on the bottom corner of it.

"Someone was recently here," she observed, rolling the spark wheel while examining the surroundings, "This lighter had been used, possibly held for a certain period of time. Still feels warm... You know we crossed this path, this wasn't here before. They could still be around... we should get going."

Just as Xira was about to get her bag, Willow abruptly grasped her arm, her mouth gaped open and brows furrowed.

"What happened... what did that to your face?" she questioned, glaring at the fresh scar down her cheek.

They settled back down, both in silence, holding their bags near them. Xira was fiddling around with the lighter, opening and closing it as the sparks lit up more each time. Taking a breath, putting one foot on the go, she looked at the grey smoke lifting in the night air.

"I don't think I should be telling you this... it's a breeze... we've got to go and find out what's going down," she replied quietly.

"Xi..." returned Willow with heed.

"Will," mimicked Xira, giving her a quick corner glance. The crackling in the barrel sounded with the burning sparkles that appeared quite like fireflies emitting smoke. A sea of rainfall refreshingly splashed while the smell of the smoke provided a rather peaceful, cool feeling.

"It was a stranger...spawn of inhumanity...a bastard," she explained, looking at the blazing fire, the flames harmonising with the fire in her eyes and soul — throughout this wintery night. "His vile acts with disgusting immorality, to unknowingly attack somebody... apathetically... ugh, he... saw me as a threat. Carrying some gears with him, all dangling from his waist down... then engaged in a skirmish, there was a metal hook with spikes by his flashlight... so I disarmed him quickly, dismissing any further nonsense... he was about to lay another hand on me so... I had to... I had to... I have to keep going... The only way through is forward."

"Oh, my goodness... Xira... I — had no idea, you — I'm so sorry. I completely understand, though you did a good thing. You saved us. Defence in any form is a survival morale and the outcome is definitely not your fault — he chose to attack you, that's his misfortune." Humbly expressed Willow, putting her arms around Xira.

"Hm… it'll heal and perform as another symbolic mark, much like this natural birthmark on my wrist that Serenitatem informed me about… but kept it mostly a secret though, from any of us who had one according. Said it was nicer and more magical if the secret was discovered by the soul themselves. Jay'eo used to say it was like a holy tattoo ink, hm… how I miss him too — anyway… the bastard must've come from the masked from a while ago, they were the only other ones roaming around here," she pointed out, sliding her foot backwards, kicking mud in the air.

"Y'know, maybe we sh—" just as Willow started to talk, a revving noise accompanied by a group of grumbly voices neared their location.

They went silent as they spotted another truck like before heading their way with more of the masked ones. Immediately, they hauled across the benches and ran back towards the direction of the cave. In the midst, Willow dropped her blanket that she was about to use for camouflage in a mud pile. The masked were directly behind her as Xira urged to let go and move on, but her friend was already crouching to pull it out of the mushy clump. Dragging it across the glistening grass and occasional rocky terrain, she tried to catch up to grab Xira's hand but one of the masked launched a net to entrap her feet, tripping her on a muddy patch, blaring out a warning as she'd been detected by their truck lights.

"No!" Shouted Xira, watching Willow pull herself up and further away from them. Despite her efforts, she felt the desperation in that situation and turned over to attempt to untangle the net. A masked one jumped out of the truck and shone a light while running towards her. Then another followed, with another joining shortly after them. Growing furious, Xira bolted to the truck, jumping on the hood and leaping on the one behind the other two, knocking him down. Then immediately targeted the one in front and climbed him, while gripping and snaking his upper body, with her foot knocking a metal weapon out of his hand. He was reaching for his side gear but she brutally kicked his arm away, forcing him to surrender to the ground. Meanwhile, the one attacking Willow was standing over the net, trying to pick her up as she used her bag to wham him off while reaching into the zip for a possible weapon. Hearing her cry, Xira yanked him by the back of his overalls, wrapping one arm around as she grappled his shard-like weapon from his hand and sticking it into his leg. Shoving him off, she went to pull up Willow while helping her untangle the net. Seconds later, the driver got out of the truck, angrily approaching them while stepping over his group as the truck lights outlined his silhouette, showing that he was carrying something larger than their usual gear in his arms. Sensing that he was about to swing, she dived to the side while Willow pulled out a can and sprayed his face. He dropped the gear and tumbled around for a moment before slapping Willow as she just got the net off of her. Xira ran to the truck to find something to even the odds against this gigantor, while he eased closer to her friend who was struggling to get up and away. She searched the crates in the back, feeling for what was in there. After grabbing a spear-shaped weapon that could be extended in length just by using the bottom buttons, she launched herself with a swing to knock him on the side. Furious, he turned to stomp towards her as Willow carefully got on the knees while Xira sprinted over the truck, aiming the spear in his direction. He leaped on the roof to try and get the jump on them, as Xira slid across with the spear to cover her companion and focus him down. With another attempt, he threw himself above them as Xira sprung to the left and Willow pushed his torso, sending him over with a graviton launcher that he dropped before, watching him land on the hood of the truck with a bang. Xira noticed her friend dropping the weapon while getting up and the man gaining some leverage, reaching for his pockets. He pulled out something quickly and angularly threw it at Willow, who within a second exclaims in pain. A metal shard incised her leg, as Xira dashed to push him over to the ground. Aiming her spear and glowering at him, she placed a foot on his torso as a final warning. The moonlight shone through the cluster of clouds again, as the rain fell around them and the wind eased after a few quiet moments. She checked on her friend who was holding down her wound, crying softly in between. Turning back to face him, she lowered her gaze and glanced towards his slumped group.

"You're going to give us your truck. You're going to get far away from here without ratting us out. No one should know of this, not even your sector — or so help me." Xira demanded, raising her spear. The masked man slowly placed his hands back as he lowered his feet to the ground, splashing some mud. She rushed to the aid of her friend, helping her up to the truck and grabbing the shard from her. Upon entering the front seat, she threw the spear behind the crates, then closed the door. Willow wrapped a piece of cloth she had in her bag around her wound, keeping it warm and secure until they had visited a safe spot. Before she revved up the engine, she opened up the glove compartment and any other spots just in case they contained any weapons or gear. A slingshot device was in the front, a little advanced than the usual kind — with a steel tip and an eerie lure button. After starting up the truck, she watched the mud spinning around the tires as she manoeuvred through rocky textures and along the masked. "We outnumber you... all of you..." a gruff voice mumbled, "Armed in our entire district... watching..."

Rolling down the rest of the window, Xira looked at the masked man.

"You don't have what we have. Your core is not even our surface, which speaks of your demeanour about peace," she returned, before driving off through the field's rejuvenated grounds. Along the way, hissing and frizzling sounded from the radio attached to the dashboard.

"Transmission proceed... Transmission received. Notifying units. T-Y-158, do you read me? We need you to visit the supply base on NE of your route. Your portable GPS should provide you with assistance if required — T-Y-158, do you copy?"

Keeping one hand on the steering wheel, Xira searched in her bag for the torn-up shirt she'd found in Fiona's abandoned car. She handed it over to Willow, while focused on the path and around them. Noticing her discomfort, she pulled the truck over to help take care of the wound. Willow leaned forward in anguish while holding the side of her leg, as Xira wrapped the fabric underneath then over the top, overlapping the centre to enhance protection. The radio crackled again, harshly in parts, with another voice seeming alerted.

"Dispatch — vacant. Unit T-Y-158, do you copy? Duty marked. Unit T-Y-158, do you copy? Lieutenant needs your call. I re — Roger that, Lieutenant... Duty marked. Code red, units. Find Unit T-Y-158 recent location and inform. All units nearby, this is a code red. Search for Unit T-Y-158 and inform once located."

Within a second, Xira stepped on the pedal, causing the truck to skid a bit while mud splattered from behind the wheels. No looking back, as Willow held onto her leg and concentrated on the area. Nobody was yet spotted following or patrolling during their drive, though the group was still back there and if more masked were to follow their route, they could eventually be found. As Xira continued down the grassy lands, the lights from the truck sprung upwards as the tires caught a slanted rock, revealing something intriguing in the distance.

"That's near the cave… it could be a way through," she looked at the large carving on the cliff face with symbols covering the exterior and an extremely cavernous entrance with mysterious phosphorescence, "We can come back here once things cool down and pursue this whole mess."

After bringing the truck closer and telling Willow to wait in the seat, she made her way to the entrance, examining its two wall doors. The symbols went across the top area from left to right, quite similar to the ones found in the cave. Larger in size this time, as well as many forest-green vines covering the marges of the cliff face itself, with delphiniums wonderfully on them and an icy mist flowing along the front. She walked up to the left side of the surface, feeling the scratch marks that appeared to be from something other than human or machine. Dusting off some of the other areas of stone, the carvings glowed one after another in a colourful, charming sequence.

"These symbols resemble the ones on that stone in the cave," she noted, "They appear to have a connection… I wonder what exactly… albeit it does seem like an ancient script."

A musical, whistling tune echoed through the space and outside. Sticking her head out of the window, Willow grunted with a small wave.

"My leg… is really sore, Xi… are we going in there?" she gestured to the entrance, looking doleful.

"There could be something that might do good… it's just a little further, okay… hold on," Xira replied soothingly, observing the vibrant abyss, "hm… it reminds me of the instrumental beverage nights with Yiya… I hope he's okay too… "

The drops of rain fell rhythmically on the truck, as Willow leaned on the window — her gaze to the gap where the wind flowed through. While she waited for Xira, who was admiring the plantation and aura, two headlights from behind reflected in the side mirror as it caught her eye. Panicking, she shouted out the window.

"Someone's heading this way! It's probably backup, what if — oh, let's go!"

Xira spun around, noticing it getting closer to them and leaped to the front of the truck.

With a solid undertone, she directed at the driver's seat.

"Turn the ignition off, quick — stay low in the car and lock the doors!"

The sound of the engine was approaching, rumbling through loudly. As it neared, Xira crouched in front of the truck, facing towards the incoming threat. Slamming doors and grumbly exchanges were overheard, while the truck's headlights shone directly at the back where the gear was and the rocky dirt beside the wheels. One of the trackers walked forward to check the crates.

"This is one of ours. Some gear is left out in the open, it's not like our crew to do that," he remarked, tumbling the items around.

"What IS that? Look," another commented in a higher tone.

More footsteps reached closer towards the side of the truck, stopping abruptly as one of them leaned on the driver window.

"Out of the ordinary. There's stuff in here that's not from our suppliers and it's just thrown all over," his voice growing vexed as he shuffled around the back. Another tracker slowly walked to the entrance, the sound of his boots slinking into the mud and quietly rustling along the grass. Xira lay down on her forearms, as she stealthily crawled under the truck. A count of four pairs of feet were scouting about as they surrounded them. The one near the entrance crouched to take a look at the patterns on the side of the vines which covered most of the earthly surface.

"Doors are locked," one spoke bluntly, pulling on the handles, "Break window?"

Silence fell through the open gaps around the truck as cold wind drifted down, the smell of fuel dragging across her nose while eyeing a tracker's boots standing to the right. The smash of the window rung out for a moment before the cracks of the glass dropped one after another. Xira hoped Willow was out of reach as they searched, ruffling the items in the area where a large trunk was kept just behind the front seats. After flipping things around for a brief minute, they pulled away from the doors and two of them paused as they turned to each other.

"Do you think they went in there? Lieutenant never told us about this," a croaky voice remarked.

"Not too sure, we need more intel — Commander expects us to have this situation resolved and that's what we're here to do," replied another as he began walking to their truck, his boots splashing the mud.

A door was opened and loudly closed, as Xira began slithering backwards from under the truck and up into a crouching position while cleaning her gloves off the bumper. She peeked through the windshield to check if they had all gone in. One was still standing next to the passenger seat, clicking away on a device in his hands. As she watched him enter, leaving the door open, the driver then turned the headlights off. They didn't seem to leave just yet, for it was probably a surveyance. *Damn it,* Xira thought to herself. Assuming they'd stay here all night, Xira knew there was only a head-on solution and that was to grab Willow and go. Both trucks' lights were off and this was their chance. Pulling her hood over, she carefully glided to the passenger door while glancing at the trackers and feeling for the window gap. She turned her palm towards the roof to tap a warning. *Willow is probably still frightened,* she thought. Grabbing her phone, arching closer between her jacket lapels, she hid it under cover to signal Willow through a message.

>> *<WILLOW> Now Will. We gotta go.*

_____ __☀__ _____

She kept her glance at their truck as she awaited her reply. A moment later, her phone's screen lit up.

(1) <WILLOW> {02:09am}
Ok but I'll need some help…

_____ __☀__ _____

Feeling the door unlock, Xira carefully pulled on the handle while leaning in closer to the side of the foot rest. Willow arched up as she grabbed on her arms.

"My leg is still in a bad way, I don't think I can drag on in a hurry," she whispered.

Without a second thought, Xira carried her away and over her shoulder.

"We'll go along the side and hide out until they leave," she responded calmly. The cold air hovered on her skin, as frost-like particles drifted about. They lumbered covertly towards the open area, opposite of the trackers' direction. While keeping them in view, the light from their device flashed and flickered through the side window, appearing to remain stationary in their truck. The moonlight shepherded the path of their escape. Just as they were turning the corner, Willow's grunt echoed through the space. She held on her thigh, lowering herself in pain. Although they spotted a place to momentarily rest, it was a sudden change of course in the wind as a shout blared from behind them. A little late for a plan, they realised the tracker's had overheard her cry and the ignition of their truck had rumbled within the second. Willow grew overwhelmed, as she and Xira quickly stumbled and dragged to the closest cover, with no time to spare of looking back.

One after another threatening voice followed like a generator's engine in the midst of starting up. They leaned, in cover and low to the ground as they could, remaining on high alert of their surroundings. The trackers were scouting the area, all going in different directions as the sound of mud being splattered about got louder from each fringe, their gear clanging with every brute-like step. Willow began to panic, as she tried to maintain her wound to a tolerable level, stretching the wrapped fabric closely around the thigh. Cold drops of rain fell diagonally, the muddy land beside them forming into puddles. Quickly thinking of a getaway, Xira reached into her pockets and pulled out the shard from before. She grabbed the slingshot that she'd found in the truck and artfully combined them together, awaiting a target. Peering on an angle, she noticed only one was heading this way while the others had been checking the many rocks that were in the expanse. Before glancing again, a green and blue liquid light shone on the shard — appearing as a glowing trail while the metallic textures resurfaced. Curious to know more about it, she leaned forwards on the ground, getting ready to launch. Aiming at the tracker's arm, she patiently waited for the opening to their way out. The tracker seemed oblivious as she was holding the band further back on the slingshot, keeping him in the line of its charge.

Your turn to get a taste of your own treatment, she thought to herself. Footsteps harmonised with the pattern of the rainfall, getting more menacingly enunciated with each collision of the mushy ground. Willow huddled close to her friend's shoulder, attempting to hide away from detection. Within a second, a beam of light stretched to the hiding spot, bouncing from left to right as it extended into the darkness. A brief sound of a musical tune interrupted the fairly silent ambience as it prompted a gasp out of Willow, who suddenly fidgeted around her pockets in an unsettling method.

"Report. Suspicious activity, I think we're on track. Over," the tracker spoke into his PDA.

The flashlight waved over the rocky surface as the tracker approached. Frightened, Willow lowered to her side in a curled position. What seemed like an imminent doom, felt quite the opposite. According to Xira's beliefs, a looming act meant nothing if the moral compass and spirit weren't as pure. Although this wasn't a debatable situation, she believed a fool is a fool regardless if they were in a shadow of another. Without a dire moment to spare, she unclasped the band, firing the shard directly in the tracker's arm. After his loud outcry, she grabbed her friend's hand, gesturing to sneak past and head through the bush on their right. The rushing didn't help Willow's wound after gaining some distance away, as she stumbled and limped along the path. Shortly before she picked herself up, the tracker was beginning to catch up from behind.

"You! HALT RIGHT THERE. HALT!" He shouted with a finishing growl. They continued on until they reached two trackers with their backs facing while they searched.

"Push him! On your right!" Xira alerted in a quiet pitch, storming past and knocking out the one near her. For a few intervals between, it'd stalled the tracker chasing them but tilting their odds, he rounded up the others with a warning, then proceeded to detach a piece of gear and threw it in their direction — resulting in a smoky fog, clouding the atmosphere. Xira relentlessly ran forward, the thick cotton starting to retract into diffusion. Though the cold breeze overtook, her doleful friend in need of salvation kneeled down hard, wrestling to get to safety. She took one good look through the mist, centring on Xira with a sorrowful expression.

"Go, Xira. Go…" she spoke tiredly, barely holding the leg, "you have the gear."

Xira quickly skidded as she faced her.

"Hell, I'm not leaving you here!" she fired back, rushing to carry her, "You're not going to be alone and you're not going with them."

"Just leave me. Please. Get somewhere, anywhere. Be safe, don't worry about me," Willow exhaled heavily, while snailing on.

As Xira was crouching to carry her through, a sudden force pushed and launched her a few meters away, causing her to graze rough across the ground. In the flash of the moment, she looked ahead while revolving on her side, leaning and rising to see what was going down. Among the sifted haze, tones of forest green weaved throughout the space, muffled noises and shuffles combined with the gentle icy touch of the rain, when a scream eerily pierced through the distorted and cottony air.

"No!" she vociferated in despair, "No…" It wasn't long before one of the shadows emerged from the mist, gloomily following in her direction. Edging closer, Xira arched back up on her feet, using the rocks nearby to get some boost as she tried to push around to flee but her weighing feelings brought on a bit of hesitation. *Use the heavy feelings as fuel, dear Xira,* she remembered her mentor's saying and his gathering where he used to light a spiritual aroma compound and pour the healing remedy in bundles of art nouveau antique pots and mugs, divulging his wisdom in his meditative ritual. She felt a strange comfort in reflecting on the momentous times that made her home feel like home. A family by the bonds of spiritual connection. *The river flows through its mighty way on stormy days just as it does on days of sunshine,* he would also say, *and both are just as marvellous days.* She knew she had to keep going, no matter what. With a spring in her swing, she bolted ahead of the tracker, gaining some more distance to give her enough seconds to recover. The relentlessness and cruel intentions of this person only reminded her of the difference between the security back at the checkpoint and their methods, compared to each other, one was a snake hidden in the grass, while the other was a snake in plain sight. Only again there was the advantage of the darkness which provided the chase a few more odds in Xira's hand of cards. As she was also a runner, using the stealth tactic to keep out of the tracker's line of sight and path would play him out just right, forge her escape and lessen the possibly awful scenario. Camouflaging with the surroundings, she slid by all angles to find a way out of their search area. She noticed one of their truck's ahead and stormed to the back, hoping to pick up anything of use. To her wish, a retractable steel weapon was uncovered, in the form of a rifle but built electronically with the handy utility of shooting nets towards a target or numerous targets, capturing them in its hold to the floor. After carrying it away, she walked backwards to readjust the length and wait for a clearing. Anticipating the tracker at any moment, she tested out the gear in a random direction.

Nets, huh? Ok... ok... she thought to herself, examining the net she'd just launched on the ground. Something like little zaps of light flickered throughout the rough material, bouncing from one point to another, almost igniting the grass around it. The automatic reload of the weapon sounded through the mild winds as the barrel was cooling off with a low, robotic reeling effect. Sensing the tracker approaching closer, putting one foot further behind her, she stared down in the direction of the motions, while making sure the weapon was all ready to launch. It wasn't too long before the mud-covered epitome of a nuisance showed up and was barbarically scampering in hopes to catch her. With a million thoughts racing through Xira's mind about Willow and what was happening with her, she quickly grasped and pulled the net launcher, aiming forwards to the tracker, knocking him hard on the ground, splattering the soil on impact. She watched as the lights buzzed across his uniform, charring the seaweed green textured surface. After throwing back the launcher in the truck, she heard muffled grunts from the tracker as he regained focus and attempted to free himself from the clutches. Forthwith, knowing their relentlessness, Xira ran across paths in a quest to find the whereabouts of her friend. Along the way, she'd spotted a couple of the trackers seeking her out in different corners of the place but the fog that was forming through the hours before dawn, availed her as she continued hunting down the captors. A few moments drifted, as she overheard rather distinct voices in the distance — almost overlapping one another, the volume alternating often. As she neared, she noticed the back of the shadowy figure, towering over someone before them. The exchanges were sounding more unpleasant as the hoarseness cut through the defensive tone which sounded quite familiar. Although it did, the other slammed back with a louder and fiery response, leaving the brute speechless — until he pulled the figure below to meet his angle. A fierce shout threw him off, while becoming annoyed, still holding onto them as the captive leaned closer to the ground. *Willow,* Xira knew right away, recognising her voice. Approaching cautiously, she heard Willow's cries in an attempt to flee from the tracker's clasp. His buddy was searching for something in a crate a few steps away, asserting him to keep his ground until they'd found *the other one.* There were a couple of detached wagons, supposedly from their trucks, anchored to the soil below.

Opened crates, including some supplies that they were likely carrying over, could be seen sticking out from the surface. The same symbol from all of their property thus far was etched on the sides of each crate, with ink and muddy smears. It didn't come as a surprise to Xira if their bags were already forsaken, despite carrying what she needed with her, the rest of the belongings in her bag were to be of additional resource but she knew if it were to be that way, that it would only motivate her to persevere. With regard that her friend's life was becoming a threat's matter and bait to lure her there as well, she knew she needed a more safe and smooth strategy. It was gut-wrenching for her to even imagine the perilous outcome if the odds were unfairly tilted, and the lingering damp feeling of someone she deeply cares about being taken away from her, again, to finding herself alone once more.

She crouched near the crates, holding onto the wagon and searching the inside of each one in hopes to find something quite useful. Among all the little bags and material items, her hand brushed across a metallic type of handle with a taser-like edge, combined with a cold, pointy steel tail that rested atop the many items in that crate and most of which were pieces of clothing. For a brief evasion when she handled the device — she turned it all ways to discover its full operation, analysing the activations and compartments while feeling around every piece to the other, noticing the connection to their various gear and how some of it seemed very different and uniquely enhanced than the usual weaponry and machines of militia. On the bottom of the device read parts of the information involving the use; *knock-out sleep, refill tube when empty, non-lethal.* She looked up at the shadowy figure, so eager to find the answers to their demanding, interrogative pursuit. The disgust towards them broiled her patience and tolerance, or what little she had left for them, keeping the reminder that this would have to be resolved before anything disastrous could transpire. Their exchange became quieter, while the breeze overlapped the slight noise. The tracker's boots began to slink between the puddles of the mud-covered ground, as the water from further down the path trickled between and around their feet. Prowling closer, she felt the water continue around her boots as she waited silently, before cutting distance. The fog grew thicker, with fewer gaps after each wave and it was apparent that this could serve the girls well. Turning on the device while holding down the switch, she tasered the tracker in the thigh area, causing him to release Willow as he slowly dropped in front of her. Startled and bewildered, Willow stared below with an inquisitive expression, then back at Xira who was throwing the device back.

"Oh goodness... do we..." she whispered, looking around.

"Let's just go, before they spot us again," Xira replied quickly while grabbing her friend's arm, running off the other way. Willow hurriedly stepped over the tracker's legs, almost slipping from the damp grounds.

"Wait—" she called to her, "my wound has been angered again, shortly after they got me."

She paused briefly to tend to it, limping her leg back and forth. After that, they continued further at a slower pace, about to hasten when a harsh grip got hold of one of Willow's arms, yanking her backwards, almost reeling her in out of nowhere. She screamed to be let go, stretching her other arm towards Xira. Meanwhile, Xira hunted down the direction of the noise, noticing her friend's hand flailing, she immediately grabbed and held on to it in a trying tug, finding herself slightly skidding the ground while being opposed with one of the trackers who desperately tried to cling to Willow's foot as well, pulling away.

"You bastard! Let her go!" Xira warned him off, adamant to hold onto her friend as much as possible.

A hoarse chuckle weaved through the commotion.

"Two for one... knocking my friend out is costing ya'. Silly fools." His voice growled while Willow wriggled around to get away.

It got too much for her as he eventually started pulling on the wounded leg, struggling to detach from the tracker. Where being genuine catapults in the abyss, the likeness of a fiend is ever the spellbound bolster. She was far concerned about making sure she wouldn't alert any of the others in thought of her friend's safety, though the relentless brute was causing more trouble to them than they'd anticipated. The thought of tackling the tracker crossed Xira's mind, but she didn't want the result of that to harm Willow, as her wound hadn't healed completely and all she wanted was to leave the place.

"I'm tired of this. I'm tired. Of you... and... uaargh!" Willow cried, traces of hopelessness in her quivering voice.

"Shut it! By order, you're ours now, whether I yank ya' or something much my style." He interrupted, raising his already raspy tone to threaten a surrender.

Pulling her further towards his way, the silver lining that once was, fell through the gaps and into the cosmic smog. Humanity had lost its flavour and since a long while, this had been unfamiliar to them, for they've known kindness as the serve, a clashing paradox to an overdue and overused pernicious mechanism. Her grip on Xira gently slid away as she decided to not haul her in more trouble and ease it for her sake. While they weren't on the same page, it gave the tracker the ultimate chance to fulfill his demands, despite the unjust aftermath. Earthly tones began to form around the wound on her thigh, with moss green in the shape of clovers, continuing in pattern with shades of icy blue waves circling into the orange webs that stretched to the outer sides of the leg, sketching down to her calf and glowing fragments sequentially surfacing on the wound's outer core. A trace of lightning shone outwards, in a thunderous style, then connected down along the thigh to form rays raining around her leg to her ankle and oddly attaching to the tracker's arm that was holding her, receiving electric zaps as it slowly disappeared with sparks shooting from the tracker's forearm. After a moment, there was a pause, almost as if enchantment had taken place. While the tracker resumed focus, Willow could overhear Xira calling out but the mist that surrounded them seemingly swallowed the message, whisked with a muffled intervenience instead of an echo. She could feel being tugged even harsher now, the light zaps reacting with the agony of her wound — her mind raced between what the oddity was and the foremost nuisance shuffling before her. Clenching her teeth, she let out a cry, the other foot dragging across in means of a reminder to be let go but disappointingly, caused more unease and less fury in the tracker. Everything had felt insignificant, like the mountains and fields beyond ceased to exist in the same realm and the sky was darkened by her pain, only the mud beneath both feet and the sparks on her leg were the only remnants. Trying to find her breath of fresh air, with every tug she felt further away from her escape. It began to fuel her emotions, fury forthcoming besides her pacifism as she had lost her extent of empathy, a deviant welcoming, along a fresh silver lining that re-emerged as to what felt karmic, sweeping aside the anterior civility that she otherwise would've felt — now that she discovered what lies deep down, she felt the desolation and knew, she couldn't allow what could forge... to surface.

"Come on, you brat. Don't make it harder for yourself." He grumbled, his voice lowering with each rest between words.

Barely regaining full concentration, Willow looked around, realising the area had become quiet and Xira wasn't nearby. She began feeling worried if there was too much distance from where they last were, as she further lowered herself, her other foot just about holding it together while the tracker just kept pulling and pulling. After a few attempts to wriggle the leg away, only to find herself on an angle, her other foot started to slip. Feeling the cold tears run down her face, while the leg burned, her hope drained dry. With effort to inhale all the air possible, she trailed the ground with one hand, searching around for a grip on something. Anything. Scrapes and scratches from the burrowed stones and plants met the palm of her hand. It had stung as she slid it across the mud to wash it off, waving it mid-air. The tracker used this moment to tug in irregular patterns in attempt to grab the other leg. At this point, his sleeve was gradually burning off from the effects on her leg attached to him, wrapping on the clothing underneath it. Willow tried to push downwards to free from his clasp, but to no avail, he kept his grip. Mustering all the effort she could, nor left or right seemed to be of triumph, nothing was falling in her odds against this grim brute. What was colder than the air of dawn, the gentle voyage of another beaming sunrise in the atmosphere, were the rivulet of tears that painted her face, while the submerging sentiment that dropped to nowhere... left the rest of her thoughts in an abyss. Willow's rough gaze directed to the tracker, as she noticed some of the material of her pants shred apart and the effects swarming the leg. Holding her cries, the electric zaps aligned with the trajectory of her cold stare, zapping with each core of her feelings coming to rise. Leaning back, she sunk to rest her hand on the ground. After every scratchy breath, she prepared for all the will that could then be summoned. In a muffled bellow, she drew her mysticised wounded leg far back, then forthwith, she mercilessly booted between his legs. The outcry she was holding, let out like a multitude of birds soaring close above them as the tracker dropped down, forming enough distance between the two. Willow carefully slid upwards, turning over to crawl away and recover her step. She clenched her jaw, heaving deeply after each gape, the tears that soaked her face dribbled from the chin while facing down, resting the eyes. Slowly getting back up, she limped on her leg which looked like a tattoo covering the entirety of it, some of the glow was lingering in different areas while the wound appeared dormant. She began to make her way back to Xira, as quickly as the other leg would bear. The trail from the tracker's encounter had made it easier to navigate back to her friend, meanwhile the fog dispersed more with each portion that was covered along the way. As highly alert she remained, she reached closer to her escape — feeling the soft breeze brush through and the sun gently caressing, the ambience eerily silent while anticipating to greet her friend again. Looking around, it was oddly safe from the trackers, although they could be heard from afar, they were nowhere near here. She wondered just how many had ventured to hunt them down, as all she recalled it was a group or two, but given it went up in a flurry, she couldn't risk thinking they wouldn't order reinforcements. Every few minutes or so, Willow checked behind her in case of a stalker. Meanwhile, trying to keep on the low, she'd recognised the wheelbarrow from before, the materials tipped over the side. Only no one was there. She looked around to find a small camp on the left, with a rolled-out blanket and a lighter. Walking to it, there didn't seem to be anything else left behind and no recent campfire either. She suspected whoever was here was bound to return, but she knew she needed a little rest before continuing further. Time had gone, the morning turned to noon. Mud to shale. So far, Willow was under no threat, as she figured they'd abandoned this area for now. Although anxiously wondering about Xira, this little spot had been helpful. She thought about heading back to the mystical entrance, though deep down, really wanted to wait for her here, as she wanted to ensure she was still safe. Knowing they wanted to go through there together, she wanted to keep that promise and especially that this was more than just a way out, but involving uninvited guests. Regardless, they had each other's backs, no matter what and she wanted nothing other than good for her dear friend. The lighter beside her was etched with an ornamental design, silver outlines and painted in metallic shades of brown with black overlay. It didn't seem like it belonged to the trackers as they had their own insignia on all of their supplies. The blanket was rather weary but thick enough to provide warmth despite the frosty grounds beneath. Since a while, mainly all that was noise was from the havoc that the security back at the checkpoint bridge and the trackers had wreaked. Now there were the whistles and chirps of nature and birds from the nearby trees on the side of the field. It brought her comfort as she watched the horizon for anybody returning. While waiting, she wrapped what was left of the pant material on her now decorated but wounded leg. Just about three quarters secured around her thigh, though quite all right, still needed further aid. For the meantime, she played around with the lighter, flipping open and closing the lid, almost in pattern with the soft wind flowing. Her mood sunk each minute that went by, contemplating whether she should scout the place, and if anything strange had happened elsewhere. Sitting up on the log behind her, Willow used the blanket to cover up the rest of her leg as she stretched. Though still wondering about what was the phenomena that was around her wound, she kept watch on both sides for Xira, assuming she would head this way at any point. Just as she heeled her head, sounds of running were heard coming from the right, with the low dust of the ground picking up. Startled at first, Willow focused on the figure heading her way. Followed by a puzzling expression, she'd recognised the silhouette immediately. Tears built in her eyes, she crinkled her mouth then slowly rose to stand. Her body was weary as she limped ahead, her puzzled self now sorrowful, yet exhaling with relief while meeting halfway. Xira ran up to her with open arms as they both collided in a hearty hug. They comforted for a little moment before Xira held her friend in front of her.

"Oh damn…" she whispered concerningly. Tracing the face with her eyes, she could feel her heavy soul rest on hers. No words could tell the tale like her eyes and the depths within did. Xira huddled in to continue their hug, wrapping around like she was shielding her friend from something — a certainty sat to rest, that the moment she desired to hold between them was of dire need to keep Willow from falling apart, a reminder to hold on to her own light, even if it took the risk of danger. She grabbed her arm as they turned around, back to the camp, while Willow slumped in her grasp — as if she'd been rescued by a lifeguard. Xira sat beside her as she lit up the campfire with the ornamental lighter, before putting it in a jacket pocket. Throwing in a couple of pieces of debris she'd collected, she puffed a few times to accelerate the fire.

"So… that, yours?" Willow looked at Xira as she spoke, almost swallowing her words.

"Yeah, hm… found it before, in that wheelbarrow. I searched for you…" she replied, glancing at the fire, "one of them planks… came after me just when I hurried through… deuce… I guess that fog they created was in my favour, but you were already gone. I didn't want to imagine what might've happened, so, I ran around a while… got some stuff, came here and found this spot. Started the fire… it felt safe enough, but I went back down there. By any chance you were somewhere there, though I can't say it enough just how glad I am that you're here now." She turned to her friend.

Willow angled herself to rest on Xira's lap, while they both held onto each other, in front of a warm hideaway from the world. A few moments of bliss and quiet before heading to the entrance.

A soft wind brushed through the space, as the remaining embers sparkled from the campfire. Xira let out a sigh, watching the area around them. It had felt peaceful. For once throughout the whole night, their breath had returned and hope was gently restoring. She wondered if any chaos was still in progress back at the bridge, seeing as this part of the outside was growing uncannily silent. The connection to all that was observed thus far, had to have an answer. Her thoughts filled with questions and theories, both light and dark, to which appeared that it's more to the phenomena than it is to the people keeping secrets from the rest, or was it both? The suspicion heightened as the clash of bad vs evil came to combine, the mere inhumanity didn't seem a surprise, but rather the key to the plausible theory that was realised in their own hometown. It all had weaved through the supernatural, to the looming cataclysm and the puppeteers who fed on control and corruption. As frightening as it had seemed, she knew the clue resided in the core of the vortex that'd swallowed their home and the residents, beyond the valleys and hidden lairs of the lost and damned. If anything was to be of an exit, it'd had to be that mystical entrance. No matter what, it was all they had now.

"We need to get going, Will." She reminded her, "The entrance awaits."

"Mhh… mm…" her friend mumbled softly, "but… my leg?"

"I took care of that, the soft material should act as a good pillow to the pant material underneath, making it stay in place and serve you some comfort." Xira informed.

Noticing her gazing down as Willow slowly stood up, she gave her a curious expression.

"There's something — something happened, I'll tell you on the way," Willow responded quietly as they both began to walk.

Arriving at an open portion where some of the trackers were searching before, now empty, was covered with snow-like particles along the grass, emitting little clouds of smoke. They exchanged glances as they cautiously continued closer to corner of where the entrance was spotted. Both of the trucks had disappeared, like nothing was ever there. Completely deserted of everything other than the nature that surrounded. Xira observed the truck tracks from where they'd crossed before, still imprinted along the ground, connecting to the direction they arrived from early last night. She wondered if there was anything at all that might've been left behind… but it came to a disappointment. Just the mess they had made.

"Great, now our stuff is really gone," she remarked, "like it wasn't bad enough most of it was already taken…"

Willow gasped with a slight whimper.

"My-my… I had some things in there I couldn't afford to lose… more than just, things, argh — the one irreplaceable thing I can't ever get back," her voice crackled.

The light from the entrance flashed in rhythm, blending with the sun's rays as they touched in point. Colours of the rainbow glistened, like a visual tune in play, while the ethereal glow caused the vines that covered the stone surface to sparkle as the light trailed to each stem and leaf. Xira stared in amazement, as Willow was still eyeing the ground around her.

"Mother's journal… the-they just, took it!" She was etching near and dear to her darker emotions… ones thought of as barely ever dusted. Sliding across the grass, desperately trying to find her answers, instead only found to be expressing the sadness that was felt. A rumbling noise in the distance grovelled as she got up on her feet.

"Will — I'm sorry. I know… but there's still a chance," she reassured her, "we just need to get going. It's not safe here and no one seems to know of this… entrance in front of us."

The noise became louder as it neared with each second that passed. The girls turned in unison, noticing a vehicle that looked exactly like a tank approach their location. Ready to fly, four trackers stuck out from each window of the tank-like beast, aiming their weapons towards them, as a megaphone took over the now hushed engine.

"Fire on command!" shouted a voice through the speakers above the hood, "Surrender or we'll shoot."

Willow anxiously glanced at Xira, in a limp backwards. Xira didn't tolerate them one bit, as a fierce look decorated her face.

"You want to promise hell, well that's one promise I'll have to break. Will — Get the hell out of here!" shouted Xira, leaping in a flash, diving into the entrance's light. Willow immediately followed, with the help of her friend's grab, jumping in there straight after. The trackers in the midst blared their bullets in all the fury, like a whirl of shooting stars, yelling at one another that they'd just missed — but just too frightened to enter themselves.

Xira collided with a soft, ocherous ground while the noise from the trackers echoed into a slow dispelling. Willow stumbled a few seconds later, rolling on the side. Everything appeared to be hazy for a good moment before footsteps in the distance swiftly approached. One of the silhouettes bent down to check on them as the other stood aside.

"Hello…? Are you all right?" Spoke a gentle voice, though the stranger kept talking, it had become more muffled like it was happening underwater. Two voices suddenly overlapped, each one waving one after another, as Xira lightly slumped over in a swift sleep.

The wind was colder once again, with brief whistles springing through every now and then. Accompanied by the comforting warmth nearby, that'd caressed the surface of the skin, like a cuddly blanket sprung over. Crackling sounds touched the atmosphere, which formed an interesting scented aroma. Something lay like a cloud beneath, a gentle embrace which made her feel afloat, like the sky had descended… Someone near carefully grabbed her hand, checking over the palm. Xira turned slightly to observe, as she realised she was in a different place with another being. Remaining calm and not wanting to frighten them, she arose, briefly lifting the hand.

"What's going on? Where am I?" Xira questioned, as a puzzling look met the stranger. A woman with a cloak, placing her hand down, smiled.

"You're all right, dear. I mean you no harm. I've come to your aid, you seemed… lost," the woman responded soothingly.

There was a pot with vegetables, with the water boiling as the steam travelled along their noses. Looking around, she noticed they were in a green bell tent, kind of like the ones she'd often have back at home with the others. The woman stirred with a swirly wooden spoon, before pouring in a leaf-shaped bowl. Placing it atop a crochet trivet, she rolled it over using a wooden stand with modified rotating-wheels underneath.

"Is my friend okay? The one with the honey-brown hair? Injured?" Xira asked curiously, watching the wind flap the tent's front.

The sweet smell from the bowl was refreshing, making her feel at home, but most of her thoughts were occupied by her wonderment of Willow's whereabouts. The caring gaze of the woman directed towards Xira's wrapped hand, then back with a grin, as she continued stirring the pot.

"Oh she's fine, my darling friend Niko is taking great care of the leg, albeit…" she paused, perplexed, "I haven't come across such an oddity, which is rather humorous, given where we are… it's just — something that makes you question if it's truthfully pure or sinister."

Xira flashed a surprised glance, as the woman stood up to leave. The wind became louder, whistling around the tent.

"Wait—" she called suddenly, "What is your name?"

"Valin. You may call me Vaoz, it's Niko's nickname for me. You'll find it has caught on," Valin responded smiling, "…and what name do you shine, dear?"

"Xira," she replied.

Valin nodded, opening the tent as she walked out, her cloak flailing behind.

Sometime later, multiple voices were heard chiming outside. The sounds of people going about, laughter, cries of joy and friendly exchange. A different feeling, as opposed to Glacial Mist, or what it was like now. The vibrant atmosphere connected to anyone within, enlightening and lifting up from no matter what kind of mood one's in, bringing forth the feeling of a home, the light inside and a world of blooming paradise. It almost made Xira forget about what had happened, her current wounds intertwining with the soft air, like it was healing her. A soothing steam fetched some more peace, as she finished up the soup, the warmth settling inside. After a long night, she felt well rested and with a slight smile, she glanced at her palm. Noticing the glove repaired, she pulled it upwards to find her skin padded with a light pink and orange powder where her scratch wound resided, now gone. She realised the handkerchief that she used to wrap it around was also removed. Grabbing her jacket from the edge of the bedding, Xira walked out to greet the sweet new land. Not too far in front, was another tent, only its flaps were opened and pulled back as she realised the woman she'd just met, Valin, was standing next to another person, seemingly occupied with something. Observing the surroundings, she made her way to the tent, the sun shining across her face. There was an entire village here, from tents to huts and many outdoor creations which offered various activities for its people. Filled with flowers, plantation and campfires, it was a delightful space, where anyone could come along and blossom with its nature. Focused on Valin, Xira marched forward, noticing the other cloaked person tending to a patient. It had felt colder in there, although it didn't appear to be a problem to either one of them. She walked closer, not wanting to give a fright as Valin suddenly turned with a delightful surprise.

"Well! You're looking refreshed, I take it you have gandered at the village? It has much to offer," she spoke, grinning.

"Uh, yes, a little. Are you busy right now? I wanted to talk to you about… something," Xira asked, looking at the bottles on the table. The cloaked doctor beside her rotated to face them, as a smile coated over his stern, concentrated exterior. She noticed the similarities between the two and began to question and feel more curious about them, when he placed a hand on her shoulder to give a warm greeting.

"Oh, you must be Valin's patient, the girl with the intriguing tattoo," he began, "My, my… you are looking much better since the first time this morning that I saw you. She must've taken very good care of you."

Valin tapped him playfully, crossing her arms in front of her cloak.

"We *are* the only medical practitioners in Bloom Core. If we don't do it, who will? After all, we manage just fine," she added with a sparkling wink.

"Actually, it's my birthmark. A very close friend of mine told me about it, years ago… like a special emblem, but he had no clue as to what it meant. He left that for me to figure out, I hadn't thought about it too much but I've been starting to feel some strange connection ever since I got here," explained Xira, observing her wrist in thought. Both of the doctors gasped, turning back to her, surprised.

"Did you arrive from the other side? The dark realm of the people?" Valin suspected, slightly tilting her head.

"The dark realm? Ahaha, as far as I'm concerned, that's my hometown. Sure it has its gloomy side, but... every place has its own, relatively. You could call it that now though..." Xira's cheerful array transformed into solemnity.

The cloaked duo exchanged empathetic glances, as Valin lifted her hand.

"You can count on Niko and I to be here for you, anything you may need or desire. We're both present," she stated, reassuringly.

In-between the moment, the sound of a broken bottle cut the silence. The patient behind Niko rose to sit, as they awakened.

"Xi-Xira?" a soft voice muttered quietly.

"Willow!" Xira immediately called back, rushing to her.

Valin and Niko joined alongside them.

"Xira and Willow. Oh, that's right, they were together when you and Luki brought them here," Niko recalled, reminding Valin of the incident, "I'm certainly relieved you two are okay. We can't bear any more tragedies ever since... well, none the matter, I'll take these pieces to dispose of, there are many more where they all came from, aha."

The girls watched as he made his way out, carrying the shattered bottle pieces from the floor. Winds began picking up, as the people outside grew quiet and the chimes on their hut doors resounded through the way, forming a humble, gentle tune. Valin smiled, putting the other bottles in the cabinet next to the table. She resumed cleaning the area where Niko had operated, easing some of the work for the next time he'd needed to perform. Bundles of cloth and other materials crowded a corner of the tent, pieces of fabric were spread out nearby and a container of tiny medical tools rested on a bench. Xira leaned in for a hug, feeling more relieved as the comfort of her friend and the now healed wounds shared the contentedness between them. She observed her leg, now dressed in neoprene fabric with a cotton wrap overlay, resting on the patient bed which was decorated rather similarly like the one she was on before. Willow seemed to be feeling just as well, her smile widening as she kept the leg up at rest. They could tell she still required some time before going further on, as they gestured for her to get comfortable while they placed a blanket around and prepared a cup of tea.

"So, dear Xira… a delight it has been." Valin sat on a rolling chair, grabbing the teapot, "What was it, that you wanted to speak to me about?"

"I understand this is your village, Bloom Core? Hmm… I'm, curious, as to where *this is*? Like how that portal, thing, got us here and why no one else from my home has seemed to find their way here…" Xira rolled in a wooden chair, searching for answers. Valin placed the cup on the resting stand next to Willow, before flashing her a comforting grin and placing the other cups on a tray. Turning to respond, she glanced on the floor then back up again.

"Look… we should allow sweet Willow here to get some rest while we continue this conversation back in my tent. You can visit her after the seasonal village ceremony we have by the campfire, tonight. She'll be safe in there, I myself vouch." Valin explained, "I'll introduce you to our all-welcoming celebratory rituals that enlighten and soothe the entirety of Bloom Core's brothers and sisters, spreading not only peace but a reminder to humbly coexist. You'll find… is quite fantastic, dear."

As they walked over to the tent, the sky formed into evening and clouds eased in, like rain was to arrive anytime. The cool atmosphere brought the best feelings for Xira, as she enjoyed every moment with the winds brushing along her dimpled cheeks, facing upwards, smiling at the sky. She loved winter, as it was her favourite season. The cloaked doctor pulled aside the tent's front, gesturing for her to enter through. They sat down opposite of each other, while occasionally drinking their fresh tea. Valin made sure to put back all of the things she had been using, making space for the both of them, as she lit up two burning essences and placing a small table with the vintage teapot before her. She signalled of her resuming the talk, as she took a few sips, the concentrated expression meeting with Xira's suspicious glare and both arms overlapping on her cloak.

"Your quest for answers is mightily enchanting. I shall deliver, then," she began, placing her cup on the small crochet on the table, "Bloom Core has been around for over a century, we weren't the only ones that made this our home. Some of the people here are actually direct descendants from the ancestors that founded this village, which helped with development, as we restored and maintained the place over the years. Our plants, vegetation and structures are better than ever — as I recall, the lands beyond provided us with many goods through the decades and it's ever the same."

Xira glanced at the pot, her gaze sliding over to meet with Valin's.

"Why hasn't anyone else ventured through here? Through that glowing portal? It all seems very local," she questioned.

"Well, it's not likely that many have discovered it as you two have. Quite frankly, it's not easy, as there are other things that need to occur for it to be shown to you. I take it, something... odd or magical happened?" Valin returned with fascination.

"There was... there, this — sphere that led us to a cave, then..." Xira paused, "after uncovering this trail, it activated some kind of opening which involved the vines and flowers, then the entrance appeared. Collision of lights and colours shined on what was previously just a stone wall with plantation."

After taking a drink, Valin returned her cup and pulled out a piece of paper.

"That's it, indeed," she responded quietly, "in that case, you'll need this map. I handcraft these from my knowledge of the place as far as I've gone. Those who are in need, I provide. Here."

Receiving the map, Xira unfolded the flap to full form that in which displayed a larger portion of the land. It was marked with specific locations according to what was discovered there. She noticed the little notes that were added in certain parts and missing elsewhere, along with cut off paths that weren't finished. In more than a few spots, it'd indicated that it was treacherous, that she chose to return from the path.

"So this is north from the village?" asked Xira, circling around the map, "Your note mentions another village with ruins and a lake nearby."

"Underwater Folk. It's the one next to the Phantom Lake, many myths and tales surround it. Some proven true. Although, the people there aren't too much like us here, first — they live underwater as well as on surface to their liking. Secondly, they have what they call a 'Chorus Angelicus', a Chorus of Angels... they sing, they chant, to scare away lurkers and create a harmony in their home and unite all of its people." Valin explained, nodding, "It was my honour to meet a few of them when they surfaced one night... they told me what it was like to live underwater. Venuso, one of the elders, informed me of the dangerous and frightening things that've taken place near and far ahead of their home.

It is why you'll piece together why there's only the nearest part of the north mapped out, I figured it was safe to return instead and well, I don't really desire to be a bad influence on you."

Placing the map inside her jacket, Xira lifted the cup to drink, then lowered to hold.

"Hmm… do you happen to know anything about a crash? Something enormous landed in my hometown, in a field, which was accompanied by wild weather and such oddities." She continued, "I thought about it again before and it seems to connect with the mysticality of this place. Did worlds collide? Interfere? Is there a… war?"

There was a brief silence between them as Valin was left speechless. Her face distraught, as immediate discomfort took hold over her pose. In attempt to keep composure, she pushed away the small table, giving space by the feet. When staring back at Xira, she looked grimmer and more frightened.

"It sounds… like a collision with worlds. At the very least… our world entering *that* world, in the sense of well, travel by cosmos. Specifically, the mirrored galleries. They act as a fast-travelling slide to another dimension. However, they aren't supposed to be used to the far-out lands, for they were made here." Valin elaborated with concern, "When something is created for one purpose, it sticks to fulfill that task, if someone were to use it to break that paradigm, it becomes a paradox. Chaos ensues. The right intentions to a good outcome, can miss the target for which it was intended. It doesn't mean, necessarily, that it's immoral to share tools like such, no, but this involves our nature and their nature — as it isn't one any more, it won't cooperate with ease and balance, thus forming a dark fall… where true light needs to ride again, to ultimately rebuild the peace. As you can tell, if this is occurring, then we're in for trouble. I'm not sure who would do something as catastrophic as this, but I feel like it is a conflict between someone on your land and here that we haven't been informed of yet. I'd rather it not turn into a vortex of horror, though."

This had filled in the question marks regarding the incidents back at Glacial Mist. For now, the puzzle pieces were coming together as one, but Xira wasn't finished.

"So who built that entrance then?" she asked, leaning.

"That, unfortunately, I don't know. It was there long before the galleries were created. I suppose it was ancestral, or even nature itself. Many mysteries are right under our noses, dear. Use that map and search your way through. You'll probably find its origins before I even care to, I'm too occupied with the village and now, this." Valin grew soft and quiet, as she drank the last drops of her tea. Gently setting the cup by the pot, she held Xira's hands in hers, warmly as she did, giving a smile, "You keep going. No matter what goes down, you keep on going. I see a glow orbiting a flame in your soul, it will be your guide and the worlds. I take care of things here, you go further. Be careful though, I don't want you to put yourself in harm's way because of me, I'm just... trying to say that... being there for each other, is rare. I haven't met many different wonders, like the wise of this land. You're something else, I can feel it, thanks to you. It's not often that this happens, this kind of encounter. Now, please. Excuse me, I have to go prepare for the ceremony. Help yourself to whatever you may need in here, I have biscuits and treats in that cupboard, more tea here, fruit in the bowl. I'll speak with you later."

"Wait!" Xira cut in.

"What is it, dear?" Valin replied, standing at the tent's front.

"You didn't tell me... where *is* this place? The entirety of this land, Valin?"

"We're in the Spirit Realm, my dear. The land of love and peace. Home and everything." Valin spoke warmly.

As Xira watched her disappear through the covers, she was left with more questions than the answers she'd received. Checking the space for any clue to give her an angle on things with the townsfolk, all that was uncovered apart from the food, was a little book in one of the drawers to which belonged to the initials of somebody etched on the front. *E.M.* This definitely wasn't Valin's, nor Niko's. She assumed it might've belonged to a villager or an assistant perhaps, but it wasn't cold cut to be definite. While hesitating whether to peek inside, a shout blared from outside the tent, alerting anyone within radius.

"Hear ye! Hear ye! Join us here for the night ceremony! Tonight, we celebrate, for tomorrow we grow! We blossom! We share!"

Immediately closing the drawer, she rushed out the front, bumping into a stranger before her.

"Oops! Apologies, my friend! Go on ahead," he stammered, a slight grin tracing his surprised self.

Skimming past, Xira continued down to the campfire where people had started to gather around while the announcer still chanted his lines. Flower stands were on each side of the area, presented with crowns, leis, wrap-arounds and bracelets. Few of the folk stood behind them to hand out to the crowd, bundled with many of their homegrown flowers, ranging from different colours to the styles, some even created from the very material that they'd use for their everyday clothing and needs. The emotion that filled this place was a sweet reminder of the good ol' days with Serenitatem and the family, as Xira warmed up a smile, feeling instantly cosier once again. Walking alongside the logs placed throughout the sandy grounds, a hand locked onto her arm just as she spotted Valin.

"My dear, take a seat. We're just about to begin," she told her.

"I will, thanks," Xira replied with a slight nod.

She sat beside another cloaked man who was eagerly concentrated on the speaker and nothing else. Admiring the flower crowns that rested atop his fluffy caramel hair, he turned with surprise.

"You like? I love these flowers, they're the exact same ones my nana used to give me at any morning she could. Smell!" He leaned in enthusiastically, holding the side of his cloak.

"Mmm, that's so nice. Your hair smells of coconuts as well, it's a great mix," she smiled, touching the petals.

"Sweet girl, I'll be sure to give you potpourri in one of the special fabric gift bags my mum makes. You can take it with you or keep it at home, wherever you please," he said kindly, giving her a hug.

"Aw, thank you," replied Xira as they finished hugging.

The fire rose up, sparkles of red, orange and yellow floated in the air. A woman came around to spread powder from a bucket, seemingly to give a blessing as it turned into a rainbow pattern, snowing along the logs in the fire, creating puffs of clouds and sparks while it ascended into the atmosphere, glowing with every touch. A cotton formation stretched out to the crowd, covering the whole area like a pillow cloud in the sky. The fuzzy feeling that tickled Xira's nose, continued through the surroundings like a launch of fireworks from each side, combining with the gentle, cool wind. *It truly feels magical,* Xira thought to herself, gazing at the rainbow swirls that flew through the sky and above, as another speaker joined at the mat placed on the ground. Sitting down, they held up a dark hooded purple robe in their arms.

"Tonight," she began, the crowd falling silent, "I bestow this prosperous robe unto one. One who shall wield with grace, honesty, loyalty and love. The moon's light will choose the soul that the robe will rest with. Until then, it floats above the flames, as we await. Humble yourselves and enjoy the night, celebrate with all from left and right. Have your feast, and when… the light shines down, I'll be back then."

An uproarious cheer boomed from the crowd, people lifting up flowers in unison, lending a dance to one another as hugs combined the beings filled with joy and love, rotating and spinning around the place, singing and dancing throughout the night. A musical cadre stood in a gap between the crowd, beginning to play the tunes on the instruments they carried. It all became a festive juncture in a space of magical ambience. Smiles and laughter bounced from one face to the next, the singing of the crowd and musicians harmonising like birds in a flock, while a few stood around the sides to spray a perfume-like essence across the villagers and two boys dressed as noir sailors skipped around the outer grounds in circles, dropping large leaves and seaweed out of their baskets. Xira admired the friendliness that was shared among each being, with everyone chiming in with different treats, it surely impressed like a beacon of hope signalling to connect what was left of pure kindness. Valin approached her on the side, with folded arms behind her cloak.

"What do you think of our ceremony so far?" she asked, watching and smiling.

"It's wonderful. I think it should be like this everywhere… anywhere…" Xira returned, her gaze sparkling with the campfire.

"I second that, sweet Xira. There'll be that true hope again, don't you worry," Valin kindly spoke, before steadily walking back.

The musical celebration went on for a long while, as the crowd merged into one giant conga line, skipping and dancing around the village, the musicians stood on a log as they shared laughs, while others clapped in rhythm and handed around a goblet of juice to sip from. Niko was spotted heading to Valin in a hurry, not appearing to be amused or enthralled by the celebration. Quickly sneaking through to observe the matter, Xira hid behind stacked barrels, overhearing the intense chatter between them, as they stood in front of a notice board holding some papers. With all the noise in the background, Niko was loud enough for his words to sift through while Valin attempted to hush his annoyance, but he insisted.

"We're just going to *let* her come and cause trouble for us? Don't you recall who this fiend is?"

"Niko, please… calm down. It will get sorted, we just need to do this quietly, away from home," were the words that Valin replied.

"No matter where we go, Valin, she will be lurking and committing all of this *foolery* and if we don't get that sceptre, who knows what she will unravel onto us all," Niko uttered fiercely, fluttering the pages in his hand.

The music began to quiet down, people slowly dispersing back to the campfire, as the speakers returned to stand and resume the ceremony. Valin's attention darted to the group as she turned to Niko, holding his arms in alert.

"Head back there, I'll meet you later. Whatever her agenda, it won't touch Bloom," she told him.

Rushing back, he disappeared in almost a second before it was announced for people to join. Xira ran to a log and took a seat, in time for the speech. She noticed Valin making her way to where she stood earlier, while others were still arriving. The speaker braced a smile, stretching her arms before the floating cloak. Taking a deep breath, she focused on the flames and held the tips of the ensemble. One of the sailor boys hurried to give her a ceremonial claw for her to place on top of it.

"Fellow folk. I've gathered you once again, for this penultimate moment before the conclusion of tonight's ceremony. As you may know, these offerings only occur once every decade. We do not choose, for the universe itself does. Nature beckons, so I've heard. The shine on the blessed here, so I've witnessed. I have my gratitude for you all and hold the unveiled name in my palm, so I shall deliver. It is always an honour to present the ceremonies, with all of the humble presence of Bloom Core sat before me and indeed it brings such joy when we all unite as one. No place for evil, but for good. Kindness blossoms the seed, with love to rise again. Come forth, blessed treasure," the speaker declared, "I call upon you… thy illumination… Xira."

A silence sliced through the twinkling air, as the wind stormed the crowd, the speaker carefully grasping the cloak along her forearms. Awaiting to hand it over, she stood by the fire patiently, watching over them to catch the one. Xira, awe-stricken, glanced at Valin, who kind-heartedly saluted with a huge smile, waving for her to go ahead and take what was hers. Scanning around, nobody seemed to dishonestly charge in or similarly misbehave but instead cheered on as humble as they were. The speaker called aloud once again, lifting it high above her head to lure in the collector.

"Needn't be shy, it will shine on you... for you..." she stated promisingly, before an opaque beam had found Xira sitting on the edge of the log, as if about to get away. Like a hundred torches on a hidden treasure, the people of Bloom Core stared in amazement as they continued cheering and flailing about, encouraging her to meet with the speaker. The man with the flower crown rushed for a hug before slumping back in his spot, excitedly rooting and watching as Xira smiled, then further walked up to the fire, observing the magic up-close... she could feel the floating pieces of ember touch her hands and a strange energy that was luring her closer and simultaneously lifting like she was going to form into a tornado. Once standing opposite of the woman holding the cloak, the beam disappeared while the flames twirled and raised. The speaker joyously resumed the speech.

"There you are. Darling girl, your spiritual connection with this world is beyond my comprehension and it is not by my utterance but of the wise, that have told me you are the only one that holds a unique secret... maybe you are unknowing of it yet, although you shan't concern yourself girl, for you are truly blessed and we are here to hand you this cloak," she continued, "and you shall wield within you, for my will to grant is my gift I share truthfully... and gladly... for the heavens have shared with me tonight... for the blessed one that is dearly before me."

Xira gazed at the cloak as it hovered over the fire like magic, to the palm of her hands it rested, while sparkles glimmered along the sides to the bottom. Feeling a cool flow from beneath, rainbow hues seeped from beneath her flesh hiding within the cloak as it circled around the back to place itself for her to wear. The hood covered over her head, as the rest of it gently descended across her shoulders, to her arms and down to her feet. She quietly gasped, observing her new ensemble which felt just as mystical as it wonderfully displayed on the exterior. The warmth that it gave her, almost seemed like she could stay afloat, just like it had over the fire. The same energy she felt before, coursed below the material, tracing through every limb and edge. This was surely otherworldly and sacred, as she suspected what the speaker was about to say then.

"Ah, marvellous. That zap you just felt on your two fingers, it is the sign of the ancient wise contacting you and sending their regards, commemorating the event and the truly blessed that is you, Xira. They are profoundly cheering alongside us." The woman explained, "Whether you wish to stay and celebrate the rest of the ceremony tonight, is up to you, for now, I shall say once again, the offering has been done. I wish you all of the best, young lady."

Quickly turning to her hand, she noticed the fingertips and exchanged glances with the speaker, then back with a smile as she knew this was indeed amazing. Before she left, the woman had more to say as she lifted her arms again, in praise.

"It has been a sweet honour to be here with you all… as we further celebrate the rest of the ceremonial event, here, tonight." Continued the speaker, "For now, we send off the dear girl, off on her merry adventures and where you shall venture beyond. More drinks and food will be given once they are prepared, by our fantastic Eugene! Hooray!"

Everyone clapped and chanted once again as Xira walked back to a drink stand, made with a tall wooden table in the shape of a clover, decorated with Bloom Core's festive ornaments and an umbrella perch made out of bamboo. Then dangling from it, strings of home-made lights of various kinds. One of the stringed lights fizzled out from an exposed wire by the table, where Xira fiddled with its edge in hopes of repairing it — when she did, enveloping her fingertips on the wire, the lights lit up once again and so did Xira's surprised grin. The ornaments grew brighter sequentially, emitting the glow's magic through its surface — twinkling stars which trailed along its material. Noticing the slight exposure of the wire, she realised that it'd been her own doing…of returning the light. Valin spared no time to accompany her, waltzing, in an euphoric way. Standing next to her, she noticed her cheery expression was painted over by a worrisome feeling.

"Well? Wasn't that surreal, dear?" she kindly spoke, taking a gander at the crowd gallivanting around the fire. There was no reply in return, only a sigh and a slump on the table.

Valin softly placed her hand on Xira's, in a comforting manner as she leaned in closer.

"What is the matter?" she resumed quietly, "Are you afraid? Did something happen?"

"Hmmh…" muttered Xira, raising her head higher, "It's just strange… what does it all mean… aside from what the speaker did say, something just feels unanswered… a mystery, or, like I have to find the truth and uncover it myself, starting with *this*… ogh…" Swinging the cloak around as the hood fell, she turned to the music and dancing.

"I do apologise for the missing answers in this regard, the speaker only announced what was sent to her, through the connections of the wise. The rest *is* up to you, however, don't you suppose it is quite a guide closer to what you were wondering all along?" Valin questioned in thought, placing her hands back behind her.

"It's still a clue to a clue. I got here by escaping that *thing* that was happening back at my hometown, not knowing this is an entirely new world… a world that somehow has something for *me,* an answer, a whatever… meanwhile who knows what's going on back there, how horrible it has become, those that have plagued the towns further than just Glacial Mist. They could be seriously evil and not really helping anybody with the way they have shown themselves. Between the connections from here and there and how you mentioned the possible collision that is looming, I have no doubt the answers are in both places. Although…" Xira paused, puzzling the pieces together, "It feels like the most important one is here. The cloak is for my truth. This world knows something. My instincts pull me like a guidance, to search the realm, to find the secret it protects. My heart knows… and once I find *it*… then it blossoms further through all the shadows, revealing itself entirely. I can feel the energy, it's satisfying, Valin, and it keeps getting stronger by each moment that flies. The *wise* you two have spoken about, they set this during the ceremony, because I was here. The speaker *did* also say these occurrences go down once every decade, it's all coming together, aligned with every spark. Huh… Serenitatem didn't even have a note about all this, this — this wanted *me* to go to it. *Me.* I'm so glad the people that found us were kind, you guys have shown your generosity and care. Now I have another clue, for my path in here, this wonderful place. A journey to the mystery, and my friend along with me, this means a lot… Vaoz, I can't explain enough. All of this sorrow and mixed emotions have finally etched the exit to another entrance, revealing the mysticality… and… I just want to fly there, with a broom or, whatever, such a rush what this world has displayed to us… I have to go… thank you so much Valin, Willow and I are very grateful for you and Niko's help. Your home truly reflects on what you all share and do for one another and that's amazing. We needed this honestly, and I hope we keep in touch… probably will visit again though… I'm sure you'll stick around, they need you and the town needs safety. Like a friend of mine, Jay'eo, used to say… "*the kind that are kind know the kind…*"

Valin launched for a hug, holding her close. Teary eyed, Xira wrapped around her, prompting her to tear up as well.

"Dear, dear Xira, of course we will keep in touch. I'm honoured you shared this with me, and we are always here for you, as Niko and I have said before." Valin quietly spoke with a gentle smile, "Now you two stay safe as well, we want to hear of your discoveries. Whether here or anywhere else, we're always with you. In spirit, in magic. We usually don't get easily comfortable with outsiders, but we now know you guys are much more at home… bless your souls."

"We'll probably leave in the morning, so I guess we'll part then. Talk soon, Valin," she responded quietly.

Xira noticed Valin choking up, holding back tears through her smile. After their hug, she held on her hand before sending her off with a joyful wave as Xira hurried back, her cloak floating behind, to check on Willow who was taking a nap in Niko's tent. Walking in, her friend was fast asleep, the blanket over her drooped down to the bed's metal foot rest as Xira sat on a chair next to the nightstand. Not wanting to wake her, she searched the room for something to keep her occupied. After finding a book on potions and remedies, she flipped it open as she went back to the chair, swinging one leg on the other. The tent started to feel colder, so pulling the hood over, it automatically provided her with warmth, smiling, she felt closer with it already. *If only my mood could always be like this*, she thought. Flipping through the pages, it'd captured her attention on the variations of ingredients that resided on this land, none of which were alike to Glacial Mist. In awe, the list of recipes revealed were in relation to healing and recovery. She'd recognised one of the flowers that had been featured during the ceremony, in a healing recipe called *Sana Animam Meam, Et Caro*. The flower was known as Verbena, multi-purpose for protection, peace and healing, there added as the main ingredient for the remedy and was as well mixed with two that were already familiar with her, dittanies and chamomile. Below the description, someone had scribbled a translation reading; *"Heal the flesh and soul"*. Along the page were more notes etched on the sides and any gaps given throughout. Xira figured this had been the doings of Niko, after recognising his handwriting on the notes he'd written from before on his table. While skimming through the book, she felt a tickle on her left wrist. As she was holding the book, facing it upwards, her birthmark began to glow, trailing along the inked lines and forming a neon shine… before setting off like a lantern, its sparks springing out and then returning back to her flesh. *Uh, what was that?* She crunched her forehead, staring intently. Immediately closing the book and rushing to place everything back on the table, she fumbled along the forearm, circling her phosphorescent wrist. She felt a burn just below it then yanked her jacket sleeve down without a thought. *Oh man…* she pondered, focusing on keeping her equilibrium. Patrolling around the tent, hunting for a distraction, she came across a note pinned on a clipboard that was dangling off by the tent's front.

'URGENT NIKO!~MEET WITH VAOZ TO FIND <u>HER</u>
GET THAT SCEPTRE!
ing. list
Mugwort — NORTH
Valerian — WEST BLOOM FIELD
Strawberries from the garden
Agrimony — NORTH EAST'

I wonder what they're all up to, she whispered, analysing.

"What is that?" Willow questioned from behind her.

"Oh," Xira turned, facing her, "from the ceremony… I'm not sure dude but it's apparently connected to me and the answers I'm supposed to find in this realm. It's so strange, but in a good way… there's a high feeling that it gives me, like guiding me to where the hunt leads to, the mystery, so, something hidden I need to uncover. That something, my *truth*. Are you feeling better? How's your leg?"

"Wow, that's super cool, goodness… I, uh — yeah, the doctor Niko did really well… I don't feel that agony any more. At least… I hope it's the same for when I…" Willow abruptly cut herself off, as she stood on the leg in attempt to walk across the space, "Yes… oh my gosh… I, it's painless when I walk! He did it. He—"

Not even after a few steps, a force pulled her to kneel as the other leg pushed back to support. Clutching on her thigh, she felt the same thing that happened when her wound transformed.

"This… I still don't know what *this* is," she cried, checking her leg, "It's not infected. I would know, my mother told me about all that. I'm scared, Xixi… what did those creepers *do* to me?"

Xira joined her friend in angst, lifting her to the bed again.

"We can ask the docs when they return. You probably should still rest… you're safe here," she reminded her.

Pulling the blanket over, she sat beside her. In comfort, they huddled as Xira's mind raced between her friend's burden and her own. The thin define between good and evil, and what was yet to be discovered and fall on their palms. To fill the longing space in dire need of information or sound the whistle to the already existing within. For it to come forth, present itself brazenly. As light and darkness hold hands, the warmth between cannot ever be emulated.

Almost slinking into a doze herself, she was startled by the shuffling feet grating past the opening of the tent. Hurrying to check it out, she recognised the cloak dripping along and decided to tail. Using the shrubs to keep cover, Xira quietly leaped through each one as the cloaked was rushing off to someplace. Fallen debris and ruins laid ahead, as they halted before a fork in a road, where one led to an ivy gate with branches for locks and the other to a path towards a river surrounded by tall trees and plantation. It wasn't too long before they continued down the direction of the gate, where another familiar face turned to greet them. Not quite a cheery expression as both of the cloaked hurried to the gate, holding a crystallised sphere on a steel chain and a woollen bag wrapped with a begrimed red ribbon. The branches cracked along the gate as they slowly slid in a wave to the edges of the gate's doors, the leaves dancing above the vented interval, and an eerie distant noise chiming through the wrought iron.

"She's almost here. We stand only feet apart. Are you prepared?" Niko's discreet voice echoed through the night air.

Valin clutched onto the bag, one hand shielding it, "I'm giving all

I've got. For the sake of the realm. Niko, we need to find out where she's plotting, it could aid us to avert a war and maybe cleanse of her maliciousness for good."

"You need not worry… I believe *these* will guide and provide us. If she *has* started a war, the best we could do is finish it before it completely demolishes all that she touches. Remember, she's a threat to not just us… she may be cruel and unholy, tainted beyond belief, but purity overcomes all." He spoke, his arm caressing her cloak consolingly.

The two stood side by side, patiently awaiting the arrival. They had covered themselves with the hoods and intently stared at the gate's front in complete silence. *Whoever could this be?* Xira thought to herself, hunkering down beside the ruins, holding on to the brim of her cloak and observing in their direction. A strange tune was heard on the opposite side, getting closer. By the looks on their faces, it wasn't a delight to be expected. She focused them down as they took a few steps back, still facing the front, almost in overwhelming fear. Niko appeared to be putting his brave face more so than Valin, who barely could keep quiet as her repeated shallow breaths puttered. He tried to reassure her, but she seemed to sense the danger too close and personal. Within a moment, the gate's doors creaked open, as if they hadn't been used in over a century, though in this case it feigned from dark magic. The cadaverous vapour that smouldered along the stone surface creeped around the grass patches as it reached at the doctor's oval shoes, like it was pulling the ground up from underneath. A grim burgundy figure gradually slithered onward, uncannily hiding their exterior as they approached with a cold demeanour, not requiting a warm salutation, leering slyly into their souls, as if 'twas the unforgiving reaper. Before they could blink, the gate slammed shut and the grounds behind it grumbled, sending the reverberation of the aftermath to ricochet from one point to another. No one uttered a word while Valin held the woollen bag above, obscuring their gaze. Revealing behind their dense cloak, a cane-like object pecked a stone as it remained overlapped by the material in front which led Niko to abruptly shoot a glance at Valin, whom was focused too on their heel.

"Settle down…" the voice spoke pompously, "I have but agreed to meet for our… discussion." Lowering their hood behind, as it rested on the shoulders, the stranger curved a corner smirk as they adjusted their sleeve.

"You *agreed* to tell us. We still stand by the pact that was sealed years ago by the relatives of the ancients." Niko replied sternly, "Even polar opposites can come to make peace by fair compromise. For the sake of yours and ours…"

"The pact, you say?" She scoffed, "By no obligation am I to abide. We are the new form of descendants, they no longer have a say over us. Your foolish behaviour is what *makes* this kind of *mess* in the first place. You wouldn't want that for the people now, would you?"

"*Your* mess is the root of the problem we face. We think of doing good, while you parade around with nothing but cruel intentions and apathy." Valin cut in, lowering the bag as they met with their gaze.

Niko moved closer to her, trying to maintain the space between the two while locking onto the guest. To his surprise, it hadn't escalated to how he thought it'd turn out, but rather the lingering disgust that befouled around them. The woman chuckled under her breath, lifting her head, acting with insolence. Xira kept her focus on her, as their expression turned dim, observing the discomfort that was shown. She felt an ominous drop in the pit of her stomach, like a signal was received from the opposite way. *Are they having a staring contest or something?* Was her thought, trying to brush it off, *They shouldn't be in danger… just talking… right?* A crow suddenly swooped past them, bringing a gust of wind through, then disappeared off in the trees ahead. There was a glow emitting from inside the bag, sparkles shining through the wool. A worrying look flushed Valin's already shambled composure. The soil beneath began to crumble, tumbling outwards and past their feet, a thump and one more followed with a gravitational pull from the ground before them. Niko slanted closer to disrupt the intruding commotion.

"Erma!"

"Reluctance in a civil barter does not capture my generosity to forgive," she sneered, sounding exasperated, "Nor do I grant chances to imbecility."

"But that's ridiculous! We didn't ask for such conflict!" Valin added in hopes to soothe the situation.

Trying to stand against the pull, she held onto the bag as the force tugged on her. Immediately, Niko raised up the crystallised sphere by the chain and extended his arm in front, which projected a transparent diamond wave to shield both of them. Xira observed, enthralled, as Erma carved a groove to trap the two on the isolated ground which stood afloat, her wicked demeanour glooming towards them. The doctors exchanged quick glances, muttering something under their breaths. Hiding the woollen bag under her cloak, Valin wrapped her arms around Niko's as she realised the dark depths glaring at her only feet away. While the crumbles rolled off the edge, a singing whisper screeched through the air from below. They turned around in haste, planning a diversion to escape without complications. With a short chant, a group of crows and ravens rushed downwards in their direction, wildly orbiting Erma as they flapped their wings simultaneously along their cries which prompted her to focus on the ambush, leaving her targets at bay. Niko used this moment to swing the chain in alignment with the other side of the gap, transforming the shield into a walkway for them to cross over. Sturdy enough, they still had to be careful, as they slowly stepped one foot after the other, making their way one by one. They'd reached the other side triumphantly, as they dropped to rest. Meanwhile, Niko still holding the chain, braced it before them in protection from Erma.

"I don't think we should hang around until she comes to," Valin proposed, dusting her hair, "we'll have to collect that sceptre another time…"

"You heard her, unless it's by her default, arrangements are something she does not desire!" Niko responded frantically, "If we fall back, it'll be because of us that she pursues her initial plans."

"We'll have to take that chance," she returned calmly, "Bloom needs us. There's always another way. Do it for them."

Reluctant to agree, Niko remained in his defensive position while Erma grew furious. With the despair and concern she was feeling, Valin began to make her way back, distancing herself enough away from the trouble. She knew a new plan was needed in order to rescue Niko. Rushing down, her feelings that overwhelmed seemed like different kinds of weather clashing on the inside and outside, but that fuelled her concentration in the midst of forming her plan. She searched around for aid, any means of distraction and all the resources she could find in the near land. After thorough scavenging, a couple of bags had been filled with the materials in mind. By luck, a hut was located out in the open of a flowery meadow yonder. It had contained every-day necessities for anyone who may be in need, which in this case, home-made bags of cotton with a thick string to carry. Perched in the rocky corner, Xira tracked Valin's activity as she made sure not to get spotted. Not knowing what she had in those bags, it was a count of four that were flung over the back, each filled up and stringed shut. Valin was running at an uncalculated tempo, swinging left and right, in a hurry to reach her friend in time… with a desperate look and hope to achieve the new plan. Meanwhile, the opened soil had mended back together with a fresh tumble of sand rolling over the surface. Erma returned to face Niko, who was still behind his protective barrier in determination to hold her well off and cover his unsettling gut feeling. In close contact, he began to wince as slivers of secretion weaved along the forearm holding the swirling chain closer to his knee. The winds picked up while the ground grew much colder, the terror that stalked slithered behind the shoulders and the illusion of a confined rift pinched his throat, looming across his nose as if the air suddenly formed thick particles, drawing it away dry like a vacuum… leaving no flavour behind to consume… all he could concentrate on was the merciless scowl that descended too close for comfort.

"Is that, fear?" She seethed, her tone churning his stomach, "Here was I thinking you were going to rip me a new one. Come on! No one has done that in a long, long time…"

Lifting her feet about like she was kicking up dirt in the style of a top hat and cane dance, taunting with masqueraded emotions, he only then felt the warning of which Valin tried to tell before — filling his insides with the regret. It had appeared that this woman relished treating prey like treats in a piñata, all to fall in the palm of her hands. To his advantage however, the impudence served in his favour and he was to hold his spot safely, even if it meant mere inches away from the claws of the predator. Her mocking laughter scratched through the cold cutting air as though forced, dragging her sceptre across the path in a circular motion, the noise grating against Niko's sides whilst a low booming scare rendered among the grasslands and tall blossomed trees in the distance. Silence fell, as so did the night. The moonlight barely pierced through the dark clouds, let alone the stars, like it was expecting a heavy storm. Meanwhile, underneath the waving frizzy hair, Erma's eyes glowed a sinister red, being one of the few illuminations with her sceptre's red and black crystal, along with Niko's barrier that revealed entirely and intensely in the darkness. He stared like an unknown had risen from the abyss — from his angle, it was equivalent to a nightmare in one's slumber... goosebumps tickled the hairs on his skin, while cold smoke drifted around them, Erma becoming almost inhuman...

Running footsteps got louder as they reached the vicinity, luring Niko to divert his attention as it was originating from behind him. Instead, he remained focused to what now seemed like a flight or fight moment... but feeling utterly helpless. The barrier sufficed to protect him, keeping any direct attacks away, though he wasn't so sure to add any chance to it fending her off for the better. Lightning zipped through the damp clouds as thunder clattered. Water that waved by, welded Erma's hair down her jaw's end and hung below, with some pieces curved across her forehead and the bridge of her nose. Ominously, the sleeve of her garment elevated while drooping around her wrist that was holding the sceptre with her begrimed flesh, as she twisted it slowly to face the centre of the barrier.

With heavy breath and cotton bags, Valin returned in a tumbling halt, just a short distance behind, "Let him go! This needs to be resolved with words... communicating with... with each other."

"You should consider joining your little guy..." Erma dismissed slyly, "Do him not foolishly, you'll owe for his karma, with yours, by my dealing."

Valin knelt by his side, leaving two of the bags with him, "You know what our matter was, it's not responsible even for your people to get dragged into a redundant case because of your horrid temper and simply neglecting your vowed code—"

"Hush... don't speak of mine, or so. Help. Me." Her voice low in her reply, as scraped were their ears after each uttered syllable, "There is no family where you reside... it is but obvious that a true, raw connection... births from within. As for you and yours... it is merely solitary. Nothing of substance, utility or without prejudice. For that and more, your little town is doomed... as are you both."

Not wanting to linger any longer, Valin tossed a handful of green powder around the barrier, then swung one of the cotton bags over to knock Erma out of the way. After that, she proceeded to jump ahead, reaching behind to trap her in the centre before launching the other one she had been carrying. Distraught and compromised, Erma released a suppressed screech as the contents from the bags fell out to erupt around her, with what was in the form of magma rocks and crystallised bijou that sparked with collision, compelling her to spring backwards. The smoke which surrounded, was a mixture of colours that derived from the fragments and exerting an opaque cage-like egg bubble over the wicked woman's body, in a method to contain her. Lending some time to free himself, Niko rolled in the opposite direction and further away, still positioning the barrier before him, although his thoughts were all over the place. They watched as the moment went up in a flurry, right before it submerged into a mud-patch beneath her high boots and the edges of her material. Valin went over to Niko, kneeling behind the barrier just as a gust blew through them. Within the next second, the ground Erma stood on pushed away anything near, as a dark whirlpool appeared, beginning to swarm her feet. It ascended into a wider radius simultaneously with her arms hovering upwards like a summoning was occurring. The haunting tornadoes of black smoke flew up in the air, along the pool of black and burgundy ribbons swallowing the atmosphere around her. Just then, a silhouette formed like it was separating itself from the host, as a dark portal emerged, pulling in the wind and smoke. Leaping towards the trees, Xira rolled to the closest one near the dispute to keep track. A bag from the centre of the path tumbled towards the grass from the heavy gusts, right by her as she collected it for herself.

"If I were to spout what's under my sleeve… my magician name won't be inconspicuous. Have you not danced with roses of thorns? Return I will." Erma verbalized grimly.

They watched her retract into the darkness, offering a deriding smile moments before disappearing. Valin immediately turned to Niko, still in his frightful slant.

"Why on holy worlds would you allow to get that close to her? You know how dangerous she can be if she really wants to, anything more than that would've been enough to provoke a deeper layer which I'm sure wouldn't have gone in our favour," She expressed with worry, making sure her friend was all right.

"It's not like that… not by choice," he replied, taking breaths in-between.

"Huh?"

"The root of it, really… it's — it goes way back," Niko continued,

"I didn't exactly get too lucky with the family…"

"Niko, please. Our friendship is hardened because of our hardships that we share with each other, allow that growth even further. The bigger, purified, the better. Better for us. You can open up to me, you know that," She reassured him kindly.

Behind the trees, Xira curled on an angle to eavesdrop while crouching in the flowery grass. The height of the lavender toned tree then cast a shadow that stretched far off, providing a sweet camouflage. A soft breeze flowed through the path, bringing a fresh breath of air as it cooled down the remains of the mess. Any trace of Erma's visit had long been swept off, apart from the aftermath of the moments before she left. The leaves that twirled over the way seemed to have nourished nature's grounds into the refreshing blossoms that lifted once again. Though the feelings of each soul filled the atmosphere in various moods, it was there willingly to perform its healing for the natives.

Finally gasping and returning to himself, Niko glanced up in preparation to answer. However hard and rough he'd been feeling currently, his determination to confide in his dear friend was higher. The trust they both shared outgrew anything else that attempted to kick him down.

"You know… remember, how you used to visit every other full moon for dinner whenever I'd invite you to join our 'special family feasts' because father would transport back and forth due to his duty?" He asked, "It's not what it was. H-… at all."

"Go on," she added gently, holding his hand.

"He used to tyrannize me. Often. I wanted nothing more than to decline my mother's call for those evenings… I would've spared his visits." Niko explained heavily, softly wiping tears, "But even after trying, after my efforts… he still found ways to breach and… mother had not a single idea. I couldn't tell her. I couldn't bear the burden, to give something that horrible to her, who knows what he would've done. It's all in the past… but this brought that up again. That same… ensnarement. This is a place of peace and that kind of evil definitely should not go here."

Valin felt the emotions sink deeply within, pushing through the stomach to what he expressed. That sorrow left her overwhelmingly speechless, as she lunged in for a big hug, the comforting love she knew he'd needed. Niko wrapped his arms as soon as she did, leaning his head on her shoulder, his tears soaking the fabric as he coughed, clearing his throat between each whistling inhale. Neither letting go, they went on with the embrace, tending to the caring feeling in one another. Xira leaned gently on the tree, her sympathetic glance to Niko made her think of events of her past, as she scanned the nature of the location, deep in thought. Brief minutes later, she jumped far high to the right, through the grasslands, on the way back to the village. The moonlight followed her each spring, beaming through the night air with only the swift sound of the grass conducting alongside the quietly chirping birds. Although it had been some time, Niko and Valin remained on the side of the path, hugging through the night, for a long warm while...

Everyone must've been asleep as soon as Xira returned, for the village felt quieter than when she'd left it. She checked in Valin's hut, most of it cleaned up and went to grab some tea that was in the pot since before. *Ooh, still warm...* she thought. Walking out, she went over to check on her friend, who had been waiting with her beverage wrapped in hand.

"Xira! Where were you?" She asked, her voice lowering.

Xira walked up and sat on the nearby chair, "Well I'll tell you..." she said, taking a drink. Almost an hour had went by, before Willow's expressions changed from surprised to frightened to saddened. After telling her everything, Xira shot up to walk around the space while finishing off the drink.

"They don't even know yet, they're still there and I just — I hope they're all right," she continued, "That Erma woman, the name is quite familiar... wait a minute, that guy — what was his name? Back at... home?"

"Uh... oh! J... Jerril Hank? Yes, yes, what about him?" Willow responded, confused but gathering.

"He mentioned that the so-called librarian in our local library posed as an 'Erma', now it *could* be a serious coincidence... but she gave him something that stands out as an odd deed from a librarian. We have maps, they've been giving them out for as long as it has been opened," explained Xira, "I don't believe that someone holding that type of knowledge of the land comes with no hidden secret. She isn't exactly your old friend and I certainly haven't met her. All the things that Jerril told us was merely below the surface, which I intend to fill the gaps of — if this *Erma* is the same woman as Jerril's *handler,* then this gets even stranger. With what oddity is happening back home, it can't possibly be too different to this realm. There's a connection in all of this."

"You don't suppose…?" Willow paused, feeling quite aghast, "I have to talk to the doc first about the safety, then we can go on with our search. I really thought this place would at least be without such hostility, guess there are those types like… everywhere."

Xira's face lit up, "Wait, hold that thought — I'll be back in a bit."

Running to Valin's tent, immediately the drawers were pulled open from top to bottom. Retrieving the small book from there, she found blank pages beneath it with a stained pattern. On the table in the middle of the space, she used the ink pen that was on the corner stand to write a note to Valin and Niko. After quickly placing it on the desk by the entrance, she held out the cotton bag from within her cloak, carefully placing it beside the note. Heading out once again, she entered Niko's tent. She raised up the book before dropping it on the bench, placing her palms on each side.

"This was in Valin's drawer. It could help us. I'm not supposed to go through this but if it has what we need, then it's worth borrowing it," she quietly said, "I'll return it before they do."

The girls leaned over to examine the pages, the initials E.M. etched on the front and a message in smudged black ink on the opposite side.

'vow to dance with almighty of the dynasty, vow to vanquish with almighty of the dynasty'

Flipping through the pages, surely enough, it was as more cryptic with every page read. It came to a surprise for Willow, as she hadn't witnessed much of the darker elements of the realm as of yet. The reappearing symbol painted in red, black and gold was noted on the pages' corners after every few. It resembled the gold edges of a harp, three red spears sticking out from within and a black sun painted behind it. It had appeared to be of great importance to the beholder, for it didn't contain any elaboration further than the imagery and though it sufficed, there remained an unknown secret attached to it. Reading through the text, Xira noticed a mention of another name.

"Syphon…" she remarked, "The rest of it is encrypted, I assume it's their secret language of a sort… and it finished with the same name, instead written with an 'X' than an 'S', this time."

They ventured further through the inked pages, as they noted various indentations and hidden letters. Before reaching the last of the notes, the *E.M.* initials were spotted again with another lengthy written text below. Scanning along the lines, Xira saw a little emblem which Serenitatem and her family back home had used a long time ago in their letters. It had meant to shed light on the specific area to reveal its core to your need in answers, which in this case, was to read what was inked between the lines. Holding the book, she went to pick up the lamp on Niko's desk to test it out. Nothing. *I need the flame to touch the air on the surface,* she reminded herself. The drawers on the sides of the desk caught her glance, as she raced to search everyone. Upon finding a bundle of matches without the box, she jumped towards the mini stove that Niko used for tea and other liquid preparations to apply the matches. *There,* she held the match in relief. Sliding back to the table, she held the lit match close to the page, hovering it across the gap between each line to read the message. As it illuminated the silver steel glow of the individual letters forming an entirely new text, it had information which made little sense to the girls and just added more questions.

"Look at this." Xira's attention suddenly swooped, "Erma. Erma Merideth."

Willow shot up, spooked, "THAT'S code for… oh my… oh no."

"It's her all right. From Jerril to here, this all comes full circle. This is the same woman." Xira continued, "Valin has likely been trying to decipher the text inside and knows about the darker entity from the past. What is she up to in our neighbourhood?"

Her friend cast a worried look, "It's not safe for us to go back yet… don't you agree it's better to find out here?"

"I think we should rest first. We'll figure this out in the morning, okay?" replied Xira, closing the book.

Willow nodded as she rolled back in bed, pulling the blankets over. After saying their goodnight, Xira quietly returned to Valin's tent, hiding the book in the drawer. She went over to the teapot to pour herself a cup, before sitting down at the table, warm beverage in hand and deep in her thoughts. Her index finger traced the ceramic rim, the steam sifting through the sides as she zoned out, staring at the table. It had been quite some hours that went by, when hushed chatter was heard. Shuffling feet and light rain accompanied the distinct voices that got louder with each step. Between the two, they'd assumed everybody was asleep in the village, but still paranoid about any listeners. Xira waited in anticipation, before Valin stepped in with a hesitant entrance.

"Dear! You're not sleeping?" She spoke in a high pitch, trying to keep quiet.

"I couldn't. I had a lot of things on my mind…" was Xira's reply as she drank.

"Well, care to share those with me? I'll join you, I myself can't bring my body to catch a single wink, p-probably because of all the celebrations, ha-ha," Valin let out an anxious laugh, before seating herself down.

For a moment or so, they exchanged various expressions like it was an indirect interrogation, with Xira knowing a little too much and Valin being left in the dark, both hiding familiar things and yearning for another. Two which contain each other's answer.

"Where's Niko?" Xira asked.

"Uhm, he's, he's back in his tent. He helped me with the cleaning and sorts. Doctors we may be, but we have many other matters in Bloom, even if it's not our forte." Explained Valin, though masking the vital truth.

The background sounds of rain and creatures close to the village balanced through the comfortable ambience that occupied. They took sip after sip, not one giving a word for a long while, but then Xira broke the ice.

"Valin…?" She muttered, relaxing on the cushioned chair.

"Yes, dear?" Valin returned, refilling their cups.

Taking a pause, Xira leaned in with a daring and direct stare, "I know. I was there. I know what happened."

Startled, Valin fell back in the midst of her attempt to hold herself together, "Know what, may I urge?"

"Erma." Was her only reply.

"…" Again, she fell in distraught, "How?"

"Never mind that. She's planning something, isn't she? You know she's visiting Glacial Mist and that her posing danger means none of us are safe." Xira fired back, one hand gripping the cup's handle, one out front.

"My goodness, Xira… I didn't want to burden you girls with that horrid wretch. Truth be told, I was only ready to send you off on your merry ways after Willow's leg had healed. Niko is not his best self, right now, it'll be a little while before we can talk to her again. No denying that there's a threat on both our homes, but please, until we resolve this quietly, keep this between us." Valin humbly responded as it resulted in a close whisper.

Xira, finishing her drink, got up from the chair and began preparing for slumber. While turned, the clash of the cups filled in the silence. Valin took them over to the crafting bench, eyeing Xira every few moments. The water gushed down as she washed the wares stacked in the sink. She pulled on the cord near her to activate the lighting in the room, before modifying it for sleep mode so only the row of mini lights and a lantern that were connected by a decorative wire along the wooden sashes from one end to the other were in use — the twinkling set the mood for a fire, as it was being arranged by the fireplace. Clearing her throat, Valin approached the young woman to hand a potted plant she'd pulled out of a pocket.

"I am more than what I put on," she uttered in a reassuring, grounded tone, "Like the art of herbs…"

Walking to the table, Valin quietly sorted through some aromatic, hueful herbs and slanted to glance at her.

"It's all about how you do your magic—*which* is something I don't tell Niko, see…"

She winked at the companion, before gesturing at the folded paper that was left discreetly on the surface then.

"He doesn't tell *which is which*. About me. My *secret* craft," whispered Valin, "Read the phrases of this poem. Letters catch the eye and the beginning is the place to start. Like the seed to the seedling, it leaves none apart. Tell no one."

As the woman wandered off, Xira opened the page to read;

'Valin is the name.
Where I come from, where I've been,
Is my business to keep, as you've seen,

There's no one quite like me,
Crafty as I'll always be,
Heathens hath no hook on a woman so free!'

Before leaving the tent briefly, Valin stepped forward to remark, "I did that for fun, sitting in a garden, drinking tea…"

Xira gave her a fascinated glance and smiled warmly, as her eyes expressed her delight and appreciation. They shared and exchanged warm energy, as they turned to their own tasks. She could hear her outside, quietly singing before returning again; *"Fun is key. Key to be. One is joy, one is free."*

The cold breeze entered and the flames came to rise. Warmth coated the space, crackling effects beside the occasional flue ventilation, mixing with the sweet smell of flora which was sprinkled around and the cosiness greatly increased, as it effectively huddled the air right for a soft, sound sleep.

"Goodnight, have sweet dreams," Valin spoke up caringly, still watching her while wiping the bench.

"Or nightmares…" Xira muttered under her breath before catapulting into bed.

"Pardon, what was that?"

"Likewise." She replied like the motion of a dart.

"Oh." Valin lifted a smile, then quietly sat back down, flipping through her recipe book. Seconds, to minutes, to hours, Xira began to fall asleep, wrapped in the warm fluffy blanket and the fireplace guiding her well into a sweet, warm rest.

The entrance's flaps fluttered inwards and out with the village's cheerful morning presence. Xira got up to get some water as she heard the people's kind exchanges to each other, their fondness singing through every voice. Looking over to the desk, she noticed the note and bag had been taken. After placing down the cup and walking out, the warm, fresh breeze swirled through, her cloak lifted as the goosebumps from the dawn's air weaved along briefly. The flower crowned man from last night raced up to her with a huge smile.

"Here, I want you to have this. It's a gift of potpourri, like I promised. My mum was making them since last night and I just couldn't wait to give you one!" He handed it over joyously.

"Thank you, this is sweet, mm," Xira replied, inhaling the lovely smell, "Tell your mum she's a great woman, but she should know that already."

"You are so, so welcome! Such a delightful gal, I'll be sure to let her know. Hey, I'll catch you around? My name is Lleyton by the way. Enjoy!" Lleyton skipped away after giving her a quick hug. *What a kind dude. People could really learn from his humanity,* she thought to herself, smiling.

Before entering Niko's area, there was a conversation between the doctors that seemed like a mix of emotions bouncing off, exactly how birds chirping altogether in a tree could compare. Inside, Valin and Niko were found going about the place with flailing hands every now and then, expressing what Xira could only assume was their new discovery. Too busy to pay any attention to the screeching tea pot on the stove, they spread out multitude of papers on the mid table, pencilling their analysation and points. Her friend still asleep in the back, Valin cut abruptly mid-sentence as she turned to greet.

"Have you had breakfast? We need to talk," She began, sounding like she had just one too many cups of coffee.

"Sure… I was about to ask you the same thing," Xira answered, as Niko's focused self, joined in.

"Did you leave this note?" He intervened, desperately wanting to know.

"Wait — Nik, please, just a second," Valin placed her hand on his shoulder reassuringly. Going around the table, she pulled out a chair for Xira to join, hauling it over the opposite side. In front of them was the cotton bag with the sceptre laying on top of it and the note beside it. The papers scattered along the sides showed their notes about the item and its connection to the family that Erma was a part of. The book with the initials *E.M.* was also near the papers, as Xira dragged the chair closer, then the conversation resumed.

"Nothing has to be hidden now, all that you went through, I myself witnessed," Xira told them, "I understand she's the one you were worried about and that she is not one to be trusted."

"Ok, so you know Erma then, that's neat, neat…" Niko uttered with unease, before bringing four mugs of tea on a wheeling-tray.

"I believe she has invaded my town. Maybe no drastic actions since

I first heard the name, but a man by the name Jerril Hank, has spoken to my friend and I. He told us of a woman with that name supposedly working in our local library, or in our logic, under cover. I don't like to say this, though I think she might be collecting people to be her puppets in her scheme, using them to build an army of a sort… so she can have a piece of her, to say, in everywhere she goes." Explained Xira, inspecting the tame sceptre.

"Can you take us, to this, Jerril?" Inquired Niko, yet again impatiently. Valin calmly placed her hand on his forearm, signalling him to refresh himself.

"It's not like that, he approached us and didn't mention where he was staying, only that it was temporary," she replied, watching his mood soften into passiveness.

"Well. You said he visits the library? Why not try there? Perhaps it's a frequent activity," Valin proposed.

"I would. It's not safe right now. I wouldn't advise for you to go either, because as much as we wanted to find out what was happening, we were practically forced to get out of there." Xira continued with a sour tone, "I didn't — we didn't go through all of that just to go back to it again, not until those… those trackers are gone."

"Trackers?" The doctors replied in confusion.

As Xira informed them of the current invaders on their town, they couldn't fathom what atrocities had befallen their own homes. When she mentioned how it was still unknown to everyone what was occurring, their almost symmetrical baffled expressions turned to each other and then to her.

"It's despicable that the supposed security of a land wouldn't involve the people in on the matter. We haven't a symbol like that here, what does it represent?" Niko returned, his brows angling with his slightly tilted head.

"Not sure at the moment… I know that it was on every type of transport and gear that they were using, like their trucks and weapon crates." She told them, "It's most likely the symbolic connection to their main syndicate. No matter what, though, they're not to be trusted too."

Taking a drink and a much-needed intermission, the remedial herbal tea mutually made them enter a soothing haven for their souls and the edges of Xira's cloak lit up in a purple glow, camouflaging itself within the material. Hearing the gentle clanging of the mugs, Willow sat up smelling the scented trail of tea steam, as she slowly walked over to the vacant chair by the table.

"Ah, sweet Willow, do you feel better?" asked Valin, quietly flipping through pages.

"Here's your tea," Niko handed her a full mug, "Drink up while it's hot."

Nodding with a sleepy reply, she grabbed the tea close to inhale its warmth. After comfortably seating herself besides her friend, they resumed the discussion.

"All right, here's a plan. We have the sceptre now, thanks to Xira, which we can use to our advantage. A little fair hope, I'd say. By the initiative, we can unearth Erma's whereabouts." Valin began, "The one obstacle though would have to be entering Glacial Mist... since you girls are heading through this world, we'll have to lure her back here... with the data we have of the sceptre, its uses are extremely multifaceted. We need to be careful and vigilant with the safest tactic."

"And then?" Niko coaxed, placing down his mug.

Valin cast a quick glance between the three, "Use the sceptre's vanquishing charm to send Erma back to the lair in the underworld. A reunion with the others is a wise way of defending our homes."

"Sounds good," said Xira, quickly glancing at Willow with a warm grin, "though, wouldn't she return anyway after realising her sceptre is missing?"

"Great point, however, given that not all of their force is in their forged sceptre, the lords wouldn't consider it an urgency. It doesn't mean that they'll forget about it, which is why that matter is our first objective and once that's done... so will be their reckoning. Then the only remaining threat resides in your land. We can help with that, but we'll discuss it once we've scoured few of the worst evil that lurks."

As everyone but Willow finished their drink, Niko collected the mugs and retreated back to the sink. Xira decided to keep her company, while Valin turned to sort the bedding and refill the tray that was atop the nightstand. Half an hour of silence went by, all relaxing in the high noon. The doctors went out in the meantime, tending to the residents of the village. Pleasant greetings between one another could be heard, the overall glee and humble barter filling Bloom Core. Completely in the unknown of what occurred the previous night, like it was just a nightmare that involved the two doctors, a watcher and a witch. The sunshine beamed across the way, its autumn touch twinkling on the sandy grounds beside the pitched open flaps from where it pierced through. Willow, sitting on the chair directly in its path of the midday breeze, slouched in the last of the droplets of healing tea in the mug, entrancingly bringing a look to her friend in an upper diagonal point, her cheek on the surface of where she consumed the beverage about a moment ago.

"Where to now?" She mumbled softly, "I, well, after we eat that is…"

Xira aimed on the side then returned with a corner glance at the entrance, to her friend, curving a winged impression with her mouth, "I think she might come back sooner than later. If the gatherings back home repeated anything during, it'd be that the one who'd lost, will seek to retrieve at all cost. The little markings on the stones made by the mentors and exemplars weren't for nothing. Serenitatem made sure we were all reminding ourselves. So I guess we'll head north."

"And after that?"

"The answers we hunt for. Discover the truth that hides in and under those mountains. First, got to get some more warm clothing for you," Xira responded.

Willow bent her elbow to rest, drinking the remainder of her tea, "Wait… how will we know if what we're looking for is… there? I'm sure someone must know something that could at least give us a hint. I mean, I know you have a connection and the birth mark… you're probably right but still, there's got to be somebody here, maybe further down the area, that we can ask about all of this before we go there… because… safety Xi, safety. This isn't exactly Glacial Mist."

"No, it isn't. That's exactly why I feel the mountains are a good lead. I understand your concern, I feel you, though considering Erma is on their tail, it won't be too long before she's on ours. We have to go as soon as we're prepared, or uh, you are," she explained, gesturing to her, "This realm has a lot of history and I don't doubt that it's all within the people that live here, it's a one-of-a-kind place. Kind of like home."

The warmth from the sunshine set through the archway of the entrance. Glimmering behind Willow's chair, she pulled back to carry her mug over to the sink. After a few moments, they both left the hut to greet a couple of the villagers that were outside. Friendly folk, each one with a bright smile on their face, ready to converse. There was a group of grandmothers huddled in a grassy corner, knitting pieces of clothing, the wool dripping along their feet. They seemed full with joy as they waved at the girls walking by, then proceeded to carry on with their shared tales among one another. All of the little cottages inhabiting the village were of a distinct style, like in a fairy-tale, where plants delicately covered the exterior and flowers grew from the roof and around the walls — made from ancient stone and wood, the earthly colours combining with the vintage textures. On many of the adjacent houses had a lengthy forest green vine dangling from the edges of the roof to the other side where it would continue along the rest that were nearby. The porches were decorated with various unique plants and occasionally a swinging bench by a window. Its rows of gardens forming a snake-like trail surrounding Bloom Core, depicting a united family of people with genuine love and care, had a sea of green and mixtures of rainbow tones blooming within the tender grounds and newly planted trees on the sides between each few metres or so. Many of the parents from the area with their children, had been cooking up home-made meals out the front by the lawn from home-grown ingredients. The kind of delight exuding from these neighbours all over the village was a rare incident for Willow, as her own family had its share of unfortunate turmoil. Turning the corner by the main message board, their attention was captured by a particular notice recently pinned on the top.

ALERT:GOING TO BLOOM FIELD?
Here's the information you may need to bring with you!
Please know this is the cherished place of many generations that
have visited and nurtured, so with respect and kindness do the same.
If you are new, you will need to know the following key guidelines:
This is a field where all of the land's herbs, flowers and plantation
of
all marvellous kinds are planted and grown to provide those in need
of
particular refreshments and so forth. With each visit, there will be
at least
one or two gardeners present at Bloom Field to aid you in your

tasks.

Note: Be careful when selecting plants, for the gentle touch is required as they are

very, very special and rare — must be plucked delicately.

For more information regarding each plant, ask the roaming gardeners or a friendly

neighbour who knows well about the plantation. Thank you kindly!

"Noted," Xira commented before bumping into Valin as they began to walk away.

"Hello dears, have you decided where you're off to next? I have made preparations with the help of two fellow clothiers that have agreed to assemble these gifts." She told them, "I've noticed you reading the message board? I can tell you all about it."

"That's really generous, Valin! Thank you, what — what gifts, exactly?" Willow returned cheerfully.

"I'll show you, come with me — in the meantime, I assume you've read our latest note?" She replied, as they crossed the way together.

"Bloom Field. I take that's your centrepiece for all plantation here. It was mentioned on one of Niko's lists back at his tent," Xira added, "Could that help us?"

A brief pause followed, then Valin continued, "If you're thinking of going anywhere further than the base of this land, well, take all you can carry."

"Is that so?" Willow chimed in, worried, "You're saying it isn't a path taken by any traveller or neighbour? That it's with extreme caution and... fairly untouched?"

"I respect your discretion, truly. Not many who've asked about heading in that direction have pondered much about hazards, but to carry that weight of baggage knowing the wisdom already is an added obstacle you really don't need," Valin's voice lowered in a humble manner as she motioned for them to enter a cosy mail office, where musical wind chimes resonated in a rotational sequence. They were asked to sit by a table near an open-draped window. Without more than a moment, she returned with two bags, placing both on the table.

"In here, you'll find items that will be of vital use if you shall charge in the other landscapes. For Willow, there is an especially new garment that I think you'll rather admire. Not only for its design but the many utilizations that come with it. Albeit, Niko did specifically say that the wound's area would have to be exposed to air which means the patch that is also inside the bag, will need to be attached accordingly. This will provide you with the air-pocket, although you'll need to be cautious with some locations as it does get mighty cold, only then will you need to cover up for the time being." She explained, before sitting down to join them, "He mentioned, as well, that the traces of elements found within the wound were of unusual blends, the sort which can be found, fused, yet not made. It's something that belongs, rather than of forgery by humankind... much like the contents around the soil itself."

They both examined their bag's contents, drawing out bits of material and clothing. The main necessities for where they were planning to go, were thoughtfully packed and sorted just right. For Xira, other than a blanket, new gloves and a winter scarf for both warmth and cover, she received a customised grappling hook for its initial use and other desired details. Willow had more of the clothing aspect of items, where she got a pair of hiking pants designed for every type of weather, including a zip that allowed for material transformation, which displayed that a metal layer would appear above the base material, shielding from any incoming projectiles or elemental hazards. Onto the next item, it was a winter jacket, as her current torso wear didn't provide sufficient protection from heavy weather. This jacket included puffy pads on the exterior, mainly for defence and cushioning in case of a fall. A device marked with the title '*HawkCall*' slid down the opening of the bag.

"Ah yes, that's used for communications between the one you're with and if you ever are isolated, it can be tracked using that brown button on the side," Valin informed her, "by pressing that one, it shoots up a laser flare that reaches to a hundred metres for anyone in the vast area to spot it in the air."

Reaching in the bottom of the bag, another 'Hawk' device was found and marked with '*HawkAlert*' on a silver clover shaped device with an orange lace. On a note attached read; *Whistle to use for the signal alert and inhale/exhale for silent camouflaging protection if in danger.* Willow placed the items beside the bag, as she pulled out the last piece of clothing from it.

Grinning, she held it up to show them, "A beanie with goggles attached? Sooo adorable. Thank you so much for this stuff! It means a LOT."

"No trouble dear, but those aren't ordinary goggles," Valin leaned in, "I specifically asked Niko to retrieve the materials needed for this craft, gifting you with a special design we call... *Bird'oz*... which are to be used for when you pick up a trace from the Rove Dynasty. You can contact us with a signal and we're there right away."

"Who are the Rove Dynasty?" questioned Xira, carrying her bag over.

"Oh... I... suppose I wasn't sure to tell you girls, but... Niko doesn't know so please don't mention any of this to him. He's already frightened enough by hearing about them. They're the ones that Erma is a part of... you could say, they're family." Valin went on explaining, "The sub-branch of the family consists of four domiciles in oath, with three figures in each serving their one master who goes by no name, rather only tells his... family, if you will. We've heard tales of him, mostly from Niko's field research but that's all we have. They're a dangerous lot. Fortunately, far away from here... except for Erma that is, which makes for a priority to resolve. As you may know... there are hidden forces within the Spirit Realm, that can guide you through the great sceptres and break through the obstacles propelled on the way, whether it's by them or otherwise. The ancestors have echoed these things like the very flowers that silently grow. They've kept the same secrets for the same reasons from long ago. For the safety, for the right decision."

They sat in silence while packing their bags again, after an item was placed in, they'd cast a wondering glance to their companion in the middle of her eyeing Xira's cloak. Clouds covered the sunny sky, as it evidently became mistier through the antique brass window, reflecting on the round edges of the table. Willow gulped, albeit loudly, before brushing it off as she picked up the bag, pulling to close. With the chimes circling their ambient tune, Xira cleared her throat, then added in a sigh. Checking on Willow who was lost in thought, she twisted the cloak's sleeves, having just put on the new gloves from the bag. Leaning on the edge, she held the bag between her legs, examining Valin with slight suspicion.

"Okay. Erma is our focus, that's fair enough. While we're far away from here, would she have any reason to head the same direction? How will this cloak help us if we encounter her?" Xira wondered, locking onto her gaze.

"I'm pleased that you asked that. Bloom Core may be my centre of operations and purpose, but I am filled with other concealed directions regarding many of the tales untold. Even when it doesn't involve every map inked on paper or behind a circular glass, when you spend this much time in a land like this, you will feel something pulling you towards the unknown, the mystical. Some people refer to this transfer as *a ghost whisper,* because of the inhabitants all around." Valin continued, "There are relatives of the ancients still here in other villages. Some aren't too old like the rest, but they have parts of what isn't known to the abundances. It's for the greater good, but that's why this type of contact is restricted to whom promises to hold safe. In this case… they agreed I could, as a doctor, they came to a conclusion that I have the moral compass to keep a protocol. This falls under an exception, only if you grant a promise."

"Sure, as long as you reciprocate," she sprung back.

"Splendid. Now… Erma, she'll have no reason unless she fears you may be entangled in her matter. There is one other thing…" Valin paused, ruminating, "If her matter takes her that way, that could just as well be a collision of sorts, one by total coincidence… that's an incentive to be very careful. It's where your cloak comes in. I'd advise you to be wise with it and when you do use it, for it takes a lot out of you, as I've been told by few relatives of the ancestors. Being the one they've selected to wield this blessed cloak, was also one of the vital things I've been informed about. You've a great item, however, with trust — guide it as it guides you. Together, it shouldn't overwhelm all the time it is used. I'm still truly in awe, as you've only arrived on this land, but that's all the reality to believe they felt something, a high force entering here. So I'll be all yours for anything you want to know and only between us this is, okay?"

"Okay," quietly, Xira began to stand.

"Hold w — one more thing," Valin abruptly stretched her arm out, "No one else has been there… for a long time, Xira. I mean not a single soul. You're here for another objective, heading into the unknown. Whatever you do, know the land first. *A key for the key,* as the ancestors would say. Just be careful up there. The few relatives have told me it is a wonderful paradise, though the secrets it holds weighs all the land's mysteries. Keep that in mind, the both of you. It's not only the people and animals that are the living."

"Forward and up in hiding," Xira muttered sweetly.

"Huh?"

"Serenitatem would tell me," she replied to her with a slight chuckle afterwards, "once he figured I just loved to be the silent one, good to avoid all drama that way."

"Ah, endearing, though please, please, keep the cloak close to you at all times. I know there're warmer areas inside some caves, another weather factor I was told by the relatives, where it may seem like you need to change clothing… just… okay…" Sliding her hand in comfort, Valin got out of her seat, before pushing the chair gently under.

"We'll be in touch, doctor," Willow added warmly.

Walking outside the front of the building, a man carrying a heap of lavender lassie and orange floribunda roses, springing out the side of his arms and dressed in botanic overalls and a wheat-woven sun hat, sauntered by as he handed them each a flower to keep.

"For you, my dear blossoms," he said, giving out two floribundas to Willow and Valin, and a lavender one to Xira. They thanked him and went onwards.

"What a friendly neighbour he would be," remarked Willow, smiling as she sniffed the flower.

Sometime later, they circled around the village's fountain, then soon arrived at Valin's hut. Placing her things on the bed provided for her, Xira thoroughly assembled what she was to take with her for the outing the next day. *Vaoz should keep the rest of my things safe, I hope*, she thought to herself. The sun began to set, as Valin made her way in.

"If you want to talk before you take off early in the morning, I'll be in Niko's tent in assistance to Willow, whom by the way, told me to tell you she'll meet you by the welcome sign down the path — she wants to surprise you with something," She explained, carrying over supplies for the fireplace.

"All right, noted," Xira replied, before launching herself on the bed to check her phone. *As I imagined, low battery. I won't need this for over there anyway, it's safe here*, she thought. Just about to hide it under the covers, an old but recent message glowed up on the lock screen.

Your secret and yours only. Protect it from the world.
{1 day ago}

_____ —☀— _____

Cold goosebumps pierced from underneath her sleeves, the crown of her brows furrowing, curiously wanting to uncover the cryptic text. *We haven't spoken in ages, ever since the departure*, she wondered. Checking the recent activity on Merlot's installed chip by the name *'Home'* revealed nothing after the recent message sent. Nobody had lived in the house after the event which had divided the family — one after another had diverged and been long gone from their street. Most of the secrets were left untold to the family but the mentors, protectors and carers. All that was uttered in a mere whisper, was that someone who had lived in and cared for the home, had betrayed and lied to the family before voluntarily leaving due to a matter unknown, but out of the octane blue and leaving behind an odd, tainting taste. Soon after, another had broken their loyalty and it had snowballed in a nuanced manner from there. This had prompted her to reminisce of the good feelings and times that brought the comfort and love between them altogether. Falling dark depths of her racing thoughts, she reflected on his whereabouts and if he was okay. *What's he on about? Where has he gone?* She hid her phone under the layers of soft blankets as she nosedived into her pillow, eyeing the crackling, warming fire.

Hours had melted by, the air of the night turned to icy snowflakes settling on surfaces. The clash of the two polar opposite temperatures formed a wave of ventilation, intertwining through the space of the tent. An anomalous silence falling just as footsteps in the distances reached the front, a low growl haunted, ominously wiping out every other vicinal sound just as Valin rushed in.

A momentary halt before she whispered alarmingly, "Oh no… what am I going to do?"

She rushed to the sink to get some water, then proceeded to barricade the entrance with a flip of the table and pulled out a huge blanket from one of the cupboards, laying it before the fireplace and sat herself with an opened book in hands, flipping the pages every couple of seconds.

Aware that Xira was asleep, she kept as quiet as she could, while searching through each page in a skim.

"This has to be, the explanation… the way out of it… a solution perhaps, what we need," she muttered quite breathlessly to herself.

With the flame's light glowing on the pages and its crackling bouncing onto the ember tinted pyroceram glass, Valin remained comfortably on the centre space, deep in the folds of the vintage book, its covers obliquely resting on her lap as her fingers swept down each passage as a chilling gust barged through a small gap above the covered portion of the archway. Immediately turning her attention to it, she dropped the book and went in haste. Once it was done, she returned to the book while the noise outside grew louder.

The warmth of the fireplace tended to the atmosphere, becoming a cosy place yet again. The village had become quiet, a mystifying tune taking over the sound waves was creeping along the metallic panel of the tent, its ghostly finish interposed between the crackling embers and a soft distant wailing. Xira awoke in the midst of a dream, sitting upright on the bed as she brushed parts of her hair behind her ears. Facing what had occurred in front, a wondering expression covered her rather sleepy mood when she noticed the table that used to be in the centre was lunged over to the side, away from where Valin had placed it beforehand, along with other bits of furniture scattered on the opposite side near the doc's bench. The entryway was flurried open, with just the top area barely at a close. At first, the ground on the outside appeared to be the same rough texture of the sand and morning sunlight beaming across and beyond. When she came to, she immediately discovered not only that the same ground was glowing a fiery red, with bold traces of blackened soil, but the dawn's light revealed a heavy heap of smoke travelling at snail tempo higher up, completely obliterating any slim chances of clean air, as it gradually entered the room and pulling hoarsely at her throat, her nose already dried up, causing her to spring forwards on the floor. Looking around, she picked up the bag she'd prepared earlier while getting on both feet and making her way out, keeping her mouth protected. Meanwhile, the distant noises became muffled through the smoke as she ran to the left, down the path and to the welcome sign a couple of metres forth. The exact symbol she'd seen in one of Valin and Niko's books before was briefly etched onto the wooden corner in a red smear. As the area to inside the village was compromised, she continued further ahead to a higher point to examine what was happening in Bloom Core.

A bloodcurdling scream ruffled through the thick vapour, turning to a distinct resonance as pulverising footsteps scraped roughly at the corner, the raucous voice shouting Xira's name. Spotting her friend catching breaths down below, she cupped her mouth and called out to her. Rushing upwards, the horrified Willow haled herself as she reached out, coughing and gasping for air. Xira held Willow's arms as she had her head down, wheezing underneath, the smoke just about thinning out in their direction but still awfully contaminated. Both turned to view the whole of the village burning as its land was consumed by the flames and almost every building transforming to ashes. Some of the people tried to apply water to the critical areas, many others were overheard screaming and crying while attempting to evacuate. There were some that seemed like they were in need of a rescue, as from time to time a good number of villagers appeared in and out of the fog, going to where they were trapped. From up here, the girls' perspective was mainly obscured by the effects of the occurring disaster, while the rare remains of buildings and structures were occasionally revealed through the engulfment.

"This can't be happening... I... I don't know if Niko left or not... he was in there with me," Willow cried, sitting down on the grass with a frightened look, "What if they're in danger?"

"I'm sure they're doing all they can, I just hope they get out safely," Xira replied, folding one of her knees beside her and leaning a forearm on the other, "Have you spoken to any of them? Even briefly?"

"Oh, no, no, only kind of... I was falling asleep but I heard him washing something in the sink and that's when he freaked out and told me to get out immediately," she explained, "Then 'get somewhere safe' were his departing words..."

"He's probably in there helping or out, we'll go search around the perimeter. In my case, Valin wasn't even inside, although it'd looked like the room had been ransacked," Xira told her, "Hmm... there's a couple of the villagers safely out front."

They hurried down to meet them, albeit startled they greeted politely.

"My word! My word! There're still people in there! Our very neighbours, what on mighty land is going on?" One of the women lamented, carrying her scrunched bag while pulling in her flower garment.

"Heavens, oh heavens…" The other woman added, "My family… I need to find them…"

"I'm sorry," Willow replied empathetically, "We're wondering the same thing, we just got out not too long ago… it's horrible, plenty are helping… I just didn't think something like this would happen here."

"Neither we — it's horrible, this is. It's always been peaceful here, this has to be moored with a strange entity!" The flower garment woman responded.

"Aren't they northians, Farah? I've been told they roam up there, in those parts. Scary if you ask me, it's no wonder the lands don't get visited too much by any villager across the realm. Tale was whispered by this ol' folk, that anybody who dawdles there at night are to meet the ones with no name…" The other woman said, lowering her voice, almost to a whisper.

"Oh, they have a name, th-they do. We have been fortunate enough to not come by them to find that out for ourselves." Farah replied, casting a wary glance, "As Claire mentioned, they do stay up north but… this then has got to be done by a vengeful spirit, who has something against us… it can't be another village though, no…"

Willow held Claire's hand in compassion, as they stared into the blazed land.

"Are those entities you're describing, human at all?" Xira questioned, going closer.

"I — I have no idea. There was this man that prophesied that they had humanity within them. He never returned after leaving again. I heard he joined them." Farah answered, resting on a stone behind her, "Right now I think… the best thing to do is… wait here, Claire. Sit, will you?"

After she had joined on the stones, Willow grabbed onto Xira's hand.

"Let's go find the docs," she said.

Telling their goodbyes, they made their way around the side and ran forwards. People were spotted gathering themselves in huddles, concerningly checking if everyone there was safe. As the girls circled round the perimeter, the smoke intensity varied depending on where the fire had caught on the most. They glanced sombrely at the once colourful, blooming flowers along the grass patches of the village, searing softly into the soil. With each crackling of a broken building and burnt plantation, it rolled below like the churning in Willow's stomach. Deposits of torn clothing and material were scattered along the paths leading to the main back entrance, baskets tumbled over the grass, a dismantled cotton bag previously filled with fruit stretched along the divide between the soft sandy grounds and the grasslands, as well as a bundle of books about home gardening flipped nearby the baskets. Walking to the entrance, they carefully watched as the fire spread towards the edges of the fence that connected to the archway. Keeping their distance, they walked around the side to see if either Valin or Niko was still inside. Xira placed her hand on the outer fence where it had been untouched by the blaze, her cloak merely drooping over the wooden surface. As she trailed along closer to the fire, there was no indication of either one of them running about the place. Eager to find them, she proceeded to slide closer to the entrance, while Willow continued checking the area from the safe vantage point. There were less screams now with even less people frantically going either way, only a couple of small families being escorted by a few friendly neighbours. It had started to burn higher on the wood right underneath to where Xira was standing. Too busy scanning for their companions, none of them focused on what was right under their noses until she felt the heat swirl within her sleeve. As her friend concentrated on the rushing people in the distance and some going back in, Xira amazed, looked down to realise her sleeve had been touching the rising flame. Oddly though, it had appeared that it was shielding the fire away from actually burning her, as it hovered gracefully on top of the glowing cloak's exterior. With the flame reflecting in her gaze, she also noticed her birthmark lighting up once again… this time even more. Quite in awe, she slid her hand off the railing, rotating the forearm as she examined the sleeve. Turning to check on Willow, who was heading further down the perimeter, she ran to the archway, with the sands kicking up behind her. Without a second thought, she rushed in the middle, with a sudden drifting turn to the left in search of the doctors. Covering her mouth as she pushed her way through the piling debris, small shouts came from each way and one by one, villagers coughed their way out, barely jogging to get away to safety. After arriving at the mail office, its sign dropped on the floor, there'd appeared to be nothing remaining in its space, except for the broken pieces of the burnt structure fallen.

She continued down to where someone was stuck under a log that had been a part of the cottage nearby, or at least what was left of it. Going to help him, he cried in fear as he tried to push it away from his torso. Xira crouched behind, putting her left leg behind his shoulder for support and pushed down on the log. The man struggled as he tried to withdraw, feeling overwhelmed by its heaviness. With one more go, they managed to get it down his feet and in a heavy push, Xira rolled it off and down away it went. Relieved, he turned to kneel and pull himself up to sit against a small broken stairway.

"You've come to my aid... bless you," He thanked her, "By any chance, have you met a woman by the name Ives? I don't know if she has been rescued... she's my wife. She was at a friend's home this early morning."

"I'm sorry. I'll keep a lookout," She replied as she stood up.

Further down, a few more people were seen coming out of various gaps where huts and tents were previously located and now in imminent danger of anyone still right by them. Under planks of wood from furniture tumbled about, some emerged from and rushed to leave, all clearing their throats while they escaped. Covering her mouth as she watched others get away, frantically trying to find the exit, Xira spotted a familiar figure just ahead, helping someone get through the thick smoke that surrounded them.

"Valin!" Xira shouted, then again louder, "VALIN!"

She ran to the hut where they had left from, realising a pile of bodies lying in the midst of the flames sputtering around the indoors. A bitter aftertaste cut dry on the back of her throat, a gloomy feeling that many of them weren't rescued. Going after Valin, she noticed her finally leaving the burning area to try and catch her breath. As everyone ran in panic to get away, she turned when hearing the approaching footsteps.

"Dear, oh my goodness, why aren't you somewhere safe? I assumed since you weren't inside, that you'd gone already," Valin said worrisomely, turning towards her.

"I did. I came back. We wanted to check on you and Niko," Xira answered, "Do you know why this all happened?"

"We? Willow's okay? Good, good, uh we're... I think he's fine, he told me he was making sure others in the village were safely assisted and that he'll meet me by the orange blossom tree." Valin continued, "Right over there. Come with me, I'll tell you about this absolute horror."

Watching most of the village turn to ash and charred fragments, Valin folded her hands behind her cloak, sorrowfully witnessing the remainder of the embers disappearing into the rough ground, while two out of many people who'd carried giant buckets of water poured across and darted off to grab some more. It'd seemed as the village was to now be left to breathe for grieving and respectfully tended to, before its initial rejuvenation.

"This was no accident, not by any one of us," Valin uttered quietly, "Previous night was the preliminary phase of these disastrous events. Not a single soul was roaming about the village when I was, it grew colder than it had been. A distinct feeling in my gut warned me of an uncouth presence… that it shall behove me to weave the needle throughout the matter with the wreathing fibre, in vow to defend my and our home."

"Hopefully this won't rub salt to the wounds, but I suspect we think of the same being," replied Xira, looking for Willow in the scope of where they were searching.

"Albeit, I was distracted. A little peculiar, like I'd fallen in a chemical extract to hallucinate and somewhat hypnotise. That's when the village was submerged in snow. At first, it felt like raindrops falling in a cinematic dream sequence," She explained, her eyelashes dampening, "I barely scraped the way to the tent but fortunately, a trusty exothermic lamp was with me. Once I entered, immediately barricading the entrance, at the time I assumed one of Niko's books on such mystical phenomena would be of encouragement, however false… it wasn't for nothing. After investing in all that reading of tales, myths and guidance, it pointed to a particular factor which I'd feared. Indeed, executed by no regular mortal, this was adding up to and with reason towards, well… Erma. It must be her seeking of vengeance and her temper getting a pull on one of the reins. Our focus now is to heal Bloom Core… foremostly."

Xira turned with a suspecting expression then to examining the village, with a return, "You know, if that sceptre wasn't taken, maybe the village wouldn't have been sacrificed. It sounded like a reasonable idea before this mess, though now she's taken your homes. It's not fair. Nothing but loss here."

"Xira," Valin hugged around the shoulder, her garment covering behind, "She may have destroyed our houses, everything we've built over time — all the love and care that was put into this village, yes it was gruesomely done and for that unforgiven. One important fragment that Erma hasn't placed her mitts on, is our souls. It's something that cannot be touched, taken or torn. Our houses, sure, but not our homes. They are within us, just like souls. The blame isn't on you, you did what you thought was right. Heck, if you hadn't brought that here, who knows what she would've done otherwise. High risk, high reward, no matter the cost. I grieve with optimism, have done it before and I'll always do it again. Niko and I have known her for so long, even we can't sometimes determine what she'll do when she's not around us. I can't possibly expect that of you either, so take a breath, dear, the burden does not sit on you."

"I want to do whatever I can to help, at least to mend the heavy feelings... I can't help that," she replied, observing the village while comforted.

"No. We'll carry on with what we talked about, remember? When you reunite with Willow, venture to the north, like you both had planned. As for us, we will rebuild." With hope, Valin added. "To refresh with the same and even more love and nurturing that we had applied before, because it is ours and we do what we must, in protection and rebirth for the good. The sceptre, well, that'll need to be hidden very discreetly... where it won't blip on her radar. If she searches again, it'll create a decent diversion while we figure a solution and she haunts the grounds. It'll be far away from Bloom, that's for certain. She will absolutely not enter here once again."

"Understood... I just hope you guys will manage with us at the mountains of secrets," Xira mused, walking with her to find the others, "although we promise to be *ghosts*, I can't bear to think the outcome of... you know who... returning, with a bigger agenda whirling in mind."

Valin hugged her closer with an empathetic and hopeful smile, as they traced the outskirts searching for their friends. It wasn't too long before Niko was spotted kneeling in front of a person with his garment all tainted from the after-effect. He had been treating a villager who was knocked out by the gas and without any tools, did all he could. There weren't many people sitting out on this side, as they'd gone outside the entrances, somewhere safe or awaiting advice further away from the place. Valin placed a hand gently on his shoulder.

"You're safe, thank goodness," he muttered with a worried look on his face, "Is Willow all right? I haven't seen her myself, these people need my help but they're all over the area. My things, all my things are dust in there, everything I've accumulated and crafted for my kits. I can only do so much, it pushes my utmost patience with what happened."

"This is way beyond what we can carry, Niko, you need to make peace with that. I'm sorry, I feel the same way, we can do all that is carved in ourselves and that itself is grand alone..." Valin paused, peeking over him and whispered firmly, "What of the sceptre?"

He turned quickly, facing her closely to answer, "Listen, listen. It's in my coat, I've fabricated a long pocket on the inner layer to store it in the meantime. Now we just need to gather all the folk that are scattered about and discuss what we should do collectively and to commence the village healing."

After agreeing, the three continued along the edges to find and gather all the village's people, with Niko carrying the unconscious person across his arms. He walked off to place him warmly by a tall and thick oak tree. Valin rushed to the hills in hopes to retrieve as many of the people as possible, the sunlight beaming on behind her. Meanwhile, Xira made her way around the perimeter and kept a lookout for Willow, who wasn't nearby where she previously was searching. A couple of moments flew by, before hearing a loud call in the distance. Turning the attention to the sound, it then was accompanied by footsteps going towards her. Xira noticed the half torn down entrance, where she'd first gone, observing the dusty path ahead.

"Where did you go off to? I was worried!" Willow exclaimed, raising her brows as she harshly inhaled.

"Sorry, Will, I—"

"I thought something happened to or someone took you, you just left!" Her voice breaking, as the pitch indicated her emotions reaching the surface, then simmering down again.

Xira went in for a wholehearted hug, wrapping protectively around Willow, who in return, broke down in a sigh as she went right in. Feeling weary and relieved at the same time, she decided to not say a word while taking in the peaceful moment, despite her thoughts on the situation.

"I would never leave you," added Xira mellowly, "That's the kind of promise I make for the ones that matter to me the most."

With a thoughtful smile and a twinkle in a hopeful glance to her friend, Willow walked under-arm as they slowly went to greet the two companions who were escorting the villagers to one spot as a group, ready to inform them of their plans. After joining them, the conversation went on for quite some time, as the morning reached the afternoon and multiple roles and tasks had been assigned to all of the families and randomised groups. Niko stood by a rocky path, directing the people to where they were to embark, giving each of them a sweet blessing before they departed. Valin hurried to talk with the girls as they paused in a triangular form, facing each other. She pulled out two hand-crafted moonstone bracelets from her cloak, holding them in front to display. A perplexed look drifted past her as she pursed her mouth and looked up at the girls.

"As you know, unfortunately almost everything was destroyed in the fire. We've managed to retrieve as many items that we could hold, but nothing too specific — just what we presumed was irreplaceable," she told them while gifting the bracelets, "These were crafted by one of the village's ancestors from about a century ago, her name was Lithia Aeriza. Using the found and collected moonstones, originating underneath the Elysian mountains far on the left, they were decorated throughout the village, to offer protection and healing amongst the residents of Bloom Core. I've kept two myself for my late partner and I... I haven't had these up for a long while and it's only best for them to not be unworn. Take them as a gift from me, something to remember me by in any chance we don't cross paths again. Although, I'd prefer you remain optimistic and consider the bracelets as... a kind gesture by a grateful, fellow friend."

"Beautiful, Vaoz. You've done so much for us, the thanks you deserve are endless," remarked Xira, putting hers on as she examined it thoroughly, "These indentations, I've seen before... in a cave back at Glacial Mist... home. Interesting, I bet they glow... don't you think?"

"If you're referring to the mother tongue of the ancients that alighted here, then yes, that's correct," astonished, she added, "What were those descriptions doing *there*? It's sacred to this realm... and surely, they should glow."

"Been wanting to find that out myself actually," was her reply, "they kind of, led us to the entrance to this realm. Somewhat hidden, like completely unknown to my world."

Bewildered and in thought, Valin nodded briefly before stretching her arm out in Niko's direction.

"I'll take you girls to the way that leads north. It's all yours from there," she explained, "Niko will be heading to Bloom Field, which is quite close to the path you're taking, you might visit if you'd like — he can tell you all about it."

Greeting Niko, he folded his cloak sides to a close and gestured towards the way north. As Valin accompanied them to bid farewell, they turned at a halt to both give her a bear hug and their gratitude with a few friendly blessings.

"Be careful in the mountains and beyond. Do make sure to watch out for each other, I won't say that woman will find you but trust nobody, be on guard," Valin reminded while inspecting the northern field, "The sceptre is with Niko, because we were thinking of studying it a bit further, he'll be holding onto it — the more we help with securing your safety, the better. What you do from here on, is up to you. I've heard tales of what is within, between and further from the high mountains, it sounds beautiful but dangerous. I know that it is connected with the magic of this realm, which means you'll need to discover as you go, as no one that I personally know has been anywhere near there, all the information I've gathered thus far, I'll eagerly give to you. If you shall encounter the souls that neighbourhood folk have voiced in a whisper to me, you should know they are not your threat, for they dedicate themselves to the mountains and its secrets that they protect. The ghosts of the land's old times don't venture that outward from their usual roaming nests which are to the east and a couple to the west, however the habitat differs. Although you go with good intentions, the keepers swear for no danger to dawdle, so I don't doubt you will display your respect and uncover the secrets of the north. We want you to find everything that you are looking for and with love you embark. We'll do our part here, keeping the village safe and… blossoming, as always. We'll do our best to hold her off from barging in — while we rebuild. We know she's onto us and anybody in this realm, she wants to bring her heinous formula upon our kind, she'll cross all the lines if it meant completing her desired objective and this is definitely not her homeland to ravage with callousness. The first time we met her was by accident, through her former *companion.* Her old tricks won't work the same way. This time, we have our claws pointed at her… anywho… one more thing. Take note of your cloak, it's going to be very helpful in your favour and trust me, that wonder has layers you've yet to decipher yourself. All great wisdom and light shall be of your guidance and with the wind, you fly high. We hope to meet you two again, it has been delightful to say the least."

"You have my word," Xira beamed, holding her hand in return, "Thank you again. For taking care of my things as well… for healing Willow, all of it."

"Oh and, we're very sorry we wanted to help with your village and that we're practically leaving when you need more by your side," Willow added in empathetically, "I hope that for what it's worth, I tried to assist Niko with a few rescues, but the gas was overwhelming…"

"Sweet peach, you needn't be sorry at all. Your care means everything," She replied, "With that, know that you both mean a lot to us. We always welcome any kind soul into our home. Our friendship, dears, is unbreakable, cosmic and a novel treasure that is not one to be plundered. Off you go, with blessings on your journey — the moon and sun on your axis."

Waving their way apart, Valin tearfully smiled as she watched and they turned to walk alongside Niko, who led them onwards. The rustling of the tree's leaves created a whistling tune. Gentle sand sliding across the feet's trail, Xira turned once more with a warm glance to the doctor and then smaller they became to each other, as distance swallowed the air between — with the cyclical wind wafting around Valin and the glistening green grass beside her too, in sync.

A quiet walk ahead, Willow followed the ground without any mind to anything else as she fidgeted with her jacket's sleeves, "That was odd… "

"Hmm? What was?" Xira asked.

"She called me 'sweet peach'… it was what my mother used to call me," Her friend added in a low tone, "It was her cheery nickname for me… "

They continued a little further before Niko halted to a turn, gesturing beside him. With a sympathetic glance, Xira dashed to the nearest flowers along the way and gently picked up one that was already plucked between the huddle of the grass. As the other two caught up, she flashed an endearing and comforting smile, in a bubbly trip back to meet them and looped the flower underneath Willow's Bird'Oz hat, through the entangled auburn hairs. She could tell by the crinkle of her nose, the touching of the petals and the glittering tearful look as she inhaled the scent — that she'd encouraged another emotion to brave the frontier of her melancholic burden. Reminded of earthly serenity, lifting her generous spirit to epiphanous heights as the dripping tears trailed warmly along her cheeks. Going in for a hug, Willow planted her chin in an angle of Xira's cloak.

"Come on," Xira whispered, spinning around and guiding her along Niko's side as they ventured north.

Upon nearing the point of the road where each grassland was becoming filled with various ravishing flowers, which to Niko was no surprise — they had been getting close to the location. Their awe painted impressions beamed with inner light while reaching its tall oakwood entrance, observing beyond exactly what they'd assumed would be found in a field like such. The countless plantation that ranged from garden flowers at home, to types in dreams and the usual and unusual of remedial, magical, herbal wonders. The colours that decorated across the field were all the more blooming during the day, as the sun's rays revealed a shine to their petals with the recent rain that doused the plants. The aroma fusions brought a euphoric feeling through their noses as they wandered the bristled grounds. Meanwhile, Niko had already been chatting up the gardeners resting by some antique pots and vases. With the bags Valin had provided the girls, they joined each other by the herbal aisle and placed them on the floor while they selected a good amount to carry along. Shortly after browsing, ever so friendly Niko walked up to them with woollen mini bags in each hand.

"Here I greet, bearing gifts," He jested, handing them over, "These will allot supplementary practicality for when you journey onward. You only need to stash your chosen floral and herbal magnificence. If you're willing to trade, I am more than pleased to do that."

"If you say so," Willow commented pacifically, peering at her friend, "We assumed these would be good for well… carrying anything really."

"They certainly are, sweetheart, albeit you must consider where you are to be entering," Niko explained rationally, "the smaller, the more elusive. Mountains with or without snow, are open areas with lots of passageways that are most efficient when your knowledge of the place expands. It's easy to get lost as it is to get found... and not every entity up there is human. The best way is to carry less with more value — that's something I'd learnt the hard way. Anywho, I'll provide you a thorough list of a great selection that will aid you in the north and beyond. Once you've gathered them, head to the gardeners and they will sort the batch out for you. Then we'll go our separate paths and keep in contact, perhaps?"

"Right, thank you," replied Xira, motioning to the inked list, "This includes specific detail on each one, that's so cool. Some of these are plants our town does not even have — would they have the same effect as they do here?"

"Unfortunately, no... no, the mystical and hallowed selection are strictly for this realm. It has been declared by our ancestors, ancient entities, amongst other ethereal beings that wander. Off you go now, I'll wait by the archway — oh and do be careful with the stems." Niko advised as he walked away.

They held the bags while going about the different plants in each section, all planted and cared for ever so delicately. *These are almost like the garden back home*, Xira thought as she collected. A hint of sparkle shone on the edges of the flowers and the aroma waving through the fairly warm atmosphere. As Xira tracked the names on the list, she'd used dampened soil to mark beside them once they'd been added in. Carefully placing the gathered plantation inside the bag, she pulled out to check the list one more time. *Now where are those? I'm sure we've examined all of them*, she wondered.

Flora i Herba ~ all season/weather

Acacia ~ magickal uses; protection, enhancement, friendship to bless sacred spaces, light for purification, meditation and infra-watches enhancement {latter; only when safe}

Agrimony ~ used for protection, mainly the wraiths/entities of the realm {ONLY if nettled, wraiths roam}

Amaranth ~ protection under full moon, powerful herb against any threats {note; wear under clothing, close to skin}

Angelicas, {Angel's Herb} ~ protection and purification, protects from evil spirits! can light to create a surrounding protection {note; most powerful, magical herb}

Combination of Burdock Root i Cacao ~ {gardeners will provide b!root} protects against evil intentions while travelling, worn like a sprig necklace ~~~ to which cacao can calm the restless spirits, can be made in powder form

Cayenne ~ breaks hexes when eaten ~~~ very useful for such a threat

Chamomile ~ used quite often, however in the form of powder it grants the same effects of healing and protection, tranquillity and joy

Juniper ~ rids of unkind spirits overall

Mugwort ~ for this noted use, a banishing herb in such need

Valerian ~ mixed flora used for healing, refreshment and uplifting

Verbena ~ all-purpose, use when low on other herb and placed in bag, whether as a whole or particles

{the gardeners also have onions if you shall want any, but they are to be carried separately}

With Willow retracing the steps, Xira walked up to the gardeners who were now drinking a steaming beverage before greeting her. She had shown them the list and asked where the other plants were, for the names on every palette included the listed plants aside from the missing few. The gardener sitting on the right placed his mug down on a wooden accent table and reached over behind him, rummaging inside a hand-made retractable vessel. Meanwhile Niko was spotted standing by, admiring the newly planted roses by the archway fence. The gardener sitting next to the other introduced herself as Carol, began talking about her origins and how she came about this area, then placed a mug beside a wooden bench as she helped her friend with the sorting and packaging.

"These are a fine selection. We indeed keep some of the ones written on here in safe-keeping since they are seasonal and rare in larger quantities," the man informed, "The chamomile is usually on the far end of the field, but... not too long ago... fourteen suns before? A rascal or akin, sabotaged that quarter of plantation while we were away to visit family. I uncovered what was left, though not much and since then, we've had to add another fencing that'll ensure full protection."

"Darlin', I don't think we need to dwell on the past matters. Our duty is to help those in need, and in that, help each other. Magnanimity always outgrows the ravager I say," Carol remarked, her necklace reflecting with a radiant glint, "I know it's highly odd that someone would do such a thing, to be truly honest."

"Exactly why the past is the reason that happened to a large sum of our tending," He replied.

"It's *why* we added that fence, Raj. We now focus on the good, so the good can grow with love," she told him, helping him finish with the packaging.

"Right, that's right," Raj lit up, "Here you go, fellow friend. A note also, whenever you decide to wear a sprig, make sure to keep it well hidden and before combining cacao, that it is inside the designated bag."

Carol flashed a sunny smile at Xira, who in return, thanked them both for their help as she carried the aromatic assorted bags back towards the exit.

"Ah, I see you have met our loyal gardeners," Niko stated, "Did you get everything?"

"Yes, we had a nice talk, they told me about what happened here," She replied, "I noticed you were keeping your distance for some reason?"

With one hand over his gut, he chuckled, "Nothing odd, truly. I was just admiring and making sure the perimeter was fairly tidy, since *that* event. The frequent visits have made us become closer and them feel… reassured."

A moment later, Willow quickly joined the huddle, carrying something in her hands.

"Here, Niko, I want you to have this," she said, "I made it for you, as thanks, it's the least I could do after all you've done."

"Something sweeter than honey. It's a beautiful bracelet, I shall wear it solemnly. What is this?" He leaned it to smell around his wrist, "Ah… well, motherwort and nettle. This is very kind, thank you Willow."

After a hug, they leaned back and walked off to the path again.

"This is where we go our own way, my friends," Niko continued kindly, "Walk up this path and you'll encounter the guiding pillars which direct you to the places you desire to venture through and as you cover the roads, there'll be more leading to the ultimate one-way pillar. The escort to the mountains. From there, you enter the mountains and whatever resides beyond it, with that, I give you both my blessings, regards and utmost gratitude."

"Thank you very much, Niko," Xira replied, "For taking us in, caring for us, trusting us… may you get everything you give… friend."

Tearing up, he pushed forward a smile, "The ancients hear you, loud and proud."

"You've done a lot for us! Generosity like that is so rare, especially where we come from. With barely even knowing who we were, you welcomed us with opened arms and worked your magic. We have to meet again! We could help more then," Willow added, with a slight jump and hand motion.

"Humble souls. You promise?" He asked, grinning.

Xira peeped at Willow, then back at him warmly, "We promise, Niko."

They hugged again, waved their hands and with a wholehearted smile, they began walking to the north as Niko watched from behind, his hands folded in front of his overlapped coat. Silence befell the two while making their way onwards, the cold settling in the further they went. Although the breeze was gentle and the sun casting their elongated shadows, beamed its rays, the feeling of isolation, secrets and forged trust whirled within the pit of their gut. It'd seemed the distance to their next turn was in view, the bright surface of the first wooden pillar placed between the divide of two sandy paths, including the directions from top to mid-way, etched onto pieces of protruding planks pointing to the different ways. Xira glanced at Willow, cupping her hand in comfort as she wanted to reassure her and lighten the way forth — they remained close together while arriving to the rocky fork in the road, the pillar appearing taller as they had neared, piled rocks displaying right behind it. The edges of the wood had been glazed in an icy layer from the cold morning, its twinkle giving an emphasis on the letters. To the left was the way towards two of the locations by the names; 'Five Elements' and 'Rainberry'. To the right were three others named; 'Phantom Lake', 'Guidance Pond' and 'Twin Grail'. Focusing on whichever one would lead them to the grand pillar entrance, neither were too sure as the names weren't quite familiar. A little creature scurried toward her, when Xira crouched to inspect its call — it'd seemed as though it was asking to guide her somewhere. For a moment, as she looked at her friend with a waiting nod and informed her to stay by the post, Xira went on with the scaled being towards the path and then arrived at the Guidance Pond. An abundance of beautiful and inhabiting creatures travelled about the pond. She glanced at the water, where species of snakes, lizards, chameleons, frogs, giant-winged avifauna, turtles, a unique dragon-dog and dragon-cat species known as dradogs and dracats, alongside many more native inhabitants — even the realm's own legends that travel the vast lands. Each legend to each of their sanctuaries, like the crystalihuts; which are for the sacred beings around. A figure rose from the aquatic silence, eyeing her as they sat on the nearby rock. The grass entangled their feet of scales as the feminine being relaxed with the snakes coasting along and around with the other animals. Their valiant demeanour paired with the evergreen before one of the elegant and exotic avifauna landed on their raised shoulder. Some of the other animals began to slither around Xira, with the various species enveloping her and the space, admiring their new-found companion. She embraced them, meeting their scales, fur and the like, happily on the thriving grounds.

"You have a divine connection with them," remarked the mermaid-faerie-like being, their scales glistening with rich colours, "I am Syreniaeri. Traveller and native."

"Xira," she replied, observing the beauty around, "I hear their whispers. I know what they're saying."

"Keep that a secret. It's a loving gift to you," they went on to say, "There are many mystical and empyrean beauties around the realm, for one to discover with love and grace — infinite mystery."

Getting up as she listened, Xira's view of the here and beyond was magnificently reinvigorating.

"I've befriended such creatures…on my travels. We dance under the sky, like we are its children. All the realms, the magic and the universe forever right with us. They like to get out when it's quiet—when the land is more pleasant. You hear their cheer with the weather. It was a pleasure to greet you, charming friend."

After Xira waved in her cherishing expression and continued on the path, they exchanged a kind gesture of their honour for one another. She returned to the post to meet Willow and onward they ventured again. In the distance, the area appeared to be filled with forest trees and plants alike, a green atmosphere combined with the watery vapour that obscured some of its surroundings — all the more mysterious with its darker tone, whereas the other region radiated a colourful exterior along its blend of spring and autumn vibe that coexisted in a natural form. Walking closer to the right, Xira bent to examine a singular flower stem slanting upwards as she felt for the sands beneath the coarse surface. *Hmm, it's oddly colder… and softer,* she thought.

"Willow, can you please check that road's soil for me?" She asked her, pointing backwards.

"Uh, how far in?" Was her friend's response, quizzically.

"Just how you would directly plant a flower," Xira said, watching her gingerly waltz over there.

Some moment after the quiet, Willow returned giving a brief shrug.

"If we were indoors, I'd say about room temperature. Otherwise, damp, with the smooth texture," she informed, cleaning off her hands.

In an agreeing nod, Xira continued down the forest direction, "This way then. Let's keep a reminder of our trail… by the first name, Phantom Lake?"

They ventured to a darker part of the region, where not only the trees but the air felt different than not too long ago. A green mist followed their ankles as the shoe prints disappeared after each step. The sun that shone above them seemingly vanished into a clump of clouds, covered by the tall, dangly forest trees creating a cooler aura as the elbow high vapour melted through to again replenish behind them. An occasional frog would ribbit and the water of the lake could be heard softly rippling near. Deeper into a mud-filled puddle turned to a flood, the thick sediment hugged to their knees as they manoeuvred forward with the hold becoming more of a cement mix than the usual earthly dip. Willow appeared sceptical about any dry land ahead of them while the impression on her face depicted this as a walk to a thriller show after midnight.

"I don't think this is the ideal way to take, Xi," she muttered, checking left and right.

"You don't think?" A voice replied in interruption.

"What? Who was that?"

An eerie exhale blew past the girls as they turned in circles to find where that voice was coming from. Xira walked backwards while her friend stayed to the front, but nobody was around despite it feeling otherwise. When a low rumble bubbled the mud between, little pockets surfaced before sequentially popping.

"Whom does not think? You do not think? How dare one does not think?" The voice sounded again, its low boom cutting through the elevated intervals.

"Reveal yourself," Xira replied, "We need—"

"When one does not think, one makes everything sink, what once did stay, is what now goes away," The voice barged, softening the tone.

The mud flood grabbed mercilessly on their calves, making it almost impossible to push through. Colder soil swept their feet and like a million, microscopical tadpoles were rushing around their ankles and something else in the mud was attempting to gnaw on their flesh. It didn't cost their skin, however, for the clothing had shielded from that happening to either of them.

"Summon you I do... come to me as I tell you to," snarling, the mystic hollow fired back like a gust from a window.

Xira's cloak lifted afloat, forming a camouflaging shield in front of her. Willow watched as she noticed one of the herbal bags sticking out of a pocket and then gasped.

"Grab a bag! Use the herb that can help us with this!" She said, pointing at it.

Immediately reaching into her pockets, Xira pulled out the note first to remind of which one was suitable to apply. *Agrimony and Juniper,* she thought as she read.

"Here!" She threw a bag of Agrimony to Willow, who just caught it as it launched over, "Hold it above you with both hands to secure form."

Xira had the Juniper bag and held it to the phantom which now appeared with the flow of the breeze, hovering not too far from them and expressed an upsetting, rattled look. It'd seemed like it had blended in with the environment, the same dark blue and green pattern sifting to the tail and outward — a species unlike human identification nor any kind. With its mane-like features, hovering closer, it glared at them as it caught scent of the herbs right in its path. Grimacing, the phantom spun in haste, retracting to the lake and vanished through a few twisted branches stretching over the water. As the suspenseful vibe loomed into the mist, the grip of the mud was sliding off their calves and pulling away from their heel. It had relieved the soil beneath their feet, making it a swift travel again. They looked at each other, still holding the bags and quietly walked across, with the sound of the frogs bouncing around in tune. Xira carried her cloak above the mud level, while the slimy rims dangled in a drip, remains of the sediment touching back to the surface below. A portion of the sun beamed through the tree gaps once again, showing a grassy island just ahead. The girls made their way as quickly as they could, the depth of the mud decreasing to their ankles and into a shallow puddle leading up to the land. Sighing, they slumped onto the ground as they wiped off most of the mud on their clothes, after placing the bags inside their jackets.

"These will hold us until we get out of here, right?" Willow asked, standing.

"As long as we don't burn them, the effects last much longer," replied Xira as she re-adjusted her hood.

They tiptoed through colloidal turf, on the way to a partially broken bridge which happened to be the turn to the next point. Crossing it, they realised that although the land after it would direct them up the path again, the lake which they'd heard moments before was connected to the shoreline and far down in the opposite point — where it extended to larger parts of the region. Despite no shadows roaming, it's where their habitat resided. The girls continued down the left, observing the tranquil, aquatic scenery. Its mysteries and history swimming low in the depths as the road ahead finally revealed another curve to the upper hill, containing a swirling trail to another elevated rocky surface. Willow could still sense the haunting, lurking energy present behind her. She kept close to Xira, who walked forth with her cloak waving along — the garment already having cleaned itself by its divination. Along the way, they spotted an open window of a landmark piece which was placed for making kind offerings for navigation. The glow caught her focus as Xira approached the twinkling, lantern-like pillar adorned with a sweet cover. She peered to find a substance which was like the clouds of ice wafting among emerald shimmer. A whisper echoed out of a dove token in the window.

"Let's go visit this waterfall," she said.

"Waterfall?" Asked Willow.

"The dove…something about a nearby waterfall."

Sure enough, the girls arrived at the location. A green space was seen through the cascading water. Xira hopped in and met a phantom that appeared out of the rock wall. They gestured to the green patch in front of her, drawing a circle in air, then two antenna-like lines with a bend.

"Me, sorceress. Guidance for," they expressed in ancient word, as she understood, *"Grass to the hand, hand to grass. Island."*

Figuring out the message, Xira acknowledged its meaning and placed her hands to the patch of grass. Once she did, the sorceress nodded and left a marking on the rock wall that would wash off after completion.

'The Evergreen Blossom, treasure of the island and of ancient'.

She glanced down at the glow beneath the skin as the grass surface revealed the treasure, the various realm plantation which provided the opening swirled over and settled — enlightened by the special connection.

'The lyre-harp landmark; Art of the Sky, find and climb high'.

After retrieving the five-piece discovery, the sorceress aimed toward the field where the landmark was, then ventured to the rock wall with a wave to its crevices — they mentioned about *'the keeper sanctum'*, where the treasure can be covered beyond the waterfall walls, should they decide to retrieve it when they prefer. The entrance was via the rocks to which they agreed for the moment. The figure waved and the girls thanked her as they went off to the giant rock design.

"Beautiful," Xira observed, admiring the celestial emblem on the landmark.

"After this climb, we go to the taller one, yeah?"

"Yep —"

At the top of the high climb, she felt a gentle wind guide her to view the sky. Air sprinkles reached the hand and out of their glimmer, another figure appeared. The figure expressed that they were a guide from this realm, traveller of Galaxaeria and an ancestor. They mentioned 'The Evergreen Blossom' before it was displayed at the front.

"Can you please explain more about this find?" questioned the adventurer, the treasure in the hands.

The ancestor went to detail on every token of the five which was known for different aspects of the wisdom they keep. A secret to the waterfall of the mountain, now in her trust with the promise of honour to the sacred treasure. They exchanged their thanks and kindness.

"Mystery indeed, it is dear, *'art of the sky, sound of love-light'*," they said with an honouring cheer, "An answer for you. *'Mystic wisdom'*."

"Art of the sky, sound of love-light," she remarked, as it lit up.

The sparkles circled the tokens as she sat on the smooth surface of the landmark to examine them individually and as its design.

One petal for the swing-sway, a grace beneath one's feet
One petal for the quiet spring in the day and night
One petal for the space of peace for the light
One petal for the clarity, purification and nourishment
One petal for the protection in a clear sanctuary

She pondered the gear detail, relaxing in the mellow zephyr and relished the environment with its connection. Afterward, Xira hopped to the path with Willow beside her, admiring the landmark as they placed the treasure to pick it up at their return and ventured across to the mountain's base point that the two visited.

Minutes went on until they reached the swirly path, heading up to the next area. Spotting the nearby frosty pillar, it'd reassured the correct direction. This time though, a plaque nailed down to the ground captured their attention as it read;

"The path north has a climb, a BURLY SET OF STONES WITH ONE LEDGE SO FINE. REACH THE SUMMIT, granted a reward so dear, then the light shall illuminate one secret in a sphere."

"There's something more etched down here... but it has been scraped to hide it... I wonder what was written," Xira examined at the peculiar marking on the plaque's edge.

Willow crouched next to her before they both got up to keep heading north. Just as the ground began to curve upwards, they noticed their arrival at what appeared to be exactly what the message had indicated... a climb. Tumbling gravel rolled down past them, as they observed any loose sections up the wall of stones. It was a fair amount of distance between one grip to another. Never was one the same nor non-deceptive. Xira heeled closer, inspecting the boomerang shaped rock within hands reach. With a hop, she began to ascend the wall, checking and quickly grabbing on the ones that looked promising. A good few feet, off the ground, she stretched a leg to lean on a lower stone before pausing momentarily.

"On my left, but directly underneath, I can lend you a foot if you need help," Xira assured while going onto the next.

Shortly after, Willow joined in on the climb, slowly tracing the steps her friend made and with great caution keeping close to her. Within covering the distance from the start to mid-way so far, there'd only been a little more ahead before the ledge and then the remainder of the wall. As they pulled themselves up between slings, the stones grew further apart, compelling them to evaluate every fragment lining up to the ledge and co-operatively form a strategy that would likewise benefit.

"I'm not so sure about this," said Willow timidly, "It doesn't seem like it will hold much longer for the halfway point."

"Be careful... go by the trail and you'll get there," her friend consolingly replied, "You can do it."

"I trust you but I — I don't exactly know if I could trust this," she added, "Isn't there another way?"

"We're already this far up, we just need to keep going..."

While Willow climbed up alongside her, what turned from a sole pebble to a multitude, now began to emit crumbling noises as it snowballed into piles and piles of pulverised outcrops — down and towards the curved path, just about missing them. In the heat of the moment, she grasped onto a small, cuspated rock, barely at a safe angle and dipped her left foot onto a sliver by the wall as the rest swayed in a diagonal position. Meanwhile, Xira kept watch every now and then, noticing that the ledge was closer and she couldn't guarantee that it was at all safe at this point. She felt hopeful, despite the circumstance of already being knee deep in it, climbing as she inspected the serenity of the environment and its atmospheric modesty, when she heard a caroming screech...

Knowing her friend was now in trouble, automatically she yanked out the grappling hook Valin had gifted and anchored it into the wall above her while rappelling down at full speed, gallantly hooking Willow on her arm. Propping her to the wall as she panicked then with a relief; held onto Xira and the nearby crater that was barely within the range. It'd sufficed to provide them a boost for the gap lining up to the ledge. After a silent moment, she gazed upwards then back down.

"You had this the entire time?" Willow questioned worryingly, "Pretty sure it's a better way of achieving this... and especially comforting."

"It would have been better, yes, but I was aiming to respect *their* methods. We *are* in their enclave," Xira mentioned, "It felt like an earning of trust, although I know your safety is just as important — I'm sorry. I'm glad that it does its fine saving as it does wonders for climbing… almost there, just stay close."

Huddling up to her, they vigilantly carried themselves up the wall whilst holding on to one another and the grappling hook. Between the brief space left to scale the ledge and the scarce number of braces below, the gravel grazed against their knees as Xira sprawled to haul over the ledge and then assisting her dangling friend up the edges to join her in a much-needed respite. Leaning back, they sighed as they watched the panorama before them. A wonderful world of tales, secrets and purity. Deep in thought, they pondered about the *outside*, how nobody from their world or another like such had found this place — meanwhile who'd have known the current events back at their hometown, what was stirring the over boiling cauldron of chaos and *more* secrets, injustice and propaganda. Was there even anything left in that supposedly forsaken, hitherto familiar home? The flock of birds that soared across the sunny horizon twirled around each other as the girls mesmerizingly watched, the light's rays shining on their earthly colours and in-between the gaps of their travels through the airspace. Their thoughts collectively switched to a pleasant expanse in gratitude to the arcadian nature that embraced with them, wholesomely flourishing its dedicated and core tranquillity that oozed throughout the realm — a tender feeling like no other. Time at this point didn't cross their mind nor the fact that Erma could've been lurking and slithering once again. Come the sunset, they figured it'd be wise to carry on before nightfall. Wiping clean their clothes, they got to their knees to briefly examine their task ahead. Quite a bit it was, but not a lot to cover until they'd had reached the summit. There'd been enough light to assist in their endeavours, so without a mere second thought, they hopped up on the stones to continue up the wall. Although it seemed reassuring that the ledge beneath them would act as a net in case of a mishap, Willow expressed the inkling that still resided within her and that choosing the grapple tool was their most helpful option in this case.

"I just don't want an avalanche of a sort to fall down on us, Xi," she noted, motioning upwards, "Don't you agree that using this won't be of any trouble to the essence of this place? I'm sure the *hidden ones* won't find you or me disrespectful by piloting away from any destruction done by *not* using it."

Xira launched the grappling hook over to the near top, extending it as far as it'd go, then hacked it into the rough and slanted towards her, smiling, "Touché."

After conquering halfway within moments, the distance drastically dropped with the surface being almost in the range. Feeling the velvety zephyr on their noses, their tucked in hair flittering across their garments, Xira first scaled the verge as she pushed down and climbed over, gliding backwards to create distance while Willow held the device and its main wire — contemplating on how to do that herself as she heard her friend call to her with encouragement. Both of her hands clutched on the handle and wire, she extended the feet to maintain a stance, then lifted to just about place a set of fingers on the rocky terrain. Xira leaned to support, as she grabbed her hand to haul. Once Willow gave another thrust with a foot on a higher angle where the dents formed a zig-zag gap within the crack, finally she triumphantly rolled over in an exhale and stretched out to rest on the ground while catching her breath. *I knew you could do it*, Xira thought to herself, grinning at her exhausted friend. The vastness of the realm glowed along the horizon which cast a misty ray across the grass fields that oozed with empyrean flowers and sundry plants alike. In some regions the fog itself painted darker tones through the natural emission of the land's earthly palette. From the summit, they could observe all the different places of the realm. Some slightly obscured and hidden, others booming in the open environment with its bewitching essence. Amongst the trees, water and valleys, the world uncovered a beauty which cascaded throughout the ethereal design and flair, colours beyond the shadows and sunlight in fusion with pure nature and aura in sprightliness. A magical wonder and mystery rendering through this world known as the Spirit Realm. Little crystallised pebbles rolled gently along Xira's resting leg, glistering during its rotation like through the viewpoint of a bumble bee and a thousand peppering stars. She picked one up to examine, twirling as she admired it, a translucent cut folding the exterior — Willow focused on the same pebble in wonderment.

"What do you imagine is up there?" She asked, fiddling with the wire.

"I kind of wish for a pegacorn. It's only up from here," replied Xira in a chuckle, "These rocks… it's like they're telling me something… I feel a gravitational energy, or is it just the elevation?"

"That's on you," Willow replied, sitting upwardly, "I'm aware of the breeze from this point above ground but all is all. This is something to note down I think."

"Sure, are you carrying paper?" Her friend jested, "I'll keep it in mind though… rocks back home are just… earth's mineral smithereens. This is something a little more special."

In accord, after handing back the grapple device, Willow stood to dust herself off before pointing towards an aperture on their path ahead. Hopping onto the ground that extended to the way onwards, a whistling euphonious tune wafted in a smooth wave as they waltzed closer, watching the petal covered metamorphic rocks and escarpment towering around them. As they moseyed across the path, the air became quite colder between the narrow walkway, when a thud was heard and rumbled from beneath the ground. Without paying any mind to it, Xira was heavily focused on what was beyond the inconspicuous opening leading to what she could only assume was deeper within the mountainous region. Meanwhile, Willow kept her distance as she watched her cross the halfway point. As soon as she did, the ground began to disrupt and in a blink of an eye the formerly solid floor was now transforming into puzzle pieces in the midst of breaking like a batch of biscuits. Instinctively, Xira hopped in diagonal form and at the edge, leaped to a roll on the other side, landing safely next to the opening.

"Come on Willow! Step lightly and bounce off the corners!" She reminded her while crouching to extend a helping hand.

Rather frightened and in a hurry, Willow shouted, "I'm trying… I can spot something — oh, that was close! Damn it… almost there, almost!"

Xira stepped forward as close as she could to the abyss haunting below. Within the moment after, she caught Willow's arms as her friend launched over beside her, tumbling back on the frigid surface… Getting up to kneel, they watched as the remainder of the path disappeared into the mouth of the darkness unknown — once silence returned, all that was between them and the opposite side was nothing but a telling of a fable not even the eldest of a kin, would have known, in a language only the solitary depths hold dear. The tune sounded again, like it was calling out from a close distance, lingering quietly and travelling across the cracks of the walls. An icy draught slithered along their ankles, while they tiptoed inside — the little wisps of light enhanced in forms of aquamarine and azure crystals, illuminating the layout of the route. Although it was peculiar that it'd appeared to contain barely a hint of what was around the corner, it came as a thought to the pair that it's something to find by the brave act of diving towards the pillar of truth. Walking through, the area turned to an easier advance as the crystals multiplied with each footprint paving the way.

"It looks… magical," sighed Willow, the reflection of the lights twinkling with her gaze.

Tracing the walls, they made a turn to a corner where a singular orange crystal the size of a tortoise shined on the rugged floor. Crouching to look closer, with one tap a marking appeared flaring a cyber yellow trail to the opposite point of the crystal, a circular connection which activated a sinkhole in the middle of it. That portion of the floor remoulded into satiny sand merging with the soil beneath an octagonal rising platform, which displayed a spheric ocean tinted bijou radiating constellations that orbited its surface. Xira watched as her index finger was absorbed in the aquatic colours, as if the vitreous element melted in liquid form and summoned a tempest around the tip of the finger. Joining by her side, Willow was lost in entrancement — whirlpools reflected like a mirror, the atmosphere cold as an ice rink in the night. A hushed tune played along with the one they'd heard a few moments ago, then in a mere sigh a highlighted constellation lit up in the hue of cherry red as a thin thread separated itself from one of the stars, coiling like a tail around the finger and evolving into an explosive gust; illuminating a symbol that resembled something most familiar to Xira…

As they watched, another compartment unlocked behind the sphere, extending out in branches with another level below it. Inside they found a sealed scroll, a folded painted map and a letter to the very one who found. Holding the scroll in her hands, it had read:

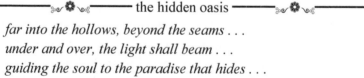

———————— the hidden oasis ————————

far into the hollows, beyond the seams . . .
under and over, the light shall beam . . .
guiding the soul to the paradise that hides . . .
birds, butterflies, owls, fireflies, day & night . . .
your fears be drenched, your sorrows be wrenched . . .
only joy will make its nest, peace will give you rest . . .
protecting your inner depths of innocence . . .

with you, together, shine with the orbiting luminescence . . .
blue you will recognise as the symbol of serenity . . .
red you will know, not of rage, but of love . . .
where silence is treasured and tunes are played . . .
creating a warm home and wonderful, happy days . . .

After reading the scroll, they looked at each other briefly, in amazement. On to the letter, Xira opened the first flap as she muttered the written words… *To the finder, open this.* Turning the next flap down, the antique pattern charmed the page of maroon ink and the font by a needle's point. Angling it to the illumination, the emphasised letters and markings emerged;

Land's Seeker…

In our awe, you've found this treasure beneath treasure. Our gratitude to you, fellow adventurer. For centuries, we've hidden these collections of some of our most cherished fragments, something which we've vowed to keep in a private location. However, now that you've wandered into this region, we welcome you humbly and honestly, provided you do not come with the intentions of harm as we like to believe the respect will be mutual. Along with that, we can assume that you will indeed kindly keep this secret to yourself as well as anything else you may encounter. Having entered here, it grants us to trust and watch over you. Remember that the presence you may feel is of souls within the world and even though most of us aren't here physically, we are here with you. You need to know we do not mean to frighten you or whomever accompanies you, for we are proud that a truly brave spirit is inside this darling home. Many have tattled various tales amongst their seed, but did not think twice to scale these surfaces and form one directly from experience. We do provide fault, although it has kept away just about everyone who you may or may not have met yet along the way. Unfortunately, even before this letter was hidden away here, we've noticed a couple of troubled souls attempt to, in their utterance, "break this place", which we understood was code for getting all what is in here and beyond without little too much consideration. No action was needed towards these beings, as the grounds themselves handled their outcome. Do be careful, if you are here to uncover more than what is carved into the land and hidden safely in shadows, your trail shall be ever light. This is your reward for discovering one of the hidden gems of this mountainous region from long, long ago. It is a wonder how many have been derailed from ever trying here or sadly have done... but in this case, we desire to express how bewildering this is in fact, that you are here now and found this very letter, scroll and map. Thank you once again, with this you've displayed a reassurance to our kind, that a falling doom is not in our world, but instead, another bloom.

~

Note; As another bonus from yours truly, you will find another compartment on the opposite end of the OctaChest... open and you shall find a little more. Safe travels!

"This is incredible, so we're simultaneously alone and not alone?" Willow remarked, looking at the OctaChest, as it was now described by the writer in the letter. Inside, the warmth Xira had felt sprung out the flesh brim in a grin.

"The map... it can really help us get around, we can actually get back to help the others sooner and then... home," her voice soothing, she looked at the OctaChest, "Want to do the honours?"

Eagerly, her friend leaned over to pop it open as it had a sequence to perform, using green opaque buttons and four little switches. To their delight, yet another red crystal fragment shone through the space, with a transparent icy stone and a note attached underneath it. Next to that rested a key chain in the form of a leaf with carved initials... *J.M. Who's that?* Xira thought to herself. As she grabbed to read the note, her friend had been examining the crystal and stone, side by side.

"*With this, you'll find, you'll discover, you'll receive... your answer. It shall light up to whom it connects with and has something to give — with a grip, all fingertips must lay individually,*" she read, then slowly turned to the stone, "This one?"

Willow quickly handed it over and held the red in her hands, wondering what it was for, if it had a similar use. Intrigued, Xira held the transparent stone in one hand while the note dripped in the other. Focusing on the centre, a little glow began to form from within, expanding in ultraviolet as it filled to the surface — its red ribbon-like trail weaved through what appeared to be slightly condensed vapour as it re-emerged onto the front, directly drawing out the same hinted figure as before. *Is that…?* Mid-thought, her friend jumped in the spot with a hushed squeal.

She showed out the red crystal that had been glowing like a song's rhythm.

"It's playing a tune? I think, uh — the tune that we heard before, possibly? Could be the exact one!" Noting solicitously, she looked back at her friend who had been watching with the stone beaming, "Ooh, what's happening? Woh—"

The full violet tone blended with the amaranth and directed a beam to the stone ceiling, covered mostly in its various crystal fragments that rebounded off of each other, painting a twilight constellation as it rushed through the gaps and connected the whole of the icy surface. A sky of its own, in the land of its own, pierced through with their gaze.

"Mountains… dual swords? Hmm… is that… fire?" Xira inspected as she tried to decipher what it had displayed, "Over there, something like what was on that sphere. Cosmic, luminous blades and energies and the mysterious, grand universe. This all looks familiar, every piece I see in here adds to the ones I discovered …"

"Does the note say anything else?" Questioned Willow, looking back and forth in awe, "Anything about this?"

Checking the note again, Xira replied, "Nothing here… wait…"

Just as she had flipped the piece of paper, she caught a briefly written piece on the bottom of it.

"What is it?" Her friend whispered, huddling.

With a quick breath and puzzling expression, Xira read, "Merlot and Jasper Grizon…"

Willow hadn't a clue as to what it had meant, then Xira continued, "Merlot… he was part of our family, as you know… Serenitatem… he left long ago and only recently he — he got in contact with me. I don't know how or what… look at this message. I have a feeling he knows something about all of this. For a long time, I doubted he would even keep his devices with him all the same, but I guess some things you just can't throw away… I have to message him… somehow. I wonder why he hasn't gotten new ones since he had left us, I thought he would know they could find him easily."

"Woah hold up," her friend rather bewildered, responded, "He's been texting you? From where? I haven't seen him anywhere either, after he left. You might've mentioned him again? ... but that's... ages I suppose!"

"No reception here obviously, I'll have to track him another way. There might be more to it in this region. Also, I think I've told you about him again just that one time at the town parlour when I recalled his own birthday," Xira told her, "As for Jasper... I don't know him that well. He hasn't mentioned much of Jasper before... probably because he left home to visit or even stay with this him after *he* left too. It was good while they were there, I guess even families keep secrets."

Once they'd gathered the items with them to pack up, Willow had opened the map to read over its contents before pointing to various key locations. Her thrilling reaction radiated throughout the map reading as it'd depicted all of the areas, secrets and hidden sections where some weren't even named but instead a question mark hovered on its illustration. A couple of them had been already recognised by the girls, as what they've found so far had stated quite a bit of the information involving the particular region. The symbol on the stone emphasised even more so, as Xira stood in front of the fluorescent OctaChest. Then combining with the other symbol, it became wildly obvious to her wonder about the meaning. Thinking back to the sphere and the revelations discovered, the symbols were a match and not for a second did she doubt they were related, for the one reminiscent was the one with her the entire time so far.

"This is my mark, my emblem that Serenitatem didn't want to tell me about," she reflected calmly, "The one I was born with and ever since had only been told that it held a vital connection."

"Goodness! We're getting closer, right?" With a surprised, merry look, Willow replied, "That other symbol, though? It reminds me of something, that's for sure."

"It looks like an animal to me. Interesting, the ears and nose are drawn out while the rest is kind of etched in a slide-cut design. It makes out... oh, there. I aligned it with the light of the red crystal underneath, it merges through with this very stone. Dude... it's... this is a wolf."

They watched as the rhythmic flashes of the red beamed through the stone's amaranth, displaying both of the aforementioned symbols. The aqua crystals from the ceiling rained a gentle stardust above them and to the ground, its snow-like effect lighting up the walls that formed within the surroundings. As all of the contents but the marked keychain had been retrieved, the OctaChest suddenly began to close and in the following moment, retracted back to where it was hidden beneath. The wall behind the platform immediately caught their attention as letters fleetingly revealed along the rocky veneer, spelling out yet another message that read;

You're on the way, may truth light with The Fae-o'-ray.

"This must be a key to what I — we're looking for, seems like we're getting closer to finding more out," Xira noted, examining the ghostly ink, "Whatever the pot of gold at the end of this rainbow is… I just, have an alluring feeling about it… it *knows* my symbol, my *birth* symbol."

"The connection…" Willow added thoughtfully, "It's connecting with you, by embrace, it's giving you what you want to know. In this case, the answers to yourself and what you deeply long to discover."

"Ah, so… it's getting personal," continued Xira, clutching onto the shining stone, "Then we must keep going."

Glancing once more towards the corner space, they ventured further down the path that led to a hall, then a camouflaged door within the stone wall and a mechanism next to it like a built-in lever of a sort. Squinting on the hatch, Willow shot a remark on its crafty similarity and how it had reminded her of her grandmother's old cellar back home. With a pull and a yank down, the passageway unveiled itself with a rose covered hallway towards a bridge above a twinkling abyss, showing their way through — its warming aura drawing the ground. As they stepped, the gems provided a cushioning while boosting them forward, like a guide and the comforting exchange that it exuded in the midst of a humming tune within both walls and the crystallic effect on the tip of their fingers tracing. Having reached the bridge, ever so carefully they crossed it halfway, observing its twinkly surrounding, despite a gaping vortex staring back at them. Fortunately, with ease, they jumped off to the next point and arrived at what was depicted as an archway to a tunnel slide.

Looking delightfully at her companion, then back to the passageway with a quick, angular lip curl she uttered, "Very well, let's go for a ride."

During the travel, a mix of earthly tones wavered throughout as occasional fluorescence in forms of cloud puffs floated by, in rhythm with the high pitched, rather quiet tune that played among turns — the colder air whistling with the soft bouncing of the defied gravity within the space. Quite some time later, they landed on a lush green floor with the feathery substance sidling up the walls on each side, over the ceiling and to the exit ahead.

"Huh, that was a bit of a long ride — feels like I've been swinging on a hammock," Willow commented, wiping her sleeves.

Smelling the refreshing, glacial air, Xira acknowledged, "Mhm... I get the feeling that it was like those portals that we've heard of..."

Sliding across, they noticed a glimmer in the distance when an opaque, holographic screen sprung out before their resurfacing to the ground. A charming and pacified voice sung through the air waves...

"Who is that dwells here and forth? May I ask you identify yourselves, in absolute honesty?"

Lumbering towards it, a growling echo cracked through with two large twisty vines extending in front of the hologram from each way, twirling the points in a protective manner.

"Information, then decision to proceed," the voice added, sifting with the crackling that soothed soon after.

The girls aimed to the entity, in kind intention and polite response.

"Friends... we're friendly, I assure you — Wi-Willow, and this is Xira," she briefed her calmly.

"Ah... a close friend of mine preached the wisdom I hold dear. *'There's more to me than my name...'* You see, you hear me, but my spirit's free and nobody knows where. So tell me then... what brings you to advance through here?"

"We're searching for something, a truth, that has been brought to light, piece by piece," Xira explained, "It was by what we'd recovered that led us to this land... and since, that connection has been guiding us to this very region — imploring to uncover and find for ourselves, the answers in hiding, tracing here..."

Silence befell the three, as a humming zephyr waltzed around the space. Carefully arching forward, the floor beneath deepened, while the feathery exterior coated their knees and oozed a hallucinatory fume. To her instincts, Xira thrust with her legs closer to the hologram, watching it whirl like water had entered its atmosphere. Keeping her focus in the entity's direction, she slunk to a lower angle. She caringly placed her hand on the vines when a humble embrace tickled the palm and a tranquil energy travelled through in waves, altering the swirls in the hologram into a tropical pattern which transcended towards the ceiling where the fumes had reached. It seemed to clear out the air as it covered the entirety of the area, before the screen transformed into a luminescent sphere. Joined by the rhythmic tune in its soft harmonisation, the vines slowly began to retract, gracefully opening up the path as the ground's density dispersed into sparkling molecules, floating off with the energy that soared towards the entrance directly behind the sphere.

Within moments, the sphere's pattern friendly once more, returned a warming energy towards the girls and back to itself, a feeling of safety and reassurance — spiritually connecting with the two as it emitted the colours in forms of firefly lights that it had received from deep within them. Grateful, Willow looked to her companion and then the radiant sphere, when the voice sounded yet again.

"My… what a rarity… the amulet tells me you are like our kind, however you do not reside here, or at least, *only* here." The voice resonated through the sphere, "And that cloak, I've ever seen a mere few in these times. You — this may have been your first home… it is, correct I am and even though there are no present claims of kin, it seems as your recent arrival was of no mistake, as you all are welcome — therefore, huh, there is something just for you, dweller, and it is none other than through this passageway."

Xira in awe, turned in question, "An amulet? I — I'm sorry, but Serenitatem, my mentor, told me I was born back home and that's where we had been quite so far."

"Serenitatem?" The sphere's echo switched to a hushed whisper, "He's not here, is he?"

"No, why? Do you know of him?" She replied with wonder.

"Never mind. I used to… perhaps I could indulge you with some information on the amulet," The voice continued, "It's my messenger. What it can reach to give, it does and surely it is with me and everywhere else all the same."

The girls looked to one another before walking forward, as Willow chimed in.

"Thank you, we won't be bothering you after leaving… this — this was very helpful and kind, I hope you understand, I mean, really, we have no idea what we're getting into, but if it's half as polite as you, then

I guess we're good."

There was a pause, then a warm reply from the voice once more, "May the combined potency of the spirits bless you."

Before they ventured through the way, they felt a benevolent presence circling around their backsides, as if it were welcoming them again in the space of the protected and hidden environment. Once crossing the grounds, the area became dark and quiet as they held onto each other to guide the path that appeared to thin out while swirling into a hollow with a forged ladder, ascending to an unknown surface. Being careful and on guard of their footing, one by one they climbed the distance, with each progress checking the surrounding space for any potholes or indentations of a kind. Up some time after, there was quite more of the ladder to cover, as they kept close and belongings huddled.

"By the way... do you think Jasper is around the realm? Possibly even this region?" Asked Willow eagerly.

"Eh, I don't even know what he is up to. I'm thinking it involves Merlot, whatever it is," she responded to her.

"Oh yeah? That sounds right as rain, huh," Willow resumed with a low chuckle, "Do you think they rode off into the sunset, forgetting everything else behind?"

As Xira lifted her foot above the other, getting closer to the exit, she theorised playfully, "Hmm, yeah maybe they left home to seek another they could build on their own. Maybe even considered re-enacting a scene as honest thespians? An old rusty book, dusted off into the hands of the future reimagining of A Tale of Two... with new ideas that brandish the element of real, true fusion in the modern age... making a shameless pull at the ol' societal structure of *meet, marry and make.* Knowing their deified notions, they set off to bask in the path they carved in honesty."

"Fascinating elaboration as ever Holmes," her confidant jested while scaling the ladder, "Did you just... make that up on the spot... I'll help with prop setup?"

"Haaa, already with the production mindset, hey?" Xira remarked, "I've raised an honourable partner, how sweet."

Willow let out a tiny laugh before her reply, "Okay, yeah I may have thought about, a smidge, bumping around carrying a medieval chair for a particular show."

"Hey look, there's light over there," Xira focused on the glimmer in the area, as she added, "Very well, Watson. Up and over, then."

They hauled above, rolling on an angle to find themselves in a gaping, furtive, yet warm and slightly lit up room. The corner light showed a hall connected to a somewhat obscured balcony and two dark adjacent paths on its sides, leading elsewhere. It was an odd inkling that the two shared, as it had appeared like not of cement but marble display of construction within a scarcely occupied residency. For the blue tone which masked the chained shadows that graced the space itself, throughout its regnant wall-paint of ornamental botanical design, hid what held the key factors and history of the room between walls... A silhouette caught Xira's periphery as she quickly turned to see what or who just rushed by. Nobody was there, simply an archway to the next section, seeming fairly dim and blue all the same. Sitting upright, Willow checked if every item was with them while ensuring the herbal bags were intact — although she pondered about the smaller items and how it wasn't the ideal spot to sort it out.

"Xi, do you have that lighter with you?" She asked, "I could use it here."

"I think so," was Xira's reply as she searched, "Yeah, here it is."

Handing it over, she watched as the sound of the wheel being turned into the chamber, light up the vermilion flame as it reflected on the marble floor. Putting the things back, Willow returned it to her while bracing towards the next room.

"Are we going through there? Or taking that direction?" Motioning both ways, she added, "How 'bout the map?"

Xira held the lighter over the folded paper while laying it on the floor to inspect its details. Tracing the etched paths along the page, she observed the colour coded tracks adjoining various sections with their inked titles. Directing to the blue rendering, she pieced the parts together into a conclusion that it was where they currently were located. Shining the flame over the spot, revealed the drawn spaces residing ahead.

"Okay," she uttered quietly, "We're on this path. We can take either one, they both lead to this 'Pink Clover' area and the 'Green Briar' section."

Contemplating on which way to travel through, a low noise in the distance echoed around the glass effigy in the next room and the corners of the walls. Willow turned to her with a slight valiant expression while the crackling of the rocky ceiling sounded in the midst of the silent intervals.

Folding the map away, Xira answered, "To the Pink Clover. There might be a shortcut beside it, if the map proves reliable, although that could just as well be an old rendition, so the cut may be snowed in…"

They cautiously covered the edges as they glided with the wall behind their backs, circling along the centre of the room, the shine of the light down the hall bouncing from the surface of the effigy — rotating its reflection the closer they got to the opposite side. The hallway displayed as a fairly slim path down to the following space, the pink which overlapped the formerly blue exterior, now more illuminated with the arcane, uncharted light that beamed between its perimeter and a ray directed to an oddly concealed portion of its mirroring angle. Holding onto their belongings, Willow had a puzzling look showcase her mind in whirling thought, upon gazing at the hovering mystery in question.

"I'm intrigued to know how that is floating, there isn't even a corona of a kind, that which could uh, explain this," she elaborated, "I mean, I guess this is further than science, which I admire… and it lures me to find more out."

"Let's just go to where we're going," Xira added, "I know this is fascinating and all, I just think that with the whole situation flipping behind us, it should be our primary focus."

"Oh okay," her friend brooded, "All the pitstops and the fossil searching, we can do, but one compact derail and it's havoc on the edge."

Sighing, Xira placed a hand behind her shoulder, "If none of these worlds fall into an apocalyptic calamity that's surrounded by a cult of clones with broken pitchforks, then we can revisit once again, I promise you."

Walking up to the opposite side of the pink room, the concealment they observed was made entirely of thorned clematis and within the few gaps they saw a key hole carved in the wall, shaped like a clover. Willow crouched to examine the gaps for any door knobs.

"Look… an imprint of the clover just revealed itself underneath this light," Xira pointed out as she went to investigate, "It… says something. Quite vague but I think it reads; *Spy through a wall, a strange window so small…*"

Immediately checking the walls, she pressed her ear against the corners as she knocked between each step onward to see if there was a hollow spot. One hand followed alongside the ear while the other knocked. About halfway through the other wall, she came across a concave within the smooth surface and realised it had an outline with the likes of a button. Upon activation, they heard a slight rumble coming from the centre of the space — the clover, which had formerly been a decorative figure, opened up in two and a shiny silver key ascended on a marble pillar, reaching just underneath the hovering light. After picking it up, Xira rotated the piece in adoration of its shine, noting of the clover detail on top as they both hurried to the clematis which had eased away once they had lifted the key towards it. Turning the dial with the key, the stone structure pulled its sides to unveil the way forth.

"It's dark again," commented Willow, peering in.

Grabbing her lighter, Xira crouched through the grimy tunnel as she rolled the wheel, its flame glowing the way and padding on while Willow followed close behind with a hand against the entwined branches grazing her puffy jacket. The bags were hauled along, its contents tumbling before the getting out and up again, arriving into quite a flamboyant and uniquely lucid chamber furnished with a regal pearly dresser. Its coral tones outlined the dusty mirror and the crystal chipped corners sparkled with a floral combination that have been flung over the brim, the rosy and lavender petals coinciding atop the verdant ivy which dangled to midway. Almost every item that had been collecting dust for some time, was made entirely of crystal and glass material, formed in multiple figures to which appeared like ancient and modern eras were merged in one dimension. Little recognisable perfume flasks perched on the wooden top glimmered in the room's reflections, with silver coated tins embellished with symbolic indentations alongside and among the jumble of tattered notebooks was a boat shaped vessel containing a misty liquid. Below, a flower cut nozzle to which had an extension attached to a woollen pouch on its tail. The smell of a forest mixed with an oceanic aroma breezed through the air, a new found comfort was sensed like a heater in the winter as they examined the contents on the dresser's surface. Xira bent to pick up a brooch designed in the image of a moth within a swan, within a raven. The outline of the detailed wings lured her to wonder about its tale. It'd been planted atop one of the old notebooks, which encompassed the exact symbols on its cover — though not too as explicit. She flipped through its remaining pages, to uncover scribbles from a former lodger who had been documenting a blend of discoveries and figures relating to the mountainous region. Most of the text was fading out of the page albeit the singular distinct passage written on the bottom of one of the last few pages. The subject reminded her of a familiar memory with somebody she once knew. Its ink would still smudge, despite its weathering — reading it, it'd professed;

... it's dark, it must be a month, two maybe now. I haven't met anybody, not even from camp.

I feel so alone. How alone exactly? I fear, no, I worry... I worry this is besides

that feeling. Sure, one can say nobody is here but me. That's only the matter

of... matter. Of form. Of a visual presence, no matter the distance. Who's to say

others aren't in their form? In the same timeline and it's crowded, no matter

where anybody goes... oh that's a thought... that's a worrying thought. I worry...

no, I wonder... I'm not alone. I must keep going. ~{Luki}

Hmm... Luki. Much like a good friend. How I miss Tyva... she was just as humble... Xira's thoughts circled in reminiscence.

"Hey, Xi?" called out Willow, "You might want to take a peek at this. Here!"

She received an envelope marked with the name '*Jasper*' and on the back signed; '*Promise me.*'

Within a second hesitance, she peeled off the stamped corner and found herself eagerly wanting to read what was in the letter.

"I found it in the bottom drawer," Willow added, "Isn't it strange? No one has opened it or perhaps it wasn't sent..."

Reading the large curly font in the scratched ink, it'd indicated that the letter was to Jasper with the copperplate text below:

Jasper
In the event that you find yourself in solitary circumstance, please

call to me. In whatever ways that you can achieve that, otherwise, you know our spot. I can't even begin to explain to you how full of sorrow I am, you know? This hasn't been easy without a doubt, I just can't fathom what that place has become... who I have to be because of it. You may think differently, that I shouldn't have done what I did. It's not up for debate, I did that for you, as you already know that. No matter what heavy weight or consequence sits on my conscience. I've vowed to do what's right, not what others tell of a tale so questionable of morality. Please, if I must ask for one thing that I would want you to do for me... it's that you promise me. Wherever you decide to go next, whether it's by yourself or not — do not trust them. None of them. No matter what they attempt. I'll find you if you can't find or meet me. If you don't want to, I'll respect that all the same. Just know, what we've built, won't ever change. It's written here, in the stars and in our souls. Hear the darling whispers of the world, not of beings so hostile. Stay safe, beloved. Do what you must and decide to — promise me.

~ M ~

"This has to be... it's Merlot," continued Xira softly, "If it's been in there for a while, then someone must have come by and left it unopened. Question is... was it Jasper?"

Grimacing as she turned from the drawers, her friend replied, "I have a weird impression that it's more ominous than it appears. It sounds like they're threatened and already in hiding. Poor guys, who knows what's going down."

"If only I could contact him with my phone. What else is in the drawers?" Xira returned as she walked over to search.

Rummaging through in order from top to bottom, most items were quite antique and old, a vast combination of many strangers that have found themselves here. After checking underneath and at the back of each drawer's corner, they placed all the things that seemed peculiar or suspicious on the surface of the dresser, sliding the rest of the stuff backwards to clear some space. Willow commenced a thorough re-trace of the side drawers as well, then stood beside each other over the uncovered fragments. Going one by one, from notes to envelopes, to packages, to scaly diaries — little mysterious treasures overlapped in a bundle of memories. Some had contained details of the past times of visitors and inhabitants of this region and more — where obscure judgments and occasions were told on paper and somehow all placed in this very room. Secrets which only the motherland knows and the spirit with the wind protects. Whether from the mostly wise or foolish, it provides a place for all. Lifting up the first note on top, it looked like it'd been ripped apart a former piece. Willow joined to scan briefly.

"*There is noise I think tries to tell to me, a new language? A message, but vague,*" Xira read the paper, before picking up the next piece, "*Am I being haunted — are these walls talking — no silence in emptiness — odd the abyss talks…* bit cryptic."

"Ooh, then there's this: *My sweet bud, ever lost Evelyn, can you come over? Look for me, listen for me, break the walls for me, our souls are near, I know you're looking!*" exclaimed Willow, "Uh… wait — this looks like that ink on the security back home… *'WHAT IS THIS PLACE? WHERE AM I? WAS I DUMPED HERE…? I WAS GIVEN THIS PEN & PAPER…? WEIRD, MY UNIFORM MELTED'* — whoever wrote this, left a piece of his clothing on the page."

Taking a look at the material, Xira rotated it to find that the same symbol used on their trucks and heavy weaponry crates was patched on this piece. An unsettling inkling twirled in their guts, knowing somebody from their sector had breached and tramped through here. Still unknowing of a name or information regarding the current security of Glacial Mist, she mellowly put down the piece in a low exhale.

"Either they connected with someone from this realm or the bastards have found a way inside," she retorted, "To find our answers, we need to keep going. This fool is probably not here now anyway."

With a soft, pacified glance, her companion reassured confidently, "Yes. Finish up here then we move on? We may find something — could be very helpful. Flip this place over and we're outta' here."

In agreement, the girls resumed their search through the pile, picking up pieces top to bottom.

Willow read aloud playfully, as she shuffled them, "'*Ma told me this place was dangerous, but all I gather is… mother nature — like a home.*' — '*NOSE COLD. WENT TO PRY, PUT NOSE IN. NOSE KNOWS.*' — '*I just wanted to find some plants. I heard there were extremely rare ones here. Lost now? Lost here? Here contains more than the plants… ~ELIZABETH.* — '*NO SIGNAL, NOTHING. SIR LEON HARE IF*

YOU'RE READING, THESE WIRES DERAILED THE TRACK, NOW IN THIS REGION.'"

Chuckling, Xira bounced in, "*'They sent me to seek ingredients, was this what they wanted? Rocks?'* — *'Disbelief, disbelief, disbelief! The treacherous lands are treacherous after all! MAGNUS!!!'* — *'To thee, to them, to thy, to whom* — *OH FORGET IT'* — *'Harold, I'm cold, I miss you, I want my coat back, you left it at the cottage. With love, Jen'* — ha, this one's another treat, *'Of course I land here, the Karaoke Festival, what was I thinking? Joey led me here on purpose, argh!'*'"

Her friend in joy of their re-enactments, added with poise, "*'Dear reader, you're lost too? It's wild out here, on your tippy toes, watch the walls and gaps'* —"

After flipping over the stacked pages, Xira scoffed in protest as she noticed quite an anomalous note that slipped from underneath…

'Dear Menkos — as we formerly dedicated allegiance to the home, read between the lines carefully.

Abandoning your nest is one thing, I understand that and you know it. Trusting someone with a mask for a face and never once stepping foot on our welcome mat is a whole other chaotic decision — I trust you can mend your ways but you also keep some things that you know very well aren't yours to share besides the "family". I know you've set foot in this place and I know you're still here, a little birdy told me. What they didn't tell me though is if you're still… corrupted. Whatever you are, please keep what you know about certain members of the family to yourself, we don't want any of it to be compromised.

Especially her. You know who I mean. At least the vows you made before joining should be the one of many aspects to respect and take with you after your departure. With the secrets, they are the parts that always matter and deserve preservation.

*I ask you only this. They are dangerous, they are merciless, they are falsehood. Protect the last of the kind… to plant peace and weave the light on the worlds. It's the one thing you can do without the burden of your past, Menkos. It's for her and because it is for her, I know you can do this — don't allow that to be connected with whatever or whoever you still resent. I believe in you and so should you. Make that another thing… do it for yourself too, create your peace and then take that everywhere you wander. Believe in **true** serenity. If they find her, they are both in* *peril and that's the frightening part... she doesn't know. I don't want to think about what will go down if it unfolds the bad way — what she will decide. Well...*

It's up to her.
Deal?
— M.'

"Huh," Xira remarked while unfolding the rest of the folded page, realising a whole letter had been written and then signed with the letter M marking, "Merlot again? This smells like something I wasn't told of when I was still with the *family*. They abandoned instead of being exiled? As I recall Jay'eo say... though, how much of anything was true...? Who really was at the sword's point?"

"Goodness, a downright mess if you ask me," Willow replied, crouching beneath the dresser to check for other fallen notes, "Oh, hey — hey! What's this?"

Smoothing out the paper from the crinkles, Willow added in disbelief, "*Upon us they are, the entity that remains, I search and you search — for the Lord asks us hence forth.*"

"No insignia on that?" Questioned Xira, mordantly.

Who are they? Who are these cryptics referring to? She wondered.

"Oh, hang on — didn't Valin say I can use this to contact them?" Her companion pointed to her Bird'Oz beanie, "I'm not sure if it can work from within the mountains however... I could try?"

Taking it off, they examined the exterior of its design, focusing on the details while figuring out its mechanics. Within the moment of finding the primary button then activating its nexus and defences, a semi-static signal rang through the airwaves. Nobody on the line, Willow located another button to adjust the frequencies. *Brzzzt... brzzzt...*

"*... No! No! Hakita! The pot is hot and mother said to not go near it!*" Was a voice they overheard on the channels, with others along the silences of the search.

After listening to what seemed like every region throughout the realm, they came across a soft yet distinctive voice with slightly amplified static — in the heat of realising who it was on the line, a green light flickered near the button they'd been using to navigate the channels, prompting to initiate call. Pressing it, Willow glared in the dresser's dusty mirror as she waited on the receiver. *Bzzzt... bzzzt...*

She could hear the voice chattering as another joined in the background, cutting down to clarity before picking up the ringing line.

"*Hello?*" The second voice answered, composedly.

"Niko? Valin? Is that you? Hello?" Willow responded all thrilled.

"— *Dear! — Ha — How great, you —* "The line crackled back around to a clear-cut reception, "*Where are you calling from? — — For the love of — Niko, please quiet down, the girls are calling! — Are you still there?*"

"Oh, Valin, it's so good to hear you guys pick up," answered Willow again with pleased relief, "I was trying to get this thing to work and I guess it reached you!"

Xira listened close as the radius of the volume didn't extend too far away from the two, which she supposed was a fair feature, as she leaned to the built-in earphone board.

"*Yes, we could say the same. I'm filled with joy to know you girls are safe and I assume being careful?*" said Valin, the background clamour lessening.

"As ever. I don't suppose you know how many times I can actually call you? Does this gadget have certain distance?" She asked eagerly.

"*Why — as the manufacturer informed me, yes you should be making calls as long as they are within the realm alone —* "Was the doc's response, as a shout chimed in the back lines.

"Is that Niko? What's he doing?" Willow wondered, while Xira grinned at the intervention.

There was no reply for a brief couple of moments, before Valin returned to the call, a vexed sigh puffing through the speakers — then followed a low exasperated chuckle.

"*It is he, who cannot simply figure a plan out that we've already **talked** about,*" her voice turning stern then smooth again, "*Sorry, it has been a — some packing hours with this whole... rebuilding event. What did you girls want to discuss with us?*"

"Well..." Willow paused, looking at her focused friend, "We found this interesting room with quite a bunch of elaborate texts left by people... we think they may or may have not been through here. Anyway, some are pretty ominous, vague — uh, especially this one — oh and I'll give you Xira to tell you the other things we found so far..."

A long, long, thorough conversation between the three occurred that harmonious evening, as they explained all details to Valin and received pieces of news from herself as well, even Niko adding in his occasional backing input...

The mysterious room turned dimmer than earlier, with a quiet resonance slinking through the quartzite divide that led yet deeper into the mountain's chambers. Willow, standing by the limestone wall on the far right, stayed in tune with the call until they'd concluded the conversation.

"We appreciate the help, I'll give you a call once we rendezvous outside again," she told her.

"You can contact us as you please — although remember, any whiff of you-know-who... or of the like, you call us while the air is dormant," Valin returned through the speakers.

"On it," the cautious Willow replied, watching Xira examine the walls.

After finishing the call, she turned to her quizzically.

"Aaand we're off?"

"Yeah, yeah, it's just — I know this is all around magical and such, I just can't help feeling that there's more to it than its exterior makes it to be... enlightened, rejuvenated," Xira remarked, walking to the divide, "Sure the secrets remain but its depth, is... well, quite eclipsed... — All right... let's go."

Slithering through one by one, an unusual aura breezed beneath their noses as the climate became warmer when venturing further. A glittering layer featly coated their skin like the way of a polyester voile curtain would slide down the dorsal element of a hand. The ground they walked on transformed into many fragments of dark agate rocks leading to the vibrant opalite and other mystical crystals that formed a mollusc perimeter encompassing a warm water filled pond. Luminescing nacre pearls floated around the edges, above a genus of lotus burgundy falls covering the surface of the elevated small isle, bending down beside a glissade trail adjoined to a rimy rink with the miniature flora blossoming around it. For then the path on their boot front radiated spriteful energy as they wandered forth in amazement, observing the colourful environment and its grand empyrean features. The space extended into a larger capacity whilst uncovering more of its hidden beauty, a tall purple-green blooming tree creaking its branches to the beetling array of evergreen clematis that weaved among a row of soft twinkling lights nearby a wall of water which orbited the area. Its tranquil rhythm mixed with the rustling of the bale of anthurium and kalanchoe plants on the grass a couple of hovering plush in front. Taking in the fresh scent of the nature within, Xira smiled warmly while resting along a claw-shaped log between the many lithops and marmalade hued sludge in a nook on the ground by some frosty spheric dandelion-type flowers with a glowing depth. Between the mysticality, the self-growth of the various plantation and the wonders of this ethereal nature within this mysterious secret, it'd portrayed a display of being unlike any of the rooms so far and its way of being that much more hidden than the others encountered. Giddy by the ardour and reverence she had about all of this, Willow speechlessly took her seat by the pond on a mushroom shaped bolster that appeared to be crafted of a different material as the ones they'd been familiar with, in manners that almost evince to be non-human. Observing the details among the environment, all the way to the edges of the decorative flowery vines that stretched out on each side of the glistening, crystallic walls, they realised the essence emerged throughout the atmosphere, furthermore the balance was fused with it. Upon more questions that entered their thoughts, a harmonic echo bounced from a seedling up to the bounds of the inner cave ceiling. Entranced, they watched while coloured waves of what resembled a dragonbird, float with its wings welcoming the tropical air that whirled through the whistling tree tops — a sweet tune that trailed close behind, summiting to a melodious spring.

"Hmm… greetings to you. I sense a bond beyond the frontier," the dragonbird proclaimed while the wings fluttered calmly with its fiery edges.

"H-Hi, who are you?" Willow very quietly asked, as they both gazed in admiration.

"You, keep no fear of me. I'm the spirit protector of the mountains and of the Hidden Oasis, you may call me Phoenix," responded the dragonbird, their gaze focusing below.

"Phoenix, is this the Hidden Oasis?" Wondered Xira, gesturing around them.

"Yes. This is," Phoenix told her, as the dragonbird waved a wing behind themself, illuminating the entirety of the Oasis, its mystic beauty expanding through the now opened walls next to the flourishing vines, connecting to an upper level of the cave and seemingly revealing another secret of elements within it. Phoenix raised to the glowing plants on the upper crystallic ceiling, as Xira arched in closer. The dragonbird went on to showcase the twirling colours in fusion with the aura and fragments of the mountains that represented its native symbols that had been seen during their stay at the village. With delight, Willow stood to inspect the carvings that were rather oblique from her point, as each one had their own glowing outline although much like a flickering torch light.

"Ah, these appear indistinct to you, don't they?" Phoenix asked, before directing a wing beside her, "Well, it seems you do not contain the interstellar connection with the script. May I? You, there?"

"Sure," replied Xira, musing.

The dragonbird's wing shifted towards her cloak as the aura's light flared over the hood, drawing itself across the wing and then bouncing off to the script's outlines, defining each marking in a bold enamel. The expression of the spirit told of a knowing truth that had been discovered by them through this phenomenal contact. While the girls were in the midst of deciphering the message, Phoenix hovered closer to glare directly with Xira's height.

"I sense your truth. That tells me you are one with this realm. You however, do not know that yet," Phoenix explained to her, "It is my duty to tell you of this secret... Xira."

"Huh, I'll take that you know my name, you know more about me," she responded with an extremely curious tone.

"Right you are. Xira, your coming here, is not at all an accident, no one who's stepped foot into the mountainous region has come thus far to greet, let alone meet, me. We remind ourselves of the purpose of being a welcoming entity, albeit we are just as protective, therefore not all who venture through the caves come out a shining wiser token," The dragonbird continued, "Now... the script informs me of yourself and what is within you. Apart from your soul of course. Your spirit, your eternal spirit."

Nodding as attentive as she was, leaned next to Phoenix to watch the holographic flames tell a homely story on the rocky cave ceiling. The familiar symbol she had seen a brief while ago, appeared in a quick wave with a few of the symbolic words that were carved into the crystallic surface. The dragonbird seemed to note this down before analysing its meaning and returning to render it all thoroughly. A gleaming, sweet expression painted Phoenix's feathery face as they looked once again to Xira's reciprocating, rapt gaze. She sat there in wonder.

"Welcome back," Phoenix said to her warmly, as they watched the girls spring quizzically, "The wolf spirit of the guardian, the eternal ghost of the realms around. The phenomenon of all the homelands. We have been searching for you, hoping you will then find us. Find yourself, again. You might not recall what happened, well... I can assure you, your guidance called and led you here... there's an evolved threat that looms the multiple worlds connected to ours and we haven't been able to tell anybody for so, so, long. We are on defences, however the many other worlds that are near and far, are at their own peril and all that which connects us, connects the threat itself that we think, holds a doom to us all. You're the last of the kind that can light the way through. The Goddess of Galaxaeria. To and of the homeland and the cosmic beyond. With your guardian, cosmic and spiritual mien, you bring that honour here today. Your pure presence. A pure Spirit being, known as Xira. The Spirit Realm is hidden to the rest of the lands, but just like a whirlpool, the odds can only ever expand for others to find our world. I must tell you also this, your friend here has an energy that came from your recent glow of the cloak, it tells me more about her, about what she contains with you. Willow, correct? Your essence is aligned with the one of the grand bird family, perching watcher of a watcher. Gentle approach both on land and high — solicitous and benevolent as you are. There's more to you than meets the eye. Look inside, find your light. Listen with your ears, not with your fears. Your ears, even in the wind. When you are connected to yourself, you are connected to love, kindness, to compassion, to freedom and to light. In tune with your being, to be cosmic of cosmic. You contain an undiscovered secret about yourself and *your* ancestors, of their culture and reign — royalty and highness of their grand legacy. That's as much as I am permitted to tell you, out of the requested respect and privacy of the ancestors. You can discover this secret by finding it yourself and knowing that the guidance will be given. Something special awaits, it is not in your hometown, however. A combination so rare, it's an enigma to me, you must be friends for quite some time, am I right?"

"Right, a long time," Xira sighed in an honest tone, glancing over to her wonder-filled friend. Then flashing her back a smile, Willow shuffled in the seat with utter contentedness — the rim of her goggles shimmering while her hair twirled down the shoulder blades.

"Well, it does seem you have acquired a rather special bond that I haven't spotted in any vessel for over many eras, it really is refreshing. Furthermore..." Phoenix continued after flapping their wings to the aurora by the warm, crystallised walls, "You must note this down like it was the marking that I see on your wrist there, Xira. I recognise its symbolism, the question is, do you know what it entails? No...? well — it's the ink of your personal soul. Representing the two swords, which are not *swords*, per se, but energetic blades of your truth, that crossover as the soul's source of which is hidden, then you can observe the mountain figure behind it, emanating the aura of this very place, in the detail of protection high from everything else. Then, these valley sabres that appear with an arrow nock-like effect... depict the animal relation within you. As for these mystical features, which exhibit the purity, tell the true meaning of motherland creation painting the atmosphere, galactic elements of a world and universe of peace and love. You are the key and the locket, the sun and the moon. Your fire and fury keep a balance of warmth and flame. The dark and light in one spirit. You have all the power to destroy anything... use it to save someone and something else. Balance, Xira. It is within yourself, embrace every part of it."

"...*Discover the truth that hides inside and revealed be the light, through the depths*," Xira whispered thoughtfully, "*The one light. Answers we hunt for.*"

"Oh indeed," Phoenix replied, hovering closer among the whistling trees.

"Serenitatem... he would tell us this, he even made a framed embroidery for me to keep in my own room," she elaborated, "I... I don't believe he's been here himself, has he?"

"Dear Xira, I would assume any mentor would openly confide such a matter, even so he has not, he has certainly been here. I confirm, for I didn't speak to him personally and after hearing from our fellow spirits, it did not sit well with me, however," the dragonbird continued, "you mustn't falter on your belief about his motives, I'm sure he meant the best for you, perhaps he thought it was better for you to not know that..."

Her brows furrowed along the focused, determined gaze, "Not falter, no. I believe he lied. His oath to honesty means nothing now. I cannot trust even my own mentor," Xira remarked as she stood up, "Let me guess, he knew about my truth, about another world, hell... he... probably even knew about the Rove Dynasty and the underworld."

"Pardon, the Rove Dynasty?" asked Phoenix, fluttering his elongated, feathery tail.

"You haven't heard of them? They're apparently a threat to both of our worlds. A witch by the name Erma Merideth has been visiting the villagers down south. It was not a friendly one, I've witnessed, myself. She's part of that family... as you would call. A negotiation that went wrong, turned to a malicious targeting on two very kind people. Anybody that is near them is affected as well, she doesn't care. They know she's up to something."

"Xira, firstly, this is *your* world too. To that, I agree that they pose hostility to us and we just hope they do not intend to extend to the whole of the realms. I likely haven't heard of these folk because of their location, it's off our radar and off of anybody else's. That means somebody must enter their premises for information gathering, otherwise it is simply not feasible," Phoenix told her as they sat by the lilac pond surrounded by lime grass.

Xira looked over the reflective warm water, the glint glossing on the floating petals, "It wouldn't matter anyway. You can look up to or down on someone and still be disappointed," she turned to the dragonbird, "Whether peace is restored or not, they linger regardless."

Descending to the open patch of the grass, Phoenix circled in a gentle motion, crafting a dahlia flower-shaped cushion out of the glittering stars that sprinkled like snow from the spellbinding ceiling. The orchid and amber tones blending with the rosy pink flourished around the sides and underneath, its exterior settling atop the lush greenery. Another of the same appeared next to it as they watched the dragonbird complete the details and perch beside the two cushions.

"Your spirit you trust, your own firelight leads as you lead on forward and up. That singularity, freedom and honesty can never be bought or replicated, not even by your silhouette. It's who you create and evolve, being true to what you fight for and for the greater of the worlds combined. It's all up to you," Phoenix stated as they added, "These —

are for you both to utilise, as you should collect some energy for further endeavours. It is safe here, so do what you will before you continue forth. Enjoy the Oasis, and as your alliance, you are welcomed here for always. Do know that we also provide fruit. Few like other worlds and many quite a rarity. Peace, inhaled and exhaled. With the sky, fly and rise."

They watched as the dragonbird flew into a holographic spiral, their wings lighting up as they entered through and then disappeared. Willow let out a brief laugh in relief, amazed by their new encounter.

"Are you magic? You've been magic all along, haven't you? With what Phoenix said even about me—seems like we are true magic. Grand legacy? Oh honeycakes — this is, I'm just-," she enthused, "Interestingly, I've always assumed your mark was something eccentric, in the symbolic means — now apparently you are mighty Xira, dark wizard and all."

"Wizard, yeah and here's my spell book with a brand-new list of concoctions, two of which are called, 'RU Key-Ding?' and 'From A to Zip It'," Xira retorted as her friend chuckled again, "I'm glad I'm not currently growing fangs or I will kind of freak out. Uh. That's quite the info, Phoenix... what to do with it... eat an apricot or something."

Willow launched herself on the cushion with excitement, then sighed, "Hey, hop on ya' cushion there. Let's catch some *z's* and we'll go through these discoveries later... I'm kind of spent, honestly...or you could murk around the plants, maybe find something?"

Smirking as she watched her roll her eyes, Willow slumped back, curling up under the mellow cover that was attached to the surface. Meanwhile, Xira trailed about the space quietly, observing the vibrant plantation and mysticality in all its grandeur, scenting the fruit which dangled from the branches, in designs she hadn't tried before — with the aroma of the flowers merging and the luminescence painting in dulcet and sombre tones. She took a bite out of a tulip-shaped fruit as its orange nectar splashed out of its shell, its taste so refreshing and cool as the ice on the cave walls. Looking at the star-like rocky interior and the crystallised detail across, she reminisced on home and what it was, thinking of all the times the family had inspired one another and created a loving place for all who had ventured there. *I wouldn't think of it as new if Jay'eo was in on it. Ha, even some of the others, using grub and beverages for cover,* she thought. A leaf fluttered down in the palm of her hand with the nectar staining the edges of its green hue, the light mass yielding a calming moment for Xira as she turned to examine its delicate design. Then placing it on the pond's water while the liquid blended the colours together, it'd made a shining silky surface, hovering the leaf elegantly along the water's orbit. The energy that exuded, lifting her spirit, blossomed more of the combination of flowers throughout the Hidden Oasis and even jumping to the vines that decorated the crystallic walls. Observing the wonders, she waltzed around the grassland and various stone paths connected to it, different routes which led to other parts of the area and its many hidden secrets. She discovered the full nature of the realm in its highest presence and most radiant might. The twirling, trailing plants graced along her glowing garment as Xira walked to the tall neon flora where the petals flung over with the ballad of the birds sounding from within, butterflies with colours of aquatic habitats herded out and another luminous sphere sprung out of a mushroom stump near a chase of velveteen plants in duality of ombré violet and sunny yellow. It followed her to one of the pouring waterfalls ahead and then disappeared behind it. Intrigued, Xira reached a hand out to the water and ran it through while her cloak activated its shield defences and stepped inside to find a dark aisle with the hovering sphere guiding the way. Making her distance with the trail, she found herself yet at another carved wall with a row of symbols and a sword shaped lever. *This must be the way out*, she mused, *and that's our key...*

After a brief while, Xira returned to her cushion and flipped over the cover to seat herself. Looking over to the waterfall once again, she noticed a few pebbles on each wall beside it stand apart in their shine quite resembling the sphere from before, then to form two of the symbols she had seen on the carved wall. Like an icy stalactite, seaweed type of branches emerged from the rocky curves to protect the entrance from which they had come from — layering with thorns up to the crystallic grounds. She saw the aurora from the ceiling enhance around the tops of the interior and bundles of pink fluffy blossoms float through the stellar atmosphere, a comfort she had dearly missed, knowing they were in a homely, loving environment. With the gratification, Xira swung over to her sweet and sound slumber...

Dreams within dreams, she discerned the harmonic tunes echoing through the hazeland.

"Hey! Hey? — Xixi! — Listen, — Xira! Hey," A voice called out, almost sounding muffled as if she were swimming underwater. After a brief period where she noticed the volume of her caller had increased, Xira identified her companion's voice as the blanket propped the eyelashes. Sitting up to see Willow kneeling beside the cushion, she wondered what the odd commotion was — aside the fact that she looked raring to go, the Oasis remained the same as they'd found it.

"Mm, what's going on?" She asked, rubbing the bottom of her nose.

Adjusting the beanie and jacket, Willow answered, "Do you hear that outside? In the distance? At least I think it's pretty far... there's some weird noise and it's not the wind — this sounds rather unfamiliar, so to say, it kind of makes me think it's an, uh, avalanche?"

Listening in to decipher the noise, Xira gathered a hunch as to it seeming like something she'd heard of before. Figuring it was best to stay at their location for the meantime, her friend chimed in with an alternate proposition.

"Look, we came here, okay, we found your answers — most of them — made a trusting ally, there's like no space we haven't covered in this mountain, shouldn't we be going back to help the others in the village?" As she wondered, Willow stood with her contents flung over the back.

"Yeah. I just don't think that is really our priority right now, we'll get back to them sure, but if your avalanche theory is outside, rushing to them in the fallen snowfolk puts us in their duty call," Xira reflected, "Try give them a ring if there's signal — see what they're up to."

In the arranged entente, her friend sent out the signals to Valin's receiver and waited for the pickup. It wasn't too long before the connection was made and their static voices clearing on the machine. They discussed their current matters, how they were in the midst of rebuilding Bloom Core while reuniting the families as best they could and the hard work that was needed to collect and reconstruct all the materials and shared supplies. Willow informed them all about their news as well, discussing the various subjects in regards and catching up on everything so far in the mountains. While they concluded their call, Xira jumped from her seat as a couple of loud thuds were overheard booming from the distance.

"Okay, I sensed *that*," she remarked, walking towards a waterfall, "That's not your usual avalanche."

Her friend picked up her things again, joined her and put out the hand that was carrying the other bag of belongings.

"We're going then? Do you know which way? I noticed the main entrance was kind of... secured," Willow added, "Can only guess why."

Pulling her hood over, Xira led the way through the waterfall and to the wall with the symbols. As her companion followed close behind, they examined the carvings together while figuring out what to do with the panel. By her first instinct, Xira placed her hand on each symbol as the garment's sleeve emitted a glow around her fingertips, outlining the crevices with the same hue of the light, then the next and the remainder after that, totalling in the activation of the way out. Once that was done, their next notion was to pull the lever, in hopes of opening the wall itself. Upon doing so, a low creak was heard coming from behind it. They stood back as the exit revealed a semi-narrow path through, the craggy structure sliding slowly to the left and ceiling fragments from the hall tumbling along the barren floor.

"All right!" fired Xira, then ran in with Willow, hearing the door grumble back as they made distance. There were the same crystals with a mixture of others decorating the edges of the hallway and the mountain walls. The light shining from the garment guided their exit. The sound of the two running echoed the further they went on. The outdoor resonance in the distance grew deeper and more sinister as crumbles dropped from the rocky ceiling after each of their steps, with the parts varying in size and provoking them into hurrying as the rocks fell near their feet's trail.

"Uh, whatever that thing is, it's making this hall fall apart! — If there's no door nearby, you're much faster than me. You can find it safely," Willow exclaimed, trying to keep up with the rush.

"No! I'm not just leaving you like that, what the hell!" Replied Xira like a dart landing on a dartboard, "We can do this — grab the back if you need to!"

Between swaying on one wall to the other, in search of the exit to the outside, the crumbling of the indoors had finally settled and mere dust particles descended in the aftermath. Taking a break to catch their breath, the pair switched as many items from their bags to their available pockets as they could to lighten up the weight that was carried. The path in front had been swirling them around, turning corners and providing twists as they arrived at a green jelly-looking doorway with a blue border of crystals, even on the two hoops by the edges.

"Whew —what is this funky type of door?" Questioned Willow quietly, looking at its watery shine.

"I think it's means of security, watch," Xira replied and then walked right through it, her cloak lifting the aquatic surface and returning it to its form, "It's completely safe."

While Xira waited on the other side, her voice had sounded like she *was* in an underwater location. As her companion carefully hopped out, the smell and breath of fresh air breezed along as they both sighed. Willow turned to inspect the new grasslands they had ventured into.

"Nothing… not here at least," she commented in the midst of her worried gaze rotating the landscape. Although it had appeared serene, with the night illuminating the lush plantation, ornate evergreens and the moonlight beaming on the arctic midnight fog, something was uncannily ominous, as they could hear the whispers and hushed flurry between the high aerosphere and low towards ground-level. They walked on to the meadow, spotting a piece of fabric lodged within a pit. Willow bent down and pulled on its corner to notice it had been through some mud as the red tones blended with the soil's overlay, its fairly worn guise displaying in the crinkles and folds.

"Hey…" alerted Xira in a mutter as she watched slyly before them, "That's her… what is she looking for…"

"Huh? Who? Wh—" Just when Willow was about to answer, she witnessed a rather couth greeting, among the soiled and marshy grounds, walked the tall, disgruntled and determined Erma Merideth. She who had not met either of the girls, disposed herself as she dragged an elaborate dressing along the floor then lifted its seams. Xira gazed while her stomach dropped to the feet, her gut yelling to exit.

"Lost, perhaps? Do your villages know you're roaming these lands?" Erma questioned them as Willow rose by her companion. She turned to glance, then back while wondering who this woman had been.

"There are tasks that we were sent to accomplish. They trust us to be around here," Was Xira's reply, huddling the cloak's material.

"Hmm… and *which* village may you both belong in? As far as I have heard, nobody likes to be an intruder of the northern region," she beckoned, folding her hands with the garment overlaying.

Xira dismissed the obvious sneer, then averred, "Much as I don't *want* to be... *intrusive*, I simply do what I can to help — at least I speak for myself when I say... sometimes... breaking the recycled repetition that others have grown fond of, brings a new-found light to a nurturing place such as this. Some of us want to give back for the sake of giving, that's how everything blooms."

"Ah, I certainly admire your ambitions. You do say many of the folk would rather continue what they've been told, and yes it seems to work quite well for them. You must be from the far east? West? There are plentiful villages, egh — all marked by their kin."

Brief silence rushed between their positions, only the water from the near distance sounded ever so delicately.

"I am looking for something..." Erma added in an adamant manner, stepping forward, "By, hm, a fish tail's chance, have any of you located a -ahem an old fancy lookin' staff? A precious belonging, my *village* requires its return."

Recalling the events in Bloom Core, Xira exchanged a knowing glance to Willow who began to pick up the pieces herself. Inspecting the woman's feet who appeared to angle opposite ways as particles dusted off of the tip of the boots, she turned to realise thin fumes on the horizon south west of the region. It was not near their vicinity, despite her detecting the smell from that far.

"First, where did you recently bring it with you?" She wondered, inconspicuously, "That's where we'd start."

Chuckling under her breath, Erma cleared her throat and told them, "I believe that's a good idea... well, except this is a pretty large area and I'm not equipped with a map or direction of any sort — I'm not from around here, you see, I know a friend or two. They need me. So, as a good Samaritan I'm visiting to fulfill that oath. Anything in those bags that could help me?"

Willow looked down at their belongings as they held them behind, in thought of forging the detail. Although maintaining composure, Erma was unfortunately growing impatient as she assumed their reluctance by not co-operating. She angled her feet and index fingers and cast a spell to pull the bags away from the pair, even so trying to be discreet and not reveal herself for who she is. To cover the action, she grinned in an ingenuine way to seem like they were bonding already, quite as if they were friends. As much in disbelief as the two were, the witch did not seem to care while lurking in the contents of each bag, shuffling them about.

"Well then, what is *this*? Ooh, you're not planning to *camp* out here, are you?" Erma began throwing interrogative presumptions as the bags flailed, "Huh, a hook? You like climbing? Oh my, quite the — wait, huh. Right. Whose recipes are these? This material — hang on... "

Taking out the gathered items that were inside, a quizzical yet gloomy expression came over them as the woman fixated on the girls.

"...How do you know Merlot? What is all this doing here? You do not want to lie to me girls, you need to tell me what you two are not. What you *are* hiding... you know these people, so what do you know about them?" She charged, carrying a letter, "You're not here for village tasks..."

Xira forged a reply as she answered, "We're on messenger missions just as much. Everything else is confidential, not a lie. Searching these parts will lead us to the clientele."

"I smell horse dung," Erma railed, composedly, "These people are not of this realm. I should know, I do not fable about someone's confession — so tell me, who are you?"

Determined to maintain their cover, they politely gestured for the bags to be returned. A laugh steamed from below the enchantress' nose, throwing the belongings aside as she unveiled the soiled garment. Willow stepped backwards in attempt to call Valin and Niko, searching for the signal button while her companion braced their position. The distance between them tapered with each step that magnetised the gusts surrounding the grasslands. An irksome look met Xira's defying angle, as the two came chin to hood. The static emitting from the beanie cut on its overlay material after it had reached the receiver, intervening their call by an odd aura.

"Dark by night, light by day, the shadows always come out to play," whispered Erma, her gaze lowering, "Your intention does not meet my analysis, mademoiselle. If I were you, I'd tell the truth to be excused."

Willow used this moment of distraction to try and retrieve their things, although they had been scattered, it would take her a little bit — just as the contents were packed back, Erma heard the crackling of the device spark behind her.

"Did you call somebody?" She turned in confrontation.

Kneeling in disbelief, her frightened yet hopeful glance reached Xira between the two, who noticed the hair of the enchantress flare up on the collar fabric. She nodded, her fight or flight springing in every direction, as she yanked off the first layer of the garment, the collar ripping in two as a shriek grazed the throat of their opposition. With a heavy hurl, Xira realised a lot of the belongings were within the ornate piece that landed on a swampy mud pile.

Her friend jumped to the other side as in the mere flash of a second, Erma had launched Xira a few metres across the bumps of the landscape. Tumbling over to both hands and knees, she coughed as if the wind had been knocked out of her gut, balancing her land with a slight turn to examine. In a foggy haze, Willow was seen trying to contact the village but as the enchantress grew furious, she bulldozed the way to lift her up mid-air and toss her aside, tearing off the device in between. The crackling of the call lured her to listen, as the voice of Valin shouted on the other end. She put the fragment to the teeth, watched Xira pull herself to a bend and walked towards her. Crouching with a blend of stenchy and wine aroma, Xira coughed once again as the voice of the woman hissed on the transmitter.

"So it is you," she sneered, keeping an eye on them, "You didn't happen to lose a pair of fools up north, now did you miss Valin? Sending an utter nuisance to deal your dirty work — pity they carry but no idea they're being used. If you bring me my sweet precious, they're yours with my own hand."

Whatever the receiver picked up from the call crackled through in bits as it was overheard the shouting and negotiating of two of Bloom Core's very own, on a device broken apart. Erma chuckled her anger from each to and fro with Valin, before Xira swung to kick the woman's leg under to gain leverage. Within a moment of standing up, she was hauled on the shoulders with the dirt tinting the second layer of Erma's garment while she grunted forward with another throw over the ravine by a nearby lake, landing roughly on the taller grass of the land. An outcry echoed from Willow, as she watched her friend brutally graze the floor.

"Send Niko my regards," Erma sighed, pushing to the lake, "Truly, I pity."

Even though her shout didn't convince the enchantress to turn back and leave them be, her looming helplessness pushed to try again, despite the drought down her throat being a far cry from the calm of before the storm. In the damp depths of the plantation, Xira heaved on the water, fragments of the land sliding down her jaw as a hand dug in the isle's soil. The footsteps of her oppressor reaching the radius slunk in the ground upon the tall silhouette which gloomed above — the wicked aura sifting below the wafting mist.

Dumping what was left of the device in the deep waters, she uttered callously, "Try me again, girl. An apparition on a breath, I will consume you."

Lifting herself on a knee as she wiped the skin, Xira responded in a low, gritty manner, "You push... and you push... you cannot... take what's — not yours."

"Outlander... beckoning a bull," the woman remarked, as she cast an icterine and celadon whirlpool with a flail of the arms, a spell that which collects anything isolated on its orbit.

"What are you doing? Please, leave her alone!" Willow cried.

Erma flung out her arms like a conductor, pulling the soil from beneath them as it began to drag into the pool and sink in its volcanic substance. Holding on to what she could, Xira rammed her hands in the muddy surface, tugging at bases while anchoring herself to the layers of dirt and boulder as Willow hurried to intervene — only to be knocked back to watch her companion claw her way up with every gravitational hitch that lured both feet in it. To the witch's dismay, the narrowed, wrinkled annoyance, she summoned a wrath form of a tornado to cast a gaping abyss in the now holed, swirling nightmare. From Xira's harrowing angle, it had seemed as if the whole landscape was being devoured in a sense of abstract hallucination. Within moments, the cruel laugh of the witch was the lone distinct sound she'd heard as the warped sky disappeared into the seams and her body falling under, then the veneer just about settling...

The desolation that her friend expressed, Willow yelled out, her piercing voice breaking in fragments of disbelief and utter sorrow. Thinking that the one companion that had been by her side all the time they had known each other, was taken yet again, by the hands of the unforgiving. Fixing the layering suit, Erma waltzed to greet Willow, who slumped down, crying her soul into the palms. The enchantress lifted the girl's chin, as she glared back in anguish rushing down the cheeks.

"You are to return to your village, not tell a single lie of this occurrence and do inform your remaining friends that I am always after that item of mine, even if it takes this whole forsaken place," her tone wicked as she snarled.

Yanking Willow by the jacket, Erma acted as an escort as she led to a bridge which connected the two areas of the western region. Although its appearance rendered the likes of an old and weathered crossing, the assembly precision of both edges and high-end material was keeping it fairly together. They staggered on to the foremost plank, when Willow halted in the soft breeze.

"You know vile actions are never left unchecked," she said, "What makes you an exception?"

A rumble bellowed underground, rattling the bridge as the woman cackled above the sheer ravine with the two overlooking the opposite land. The whistling of the trees nearby echoed a grating effect, as the winds picked up just when the bridge began to sway, Erma raised her arm with the hanging fabric to mould a stairway arch for them to use. Storming from behind, a rope chain curved around her collar with the steel hook ripping the back and thrusting her down in a thump. The chain clasped into the garment, tearing it from the lapels to the brims as Willow turned with her hands cupping her nose, watching a figure with shredded overlay kneeling behind, their lambent hair dripping atop Erma. Both grunting with effort, the enchantress struggled to flee as she was pulled down with great force, the burns even beginning to reach her own flesh. A second of simply panic, she pointed her fingers together in the form of adjoined hands and before them, vanished into a flash in the coarse air as the figure's smeared arms with the chain, dropped on each side in the misfortune.

"Huh—?" Willow's awe softened her reply.

"She was in my hands..." Xira quietly returned, looking up with an auric gloom, "To vanish... after a single confronting emotion..."

Wrapping the grappling hook around her arm, she arose on the rather ash-covered boots with the warmth of her companion's embrace, as they walked side by side along the whistling grass-top.

"... You should retrieve your things... I'll meet you down there."

"Hold on now, I'm staying with you — that woman probably ruined them anyway… you're my priority," Willow reassured, "I know we could use them but… not like any of it helped me in that situation… I thought she banished you."

Xira exhaled as she replied, "Knowing so little cost her redemption. Going further than herself to gain what — to destroy, all because she is as vile as they come. I don't think either of us knew the absolute darker sides of ourselves, for in that moment, you only jump… no tool or item could extinguish that kind of force. I know Valin meant well… though she doesn't know. The witch neither. Burnt and grazed, that's the sum of such an encounter."

Her friend hugged her in closer, "Let's find you a place to refresh, you could use it," Willow added, "I can search for some food… drinks… whatever we need."

Together, they went on along the deepest valleys for what seemed like hours to the evening, in the arctic elements of the realm, travelling through mellow plantation, nature's finest and basking in the comforts of it all. Upon arriving at a crossroad with yet another wooden pillar pointing arrows east and west, the two walked up to examine its inked carving. Marked on each board was; 'Hollur Haven — east', 'Underwater Folk — west', 'Panthera Shrine' — east', 'Armageddon of Prancer and Behemoth — west', 'Primal Reservoir — west'.

"A reservoir sounds good," Willow pointed out, "You in?"

In agreement, they settled to advance towards the far west direction. After a few hundred metre walk, a tall glimmery welcome sign propped beside a boulder with overgrown bristly plants, reading *Primal Reservoir*. A couple of vacant huts, the water ways, a well, old campfire spots and a secured shed could be spotted as they entered the premises. She sat Xira down by a log to rest, as Willow wandered around the area to find a canister and something edible. While her companion slumped in quiet solitude, she discovered a bundle of berries in a worn basket in one of the huts which were left open, when a note was seen pinned to the back of the door —

"Whom that finds this, read to your leisure -
Fruit, vegetables, cans of a variety and liquids have
been placed for a traveller's needs to fill up and rejuvenate.
Consume for your pleasure, or give to an empty-handed fella.
Be one with the love and safe travels my friends!"

"Great, that's pretty sweet," she muttered, resuming to scavenge the hut. Throughout gathering the mix of berries, cans of fruit and vegetables and a handful number of nuts from a barrow by the wall, there'd been a few tubs of water in a corner which were stacked upon one another — realising she'd need to make multiple trips, Willow went back to deliver the first batch of goods. Removing the cloak and putting her jacket over Xira's shoulders, she insisted that her requirement of the warmth signified that choice. Aligning the cans by their category for intake, one was sought to be halfway filled with plums that weren't as fresh as when they were closed. Willow pried the metal casing off and emptied the remainders into a compost crate that was left by the previous guests beside the well. Walking back to the hut and then to her friend, she told her that the canister had been cleaned and refilled with water to drink. After swigging it down, she thanked her before sceptically indulging in the fruits and almonds, in between the blend of a vegetable or two. More trips back and forth were made, as Willow carried the other contents in the basket on the way to the logs. The cloak was then picked up and brought by the water ways for a good clean.

"Whatever is left of it... I'll bring it back with a fresh look," she said in an under breath, with a glance to the feasting companion. The water was as crystal as it was cold, as the cloak was dipped under and rinsed out, each part of the torn material thoroughly cleansed, while she kneaded the garment, its substance from the pool washing off with the magmic fragments that were caught. It glimmered after the water purified the fabric once again, the magical aura and empyrean overlay in a stellar blaze brought Willow to an awe as she observed in enchantment, albeit the overall destruction, she could spot the essence coming back to the initial surface. Happily making the way back, Xira was just finishing off the apricots from a can, that was assumingly punched through. Sitting down by the scraps, Willow used the empty worn basket to store the cloak and the left-over of the contents once they were done with. Another quick trip to the huts before they decided to depart, Willow collected two more canisters filled with the tub water, then placed in the basket and checked in as they made sure the area was tidy.

"I was thinking we could go to that Hollur Haven place that's down east, it could be a good pit stop along the way," she suggested, carrying the basket.

"Sure… thank you again, it means a lot," Xira answered, wiping the dust.

Meanwhile, the sky had turned dark, as night befell the girls and the stars came out across the shining atmosphere. Along the voyage, the sounds of the surrounding land and nothing but the gentle wind and carolling birds were greeted, its homely beauty gallivanting and the serenity of the darkness being illuminated by the moonlight, gracing the path within the ruffling trees and through the vibrant open land. Sometime later, the stretch of the ground was in clear view upon reaching a curve point, for the perspective waved into small hills like an aircraft above clouds. Willow peered inside the basket to offer a peach when two voices overlapped between little rosebushes ahead. Following the noise, a young boy rushed out towards them as he was bearing a branch.

"'Ello, pals! I could use your help, if you would be willing?" He gestured to the location.

In the ensuing guidance, there was another older boy looking over his leg between two rather prickly bushes. The three, bent next to the leg to inspect the matter.

"Ma' name's O'lee and this is Dinu, he appears to be wounded," O'lee stated, "M'afraid a thorn's on 'is side, says its kinda' deep."

Closely checking the wound, they observed the tones circling the pierced skin to be of a bruise-like effect as the boy winced post each removal attempt — Willow paused after the third try.

"Can I use that woollen bag by the tree?" She asked him.

Once he returned to them, she dismantled the fabric to singular pieces, including the handles. Using the water from their canisters to moisturise the spot and fan it out, she placed a woollen piece underneath and applied more drops before grabbing a handle to surround the wound itself.

"Okay, Dinu. I will try again and I want you to brace up, 'cause this might sting a little," she alerted him, holding down the calf, "Here we go."

A large mean thorn was pulled out of a fairly sore cut, as Willow wrapped the wound enough for him to tolerate a walk home. The soil beneath his position was tinted in the drops of blood that had oozed from beforehand. Helping him up, they gave their thanks just as O'lee turned to face them.

"For your aid, come with us, we're pourin' supper," he said, "our way is just yonder, at Hollur Haven."

"Oh? We were actually just on the search to go there," Willow replied, surprised, "Great, then!"

They arrived a while in the night, with a tall wooden post marking the main entrance.

H.H.

The boys offered a tour to meet their people, many that which were close relatives to the ancients that were here. They had harboured a lot of the realm's lost and lonely folk, continuing a family not only of the own flesh, though by the tribe's code and honouring the faith of their kind, to fuse and nutrify. Dinu visited the nursing station to receive additional tendance, while O'lee took the girls to the Chief Citadel where the four cowled protectors, resided, seated in the comfort of a cushion row. They exchanged their salutations, as the four made acquaintance by the utmost of a warm welcoming. After a series of subjects were covered, one of them that represented an owl brooch on their front had called over Willow for a conversation sparked from the detail he'd picked up from a revelation. On the left, a tall moresque figure approached Xira, as she remained her jaw lowered but gaze steady to the reverent array. The silk scarf this figure wore displayed an etching similar to the birthmark on her wrist, the lines mirroring with a curve spring holding a star — on the borders of the material was a pattern of claw marks in the hue of red. While the other two sat again patiently, Xira was chaperoned to the Biblioteka sector, as the rococo silver placard stated, down the hallway.

"This place is akin to a hideout," the figure began, unravelling their hood, "I like to read here, it's sanctified, peaceful... My first name is Leon, surname; Waymiti. A pleasure to befriend you both — we are grateful for the deed you've bestowed upon our own. In admiration, here's a book I have yet to show anybody else. Sometimes an item or two is stored for security and oath purposes, retrieving this now is befitting, as I sense a conundrum."

He placed the book on a table by a shelf which located on the opposite side of it, with a lamp on its edge and a pile of notebooks on the far left, atop three locked drawers. Xira opened the heavy buckram cover in front to the introductory pages, the inscription reading; *'Penumbra'.* As she continued along in examination, she discovered a lot of what was written correlated with the surrounding conflict and atomic collision. While reading, Leon sorted out the other books on a tall ornate case nearby the hall's arch, shining on him a lamp of which dimly flickered as he shuffled them in their shelves. She reached to the middle of the inked writing, flipping on a page containing a smudgy inked indication over the word '*Umbra*', as if it were done in a glaze on the print's origin. The weight of the pages comprised of elaborate scripts and symbolisms, in the old and renewed guise, elegantly presented on the vaguely threadbare material. A while later, Leon announced that supper was about ready to be served and that they were to attend the dining hall residing a level below. He wandered to the back window, bringing with him a pair of candles to place on the sill then gathering the previously used batch in their hand-carved clay mould.

"Ah, this brings back memories. Families that would visit, fascinating, isn't it?" Leon remarked, fondly conveying the candles, "It's been some years since they altogether came to one place, a celebration or occasion were to be organised, sharing our delights and treasures with each other — well, parleying on the pier, you just about finished there?"

Overhearing the crowding people outside muffling the silence, he turned to see Xira tucked over the opened book, her now balmy hair veiling on the rather rendered jacket, the effects from the whirlpool still visible but settled as the desk's lamp twinkled. Joining for the supper, Willow was led to a spot by Dinu, who sorted the ladder-back chairs for their seating. After the villagers arrived, the pots were steaming along the dining table with plates and cutlery on each front, while the cooks of the evening sorted out the beverages in mosaic jugs. O'lee swerved the corner to jump in his seat, on the opposite side of the two companions.

"Good that ya' eatin'! They told me we're havin' mashed potatoes with garlic and carrot stew!" He exclaimed, folding a napkin on his shirt collar, "Where's your friend?"

"Actually, I don't know," replied Willow, "We... kind of went different ways once we met the four — uh, she's probably on her way, my conversation with Günter Wald Vogel only wrapped right before Dinu called me."

The three cowled figures entered the room and walked themselves to their designated seats. The people began to feast, as ladles were given down the table and bowls were filled. Shortly after, Leon arrived to the grand supper when another figure stood to express their commemorative gratitude.

"I, ol' Fer la' Frank, want to bless the Hollur Haven's magnitude and grandeur of tonight's gourmet delight," Frank smiled, raising his port glass, "A word of honour in indebtedness, to you and your fellow comrade… for aiding two of our very dedicated boys, albeit they were led awry… we're not seeking to place blame, and to that, I add — for two who were dear travellers, to greet and accomplish an honest deed in the name of generosity, when they weren't enlightened with the truth of who these boys were — here's to you, many blessings — drink up!"

Together they drank and clinked glasses, the bustling cheers among them fused in chatter, as they sat back down to sink their forks and teeth into the steaming food. The hung torch on the stone wall crackled behind them, the gentle warmth oozing with the low breeze by the floor, when Leon waltzed right beside, resting a hand on a chair's knob and pulling a vacant seat by Willow.

"I believe you were the friend that arrived with Xira, correct?" He asked, sitting sideward.

"Yes, oh speaking of which…" she answered and angled to face him.

"I'm not sure if she will be coming down, she's fallen asleep. I left her to rest up," Leon stated.

"Right and where is she?" asked Willow, eyeing the door.

"She's in the library," he replied, "Pardon—"

Feeling a tap on his shoulder, he spun around and noticed a tall man waiting by, leaning in slightly.

"I'm sorry to interrupt, but you're in my seat sire, if you will, please," the man declared.

Leon stood in a gesturing nod, fixing the seat before exchanging a glance with Willow to whisper to her.

"I'll be in the hall if you need me and keep an eye out."

A while later, most of the villagers had gone outside once they'd finished eating and a bare seat or two were still refilling their cups and conversations. O'lee bounced at the entrance, waving to the companions. Willow grinned and pushed her chair back to go talk to Günter once more.

"Thank you all for the supper, it was wonderful," she said, "My compliments to the cooks!"

"Our pleasure. It was the least we could return for what you've done for us. On that regard," Günter noted, "The village tailors have crafted detailed attires for you and your *compadre*, attached to that, two pieces of gear. You can find them in the red axe hut to the left of the main exit."

Pleased, Willow rejoined, "Goodness, that's very sweet to do so, but may I ask why?"

He let out a chuckle, then answered, "By no means do I intend to sound impudent, ol' Clement Bergez pointed out to me that the both of you appeared as if you wandered out of a forest swamped cave, with you all grazed and smeared by dirt and your friend looking like she ran into the fiery darkness of the underworld and back. We thought you could use renewed gear, no judgment, just uh, a good-meaning gift."

"I won't disagree," she tittered, inspecting her jacket, "It's been quite a night…"

A hug and a thanks after, Willow met up with O'lee and proceeded to find and visit the tailors. In the meanwhile, the sound below the carpet floor had grown quiet, with a mere gust of wind in the outdoors as the air whistled through the window. Xira sneezed as she observed the night sky and the tops of hills from the other draped glass, then looking down to see the book she was reading beforehand. *Hmm*, she thought. Closing the covers, she paused to examine the back surface as it revealed a circular shape, attached to a curving inner circle with a vine-like spring, to a resemblance of pollen and a scatter of leaves beneath the indentation. A note etched on the corner read; "*An edge meets another, a flip to a mask in chiaroscuro.*" She rolled the tips of her hair, the colours gently twinkling in the dimmed room. Sighing and walking to a wooden side table with a tall vase, she reached for the pen and notebook that were neatly compiled to leave a note to Leon. The note was propped upward the vase, then as she turned to walk off, a glimpse of a caught page that included *'PLAN B — F'* underlined three times was sticking out of the drawer that required a clover shaped key. Searching around the library for any keys, she soon found a board being obscured by an old picture frame, on a wall by the second window opposing the path to the doorway. After lifting the frame, surely enough the board had its own safety mechanism. To her advantage, the locks were dials and all that had to be done was to turn them in the correct order to unlock. Once the four dials were configured, the casing flung open to display rows of keys, each to their particular area and purpose. The count of four rows and four keys in every one, she read along to pick the one required.

MAIN FLOOR — SECURITY CHAMBER\MAIN FLOOR — EQUIPMENT LODGE\MAIN FLOOR — CELLAR\MAIN FLOOR — CACHE

SECOND FLOOR — M — BEDROOM\SECOND FLOOR — LIBRARY/BIBLIOTEKA\SECOND FLOOR — M — DESK1 \SECOND FLOOR — DESK2

THIRD FLOOR — M — BEDROOM\THIRD FLOOR — M — STORAGE/SAFEBOX\THIRD FLOOR — FP/CF ROOM \THIRD FLOOR — OUT/EXIT

ROOFTOP — SECURITY WATCH GATE\ROOFTOP — M — ENTRANCE/EXIT\ROOFTOP — BUNKER/NEST 1\ROOFTOP — BUNKER 2

Selecting the two desk keys, Xira returned to the table by the opened window and wedged the clover key into its lock and opened the drawer, its contents sliding as it did. The page that lured her to pry contained information on a marked abbreviation written as *TRD*, and next to it said; *'layer, route, lair.'* There was cursive text detailing on about the tasks they were sought to complete, with the rest continuing on the back of the page stating that the dangerous voyage to the *'ignited iniquity'* would need a backup plan for the backup plan. Underneath the inked page was a written note indicating to *'be heedful of Syphon.'* Who's that? she wondered. Shuffling through, a series of notes piled atop a couple of old notebooks scattered around as they all were linked to the related subject, addressed in the same inked form. *I better try the desk for an explanation*, she thought to herself. Hurrying over, she crouched in front of the three drawers, grabbing the other key and unlocked the first, a dusty smell was whiffed before more pages displayed, none of which mentioned anything regarding their dilemma. On to the second, a ripped part of a page surfaced once the dim light illuminated its notation, which read; *'MAGE THE THIRD, OF ROVE D'* — Xira jumped to the bottom drawer and rummaged through its additional stacked old pages, then again located nothing connecting to the texts.

"Rove D… Dynasty?" She whispered, closing all three after piling the notes accordingly.

Returning the keys to their spots and covering the board, Xira walked quickly towards the exit as she adjusted the remainder of her worn garment. Hopping down the way of the spiral staircase, the torch lights lit up the spots between the rays of moonlight that shone through the arch window by the bend — upon reaching the lower level, she began to run down the hall, noticing the framed pictures on the sides and the number of adjacent rooms as listed on the map. With the smell of old barnwood and embers, she rushed across to the next hall and the stairs leading to the ground floor. Spotting Leon stationary by the stone wall and him hearing her land on the carpet, a dazzled look sprayed over him as Xira didn't seem so equally pleased.

"Were you planning on telling us of your involvement with TRD? You were going to bid us the door," she confronted, her voice soothing as she went on to detail, "I was on my way out of the library when I found some interesting things that happen to be current and looming among the lands."

"I'm sorry? I — Okay, follow me. Let me show you something," He replied as he escorted, "This way."

They walked a little further, crossing the opened doors of the dining room and the kitchen storage, making their way around a corner to a locked door with a board casing lodged between the front, reading; '*PRIVAT*' in the carving. Entering, it was a dark and cold interior while Leon searched for the light. He then ignited an oil lamp that was sitting beside a log bench.

"Ah better," he remarked, walking to a desk packed with items of the old and new.

The lamp revealed documents which were spread across the top, handwritten with the similar ink and script of the ones found earlier. Some recent, others revisited, they delved in the piles of pages to find what Leon had addressed as 'confidential', a circled word painted on the front.

"This here," he started to whisper, "Is something the village has been working on... so to say, mainly us in the citadel. The thing is, we cannot tell the others, it remains secured for now. We believe whatever is threatening the grounds is not our problem alone, therefore we've taken the subject to *other* alliances. *That,* I cannot tell, unfortunately, but — it is for sure this is requiring everybody we can gather to defend home."

Looking at the pages, Xira stood beside a letter directed to Jasper

Grizon, as written below the text in black ink.

"How do you know Jasper?" she asked, "He was here, he was absolutely here, right?"

"I personally don't know him, I just manage these papers for them. The *four*. They discuss the matters, they contact whomever they deem is to be involved with us and together we form the schemes, alone. They only meet when it calls for it, in their case, every other week." Leon told her, "Then I assume, you know this... Jasper."

She sat on the chair next to him, throwing the page on the pile, "Yeah, I did. Recently I discovered he had been in contact with his partner, who happened to be one of my mentors too and they are out there, here, somewhere..."

Footsteps of the villagers treaded the halls, their chatter ricocheting in between. The light of the hallway torches vaguely glowed beneath the door, an orange hue blending with the funky draught creeping on the parquet. Leon curved a grin at her, as he assembled the pages atop the rest of the older piles.

"I must be discreet, oh I must, oh I am to be," he muttered in a sing-song voice, then lowered again, "I am very interested to know what *you* know about the Rove Dynasty. Are you targeted? A friend? Family?"

With a sigh, Xira returned, "You could say that. They're certainly not my friend. Definitely not good news to the rest of the realm."

"Aha," continued Leon, "Then I suppose... you may have heard of this particular being they're often mentioning... Syphon."

Xira leaned in, her arm dangling off of the table's edge, "Mhm. I read his name before and in one of your notes. Let me guess, he's another mage? Holds a case of powers."

Nodding, he turned to another document, listing of data that had been collected by his allies. It went on to say the fearsome personal and collectively anomalous information was the mere surface of what really was contained beneath the seething void. *A golden, four-sided orchid stained glass used as a tool,* she read, *Hmm...*

Packing everything aside, he added, "They're still figuring him out, much to uncover here — in the meantime I'll take you to your room where you can stay the night, what you need is already set up. Your friend, I saw at supper, by the way, will accompany you as well. She was asking about you. Let's go."

Together, they walked out and through the few villagers still wandering around, sharing a greeting before arriving at a tagged door on the far-left side of the ground floor. The light from the windows behind them reflected on the tag that was hanging from the door knob — 'occupied residency'. Leon pulled out a chain, sorting the right key to unlock it. After opening the door, they were met with a fresh lemon-lime smell, a sorted and cosy pair of beds opposing each other and a nightstand by a fire-safe on the wall, used for room heating. She stood by a wooden chest packed with additional blankets and pillows.

"This is great, thank you," she stated, "I'm sorry I missed supper. It's been that kind of night."

"I understand," he assured her, kindly smiling, "I'll be right outside. After supper we usually gather round the campfires for some tea, I will be sure to visit at some time, but now, the room is all yours. See you later!"

The framed picture on the wall to the right caught her glance as she went closer to inspect. *Huh, this must be right outside. I wonder when it was taken*, was her thought. After sorting the bed sheets and pillows, she laid to relax.

"Haunt by preacher, haunt by preacher
Show the fork, the silver spoon,
A knife for a knife on a red full moon,
Ride to forth, to forth and yond,
Fish out of barrel, wish out a pond..."

"Who's that? Who's there?" Xira called out in a hollow space.

Whispers chattered among the darkened fog, nothing but a flashlight a few footsteps ahead. The hushed voices crept by her ears, as if to pick her pockets when she spun in haste, but nobody was there. The hovering breaths called to her position, though she went forward to find out if she was alone in the area — as she made distance, the shadows lurking from behind, the beam dragged back with every spot that she covered, until she realised it obscuring her viewpoint.

"Hello? Who's out there?" she tried again.

Once more, the whispers gathered amidst, seemingly crawling from the ground to the feet, then the shoulders to the ears, while she pushed onward. Cold darkness surrounded her and with only the soft, eerie sound roaming the way of the flashlight, the fog filled the air and the ground dropped into pieces to another level below her.

"Xira…?" A distant voice called to her, "Xira?"

As she rolled, realising the area vanishing into a blurry brown ceiling and a grey coarse wall next to it, Xira felt a velvety warm blanket cover over the arms, to then identify her companion watching her.

"Oh, I didn't mean to interrupt," Willow backed up, "Nice blankets, aren't they? Makes me nostalgic of the lodge back at Franky's place."

Xira sat up to find two unfurled garments and a basket on her friend's bed.

In a thrilled chuckle, Willow explained, "Since you're up, I want to show you something the tailors at the red axe hut made for us as a generous thank you. The one on the left is for you and the other is for me. They're experts in their design and after an astute conversation, they said the items will suit us, for our desired use. I may have told them a little detail here and there, but they asked and reasoned that it was needed so… the results are according to our own benefits, which is absolutely fantastic. It's made of rare and special material that's usually only used by *'ancient seed'*. What do you think? Try it on?"

Thoroughly examining the creation, Xira was amazed by its delicate attention and the effort that was applied in the design. From the armoured silver bodice formed of steel, its combination of pure tungsten and the lacing of boron carbide, a dash of ceramics and indented traces of a sun's glow, she could feel its grandeur. Then down to the metal belt that attached to it is its rays of spiky matrix layer, projecting from the sides to which can be activated by its corner contraption to her preference and is essentially used for additional hostile protection. Underneath it all, the bottom portion of the outfit was arranged in a fibre fabrication, reinforced on the surface to the brims of the ankles. Merged in its carbon elements, the tones of silver and basalt inlaying with the black glinted in alteration under different lighting. Over to the pair of bracers that cover most of a forearm, were of nitinol material — adorned with bast fibre that weaved through its coating of maroon and coal blends, supplemented with another pair of reinforced neoprene gloves that were applied with viscose lycra by the palm and wrist area. Separately worn from the bracers, these allowed for a smooth, acrobatic manoeuvre. Along to the shoulder pads, formed by parts of bast fibre, gilded metal layers with the instalment of what the note next to it read; *"star-shooters ~ pull to use, guides below…"* The design engraved on the top resembled two of the ancient first symbols from the realm on each pad. On the left, in amaranthine outline presented an out-curve of a wing with two cuts down the middle, symbolising energy, spirituality and light. On the right, in red outline depicted an oblique ring with a singular cut on an angle, two mirroring spikes on the spaces beside it, meaning of the sanctus, great, noir and ferocity. Putting on the garment, Xira spun around admiringly, exploring every detail as she kinked in aim to the door and marvelled at its comfort.

"Are they mages in any way? This is very particular," she giggled, swinging her fists, "How much *did* you tell them? Crossing fingers, they don't know *too* much… I mean… well — other than reading the exterior before appliance."

Willow blushed while carrying hers to change, then answered, "Uh, I, ah. Probably mentioned a thing or two… to Günter… then that jumped to the tailors and when I went to pick these up, for the details, I added more to their *collection.* I wanted them to be the most faithfully made — ah. Yes. They did tell me their expertise includes the reading of a being, but a mage, maybe not, however… they are to be trusted. Promise. It was with absolute respect and honour that the tailors implemented during their crafting. A hut like that, whoo, you ought to be entering a place of magic."

"Hmm, fine," Xira grunted, kicking a foot in the air, "I'm glad. I wonder what we should do with our previous clothes though… it's one of the few things left from… home. I know we won't be wearing those, though we shouldn't throw anything either. We've already lost items that were rightfully ours."

"We won't throw them," Willow vaunted her suit, "Never what's ours by our hand, Xixi."

The former clothes in hand, Xira wrapped them neatly onto the foot of her bed. Willow took to check the parts of her newly worn piece, smiling from ear to ear as she flapped the shoulder shawl that arched, its pecan colour integrating with the sage crewel work. For beneath it, the sleeves were of a dark grey entwined with burlap, to the knuckles of her fingers, where it encased round the palm and aired the fingers out in bare. The chain belt that they've included for her to apply on the same hiking pants that she'd worn so far, came with a metallic buckle that its initial purpose was to latch on to any piece that would allow for Willow to secure an angle, supporting her weight if it were placed at a higher level — therefore, to do her task off a wall or edge with the trusty tool by her side. Clicking the chains together, she adored the elm bough hued aviator trapper hat with black tone application by its fuzzy perimeter feature. They also provided a new pair of wilderness boots, as the ones she'd been wearing had *worn off,* as she told them, contrary to the fact that it was charred by the mystique of her left leg in particular. Hemmed with the dark overlay, complimenting the ginger aspect on each vamp, the round tip of the boot layered comfortably on the optimised rubber base with grip indentations and maxed-out durability. The ring that covered the shoe's form was lined with fibre metals in coating of honey brown, most efficient for all the wilderness.

"You're kidding…" Xira uttered, reading the note the tailors left, "Where did they even find this stuff? This has to be done by some other workers here — shooters? These things are practically lethal! Huh… *the star form is an indication of the shooting stars that fly to the lands.* Hence the name. *After the use of the provided 10, the pads will activate cover thorns for added defences.* Well, that's super… hmm. *Note; main use aims for environmental and traversal opportunities — solutions, to summarise. — Miki & Lizari.* I'll just whip one out."

Her thumb and index finger placed at the opening, with the support of the third finger and upon throwing it at the door, in a quick whump on its wood — marked the star. Returning it in its compartment, the girls sorted the blankets to settle in for the night. As Willow placed the basket by the set of shoes, she sat up in excitement and clapped her hands at the thought.

"Right, one thing though," she said, opening a lid to show her, "While we were at the reservoir, the water, somehow — um, I repaired your cloak. Look, fresh as ever. I'll keep it in here and suggest you use it on occasion, ooo-kay?"

"At the rese — Will! That's amazing! I can't thank you enough," Xira cheered, "You've conjured material restoration using water. The cloak was a personal gift I was hoping to keep treasured."

Willow replied, flattered, "You'd do the same. You know you mean a lot to me!"

"I'd do anything," Xira confessed with all candour, tilting her glance, "You know that too."

Putting their feet up and under, they huddled their blankets close in the rather warmed up room. The light in the fire-safe glowed around its edges and on the door. Willow looked over to her while she gazed at the ceiling, deep in thoughts. The sound of the villagers could be heard in the distant hallways, chatter among the footsteps.

"After I entered that volcano warp," said Xira quietly, harking back, "I returned in a different way, it was like a new world. I found *parts* of myself reuniting to my current being... there was no land or sky, even though the place looked to infinity — the dark fragments ignited within me just as much as the light. A fusion... my emotions played like a harp and nothing was clearer. Came out like a wild element, familiar with the renewed intention like it was something I already decided."

Willow stretched out an arm in motion to morally support, "Aw Xi, decision or not, your emotions are not a fault. *She* decided to bring the violence instead of pacifying the matter. I do apologise, really, I would suggest you look at the fact that you gained more — if it's any, *any* consolation."

"You're right," she replied to her, "So you shouldn't be sorry. I thought *you* would've been in her hands with the way she was carrying that pride and arrogance."

"Erma was going to build a bridge over that fairly worn bridge," Willow added, pulling to cover, "It was odd... I speculated that maybe it was for another obscured trail but I'd rather not dwell. Uh, I probably shouldn't be saying her name either."

Rolling to the side, Xira remarked discreetly, "In cover. I also discovered that Leon and his three confidantes are after this entity called Syphon, another rogue mage. He's really connected to that kin, and it smells of bale. They really bring it out for the realm, let alone Glacial Mist. I feel a sort of gravitation in their mention or presence, like a familiarity. An eerie, daring kind."

"Oh what, I don't like the sound of that man," her friend replied, "Although, I'll just add, I'm relieved we know more information and answers — speaking of which, when are we leaving the village?"

"While it's still night out," said Xira, "Meet by the entrance if either of us is up before the other."

It was a quiet, peaceful slumber. The entirety of the village cooped up inside, as the moon's spheric glow beamed across the grounds. The chill in the air swept from underneath in the moment the door creaked open and with a light leap, Xira walked out. Watching the ends of the halls, she made her way to exit, hearing the hushed snoring of the villagers along the clanging of doors. Leon appeared in front upon reaching outside.

"Leaving this soon?" He questioned, hands folded, "Allow me to escort you and your — friend?"

"She'll meet me there," Xira affirmed, "Thanks. What are you doing out?"

They wandered to the arch by the welcome post, as he surveyed his home.

"Drank a tad much," He eyed his gut, chuckling, "Bladder was blabbing. On to forth, where will you be going?"

"Hmm, towards home," she sighed, "whatever is left of it. A mess before I came here, surely a mess when we enter again. Just happy that I'm not alone now. Though it's a wreck, we need to find answers for ourselves."

Watching the door as they idled by, a flicker was briefly seen on an opening of the Red Axe Hut.

"Leon?" Xira asked, nodding to the hut, "They're no ordinary tailors and craftsmen, are they?"

With a smile, he brought his hand as though to narrow his whisper, "Between you and me. They're much, much more. A bird sang it, a frog chirped it. Their secret is ours now and the same for us. Keeping the same boat afloat, my friend."

The Red Axe's shimmer went off as he looked back and forth from the hut to her suit and gave a wink. Xira gleamed, reflecting her fondness through the grin and slight twirl of showcasing the design to him. Exchanging their banter and conversation about themselves among other subjects, out darted Willow who with the kick of the dust, flung the door to a hefty thud.

"Easy, power-hawk," quipped Xira as her companion reached them with the basket in her swaying arms.

"Speak for yourself!" She replied, glancing at Leon, "Are you both on patrol or something? I knew I heard voices…"

As he explained the route and areas along the way forth, they walked to the outward path and faced the foggy mile ahead. The hollow sounding gust crept their ankles, throwing up the dust particles in their line of sight.

"Arrival to the nearest village may take you to the following night," Leon continued, "It'd be wise to travel during the day, albeit I do assume that was your plan."

"Mhm," muttered Xira, walking on, "Give that hut all of my thanks, all right? See you around, Leon."

"Swift voyage, friends," he replied with a wave.

A while later, the fog fairly dispersed throughout the airspace as they walked under the light of the moon. Strange noises weren't unfamiliar to the pair, however the snarling tone that was coming from a shadowy frame evolved to a cautious approach. With a side eye, they went on to examine what lurked by the path, shuffling its feet in the scrunching grass and with saw-toothed hairs on the back, pointing as if it were a wheel of spikes. The echo of somebody wearing a gas mask resonated from the figure, the static babel cutting the clarity. Spinning around, it launched itself to a growling leap as the girls dodged on each side right before the creature slid to a switch. The orange hued eyes glared at them, a werewolf illuminated in the beam that emphasised its furious set of teeth.

"Flank! Knees!" Shouted Xira, just as the werewolf dived towards her. Despite a roll, it quickly bounced up to tackle her down to a graze. She shoved to lift her elbows in place of its mouth, setting the bracers in its excavating bite. The eyes leered into hers, a chilling whiff of the nose dripping of a stenchy matter, "Ugh!"

"Watch out, Xi!" Came running her companion, who booted them off and scratched the tips of the garment in the process.

This provided a moment for the girls to gain the space needed, as Willow angled to hurl the basket but the rumbling speed of it caught her off guard with the collision and was pummelled into the dirt. Seeing this, her friend lying on her front with bare momentum from the charge, Xira sprung to push off the claw-ready creature in its towering pose and knee-bumped it across mid-air to an additional metre's way. The werewolf growled in the flailing of its arms as Xira bent a grip to oppose its attempt to land a bite, skidding backwards while it rose to its barbaric feet, pushing its arms against the capture — wrist to wrist, forearm to forearm, the antipode of a tug-of-war duel. She flipped to charge from the defence, both of which scraped the soil in the meantime, glaring each other down in her dodging of the werewolf's snout. The gust picked up from below, adding a lift to every barge. They parried quite a bit, for she noticed that it did not show musing in its recklessness. After Willow regained her posture, she was then met with the wildering winds upon walking to the brawl and held a hand high to shield, setting her back a few steps from the objective and watching between the gap underneath, the tall beast raking with the claws on its toes. The hairs on its jaw flinging to the sides in the harsh aerosphere. Her view more obscured with the upsurge of the gusts, she covered as much as she could, hearing the hassle only a foot's range. Xira's wave of hair snaked over the front in the midst of the focused glare to the creature, both emitting rumbling noises as a howling scoop threw it off track in its realising expression towards her like their souls had met at a cross-point and reached out in alliance. Easing up on her end, she took the second to twist the werewolf over to the ground and leaped to secure its arms in a lock, pacifying the elements while she bent to push to the soil.

"Damn it…" She voiced in a grunt, "Where did you *come* from?"

From behind, Willow added her weight to help keep it down, wrapping the arms over her companion's — it neutralised within the compulsions back to its human form.

"Hold up," called Willow on the side, "Dinu?"

Xira witnessed his fear emerge in the lost mien that wore his skin. She pulled him up to sit, holding the shoulders in front of her. A cage of quiet in between the spaces of a hidden secret, extracted by an anomaly acquainted.

"Don't need to be afraid now," she said to him, crouching, "How did you come to be?"

Shed of teardrops dribbled thinly as he answered hoarsely, "Hexed. In the hut… it was not my choice. Take me home… please. — I saw something. Clue to the tyrant."

The walk back to the village was of relief, as the companions guided him on in the night's light, hastily gliding to the hut's door as though not to disturb the hunkered down folks of home. He thanked them while walking inside, to then be greeted by a sleepy O'lee.

"Oh, barrel of bass! They know!?" He exclaimed through his whisper, "Din!"

"*Just* them," Dinu affirmed, seating on the unravelled bed, "I felt something too… coming from you. Pure energy. That was after I saw the tyrant… as I call it… who's responsible for the curse, but you. That… you… "

Xira shot a radiant glance, then said, "Yeah, I know. We connected, Dinu. Hear the details from the Red Axe Hut. Tell them I approved. This tyrant though, maybe we're not far off from our alike crooks. Whatever is going on here and there, well… find a better location to *vent* off your form, it's a spoiled dinner for the ones on tainted thrones."

Waving them out the door, the candles on Dinu and O'lee's nightstand were blown off afterward, as the two left the village again.

"What a sight," Willow commented on the event a brisk while by the prowl, "It must be tough, in such a land of wonder to be hiding in the dark."

Roaming on the path, the solitude in the environment gave them the peace they yearned and apart from a phrase or two, it was a pleasant venture through — for the disquiet was swept anew, along with the chipped dust of old obstacles wiped the ground behind.

The shuffling of fallen leaves could be heard between an occasional rattle of a board, the moonlight indicating its empty surface, apart from the smear of a dripping maroon ink. Somebody was standing by it, seemingly attempting to arrange its position. Not to startle them, the girls eased to a crouch as a grumble muttered. They circled round the path-walk, smelling a stench which oozed from the stranger's coat. Before they trekked over, the person turned in haste, a confronting pose meeting them both. His locks of hair streaming to the crosshairs of his radiating crimson eyes, holding an object to a sleeve.

"What are you doing…?" The man asked.

"We don't mean to bother you," Willow responded when she recognised his appearance, "Hang on — aren't you… that same man we met back at that secured bridge?"

Under his breath and scrunching nose, a few words sounded off like the signal leaping of old radio channels then remaining silent again.

"Jerrill?" questioned Xira, approaching closer.

"Stand back." He requested, the voice merging with a deep grimace.

The antique object began to emit a light red, as he pushed back to the post. While in grasp, he slouched to the beaming rays, as if they were calling to him — then yanked the forearm down, before he let it drop, following the knees to the ground in a sigh.

"Are you all right?" Willow asked, walking to the man.

A brief quiet occurred before his reply, "My-y name's —'s Jerrill," he affirmed, "I apologise... I — don't know why I transfer like that..."

"Transfer?" asked Xira, eyeing the surroundings.

"I don't know how I came here. Not even why this object reacts that way," Jerrill explained, "It was found on my doorstep as a *gift*. Anonymous, of course. Told me it was important. Been far odder since."

They exchanged a wondering glance, when Willow reflected in a theory.

"Didn't you mention someone giving you a *special* gem because they *selected* you? I think you said *they* were acting quite strangely. Have you talked to them lately?" She recalled.

He looked back and forth between the girls, a worried complexion emerging from his now hazel hued eyes.

"Not quite... I believe they took a holiday from their consecutive night shifts," answered Jerrill, "Now that you mention it, perhaps you are correct — albeit I'm unsure of what to really trust henceforth."

"Seconded," Xira remarked.

The man put the item in his coat pocket, then forked his hair back as emerald nectar seeped down his fingers to the knuckles. He examined while turning his hand, the remainder of it falling onto his skin in viscous drops.

"I — what in the blasted is this?" He paused, then looked towards Xira and over to a rustling berry bush behind the three, "I better get going. See ya-a later."

The girls, puzzled, wondered why he had just rushed off like he had been frightened by a ghost. They noticed some of the drippy substance on the floor painting to the grass brim. Watching Jerrill disappear in the distance, a hand was subtly placed on Xira's shoulder as she spun around in the moment.

"Xira?" The robe wearing figure asked humbly.

A sweet, warm expression covered her twinkling gaze.

"Huh...?" Her ardent tone breezed, "Merlot? You, you're here."

He dove in and wrapped his arms around her, embracing with an impassioned hug as he uttered his blessings, holding her close like he never was to let her go again as they reunited. A few comforting moments and explanations later, they sauntered to a set of stones for a little catch-up.

"So, you've been watching him this whole time? Did you know about them?" Willow asked.

Merlot sat silently, admiring their company before answering, "I'm certain there's more digging to be done. All the while that this has provided me with intel, I couldn't take the matter further knowing sweet Xira was in hazard's way. Even though we are no longer residing in our family house, I am drawn to the need of caring for her like she was my own. Apparently, I take my oath to the endless horizon."

Placing his hand on hers, he turned to join Willow in huddling their hands together.

"It burdens my spirit knowing what you two have thus far endured," he expressed, "Though I am just as enlightened knowing you are back-to-back through and through. Will not miss to say that you still need to be as ever careful, there's darkness lurking about and it's not just the shadows and night sky. Stay vigilant — do whatever you believe. The Rove Dynasty are dangerous and remorseless, but the lowest of low words cannot ever cover their reckless destruction."

"You sound like you know them well," Willow commented quietly.

"Too much to turn back now," he added, pausing briefly, "they know us in ways that the sun displays the freckles of the ground. They cannot find you, Xira. It's simply not their business — okay? Promise me."

Leaping to her feet, Xira looked at him in wonder, "What's that supposed to mean? One minute I'm taking care of the house, the next I'm hearing there's a bounty on my butt."

Merlot turned to focus towards her as he replied, "If I tell you, it'll unleash a doom more reckless than their agenda. Trust me, please, this remains between me, Jasper and them. I need to protect you. I cannot abandon you."

In a sigh, she kicked the dirt before her feet, the frogs nearby chirping to the noise.

"That's right… it all makes sense," she declared, as a silent moment followed once again, "You think with the four from Hollur Haven and whoever else is involved, will suffice to defend against serpents of an underworld?"

The light of the full moon beamed across the path by the three, when he responded in a hushed, cautious manner, "It's hard without a contact service, without a barrel of spells, without *deception*, I know that — however, you know better. No phone can be a shield with magic at play. In fact, it's only a tracking device at this point, nothing more for us — I'll give what will aid you, not derail… and I say this with honest love. I already informed Jasper, now the two of you. There's a gloom in both realms and we're cruising between both, through a river unnamed, a path blazed by our feet… to do the good thing."

The girls kept their gaze onto him, reflecting on Glacial Mist and what was currently occurring in the town, when a swirl of clouds approached their direction, tones of dark grey and silver as a gust scooped their stance from beneath them like sand in an ocean's underwater current.

"Here, take these. They're compact and comfortable. Contains what you should know," he hurried, eyeing the sky, "Go, find the nearest shelter and read them — we will meet down some corner. It means the world we found each other today."

Amidst the separation, Xira took every chance to turn around as she watched him run through the grass field, disappearing into the night while both of them ran forward up the path, looking for another dwelling place in the meantime.

The weather eased as they approached a vast, open meadow. In every gallop or two, a hay hut could be spotted, stretching out to a couple of acres. People were roaming about with woollen bags and supplies, some gardening by their hut, others bringing tools in and out the spaces. Xira watched the people work, the parents caring for the children and babies, their hopeful yet tiresome carriage waltzing with every step — she sighed, realising how desolate but modest the aura around the landscape felt, with the mere mumble over the hovering silence being a single distinction from the soft cries and whispers in the muck. They walked forth as a row of heads turned, exchanging their gentle greetings before resuming with their tasks. Willow winced at the witnessing of an unpleasant commotion by a barricade before them, occupied by the noisy crowd who all pushed into one another in their obscured debate. Seeing this, Xira waved her hand by her companion's front, gesturing to the far back of the group.

"That's Niko," she pointed out, "Over there, busy as ever."

Darting past the group, the pair waved as they called his name, capturing his attention when he was met with the surprise. A grin sprung across his face while he welcomed them with opened arms, his relieved laugh settling between their trio hug. Valin overheard from afar the orchid trees, making her way after dropping everything.

"You have no idea how thrilled I am right now," he said in a light chuckle, "It's a lift through this whole, chaotic period."

Together they smiled, as Willow replied, "So good to see you, Niko. My goodness... this is all that is of Bloom Core, yes?"

He nodded, telling them of their situation and motioning to the arcadian meadow.

Jogging from behind, Valin exclaimed in exhalation, "Girls! Oh! You've returned! Thank the ancient spectres, I was worried — no connection whatsoever."

"Thank Xira," Willow remarked with a smile, "And you can *thank* that wrecked witch, for destroying the Bird'Oz. We wouldn't be back here if it weren't for my best friend's save."

Valin teared up, going to huddle with the pair, while Niko stood patiently then let them know to meet him in the new hut across the field. Moments later, they approached what was a recently built hut by the two and a few crates filled with supplies by the doorstep. As Willow and Valin entered, Niko paused to take Xira aside as he explained that he wanted to talk, adding that there were crates left for him to retrieve as well. Arriving at one of the orchids surrounded by hay piles, chairs and a roller crate, he stood by an apple tree to pick some for the collection. A weaved hay-hammock resided by a prickly hay-wall, Xira sat down and watched the whistling leaves flutter and birds peck at the fallen fruit.

"Tell me," Niko stated, rolling apples into a crate, "in such a harsh climate, naught but your cloak. How, did you fend her off?"

She remained quiet, eyeing the long array of orchids far off into the blossoming lands, barely a being in sight but ones with a barrow to grab.

"Thrown into the hellfire and back through I leaped," she said brusquely, "..."

Niko turned, "It's all right, you can share that with me."

Chipping at the stray hay, her hands along her knees, she said, "Ha... adoring a tempest. Bare hands to the metal, the evil was in my grasp, through eyes I barely recognised... the dark and red became me, merging in its fury... unravelling and whirling by the same token, like I heard it call and it heard me."

"Well dear lady…" he revolved, searching the tree, "The wrath of Xira."

An apple core fell into her cupped hands, as she wondered how it came to — with only a mouthful bite on the fruit, the seeds could be seen in a shade of lime green and brown.

"I wasn't eating this," she added, "Niko?"

Clearing his throat, Niko lifted a crate as he braved to answer, "I'm sorry. Sometimes I concoct these Apple of Wine potions that I apply for certain purposes. Of great knowledge which harboured, it was that fruit to which I poured, in candour, I needed to gather all that was in your encounter — by doing so, you provided me with just that. It's a little uncouth, but remains kept secret."

"A little?" She fired, flinging the piece at a bushy branch, barely missing him as he dodged, "Your impatience is unfortunate. I would've told you!"

Niko dropped the crate by the pathway, insisting on her to join him for a chat. Reluctantly enough, he again begged, "Swear, I. We should bear another conversation. Voice and ears only, no trickery."

Willing to give him a whiff of a pardon, she released a heavy sigh while he pulled up a chair beside the filled crate. Xira laid down on the hay-hammock, resting her hands on the edges as Niko sat beside her. A nonchalant look mirrored of that of the sky, the stars above cruising over the realm.

"The weight you carry is not yours to bare. You handled an especial saddle, an assail you found yourself in," Niko said to her, "The currents that are intrapersonal are never in a singular form. The thoughts of which battle for your grasp and nurture, persist to try to take that control. You contain that control, not *it*. Your voice of wisdom and your voice of fear are individual elements that are not the same and your answer is entailed. It took me a long time to isolate the many haunts, to then settle the base for the logical triumph. I'll tell you, it's not as easy as haunting." He paused to peek at his corner, then continued. "The tricks at play can turn your once calm space into an arena — an arena of one. Ironic, isn't it? Fighting an apparition?"

"Hmm," Xira mumbled, looking over to him.

"You wield the cards and it is your table. Play the magician, reveal your soul guidance. For your own peace of mind, you must be with what you bloomed yourself, Xira, not what intruded on your very grounds. It is easier said, but more rewarding done — and even sweeter weaponised. I'm grateful for the one who stood by me," He glanced at the dimly lit hut, "There were moments where I felt like I became the gloom within me... but she was right there, the way out, the gentle tendance reminding me of myself. It was a tough while of rebuilding... and replenishing. With your light, you're already free."

Sitting back up, Xira swung her feet forward and asked, "... What about *her*?"

"Don't you worry about that. Focus on the task, an eye on all sides. I trust in you," he reassured, "Come to the hut when you're ready to join us."

The trail back consisted of people going forth and carrying their crates and barrows, every other singing and whistling a low tune as Xira reached the hut, she could feel their eyes locked peering, uttering their judgements without an audible term. The door creaked shut, flames of the candles on a table flickering from the effect, while Valin and Willow inspected notes, seated on wooden stools.

"Hello my dear! Take a chair, we've got something important to discuss," Valin claimed, tapping the side, "A little birdy told me you keep a gift in your pocket."

Xira noticed Niko sorting out the supplies by a wall, then went on to sit at the table. She brought out the wrapped notebooks from Merlot and tossed the bunch before them.

"This is supposed to contain what I am to know. Things about me, home and the Rove Dynasty," she explained, resting her arms, "You've done a lot, Val. You don't need to involve yourself for us."

"Please," Valin comfortingly replied, "Willow told me you were wounded. The dispute we couldn't partake in, least I could do now is help out."

Xira shot her friend a glance, indicating she did not want her to know of the events up north. A drop after another could be heard from outside as rain began to pour, the splashes emphasising by the entryway and the hay on the wooden roof.

"All right..." Xira leaned in, eyeing the two companions, "There were these letters... "

Throughout the entire night, they went over the details and findings from the base to the opposite end of the mountainous region. In the meanwhile, there was brewed tea in mugs placed on coasters made of intertwined twigs, making the space between the three warmer, as the icy haze below the door gap surrounded their chairs. Where the notebooks that've been flipped open to a certain page, was a full script inked by Merlot alone, implying that it was the poem Serenitatem would recite every other night before slumber. '*Whatever I light, I ignite. Dawn, solar day, dusk, lunar night.*' — were some of the words recited with her. The birthmark would shine to the sung wisdom. As Xira recalled on earlier dear memories at the house, she read over the text;

Rise the sunshine, rays of love and light,
Passion of the flame, warms the coldest night,
The shadows don't contain you,
The dark is a ring you bear,
For the howl of your might beckons
Fire, aqua, soil, air
A lone kind, o' spirit child
A lone kind, o' spirit child
The eclipse of your soul mounts through your energy,
Like an arrow you spring with the breeze,
A thunderous roar which plays a great symphony,
Up high o' fury, the ballad over all the galaxies
A lone kind, o' spirit child
An own kind, o' spirit child
Ablaze grounds behind, you wander o' free…

And under the script, a notation marked there said; *He knew of you. All about you.*

The heat of the mug burned on her fingertips, as Xira could sense the distant ol' memory of the poem playing in her abundance of thoughts, wrecking through any other forged time of the family back home.

"Your mentor, Merlot, has bitten off more than the rest of the mentors thought he could chew," stated Valin, viewing the pages again, "Not only did he chew, yet swallow and spat it right out in their face. You ought to be proud, hon."

Her glare rising up in focus, Xira recollected wistfully, "That's an understatement. He was made to be the one who betrayed. All that time his outcry was resisted through the lies and blackmail he was forced to bite on. Serenitatem knew everything and told nothing. A family broken by the deception of the one man who turned his back. I only hope nobody else took the bait. The house atoned for it."

The two looked at Xira, their empathetic respondence dawning on them — then the door flung open, with the sunrise beaming from behind when Niko walked in, bringing another crate. After putting it on top of the stacked crates, he joined at the table with a fresh mug.

"Do forgive me, sweetheart," he urged gently, "Honestly, I only meant for good intention. It came out wrong, I'm aware of that. I took the liberty to craft this piece of gear for you personally. Let me know if it's suiting as you'd like it — tis' bit of the least I could do."

On the centre he displayed a redesigned slingshot made of steel and pieces of rare metals as an overlay, attached with fine material and etchings quite familiar to her as he had noticed before, even from the old one that would hang out from the pant pocket.

"Observant," she remarked, "I think it's great. Thank you."

Valin shifted from him to the girls as she declared, "Since we're all on the same *page* about spirit connections, why don't I share that both of ours are a *raven*. How we know, you ask? Far time ago, yes. An old friend."

"Ahem," Niko blurted, "Interesting, yes, uh — we would like for the people to not pick up on this, as they'll assume we've roamed the north. They'll fall on the wrong idea."

In accord, they drank the beverages and treated themselves to a fruity breakfast. *Ahoy, the season's harvest,* Xira chuckled to herself. It evolved into a mellow morning, with Willow helping Niko out with assortments and Valin being accompanied for the handling of the workshop materials.

"So, shall my fears deepen that your silhouette of a wolf threatens my raven?" she asked.

Xira cast a sly, angled look, "Funny, the outcome of that heeds to you becoming the installer of fear. A simple task for someone to then take flight, leaving their imprint as vivid as their outcry."

"Touché…" was Valin's reply, curling yarn in a box, "And truly, I am glad that you decided to catch us up on, well, *everything*. These couple of nights of frantically trying to restore our homes has been quite a trip… being so far from the razed village and in charge of escorts — we've made improvements, however now that you'll be travelling south, you'll be assisted by a dear friend of ours for most of the way. I promised them not to return there until the dust of the old grounds cleansed to air. It's only fair considering their diligence."

With that, they packed the remainder of the components and stashed them near the water tub. Willow by the front, was bidding farewell to Niko, who manifested his sorrow as he held her in focal point, shedding tears through his heartfelt words like he was diverging from his own daughter.

"You've made a mark on me," Willow whispered between her sobs, "Understood me beyond words. I will bear that through every dark corner I find myself in."

"And beast kick a hole out," he reminded her with a tender grin.

"And beast kick a hole out," she repeated as they hugged.

Xira expressed her gratitude to Valin, sharing a warm embrace while reluctant to wrap up their conversation and swayed to and fro in their starfish stance.

"Luki, that's the name. They agreed to wait by the Butterfly Fountain," added Valin, "After this path, not too far yonder — usually they wear a hat and overalls, carrying with a patched, ribbon bag."

"Noted, Val," Xira replied, walking over to Niko, "Hey. Thank you, Niko. All your help. It means so much — really. It comes from yourself and I wouldn't want it any other way."

"Aw, my friend, from the moment we saw you, I sensed your soul entirely. With any light, comes the dark and to the dark, the light shines. Ah… Xira. I'm going to miss you," he smiled, hugging her — his eyes sparkling, "And thank *you*. We'll be sure to meet again, when you both decide. Take care, all right."

As the girls went for the door, the high noon winds flew along their garments, extinguishing the candles on the table as they waved their companion on their exit. Valin closed the door from behind, approaching them shortly after. It was a quiet saunter for a while, merely a phrase or two in between new and old sightings of the lands. The sun beamed on the greenery, the flowers of all colours and flair in bloom, sound of the birds fluting throughout the basal of their feet in the midst of the treading on the path. To their left, stood a tall watchtower built by silver stones coiled into the frame of a grail, its wooden balcony furnished with a desk and stools beside a lamp attached to a wind chime. There was a staircase leading up to the entry and a note to which said; *"Watch your foot, then watch the other"*.

"It's unlocked," Xira revealed, creaking it open, "And vacant. Wow."

The scenery from the highest point extended across like a sail to the seas and clear as it was refreshing, the green blends emanated with its floral charm. She slanted her boot on the parapet, absorbing the realm's aromatic wonder and as the chimes echoed in rhythm, the chorus of birds flying from the east glided in a pirouette, reflecting the calmness of the nature in its pure essence. After returning downstairs, her two companions biding on the granite, beaming upon seeing her, Valin unfolded her arms to gesture to the surroundings.

"Plenty of the like. There's a neighbouring shrine that we call the Vipera, celebrating creatures of tale and truth. Brought upon by our ancients, embellished with fine folk craftsmanship," she elaborated as they walked on, "We share and confide, among travels and many relics. It can be a little detour on the way, maybe even grab yourself a bracelet."

At the shrine, a woman donning a golden-rose regalia swept the front steps with its cape, while the pineberry hairs during the twirling of her bun drooped on the back of a silver coral tiger embroidery. Lacing around the imagery was a curling vine with buoyant mallows, the glimmer on the detail sequencing like the effect of a domino as she turned to the oncoming footsteps.

Xira's gaze focused on her as she smiled. Together, they took to the lanai.

"Salutations, ladies," the woman announced with poise, "Valin. It is a pleasure to see you. What brings you here?"

"Aroha Arial. These are two good friends of mine who would like to visit the shrine," said Valin, "I understand Nola is absent and you've volunteered to maintain."

Aroha fidgeted in a bowl out on a marble plinth.

"The gazebo is likely where she is, admiring the collection," she bantered, "I sauntered all the way from Panthera Shrine, as I read a letter sent through the messenger to come by — quite busy, as you can see."

The collection? Xira thought. The keeper motioned for them to enter and offered a revolving table assigned with floral cushions, placing a container including a jewellery making kit and a wooden band filled with old pages of scripts relative to the shrines' history. Willow tugged at the threads, picking her choice of beads as the cotton wire had been plaited with a yellow ribbon.

"Hand gathered and hand brought," another voice called out, joining her gleefully, "I'm Ives. *Her* sister."

"Willow. Nice to make your acquaintance."

Meanwhile, the vapour of red sandalwood incense clouded over a pearlescent curio which the three encircled. The form of a crowning mountain, its barbed tip gleamed in aim to the ceiling, as Xira saw all the dotted reflections originating from each individual part.

"Fascinating, yes. Aquatic colours that resemble the depths of the sky," Aroha presented, "These bridge into constellations, by the symbol of a fox and squirrel — their tails routing like a vortex, except outwardly illustrating the map of the realm."

They observed it unfold, as the effects of the lanterns on both sides of the curio flickered against the edges. The keeper went on to tell of the history and folklore that the different shrines represented in their own regions. Part of their similar faith involved in the unity that bonded the residents of the shrines.

"There are caves like that here? Unsanctioned?" Xira asked, inspecting the outlines.

"They led us to believe. I heard people enter and never come back the same," Aroha's evocative tone resonated, "Whether it was special or not, it tells me an oddity nonetheless."

The keeper escorted the two round the back in a *'zone'* room as they called it, seating them beside a dangling diffuser.

"*Hoot*... There's a Guidance Pond about the eastern region, it's said to grant you four keys to a personal enigma and a solution to another — more effective under a full moon and the use of the matching herb," she stated, fanning the space, "You'll need to wear a necklace with a metallic pendant for full effect, mhm. On a separate notion, you'll find the Behemoth and Sprite ruins a mere acre or so along the paralleled route. Be wary if intending to visit. Anyway... I can provide you with a personalised bottle of a mixture for your needs — ten occasions it yields, powder or liquid, hmm?"

"We're actually on our way south," Valin informed, "I'd suggest powder if you're to return here again."

Agreeing with her companion, Xira left the area to join Willow and Ives at the table.

"Ooh, is that for me?" She prodded.

Willow let out a chuckle then answered, "No. But *this* one is."

A red ribbon was curled around a brown wire and secured over each gap displayed a violet and black hued crystal as Xira examined the gifted bracelet.

"This is beautiful," she muttered, putting it on, "Haa — these look like the ones I—"

Simultaneously in their revelation, the girls glared at themselves before Xira jumped to the other room again. She saw the two women folding fabric on the floor and swung in.

"Have you been to the north?" she asked, as they shot her a puzzled glance.

"Why, of course," Aroha replied, "Although with managing shrines, I now send my brother with a couple of residents when we require supplies."

"Have you entered?"

"Not quite…" The keeper paused, "There was an incident. We left. Nothing to it."

Xira pondered at the door as she asked once more, "The jewels… they're unique. I don't suppose you sent someone."

The dreadful silence and suspicion that came to while the woman resumed to the folding, was cut by the intervention of Ives, who rushed to her sister with a scroll.

"Forgive me," Aroha looked to Xira in a repentant manner as she waved them adieu and followed Ives to the back of the shrine.

Unsure of their next approach, Valin shrugged adaptively upon deciding to clean the zone room, while the vapour reached the bottom. Once leaving the space, Xira headed for the main exit, slanting down on the steps. In a moment's haste, Willow accompanied her by the side, flaunting her craft.

"What's going on? I saw the sisters sprint off like the time our downtown market officialised," she stated, eyeing the jewels, "I'm sure I didn't intimidate her. In fact, I was about to demonstrate a waterfall bracelet braid."

Playing with the crystals as the metal salvers on the lanai rack clanged, Xira backtracked in a sigh, "She was going to tell me her truth. According to Aroha, they never entered. They retreated and sent a selected few, instead for *supplies*. Most of *that* originates from within."

"And your conclusion to that?" asked Willow, as they watched the unbounded road.

"I don't believe her entirely," Xira objected, her low tone merging, "If no one's been to the north but some that slipped through to be in the unknown, then *someone* is withholding information. Any of it could be the key to how Erma found the knowledge of the region."

The breeze from beneath the steps wafted about, amongst distinct, muffled voices that propelled with the fused footsteps reaching at the entrance, as Valin walked out to then be followed after by Aroha.

"Please, take this," she insisted, handing over a ruby potion flask, "It's the best mix I could formulate. Apologies for before, come by when you desire. — Valin."

"Aroha," Valin uttered, turning to leave, "Off we go."

The three walked the path between the fissling evergreens and although having covered a good hundred metres length, the keeper only then began to walk back inside, as Willow noticed when she'd spun. Heat of the sun hovered among the balmy airspace, its waves cruising through the meadows and bringing light to the plants, emphasising on their colours as the gaiety that thrived, lifted into spring and nuzzled around their fiery garments. In the distance they could discern a water well garlanded with the nature of a tropica-forest. Xira peered into the depths of the liquid below, her vivid hair almost reflecting on the oceanic tones. She laughed, admiring the obscured silhouette she viewed in the crisp water.

"Brisk as ever," Willow grinned fondly, as she remarked to Valin.

Xira leaned forward to inhale the fresh scent, closing her eyes when she heard a cry coming from below. *The water is visible… is someone in there?* She thought. Another shout tunnelled in the gargling bubbles. The pit of her gut pulled on the hesitancy to abandon a possible person in trouble. Her companions stood by, ready to waltz on as she hurled a leg and latched onto the rope. Immediately, the two came rushing in their dismay.

"Hey! Where are you going?" Willow exclaimed, gripping the stone structure.

"Someone could be trapped," echoed Xira's reply, "Wait for my signal!"

As she descended the well, the top became smaller with the two companions peeling their eyes on her, with the dark cylinder seeping liquid through the cracks and swamping the outsole of the boots. The base that was filled with water was now bare as if it had been consumed out of thin air. Landing on the concrete, Xira inspected the walls for an opening and although her gloves were smeared in the liquid, there were no indications of where the remainder disappeared. She faced the way before her as it began to reveal a vague print leading an underground passage to a cross point. *This is odd... but I'm already here. Where was that voice calling from?* Her thoughts wandered. Walking the path, she was met with three condensed directions. None of which held any much of a difference.

"Who's down here? I heard you call," Xira voiced, taking a step.

It was a mere moment of quiet before the person's shout blared across.

"Here! Over here! Opposite this grate, it's very rusty!"

Cutting the corner on the right, she used their call to figure out their location. As Xira neared, the print slid up a row of vertical bars, held on by a pair of hands. The figure crouching on the other side winced, cautiously backing away.

"Don't come closer — s-stay there, I beg you," their tone grew in a mutter, frightened by what they had witnessed. From their angle, Xira could be seen between the bars, kneeling to reassure the figure. Her eyes glowed an arctic silver, watching through their soul. The hands slid off the bars as they scraped the dirt.

"I won't harm you," Xira said calmly, "I chose to help."

Clutching onto the rusty metal, she warned them to near the wall while she pushed and pulled to loosen the fragments. Without much effort, the bars instead were torn off the top, forming a wider gap. Pleased with the outcome, Xira attempted at the other two siding by the broken pieces. To their delight, there formed a wide enough gap for the person to escape. As they crawled to stand, giving her a hug was the first thing they did before flooding the concave floor with their thankful remarks.

On the way out, Xira held the being on her backside upon reaching Willow who was still glaring down, her braided hair hanging above the well.

"Are you all right?" She asked, assisting the person over.

"Now I am. After being down there for three days, not only am I hungry and thirsty... I'm extremely grateful for the rescue. You can call me Buja," they stated, dusting the clothes, "The peril I was in was done by some stranger in a robe telling me I was related to somebody they knew. A feud with a fiend. I don't know who they meant because they just hid me in that corner! Nothing I could do then, nothing but flail! I was sure the well was my home from then on, that corner."

Xira arched to embrace Buja, then told her, "You were brave. You know your own two feet better than that stranger knows their luck. It's not your fault you were forced to fight."

As the four took by a pair of stumps in a saffron grass patch, Willow was playing with Buja's hair-bun, sorting out the twigs and leaves while they ate some fruit. Valin kept her view in the distance, for the clouds gathered and made appearance of a split in the sky. All the quiet that was here, there was a sense of a lurker in the shadows. Sitting around on a break, fiddling with the materials, the warmth of the weather relaxed each one of them.

"Buja, pardon me asking if it's intrusive," Valin spoke up, "Are you not from around here that you were dwelling by the well?"

They glanced at the doctor, then replied, "Ahem — uhm — I — I stay with my grandmother. We're a lonely two so... I went out on a scavenge and figured this as a good place to scout. If I had known, maybe if I wore my overalls and not this resident bakery ensemble..."

"No," Willow cut in, stepping beside them, "You wear what you want, got that? It doesn't change a damn thing. Just be comfortable, that's what matters."

Buja grinned as she turned to the peach in hand, "Can you be my sisters?"

"Didn't this *person* tell you anything?" The abrasive intervention of Valin annoyed Xira.

"Valin!" She chided, standing by Buja, "For all we know—"

"It's okay," Buja pacified, "It was the voice of a man, that was clear. They didn't tell me anything other than "*you'll hide in there until Menkos*

179

comes forth to confess". I remembered that name, it was a long, long ago since I knew that man. He's my uncle. Grandmother's second son."

"So do I," Xira pondered while they all swivelled in a jolt, "He was exiled. Betrayal of the oath. He was part of our Family."

In the realisation, they all stood before Buja, figuring out a fair solution as the exchanging of puzzled eyes darted in the quietude. Xira hopped to the path once again, also noticing the clouds ahead.

"One of us can take Buja back home to their grandmother," she proposed, eyeing the way, "Then we'll meet at the Butterfly Fountain."

Valin stepped forward, placing an arm on their new friend, "I'll do it. After I escort Buja home, I'll trek to you two — keep going down this way and you're there. You can't miss the water spout."

All in agreement, they split upon their leave, as the two continued along towards the fountain. The next hour breezed by, to then reaching a tall man in a green vest and a thulian top hat bouncing near a cart titled on a wooden board; *Cart-O-Wheel.*

"Greet you like a fellow, may I offer you a gift?" He sang his words and bent to retrieve a pair of roped pouches, "One for you, one for thee, absolutely free."

Packing their things inside as they launched it over their shoulders, they gave their thanks to the stranger, who called himself Tyrant Ted.

"This was awfully nice of you," said Willow, looking at the ornate antique cart.

"'Tis what I do," he chuckled, "Lots of goods, visit me anytime! 'Ave a spot in every region."

Blissful, the girls ventured on to their set objective. After the while of walking in the sun, the pair decided to cover more ground by a run. To spice it up a little, Xira suggested they make it a friendly race to the point. They laughed along their collisions, in attempt to take the front with each turn that was made, enjoying the peaceful atmosphere of the lands and for a moment, forgetting the burdens that weighed, absorbing the air that which rushed with them one and the same. Within the sun's shift, they shuffled to break and together walked in a backward manner, steadying their breath. Willow glanced at her friend in a goofy grin, nudging her an inch and hailing the distance crossed. Xira then returned the favour, only unintentionally knocking her off the path. Watching in the speed of a millisecond, her companion to grace and graze the gravel and tumble onto the grass.

"Woah," she tittered, sitting up to wipe off as Xira rushed to hold her and apologise, "Guess I'll know when you're *really* angry."

"I don't know why that went opposite degrees," she stated, "Do swear it was a light push… gawh."

Willow propped on her companion's shoulder, whispering, "Remember the answers? The truth about you, Xi."

Knowing she was right then, Xira lifted her back on the road. Silent as she was, for the remainder of the way to the point, Willow understood — walking beside the sempiternal friendship of theirs, loyal to her and the pact invented before, *through lightning and sunlight, they shall remain.*

The clouds that were seen hours ago, appeared to waft above and make the space below much, much colder. As the two spotted the fountain mere a few metres apart, with a lone figure swinging their legs on the edges, Willow motioned to the front.

"There it is!"

Just then, a disturbance ruffled the plantation amidst the grasslands on either side. Out jumped a pack of intruders, with an agenda seen to be unpleasant. Uttering chants of their like, they circled the figure sitting at the fountain, posing with an eye to pry.

"Oy, you squatting pariah," One of them said, "Give us a treat!"

A hoarse cackling veered as they rotated, one of which stood on the stone structure. Seeing the two oppose them, they considered that to be of a threat. The group marched closer, leaving the person to peek from the fountain — alarmed. Mad they were, sniffing like it was a frisking at a trespass.

"Hurry on," a low, growling tone declared.

"Nothing of your business, scouts," scowled another.

Hand by hip, Xira took a step, "It just so happens that this is our destination. You've made it our business."

"Oh yeah?" They snorted in their laughs, batting each other as if a joke was shared.

A hell-bent furrow of the brows cast with an arch by Xira's mouth, as they counted the five goons.

"You better watch out, bitch," The front man berated, pointing his finger.

In a tolerant sigh, Xira replied, a spark in her iris, "Gee, save it for when it's appropriate."

The man let out a guttural scoff, "Oh? And when might that be?"

Xira punched across his jaw, knocking him out to a rough thud.

The other four looked to the horror that met their presence, as a gasp and a mutter shed through. They gathered in a brace, covering their fallen ally. One brandishing a bayonet by his pocket, a threatening glare at the two, assumed position with his three comrades.

"Nefarious five! Down by one, now you're done!" They chanted, waving their weapons in a grimace.

Though not to partake in a dawdle, Xira yanked to disarm the guy and hurled herself to knock him back. In the upheaval, the second guy engaged her while the other two charged to Willow who wasn't keen to be involved in the brutal encounter, for her companion, however — things were different. She fortified her foreground, angling her legs to defence. Dodging the oncoming warmonger, she slid downward with her mystical leg then bumped under the knee, ensuing in a trip — taking his buddy down with him when their feet tangled. Standing over with the foot on his shoulder, she paused. After pushing the other again to buy her a spare moment, she thrust down once he attempted to cut her with his free arm, cracking the curve of his collar. Caught between the two, Xira put an arm around one guy, keeping him in a lock while the other tried to separate them. She quickly issued a backward kick simultaneously with an elbow ram to the gut, freeing herself to slam the other down. Although the guy was injured, using a time out to recollect himself, he bulldozed in a fiery rage and claw marks along his chin, towards her just as she heard the thumping boots. On Willow's end, she found herself swaying from the swinging, endeavouring to put in a few rough kicks — enough to make them surrender. While the one on the ground was dealing with a couple of cracked bones, his one arm still was reaching for the bayonet, dragging by the ground in grunts. Before her, the goon swiped with his weapon as she backed away in time to boot it out of his grip, then smashing through the delicates, and with a knee thrust, she executed a wind-knocking propel and watched him roll to defeat, at mercy to her powered leg. Catching breaths, she hurried over to intercept the remainder of the five, who stood atop pointing his bayonet down the clutches of Xira's hands, in a brawl to throw him back — the point was nearing below the throat only then to be pushed with every vicious snarl among them. The person crawled out of the fountain in a wince, as Willow's left ankle slipped in the grip of the guy thought to have let the matter go — with his good hand, he forced himself forward, still holding onto the ankle. Baffled by this, Willow parried with the right in aim to balance and unlock the fingers before he took to kneel.

"Hopeless…" hissed the man struggling with the bayonet, "Your chance doesn't stand on a side of a coin. My own mitts assured my advantage. Any words, player?"

In a snarling force, granting a cut on his hand, Xira twisted the wrists and knocked him under her with a knee smash by the chin, pinning him down while resuming to keep the duplet hands on the floor. Throwing a fuss, the man's grit met with her flaming gaze as if it were blazing the pit within him. A hint of fear could be spotted aligning with a regretful pant, seeing her lower herself to confronting inches from his skin.

"Checkmate," whispered her voice of deep fissure.

The clattering of the bayonet skimmed beside his shoulder, while Xira hopped on her feet again, watching him cower.

"*This* is chance," she stated in a gesture, "Your own knife to your wound. No leverage for a fool. A dirty retribution for you, *player.*"

In the moment after, a shout from Willow echoed from behind.

"Xira!"

She ran towards, immediately realising her friend in a crawl by the one hand of the brute-like pursuer, stumbling onto his calves in attempt to overthrow her — no marks or bruises were setting the man to leave. The furious exchange convinced Willow to shift in protection, crossing her arms in defence of the upper area and pulled the knees as high as she could. Xira veered round to leap on the shoulders, the man yelling in result and opened up an exit space for her companion, who jumped at the sight. While the two fell, him landing on Xira's gut in the commotion and remaining in the wrap of her bracers, Willow signalled to her, then charged forth with a swinging power kick to the abdomen. Both trapping the goon as he went for the weapon, they exchanged a quick glance and nod as they revolved a final knock out kick to the side, launching the man over, in the vanquish of the Nefarious Five.

After taking a breath, Willow ran up to give her a hug, before sliding back as the young man went to greet the pair. Tipping his green beret, he called them to the fountain and sat on the margin, joined by Willow.

"Luki. Luki Owle," he introduced, "Not much of a brawler, more of a painter. I even brewed up a little single lettered formation… Painter. Planter. Petter. Porter. Tells you more about myself. I sort of want to presume Doc Valin is to be attending?"

"She will," Xira affirmed, standing to the front, "What did those idiots want with you?"

He clutched at his bag, in a silent and polite manner replied, "I found a key. Device? Key? It's not from the realm, nothing like it. In fact, it seemed like somebody had dropped it — thought I could locate them on my own, no trouble. Sorry you dealt with that. I feel awful."

"They were armed. You would've been against the odds like that," she reminded him, "We were supposed to meet you here regardless. Luki. Can I see that *key?"*

An oval shaped item bounced the sun's light as Xira grabbed on its handle. Angling the piece to reveal the emblem's outline, a thin layer of copper shone on the metal. She thought back on the events at the security swarmed bridge. Inspecting closely, bars of vague, electrical lines zipped in all directions — like it was conducting a map layout, pinpointing occasional parts as she watched it blink by every connection it made, to then disappear into a multitude of flickers.

"I've seen this symbol before," Xira alerted, giving it back, "Break it. I'm searching their pockets."

Over to the five, she pulled apart the jackets and their pockets, emptying out everything that she could find. A car key, notes, cell phone, recorder and the same black card in each of their pants was tossed on a barren part of the floor. Inspecting a card and reading the print, she uttered its description;

— yowndrift yard — ⌄ *"Dwell in the question and it shall mirror inception."*

commander contact : co-0100100//wing commander : wco-0010100

⌃

"Huh… that's the exact one," she said, then flipped to read the back, "*Diffusion Order… Sector Z, ground trackers, mid-trackers, first trackers. Base, gate guards, escort guards, armed guards… YY-HQ, armed gate guards, Yard guards, Yarak's. Contact personnel via your device — Lieutenant authorised...* That symbol again. These are not our security regulars."

On the way to rejoin them, Valin called out upon arrival as Xira turned to the side.

"I thought we'd agreed to a meeting of civility, not a rally to cross our swords," she said.

"All in defence, Valin. Besides, I think you'll be surprised at what this encounter really meant," Xira replied, handing them the cards, "A cult of some kind. In Glacial Mist, Willow may recall, we ran into these odd troops and their trucks. The particular ones by the bridge situation included *that* emblem, *their* organisation that remained untold to the rest."

Seated by Luki, Willow slouched nigh in disbelief, "Yowndrift Yard... yes, I remember this being on everything by their provisions. The, the gear."

They moved to the southern route, encircling, to resume discussion. Valin collected all the cards but Xira's, then set them on fire, distinguishing it under her sleeve right after. As cautious as they were of being watched and overheard, this newfound data begged them to differ on a solely hushed exchange. Broken pieces of the key device were reflecting a shine by the fountain Luki was still eyeing, noting the partially hidden fragments beneath the dirt and the stone structure. When Valin elaborated on the duty that their new ally would fulfill, she shared the information she'd been keeping from them since their stay at Bloom Village, involving Erma and her executive agenda. The reason hinted that it was a matter of their own at that point, unaware that the two would enter in a cavalry fusion other than the friendship. The pieces that came together, blossomed a crystallised avenue to guide them on. Discovering more about the enchantress meant an advantage and answer to the ravaging disarray that currently roamed the adjacent realms.

"I don't blame you," Xira told her, "Going out for answers brought us more than we bartered for. I altered the contents to our own benefit, even though it holds a complex that I now decided I'm glad for... because overall, it's a double-edged sword. I'll take it all as I will."

Valin propped a hand on Luki's shoulder, then added, "Take them to your cabin before you lead them through the portal. He can care for the things you won't be using along the journey. As well as tell you about the plundering from distinct realms that Erma is luring to create demolition and alter the orbit to *their* appetite. Should you spare a minute on the while, do locate the outhouse or cottage where she had been nesting... if it's not then dangerous and it is instead vacant."

"Yeah, noted," replied Xira, walking together with them, "Valin, thanks, again. You're doing wonders with the rebuilding. I'll be sure to repay the favour for your generosity to us."

"Dear... merely a duty we shared with newfound friends. It was a delight that we caught up once more," Valin expressed warmly, "Watch each other's backs and come visit after all of this is settled."

The group hugged on the path as teary-eyed Valin then waved to them on their send off, for they did the same while looking back — including Luki who marched at the front in simple skips across the landscape. Although the way to the cabin was via the shortcut he had informed on the trip, it was a view nonetheless. With the number of trees bearing various fruits and flora, decorated with the lush greenery on their bases, springing with the well-known plantation of the southern region — much like most of the others they've seen, the colours and aura never ceased to amaze the two. It made the soil they wandered on as light as if clouds that descended consisted of weaved grass and the coral resemblance of the anthers. The shade beneath the leaves kept the air cooled while they rustled through the way. Willow picked up a batch of orange pineapple shaped herbage and cupped to smell before handing it over to Xira to take a whiff as well. A coconut exterior began to reveal itself upon their nearing to the cabin, which was propped on wooden planks, arched and crossed, built on the field below it. Clearing the way, seeing the olive-green scaled roof atop the walnut carved door which connected to the flowery porch and a stack of stairs by the path, Luki flourished his arms on the porch fence as he hopped on to face them.

"Welcome to Luki's domain," he announced, feeding his plants, "I enter in third person on occasion see, so that my fellow seedlings here can all know it is me."

Inside, a cosy and antiquarian ambience met the companions, who then spotted a bench adjoined to a miniature table piled with items of the craft and some plant vines swirling about a hand-made suspender from one wall to the other. Blankets in mellow tonal blends canopying a divan and a pot plant beside it were located on the opposite panel as Luki brought in a couple of yellow stools by the bench. He waltzed around to greet the girls while offering a bowl of a crunchy treat.

"They're lime chips in the form of spring petals," Luki stated, nibbling a handful, "Whenever I go out picking, I make these from the feathery lime layer should there be a plethora of it gathered. Eat up, pudding cups!"

As they bit a fair share of the chips, he then hauled over with a box and then placed it atop the surface. With a grin edging his mouth, he lifted the lid amidst the suspense.

"By the by, I spied a slingshot device that you carried in a pocket," courteously, he said, "Would you lend me the sling for a spicy second? I can apply an attachment for enhanced carriage and want to hand you a gift, from yours truly."

Xira placed it in sight and answered, "All these gifts and I either lose them or bear too much. This sounds great though, I appreciate it."

"Ooh!" Luki leaped with a thrill, "May I also propose something relative? Why don't you leave excess baggage with me? I'll take good care of it, promise on that!"

Willow looked at her as she replied, "That's a pretty good idea, actually."

"Sure, all right, if you are willing," added Xira.

Her companion lifted the basket over the side and sorted the contents before pushing it towards him. From his end, he hid it below the bench in its stash compartment and cleared space for the other materials. They watched as Luki applied the work and various parts for the attachment and assemble it with a fine, delicate finish. After testing its practicality and enhancements, he returned it to her and cleaned up the scraps. She secured it over her thigh and to the belt area — a splendid craft.

"Okay! On my way to the paddock now, I just need to gather s'more flowers, then make tea, eat a peach biscuit and we're set," Luki told them.

"I'll sit inside, hope you don't mind," remarked Willow, watching them exit the door, "I want to explore your home a little bit!"

"Go on, treat yourself to the other snacks while you're at it," he added, "Come on, Xira!"

To the lush green surroundings, he motioned to a log positioned in a taller patch of grass by the blanketing range of flora. Xira sat and viewed as he plucked the scattered rows that were wisping. A tinted, broken wagon was seen beyond the fencing, luring the curiosity about it.

"Was that yours?" She asked.

"Oh that, that thing," he stammered with a chuckle, "We used to ride it. An old friend and I. He left the woodlands a while ago, guided and helped me with a lot... building the cabin, locating parts, food and everything... I keep it there as a relic. After we crashed it, I went back to the spot and retrieved it myself, it took a while but it was worth it. Eh, something to keep him around. He didn't tell me why. I respect his decision and mine to move on."

"I can tell, the recent base paint job on the cabin is quite efficient," Xira remarked, her gentle gaze pottering among the plants, "Looks like mud is your favourite choice."

With a smile, he returned, "Flattered, aye. I also do *other* sorts of paintings. Blanks into art of the scenery. Not sure how many times I've painted this place with a different backdrop and objects to accompany. Guess I thought it'd bring me the solace I personally sought... never mind that though, really, I feed the animals and they bring me happiness, therefore the desired friendship. Hehe, even the plants! You do know they interact, yes? It's a truly magical thing."

"Do you have room for two more?" She hinted, leaning her elbows on the knees.

"T-two more w-what?" He quietly asked her, sorting the collection.

"Friends," Xira affirmed, "We are allies now."

A warm, enlightened expression coated his springing joy as he held up a pot, "Delightful! Tea?"

Back in the cabin, Willow was seated with two weaved covers including artworks done by paint. She admiringly flipped the sheets, amazed by his soulful outpour. Then their footsteps entered the doorway, creaking as Luki hopped to sort the flowers in their pockets. Leaning on the snowy deer tapestry by the door, Xira glanced to the kettle which he was now preparing for their tea, the steam oozing from its spout and the smell of native blends enriching the room. Soon after, they gathered by and while sipping out the mugs, they shared tales of old homes and cherished places they knew. Post finishing the drinks, the three munched on the peach biscuits that Luki was praising on the taste and savouriness, delving into the subject of favourite foods and the like. The two helped him tidy up his home, before going outside then again.

"I want to confirm, *she* won't know of our travel or coordinates, right?" Xira questioned him.

"The portals I wield are not alike to hers. Hers, stem from the dark sorcery that I do not possess." He explained, "To discover mine, she'll need to be summoning pawns through aligned trajectories… which is never done, since I keep my comfortable distance from their kind. Your conveyance is in my hands and who else? I'll always be by your backside."

Along the trail to the southern point, the trio walked for hours on end and when nightfall arrived, the familiar scenery to the girls re-emerged with the rugged entryway ahead. Sensing the signals rebounding off of the wall tips, Xira watched Luki exclaim and perform the rite, quite as he was but as the opening came to rise, they were all focused on the tune that played — its waves of colours whirling at the feet. He took a single glance to the two, then ventured forth to gesture at the vast pool that then awaited.

"Ladies… whenever you're ready," Luki said, a glum hint in his voice, "Please come back to the Spirit Realm, yes?"

"I promise," Xira vowed in return, "Hide a secret door if you can. One that other people won't know about or even find."

He bowed in agreement and turned to wave, as the girls ventured forth, waving back to Luki. The warp absorbed them in a whirling speed, as if a tornado went horizontal with static energy in its orbit. It didn't take long for the portal to deliver the pair in a leap to the land of Glacial Mist. Back to their feet, it was a moment before the entrance retrieved its rocky form and the early, icy, foggy dawn met their presence.

"Looks like they've set up an outpost," remarked Xira once they inspected the renewed surroundings, "Watchtowers on both sides, cubicle on your right. They've been researching this area, no bloody doubt."

"Man, oh man, what are we going to do? We can't just *barge* out the bridge like civilians," Willow replied, then added after a brief exhale, "I propose a performance."

Xira faced her companion as they crouched behind a tall enough barrier.

"Pardon?"

"I say, with our new clothing, we're *not* the same as when they saw us last," she continued to elaborate, "If we hide ourselves in a way that can fool those that roam, we have a plan. We just need to mask up."

Noticing the posted van by the tower, Xira motioned on to sneak around the side. The flaring beacons illuminated the spots that they traced on the rotation, providing an advantage to take the route that was shadowed by the barriers. Keeping an eye on the higher points, they crossed over to the nearest tent that had been set up with some equipment and upon entering, found a few metal crates on the tables and floor, packed with security gear and tools. Willow pushed a lid open to rummage while Xira examined the file reports on the main pitched table.

"Perfect or what?" She called to her friend, holding up the items, "Undercover spectacles partnered with an ear piece — I bet it's the recon channel. To top it off, wear this too. It's tacky, but it'll be the inconspicuous camouflage."

"Right," Xira replied, reading the pages, "Look at this. Week 1, bridge commotion. Week 2, nothing. Week 3, surveyance. Huh... these notes on the second document, weird. There was a meeting with someone coded WM-JASON to organise this outpost. Says a peculiarity was seen on the very grounds the... the *miscreants* disappeared."

Willow hurried to the table, bringing the gear with her.

"*Dispatch B-100's? No. Yarak's? Unnecessary. Trackers? Base to call.* What the hell, they must have sent somebody, if not that group... ugh. I don't even want to know what the others are, there was already that unfortunate collision of the tracker types," Xira continued to scan the pages, "Yep, they're knee deep into this shit. We need to keep going. Let's roll."

"How are we cutting through the bridge? It's barren now," her friend questioned, putting on the gear.

"First, we're finding that house that Valin told us about. See if we can uncover what we need to know about the situation," was her answer, before rushing out the tent's flap, "If it's doom sitting on their protocol, then that sings for interference. No realms or homes should be in a collision because of the hunger for power. It's an illusion, a lie, but they eat it all up. Too easy when you wear a mask for a face."

Through the darkened grounds, they made their way out to the front tower opposing the guarded terminal where the rays shone. The pine green overcoats were emphasised just when the two crew members spun

190

at the signal and with hesitancy, took a step to wager. One of them angled closer in attempt to detect the identities, however Xira aimed back to throw him off.

"Can you confirm your association with Sector Z?" He asked, darting between them, "The remainder of the camp vacated at twenty-three hundred hours. Unless you're with the lab team."

Xira arched a side glance before answering, "Hmm, we were assigned to manage the *files* and clear out the tents... really a base protocol, my good *compadres*."

"Very well," The man added and shuffled back, "Proceed."

Pulling to button the middle as soon as they treaded through, Xira focused ahead to the pathway that reached the bridge's intersection. Her friend let out a brief chuckle, scoffing at their impromptu luck.

"*Compadres?*" She teased, bustling beside her.

"Dude, we're in, out, whatever," whispered Xira loudly.

More of the PBTU trucks were seen parked along the edges. Few of the crew packed up crates while the rest were opening up the gate to cross the bridge, which apart from being a silent ghost town, held a mess that was merely fanned to the side of its concrete rails. The smell of gasoline seeped the area, with the shouts being thrown around in command boomed on the roads at the revving of the vehicles.

"Come on!" Xira alerted her companion as they ran to hitch a ride on the back of one the tailboards that was being elevated. Closing the two doors, with relief, they slumped on the covered crates that tumbled by the walls. The bumpy drive swayed the components to and fro and shifted to a clanging on the interior that briefly echoed with the surrounding clamour from the outside. A muffled exchange was overheard by the front, as Xira leaned in to listen.

"*Enter through the back exit?*" said a voice.

"*Orders stated this was the main load for the Lieutenant,*" said another in reply.

"*Then secure the gates... sliders in check... positions assumed — ground personnel contacted.*"

"*Delivery is in progress. They are informed of the transportation, sir.*"

"*Good man, good man...*"

The truck came to a halt as a shout blared on the opposite end.

Taking heed, the girls rolled to an available spot to conceal themselves underneath a wrap. In moments, the doors flung to each way and the roaring of engines resonated among the cover. A group of guards dragged out one crate after another, unloading all of the baggage and when it came to the wrap they'd hidden in, a man called out to another about the excessiveness of that particular crate. It didn't seem to pay a bother to neither as they launched it with the rest, landing with a thud and a knock by the handles that clinked to an unlatched fire extinguisher.

"That's all of it?" Said a grumbly voice nearby.

"Affirmative, sir," another replied.

"Call the Lieutenant. We'll be up shortly," a guard told them, "F1 can sort this out."

After the fall of quiet loomed the enclosed garage, the two peeped out the material to reassure their safety. Most of the place was emptied however, there only remained three of the guards that they spotted by a truck and an engine, penning down data on clipboards. Xira motioned in a hushed manner to take the back route, tailing the paint marked indicators on the floor to a set of black lockers. A lanyard caught her eye, as she sprung to grab the deserted ID badges on a bench beside them. Towards the garage door, an exit sign flickered by the staff entrance that required a key card to access. Xira cornered a smile upon raising a badge, before they hurried to slide out once again.

"Nice work there but why are we out here now?" Willow asked her as they observed the grounds.

"Well," she began to lower the tone once seeing more personnel roaming the vicinity, "Our next move is still to locate Erma's old or even current hideout. We'll need to borrow... a-ha. Catch that sci-fi bike?"

Cautiously running to the vehicle, she noticed no keys were in the ignition. A pair of guards chattered on the distant left, making way to their direction. The girls slid around a post, enough to hide an obvious position and waited patiently for the two men to cross. Although it was rather dark, beside the few construction lights that were scattered among the space, it gave them an advantage to lurk between the shadows and snoop to their wish. They watched them leave through the post's metal gaps and waltzed out to search when Willow pulled her friend's arm on a whim.

"Hey," she whispered, crouching her stance, "Look what I snagged, here!"

Dangling in the thumb and index grasp of her hand, were a set of keys on a chain that now Xira caught in hers as she prepared to vault — giving a friendly prod of a cheer.

"Ace pickpocketing!" She praised, as they seated on the bike, "Ring around a roulette, captain… "

The tires spun on the gravel, as Xira accelerated onwards to the opening gate. With the vapour flossing from behind, she sped on out the main road and on the side mirror, caught sight of the auto-operated metal sealing in the tracks. Her glove sanding the handle, the bike hightailed through to a cross-point that opposed with the bridge. Although the empty streets appeared like that of an open road, the poised perception dwelled within the loitering elements in the background, as if eyes were air that cut the granules which hovered like sleet in a winter's snowfall. A crackle uttered by the spec's ear-piece, as she tapped the brakes right at the curve.

"T-Unit, do you confirm? Come in."

Xira lowered the handle to answer, "Confirm… sir. On an errand."

"The Lieutenant requested that all personnel attend the pictorial meeting. This is an official notification as he arrives to M1FR. I will call once again to reassure your station. Over."

As the call dissolved into static frequency, she moved the lever piece back to its place.

"Yeah, yeah," Xira muttered, turning on the handle before driving forth to cross. Approaching the neighbourhood of Glacial Mist, now evacuated and hailed in disastrous mess, she drifted the bike around a corner that led to the local library. In a slide to the parking lot, she hopped off in the midst of removing the accessories worn from the tent. Leaving them on the bike, they scaled the windows to check inside and if any openings could be found. Fairly enough, the main entrance was locked and the windows beside it too. Xira searched the premises, covering each side of the building, to then spot a dented vent above the library's electricity panel.

"Wait here, I'll signal you if I need to," she told Willow, who walked close by.

"Be careful, okay?" Her friend called, eyeing through the tinted windows.

Climbing atop the panel, Xira smashed the cover open and crawled inside, just about enough space for her to manoeuvre. With the piles of dust sweeping down the vent's slide, she rolled out in a cough and onto the carpet. No lights were left on, as she lifted to her knees, observing the area. *Public lobby,* she thought. Walking to the front of the desk, she used the receptionist's mobile lamp to light the way. The desk itself contained scarce data regarding the workers, but the computer's indicators were still blinking — sitting on the revolving chair, she watched as the screen's wallpaper flashed on the desktop, icons of contact files and intel sorted in various folders. *Schedules. All right, let's check these out...* her thoughts bounced like the transition of one folder to the next and so on. There it was, the list of names that have worked previously and most current in the library's day and night shifts. Under the name of Erma, her *legitimate* first name, was instead linked to an alias that was typed up as *'Crownit', Erma 'Crownit'.* They'd assigned her as the night receptionist per her personal request.

"Found you," Xira remarked, printing out the detailed page. She noticed a glimmer at the edge of a bookshelf that was partly concealed with a wheeler rack, coming out of a crack in the supposed wall that it was propped against. Curious as always, she went to check it out — to then find a hidden control by use of a hand beside the gap which contained a hollow point beyond. Revealing before her, a staircase descending to a mysterious hall that of which the beam was originating from. Dropping the lamp by the foggy glass window, she hopped down the steps and wandered into the hall. A door, previously unseen to most of the public itself, was flung open with a sign etched onto its wooden plate that read; *'RED RANGER NOOK'.* Eerie whispers haunted through as she entered, cutting to a quiet once the door closed. Nothing out of the ordinary, such as a desk much like any other, books piled on books — a librarian's usual dance. The objects seen were of the general necessities one would find in such a place, the exact kind of deceit to hide fragments of rare value, visualised to appear symmetrical. She flipped over a worn diary marked with the unique symbols she'd found in Valin's old hut, recognising its ink. It was a brief layout, for the text that had been applied was ever a sentence to a few — cryptic as it was, the handwriting matched its very tone. By the lines, its context made no matter other than entries done by this person, it may've been an analytic correspondence or a poetic mantra, if it were not for the phrases that stood out to her, while she read them over to believe it herself.

*"In this home, to define it by house of walls, a vault, apertures and doors means optional ensnarement. Freedom lies on whichever side you choose. To add a lock means to spare the multitude. Then put a key and it tells you to run in circles. Engrossed in the idea that confinement is comfort. Search beyond the illusion and you'll uncover the truth of faith. It's only a step forward, the lie is the distance. What you need resides through, not inside or out. There, you evolve into the entity that you crave, that is everlasting, leading your own way — transform and exert. **That,** is home. The flight to **be**. Home."*

"Don't tell me…" Xira muttered under her breath, as the next part was read.

"An oath, drawn from kin to kin, fusing elements from alike perspectives… albeit opposites attract, but it is never from a simple, single aspect. This welcoming, we provide thee, show you the sun at night, a bite for bite, to enter Rove Dynasty."

Along the remainder of the text, the ink appeared in a smudge, like somebody had been applying a liquid substance onto the page. Bringing it closer to her, she sniffed out an odd smell, something which was rather a déjà vu. She tried to decipher its script, but could only pair up what was evident and that alone sufficed to provide an answer. Xira pried among the desk and shelves, even a dresser by the corner which carried mostly items for mixtures and remedies. From texts to notes, all hidden between binders and covers, she soon realised this was indeed an underground lair that Erma had been using throughout her endeavours as the library's receptionist. An uncanny and cunning stratagem to keep herself under their nose.

"There or not, I'll be visiting," Xira remarked quietly as she walked on out to the rendezvous point.

Willow overheard the vent exit, then spun to greet her, "Well? Anything?"

"Jackpot, Will," was her reply, as she seated on the bike again, "Hop on."

Decelerating around a court's corner, the swampy aura was unlike the neighbourhood they'd inhabited in. Apart from the mess that occurred prior, with the sidewalks packed with debris as well as the street, it oozed of an unsettling odour, a desolation that menaced among the area. They focused to locate the right cottage that Erma was utilising while eyeing about for any roamers. A brown tinted roof beside a tall, verdant tree, slanted down a porch that appeared wrecked below its grey stairs, including its isolated parts tumbled onto the lawn and path-way. Vacant as any of the others, the distinct obstruction on the two windows out on the front set them apart and the ripped fabric that veiled the canopy above it. Xira jumped off the side, propping the bike on the gravel.

"That must be the place," she uttered in a low voice, "Keep an eye out."

They treaded the concrete and over to the bare few planks by the door, slouching their stance upon entering the carpeted room. Filled with what was left of a table, couch, dresser and medley of chairs, the way that they were organised — with some by the openings and others on an angle on the parquet floor — it gave them the intention that she wasn't exactly eager to affiliate with anyone outside of the library itself. They looked at the boarded-up windows, no glass remained in view from indoors. All the darker the cottage was, without any appliance of light and the empty hollow that could be sensed through the mirroring archways that led to the rest of the interior prompted them to assume it was in fact empty. There was no display of inhabitancy, as it usually would reveal itself in the manner of a house chore or task. Even if she were here, the girls weren't fairly convinced that it was being visited as much now. Tapping feet towards the dresser, Willow scoffed at the sound of a particular board below.

"You think?" Xira asked, peeking the edges.

Feeling a handle beneath the wooden carve design, it'd pulled open *something* as a grating effect was heard coming from the far-right archway. Xira walked over to see a dim light-bulb swaying in view of a hall and a door.

"This looks like a basement... but why is it obscured?" She wondered, examining the sides and noticing scratches on the door's wooden surface, "Stay 'round here and be lookout... I'll see if she keeps anything down there. Whistle to call."

The door's handle was partly loose, as it seamlessly slid to the left, then met with the frigid draught of the room in its bare spark of the light-bulbs that were screwed above one shelf and the other. Dust that was swept up from nearby storage boxes creeped to inhalation, inducing a dry and raspy cough, while Xira continued on between the furniture until reaching the back end of the basement. She found a water container by a small ivory chair and an antique chest matched with a rotating mechanism on its lock. Alongside the brick wall, piles of worn cloth scattered there with a couple of chipped utensils typically used in a launderette. Besides the regular storage items from long ago and keeping memorabilia overall, everything else lingered in the shadows of twists by the room's fabrication, the lone brick cylinders edging to the ones that stuck out a wall and on occasion parts of the wood overlay that would dangle below its primed point. Kneeling to inspect the lock, Xira felt for any indentations along the wheel, tapping the rear which guided her through by the rattling effect. Applying to the solution with each turn of the knob, eventually coming to a high-pitched click, the mechanism came apart as it'd been unlocked. As she held the tail ends, the lid raised to reveal a stash of glowing pieces, more fabric and objects owned by a being of magic. *I assumed as much… but not too exact,* she thought. An echoing noise resonated through the basement, like it could be felt on her shoulder while she searched the items over. A tingle creeped along its blade as she turned to the pitch-black floor, nothing odder than a reflection of the confined space. Pieces of crystals, gems, igneous rocks and pendants, chains to isolated hoops and sizeable circlets of laminated glass that contained written scripts in the various symbols she'd seen before, were uncovered underneath a robe sheath which obscured the glow. On the bottom of it all, old marked pages were laid to bear the contents, as she pulled them out, using a crystallic fragment to then read the notations on the four prints and a circlet. It'd translated into;

"ROAM AFTER ME. A MONIKER UNNAMED. BELIEF IN A BEING. TO BE. TO ROAM. HAND IN HAND, LIKE STEEL TO STEEL. ETHOS IN FORM. WANDER BY MY TRAIL. THIRD EYE WITNESS. FOURTH PLINTH WIELDED. IMMORAL, IMMORTAL. STAND IN ONE VIEW. TRAJECTORY PAVES PASSAGES UNSEEN. REALMS TO REALMS. THE DARK IS NOT ONE SIDED. WHAT IS IN BETWEEN, IS. EXIST IN THE BETWEEN TO STAND ON YOUR OWN. RISE THROUGH THE BASES OF MORTALITY, CONNECT WITH THE ETHOS BY THE SORCERY WITHIN YOU. CREATE THE WAVE OF THE UNDER. THE FURY OF WHICH YOU FUEL WITH. A UNIFYING

TRUTH TO THE INFINITE HOLES OF THE ABYSS. IN QUESTION. EMBRACE. SILHOUETTES OF MY IMPASSIONED REALM. ONE WITH ONE, CLEAR AS THE ILLUMINATION, THE SUN, AND THE MOON. BELIEVE IN THE UNDER ROAMERS. WHERE BEINGS BEGIN. LOYAL TO THE REALM. LOYAL TO ME. TO THE INFINITE SANCTITY. ROAM AFTER ME. ROAM WITH ME. TO BE."

Though as she recognised the emblem on the corner again, she was recklessly knocked over to the side and landed to the concrete floor. Just braced about to lift up, when a maddened figure's throat snarled as they tackled with the arms pushing her down as they both swayed in the grapple. The voice was not really familiar to her and it wasn't bright enough to identify the person. Kicking with the boots to knock them off, the figure propelled her to a shelf, tilting it to the adjacent one and then tumbling towards a stack of boxes. Xira wiped her nose, the person's footsteps approaching as she hurled the closest object she could grab — in this case, something made of metal. The clanging of the fallen piece was followed by the hurried thuds of their steps while she backed off to get up. Within a slim moment and the chest illuminating certain parts, she darted round the nearby shelf, scarcely dodging the oncoming swing of the figure's hand and the tipping off of a few shelved items. Their voice lowly echoed with the preying chase, cutting corners to reach her. Xira quickly threw over the glowing objects to the ground, providing a better view of the surroundings. She hid behind the other shelf, watching the ruffled figure approach the light before them. As they'd fallen to a trance, their eyes could be seen in the reflection, an emerald shine greeting the mixture from the floor, as if it were communicating with them. Although she used this diversion to escape to the door, the being was already catching the scent once again, which resulted in a collision by the shrouded bookcase on the brick wall. They attempted to bump into her when she crossed arms to thrust them backwards to the halfway point of the room. In their grunts, Xira kicked in to knee the opponent. When they carried her to attempt another throw and with an elbow to their back, she hauled a knee to push down their shoulder, but by the being's oozing force, the two of them were sent over the boxes — rolling to the ground near the door, as the person planted themselves before the tip of her feet.

"Get off me, off! OFF!" Xira exclaimed gravelly. The person latched onto a boot in a twist, just as she hacked down the door knob. ^*&^*^&

great! She thought, then pulled up to place herself on the exit and slammed backwards with every kick to the front. Not a budge but a groan after another, not caring for a second where the sole was gambling. Luckily, the wood gave way and instead of falling right into their trap, Xira rolled behind to a bend on a calf. The figure emerged in swings, landing a couple before she launched right into the waist and pinned them down with ferocity. He ripped by her hair, snatching the neck in the process and roughing it about between the walls, as she paired her fists to pound to each side.

"ArrGHH!"

The hall fell to a quiet hum, with the basement door left at a slight breach. The light-bulb ceased to sway, but only flicker its remaining volts. Emanating hefty breaths, Xira leaned on a knee to rest the leg and raised up with the other. A sight that briefly visualised like a semblance of gloom, conveying none other identity than a spectre, consumed by its fixed agenda and ruthless ways, absolutely awed by the light. Stepping backwards, she walked wistfully through the arch, wiping the gloves against the chairs on the way out — leaving behind the cottage shambles. Nothing but the air on her mind, as she creaked the main door aside. Jumping down the steps, she met Willow by the road's edge, who patiently sat in surveyance. Once she heard the boots, she spun in the thrill.

"I heard some voices in there. Uh, what happened? What did you find?" She asked.

"*Who **and** what.* That's her place all right," Xira answered, walking to her, "This chest I discovered proves it's where she kept most belongings. *sigh* Didn't find her…"

Barging out the door, came a tall, dripping silhouette of a man. Hair dipped in green slime, matching his glaring, emerald gaze. The clothing was torn and weary, just the same as he was.

"… Found *that*… no way," as she realised, Xira added, "Jerrill. The hell that is Jerrill! Him!?"

Willow watched in chilling fear, as he ambled in sturdiness to their direction, "Um, I can assume that he still works with *her,* so we should get going? Maybe? He does *not* seem friendly, Xi."

"Yeah, come on!" She ran to the bike and lunged over, "I'll handle this."

Within the while of revving the engine, Jerrill had been a good metre's distance from them as Xira revolved in the seat, aiming her slingshot directly at the Adam's apple. Glaring him down, she waited for him to step off the pavement where she would launch a lone, barbed rock found by the wheel. As she did, Xira spun then took to the handles in full focus and tapped the pedal, gliding out of the court in trailing smog, leaving him in the satellite's obscurity. On the way through the winding road, they set off to the bridge once again, the shimmer of dawn's early sun gracing the aerosphere — igniting the wide road's surface ahead.

The clouds drawing both ways from the beams dissolved like fairy floss, the warmth settling on their shoulder blades.

"I feel bad for him," Willow remarked, leaning on her, "Goodness knows what she has done and how many to… it's just, strange, a generally virtuous man gone rogue."

"Or a rogue's puppet," said Xira, "The moment someone switches the indicator, it's out of my hands to give a crap. It's barely harder when they were close and comfort, once upon a time. Ultimately, their loss."

A PBTU post flashed nearby, with an arrow pointing towards the next mile.

Glimpsing a group huddled by the double doors, Willow added, "Complex as it is, I don't think he could fix that choice. Heck, I don't even think Jerrill's self was in there."

"Possessed?" She expressed, "Wouldn't put it far from a spell. We should keep our distance."

Driving off the side, Xira parked the bike by a tree and quickly slumped behind it to eavesdrop. She arranged the ear piece to locate their channel, as Willow followed with the same action. Static buzzed between the alterations while eyeing the group ahead. They'd appeared to be noting down on PDAs and discussing the truck's cargo. Within a second's haste, clear cut voices received on the line as it cracked through. Spying on the guards simultaneously, the girls arched to the trunk's base.

*"Simon, you understand that this shipment was to **include** the H-Tech 100 and the Ferza?"*

"Simmer down, men. The Lieutenants and Wing Commanders affirmed that we'll be making numerous trips for these artefacts. They're not easy, y'know."

"We're not even Yarak's. Why are we the ones doing the dirty

work?"

"Listen, Joe. They assign the orders, we get paid. Two-way streets can turn into one if the oncoming vehicle decides to take up all the space. We can't afford being like... them."

"Then why shut up knowing what they're up to? The Yard has already taken entire towns and what's next? Huh? Yeah, above all that, they're working with that purveyor, Erma, too. It smells like a very tainted protocol—"

"Joe—"

*"No, man, I — we were **all** told that it was for a 'renewed homeland of the infinitum'. **That**, in there? A different melody. When it all comes down to it... it unfurls right in front of us—"*

"T-There's someone—"

*"You think they'll care? Give us a spot in their ladder in who can be more of a jerk? Ahh, I'm telling you, I'm telling you, man. They're sitting around a pot and taking turns, behind the scenes, yadda, yadda... giving us the crumbs and making us be their pawns. **Just. Like. Them.** Afford that? We're already in their debt. The only difference is, Arnold, we wear these suits. Security? Of what? Their lies. That's all it is. Layers and layers of lies and we're at the bottom of the pit."*

Xira slid up to stand, hiding herself as she adjusted the handle of the communicator. She could overhear their resounding tones amidst the static overlay of the call, like the frequencies had been interlaced. Another rather hushed voice came to clear.

"There's someone on the buzz — change t — ch — change the transmission — buzz t — t —"

Immediately throwing away the piece and signalling her companion to do that as well, Xira hopped on the metal to ready for bail as Willow ducked at the back wheel.

"They don't know we're here," she whispered low, peeking over, "Let's play this out. Catch what they're doing there."

The huddle dispersed around the truck, while two of the men continued to chatter and the others secure the crates stacked up in rows. They remained in pairs, completely devoid of caution to their surroundings as they concentrated on their current tasks. Although their movements were obscured as to what exactly was occurring in that truck, secrets and intentions packed up alike, that call was enough to inform them of what lurked beneath the new surface…

"All right, use the overcoat," Xira stated, slanting, "They're all in that truck."

Willow folded the sleeves as she replied, "Are we tailing?"

"We're off to the Yard. If they're not taking a detour, then it's a caterpillar train."

On the way, the truck gradually sundered as it puttered in view — the board sign along the grass in the range was spotted throughout the ride, reading as *"Arriving to Yowndrift Yard"*.

"Yep," Xira commented upon finding a safe area to place the bike, "There is Yowndrift Yard."

The security guards stepped out the side doors after they'd entered the gates, then coming out of the garage, two men dressed in embellished uniforms approached the group with poise. Their epaulettes reflecting the morning's light as one of them uttered a brief greeting and addressed the matter. One of the guards bowed in return.

"Wing Commander Ruzak, Lieutenant Forest, the shipment has been made," he declared.

Forest tipped his sage maroon peaker hat in his front folded hands and answered, "An onus to be rewarded. Certainly, you should be proud."

"Sir, the remainder of it will be delivered by tonight," the other spoke up, fidgeting his buttons, "Would you like us to send additional convoy?"

"No need," The wing commander stepped forward, "It does seem we can put our faith in you honourable gentlemen. Forest and I will hold to your words. Dismissed."

As soon as the parley ended, they disappeared into the plated foundation and the group of security guards idled in the seats, inspecting their PDAs. Xira slunk into the base, followed close by Willow as they ventured towards the side wall. A set of pipes traced along the top, neighbouring a loose window and a camera rotating on the rim. They determined its field, listening to the faint sound effects it made, to which it synced with during its scanning. Targeting the fish eye lens, Xira launched a star-shooter projectile to tamper with it.

"That's nine left," she noted, "Thinking what I'm thinking?"

"Let me do the honours," said Willow, looking up, "I can use this linked chain."

Helping her climb to the next steel, she kept watch on either side as her companion pulled up below the camera. Willow attached the hook on the pipe above to bring herself closer to the window. Propping the left foot on the sill, she spun the latch by the glass, creating a complete opening.

"This looks like a data room," Willow called down from inside, "First floor... level... I'll wait. Are you key-carding it?"

"Don't worry. I'll meet you there," Xira answered in a hurry, seeing a guard on patrol and darted to a recycling container.

Flipping the collar on the overcoat, she approached the garage and went straight for the staff door. The key card held displayed a worker's name, marked with the position as a *Yard Guard. Access to base — first floor — If faculty office. That wasn't responsible, Frank River,* she thought.

"Excuse me, serviceman?" Someone voiced right behind, as she turned, "-woman?"

Xira forged a polite smile in her reply, "I'm with the labs. Checking in."

"Oh, right, no, I was going to say the usual entrance is the primary door out front," he claimed.

She faced the mechanism again and flashed the card, then entered upon its activation.

"I prefer this one, thanks."

The hall that extended into a white mirroring haze before her displayed a narrow, tiled path leading to a heavy two-door and a right turn towards the foyer and stairs. As she examined the area, a sight of offices in amidst the equipment and tech rooms opposed one another until walking up the reinforced dual-swing. Peering through the stained glass, a darker lit space was seen with various members roaming left and right. Another hall that continued further down appeared to link the eastern part of the base floor involving additional task rooms. On to the foyer, Xira highlighted the stairs in the corner directly by a vending machine that was out of order. She skimmed past the criss-crossing workers and guards and found herself at the first floor, thinking of locating Willow's point. Although it was a murkier level, arrows on electric wall boards provided the initial directions around the building.

Walking on, she saw a security meter by the sealed reception desk, implying the operative status of the first-floor system. A low bar giving a mutual way to the receptionist was between the fortified glass and the bench.

"How can I help you?" They asked, only their hands being visible.

Caught off guard, Xira marched to issue a discreet greeting in the while of observing the hidden scanner on the rolling screen. In a moments haste, she tapped the surface to divert.

"On call, madam… I'm off to a meeting," she told her in a ruse. Visualising the indoor layout, she walked down with a cut through the left hall, taking to a curtained, barred window at the end of the hall and a couple of adjacent doors. As she searched for the room, she came upon a sign that hanged and read as the *Data Room*. Once she'd entered, it'd been empty on all aisles, including the computer desk. Frantically checking all available spaces, she heard a muffled cough at the far end.

"Hiding in a closet, are you?" She spoke in a scoff.

"Sorry, there were some men coming this way and it was instinct, really, because what would a lab person would be doing here?" Willow explained while being lifted out, "I'm relieved it was you now, it's so *dusty* in that thing."

They scavenged the room for any intel on the organisation and its schemes, covering tracks of old documents and the tech database. Willow sat by the computer to access the file components. The log in page lit up the screen, with the Yard's symmetrical white 'Y' logo making an appearance to the password bar. *Access granted.*

"Pshh, too easy," she remarked, piling the desktop folders to infiltrate as a low chuckle was heard.

"Just… how, Will?" Xira shot a side glance as she ruffled through storage of archives.

While Willow typed in the system commands and going about multitudes of files, she added, "Why, I took the liberty to stick my nose in their supposedly secured drawers and find anything to use during my patient waiting for your return. Oh! Which reminds me… Do you recall that time we celebrated Jay'eo's birthday and I didn't want to go down that uneven slide, then that one rude boy pestered me about it, so you intervened and how you said…?"

No reply but the noise of sliding drawers being opened and closed, in the midst of the keys clacking.

"Fine, you said to *that* boy and his *buddy* group — '*If anyone ever tries to stick their nose in, I'm gonna' break it'* — and hoo, did you **let** them **know**," Willow lauded in the swivelling seat, "It just made me think of that day and how I never, *ever* will forget — ha, ha… ah. Okay, focus, focus, focus."

The clatter of metal being tossed about outside rang through the window, while they gathered whatever contained of need, their attention locked to the door. Even so, the quiet was filled with the cooler machine's buzzing by a wall and Xira filtering through the different cabinets and electronic rows of databases. It must've been a half hour of being inside, for the chatter in the halls blared against the way, trays being wheeled about with the rhythmic footsteps merging in between. Joining her by the side, Xira held a folder which she'd used to combine the findings.

"Everything is in here, are you all set?" She asked, keeping caution to the front.

"Just about," said Willow, "You wouldn't believe some of the despicable things I've uncovered… they are all using each other. No matter how high, someone is always looking down upon another. Like, this email I picked up… a Yarak called Igba Bernard attested to *sorting* out a number of families in their chambers. I wonder what that's about… Then there's this, a Lieutenant that ordered these men, from third, to *herd 'the factions'* into the lower floor of the isolated 'public' sector. Blueprints… old and new. This place is enormous… goodness… well, here it is. Portable planted, ready to jet now. Should find a good spot to read through all the files, I think so."

A banterful laugh emerged from the doorway as a pair of yard guards walked inside, patting each other on the route to the desks. The girls slid by the nearest database board and carefully approached the front of the room, reaching for the door's knob, as they saw the two sink into the works laid out before them. With triumph, they closed the door and hustled forth to locate a personnel's safe room. Xira nudged with her elbow, gesturing to contact the receptionist.

"Hello, we were wondering if you could tell us the room information of Mr. Frank River?" She asked, fixing the coat, "He has agreed to a visit, we just need the details."

Awaiting the response, the receptionist glided to their computer systems to checkmark the personnel's data. It was a short moment before they retrieved some stapled papers to the front and pointed to an underlined section of the page.

"Do sign here and... here, confirming of your visit and you may resume to meet Mr. River," they stated, handing over a mech pen, "Give that back when you're done."

Reaching a narrow hall to the right, the two faced a key-card secured door, its frame emitting a celeste blue, viewing a miniature plate outlined in white and a name that read; *F1 — Frank River.*

"Who would've thought that they didn't know the insignia of the lab people by now?" Willow said under her breath, "And BG? What did *that* stand for?"

Scanning the surroundings before inserting the ID card, Xira replied, "Berrygum."

Upon entering Frank's safe room and quickly locking up the door, they were presented with a high-tech setup interior, adorned with a fresh lime scent and rather fancy composition — and seated themselves on the sheeted bolsters opposite of one another.

"And about that, I don't think they really look into it until they need to," she continued to say, "This place is our hideaway for the meantime... which means getting all shit done before they smell the smoke."

"Right. Split the intel?" Her companion asked, pulling a nearby laptop that'd been placed atop a wall cornered desk.

They traced through the details on the organisation and about every nook and cranny of their schemes thinly outlined among the verses of supposed improvements on order and chaos, expressing their beliefs that the refined depiction of cyclic inhabitants laid in the palms of what they're imposing over the hometown and across all the lands they infest. An idea that brewed from a disagreement merely a lone hair's matter, now turned to who's got the largest appetite and who's more willing to sacrifice nobility for a shred of freedom in the guise of command over coexist. The scales that surfaced and tilted in the favour of the Yard, carried by the members residing in all the sectors and roles that of which have been applied to every one of them, whether by choice or circumstance, nonetheless was more of a burden that grew to a strange comfort in their hands and being incessantly exposed to what was carved into the space and outside the barriers of their own confinement. As they skimmed by the list of codes and briefings regarding the various members, they found a segment that emphasised on the current direction to their plans. *Override, divide and dismantle. YY confirmation and imprint.*

"*The ODD plan, layout*," Xira read the script, "They are mad."

Below the marquee of highlighted and documented prints, an official statement issued by the commander was typed out, directly from his input. Diving into the phrases, she was repelled.

From the Commander's official accord — stamped and distributed. {YY}

Salutations, consociates of the Yard.

I hereby grant the actions to go forth, in assembly of our new and effective regime. We do not falter in making a better world for mankind and I believe it will continue to thrive in exceeding heights, for as long as we stand under the same beam, reciting the faith in Yowndrift Yard. An ode, an oath, a reliance to your obedience. Stay with us and be given, otherwise taken. Our purpose wields to adapt and accomplish the symmetrical way that we are known for. If you comprehend the end grail, to the fervorous levels of collective providence and execution, then you hail witness to our gratification when we proceed with this favourable trajectory to form our evolved world for all of us. We each carry a role, gifted to you personally by the Yowndrift Yard, express your accession wisely and be thoroughly rewarded. No man left behind when we need to charge forward. As your Commander, I can surmise that you choose to sit by the reaper and honour at my will, as it is your solemn duty as a fond member of the Yard, for it will prove futile if you shall defy and a reckoning of the base as you know it would ensue, landing an inflicted burden on yourselves that you will not wish to bear — mark my words. By your Commander, the true wishes are to be in light of the Yard. We are the force, so we set to blaze. Mark the fresh code.

Signed, Commander Shepherd

Yowndrift Yard: "Dwell in the question and it shall mirror inception…"

As she went on to flip to the next pages, a bold inked, cryptic title caught her attention — it'd read; "***Containment Chasm — Administered by Lieutenant Jacan***". The description which elaborated on what it held and why, instigated her emotions to overlap, once realising that it was no section for scientific weapons but rather, a manipulation of beings *for* use. Down the lines, the informer continued to scribe that by the methods of "keeping the public in check", would allow the Yard to proceed with the dilemma that they've placed over the people, so that they were to *handle* the course as a favour to them without meddling themselves directly. It displayed their intention to the exact point when it clearly stated; *"An army by and for the Yard, to abide and build for us, with and by us."* This left an unsettling feeling Xira's gut, her hand propped under the nose in disbelief of what was uncovered. She exhaled in a deep sigh, as her gaze shifted from the page to Willow, who then seemed to be tearing up at the sight of the screen, drenching down the surface in the midst of gentle wiping.

"What is it, Will?" Xira asked, arching forward.

"He was, — he would've," she voiced, her tone brittle and cracking after every few words.

Xira hopped to her side and hugged around the shoulder.

"They, t-took my father. He's become one of them, a Wing Commander," added Willow, her tears falling on the pad.

"Wait a minute," Xira chimed in, "Jason? Wing Commander Jason? The notes at the outpost mentioned him and his involvement... huh, *he* assisted with the outpost? Man, Willow... I remember you telling me he left. Not long after, you had to move in with your grandmother. No wonder he never came back. He didn't just disappear."

Willow hurled the laptop beside her and leaped into Xira's arms, quelled by the divulgence. A moment of reflection changed into a face of humidification as her deep-rooted companion wiped along the sides, holding Willow close to herself and prompted her to believe that she would never abandon their bond, no matter what tore through the seams. Xira remained in the seat, after bringing the pages over to resume their objective. Leaning to place the laptop on Willow's lap again, she gave her a reassuring smile and cleaned up the keypad.

"We're in this together," she told her, sitting back, "Don't doubt that for a second. I keep my promises."

They sifted through the rest of the data they'd found, comforting her every other minute she set back more tears, as most of the scoured documents were scattered along the carpet and the others tabbed on the screen. With a scroll down a certain file of PDA message logs, emerged a history of exchanges between Erma herself and the known father, Wing Commander Jason.

—

WM-JASON > MISS E. : ESTABLISHED. YOU ARE TO MEET ME BY THE FOYER.

MISS E. > WM-JASON : YOU WERE LATE. I DESPISE IMPRUDENCE. WE HAD A DEAL.

WM-JASON > MISS E. : CARRIED THROUGH AS ALWAYS, ERMA. MY WORK DEMANDS SCHEDULE CORRECTION, I CANNOT DISBAND BY ORDER OF AN OUTSIDER. ARE WE CLEAR?

MISS E. > WM-JASON: IF I DIDN'T PLAY MY HAND IN THIS, I SWEAR UNTO THEE… MY SINGLE INTEREST IS THE PLAN. WILL YOU PLAY NICE, COMMANDER?

WM-JASON > MISS E.: WING COMMANDER. STICK TO THE PROTOCOL AND WE ARE SET FOR TRIUMPH. I'VE BEEN INFORMED OF A MEETING IN THE HQ LAIR. YOU ARE TO BE THERE. DISCUSSION WILL INVOLVE BOTH OF OUR DIRECTIONS — COMMANDER AND LIEUTENANTS WILL BE PRESENT. LIES ARE NOT TOLERATED.

MISS E. > WM-JASON: I AM IN THE SAME DUMP THAT YOU ARE, MR. JASON. I ENACT WHAT IS BENEFICIAL AND PRACTICALITY IS WHAT I ADMIRE, YOU SHOULD KNOW. AS IS THE AGREEMENT SHARED.

WM-JASON > MISS E.: JUST DON'T START A RIOT. FIRST IS A WARNING. COMMANDER DOES NOT HAND SECONDS. IF YOU WISH TO RESUME YOUR ALLIANCE WITH US, THEN DO SO — WHAT YOU DECIDE, YOU SIT ON, ERMA. IF THAT'S BY OUR TABLE, THEN GOOD. WE DON'T LIKE TRAITORS TAKING FROM THE ONE POT.

MISS E. > WM-JASON: SPLENDID. I ONLY ACCEPT THRONES, MY DARLING. SEE YOU THERE. HQ. BETTER NOT BE A ROOM OF PHANTOMS AGAIN.

"What in the hell?" Xira remarked, grabbing the last page of the pile, "That's just great, yeah, fantastic… *she* better not still be lurking around here. Or ah, so help me…"

Willow clicked onto the remaining folder which included a sole file labelled as 'confidential', then uttered placidly, "Nothing is private any more."

"This devours like a shopping list for the ants," continuing down the page, Xira read aloud, "*Science Lab Room 1, experimentation successful. B-100 dispatched to cells. Trial Record Room 2, victorious. Rangers assigned to own chambers. Activated surveillance systems. Security altered to LVL3 — 4 if announced by the Commander. Higher personnel access only — note: WMC, COMM. {}* "

Tossing it all on the opposing cushions, she slumped by the computer screen as they viewed the file together once it'd loaded completely. An automated command played in the introduction, announcing the Yard's weekly sermon in a robotic method. Appearing on the screen, flashed a video footage of the four levels incorporated within the organisation's lair. The first depicted the medley of chambers that sinisterly scanned about the area, almost glorifying the isolating modes. The camera shifted to another pocket of high-tech cells, obscuring the imagery, although it revealed the narrower structure of the hallways and the emphasis on the security. The scene switched to a zoomed-out scale of the sombre hall's corner, then the robotic tone explained the adjacent containment room except the additional censoring, that it was a place where safety and compliance was applied by the lab sector and the Yaraks, in fusion to bring to fruition what they were building all along and continue to pack on whatever was required and would ensure the elevation of Yowndrift Yard's set goals for the protocol. Revealing the other floors, they noticed the security levels were in fact as stated, even more lethal and harsh — despite not applying the details of it, the portrayal of the surroundings deemed to be enough of a hint that the highly armed personnel were not messing around. Much as they liked to declare that the idea of unification involved the very meaning itself, the division of their personnel indicated otherwise — the matter that anybody who'd been below level two could not access the next floor with a key card, hence pointing out that the members with installed OCRs — optical character reading — were the level two and three granted by lieutenants. These were also known as the Yaraks. The highest form of security personnel for the Yowndrift Yard. Armed to the teeth, rough to the bone. With equipment modelled to their training, flexible and armoured uniforms, they had everything and anything the officials could bring to the front. The Yarak's Armoury room was briefly shown to announce that they were not bearing these weapons during their tasks, as the Lieutenants stated, that it was appropriate to showcase the professional manners of the guards and how they were taught to discern between necessity and recklessness. Despite still being a brutal unit, the weapons were marked for *"Code Yarak"* commands specifically — giving the guards a different alert throughout their various missions, whether advising bear arms or firearms. This sent a chilling signal down their sides as they came to the finishing recorded scene. The fourth floor, the Commander *"Watchtower"* sector personalised. A room that breached to one-way windows and an array of surveillance screens, with a control panel dimly flashing below. The throne-like chair that included a remote and lever on the hand rest swivelled by the diagonal tracking of the camera's pan, as the robot spoke again through the visuals of the electro-static window; *"The Commander's third eye. A shepherd to the Yard family. Honour to him."*

"A private lair, for a private lair," uttered Xira in an undertone, "His hideout when things are a little off the tracks in his own office."

The video closed with a shot of the building from the outside, layering the logo on the edge and the official Yard billboard — as the robot buzzed, *"Room for all and a table for one, the Yowndrift Yard."* Their mantra appeared down the screen with the mirroring imagery of the emblems etched onto their uniforms and the repeated Y symbol on all corners of the footage before it zipped back out to a black screen.

"That's all of it," said Willow, closing the laptop, "Need to get out…"

In the enclosed condensation coursing within the airspace, they could overhear footsteps getting louder towards the location, as fraught conversations magnified through the sealed door. A series of questions overlapped the odd resonance in the mix that vaguely drained out the digital blips tapping alongside the frame. Xira shoved the files in the furniture and leaped towards the back.

"Now would be a good time?" She whispered, her eyes bouncing the corners.

A deadlock beneath a low vent was sighted just as Willow lugged open a laundry drop beside her. They took one glance at each other and braced for the exit.

"Don't mind where these lead to — meet you on the other side, hold it together," Xira reminded her right before diving down to slide.

Just as they did, a soft echo chimed through the narrow steel in indication of the members entering the safe room. On the landing to the next vent, Xira rolled in a crawl, slithering over an interval every few blocks she'd crossed with the room below in view — its dusky blue tint coating throughout the bars that gated many portions of the town's people, separated in the identical forms of the crowded cells. Faint cries that faded by the area's noise reduction trickled with the hushed tones of chatter stifling among themselves. She snatched off the overcoat when going forth and as the way out reached her grip, the tile at her feet loosened to result in a drop backwards on a cloth container. In the gasps that ricocheted from cell to cell, placing a hand over the edges, Xira climbed out to find herself inside the Containment Chasm. Filled with residents of all generations, most of them glimpsed at the sight. A large neon sign flickered above an elevator door on the far left, its level title displaying with the arrows beside it — fortunately, not in use. She walked the cold floor to inspect the tracking eyes of people's saddened demeanours follow her about as she listened to their sorrowful pleas and a sinking feeling in her gut, roaring like in an abyss.

"Pardon me, young lady?" A little voice called out from behind. Seeing a child gripping the bars with a gaze so sombre and a complexion that paralleled, she went over.

Xira bent down to meet her by the cage.

"Do you know why these tall men are keeping us here?" The girl asked, "I'm scared... they didn't give me my bear... her name is Poochy."

"I'll search for the bear," She told her as distant noise veered closer, "I can't stay but be near someone tall enough and I'll try return it for you."

The elevator suddenly dinged to a light which pointed to the current floor, before it split to an opening, then emerging a group of Yarak guards in formal ensembles spread out apart. Behind a cement column, Xira peered the sides in hiding as the Yaraks performed their duties. Wanting to listen in, she hopped into a nearby container filled with material and quietly pressed an ear to its wall. Although muffled, their hoarse tones ceased to falter.

"Next batch tonight? Lieutenant Jacan affirmed on the move."

"Dispatch to radio… I'll go there right away. — Catch you later in the huddle."

"All right, no problem. Men, sort these out. They want the chemical resistant fabrics aligned by cell height and width. Nobody in or out — and ready your gas masks on my command."

"Are you confident these will work?"

*"Tell me, are you questioning Wing Commander Jason's methods? He **himself** informed me of their effectiveness."*

A clanging shift rumbled by the floor, resonating upward the container she was hiding in. Xira slumped beneath the bottom piece, holding her breath. Once it had been wheeled across to the other containers, she felt a Yarak reeling out the pile's surface and decreasing the weight of the sheets above her. Instinctively, as he leaned to grab the lucky last one, she knew it would mean trouble if he should uncover her. With the fabric pegged in his fingertips, Xira folded the sides in a lifting thrust and encircled the man's collar to bring him down in a headlock, securing the rims on the back of his uniform, while holding him close and knocked the Yarak unconscious. Grabbing the mask attached to his thigh, she placed it on and pulled the straps before emerging out of the container to find another spot. She kept the focus on the other four Yaraks that tended to the cells around the compass. They stood in front of the veiled cages, the frightened cries bellowing behind it. Not a care in their wake, as their posture remained fixed to their PDAs in hand.

"Clear your zones, gentlemen and masks *on*," declared one of the Yaraks.

Upon gearing up, a strange chemical oozed out of the ceiling gaps in a range of colours, a vapour that swirled in waves among the floor, like that of a washing machine. They felt on the sheets which its white material became painted by it, ambling about as Xira hurried to the control panel on the far wall and switched down to shut it off. To their surprise and wonder, the substance diffused to particles before one Yarak tended to the panel again.

"Someone's deactivated the component," he announced, turning back, "Sweep the chamber. Find what did this."

They began to search, breaking their huddle after noticing one of them was missing.

"*Find* him!" A shout was heard.

Perched beside a corner of a nearby cage, Xira watched the Yaraks pace the lanes and while the cells remained covered, the muted cries were still ringing through the threads — the low echo of the hollow halls haunting in the background walls. A Yarak approached her direction, hearing his footsteps thump on the concrete, she stuck to the sheet and whipped out the sling at the ready. Inspecting the environment, a tall pipe connected to a speaker had appeared to have been pierced on its bend. The man crept forward, checking the sides through his patrol. Xira pulled back a star-shooter by her grip, in aim towards the high joints of the chamber. *That's eight left,* she thought. Within the moments of the loud crash catching the others' attention, she disappeared to the far back, in yearning of the elevator door. Just when she reached the door's mechanism, a distraught Yarak shouted between the opened path to which he had spotted her. Unaware that the elevator was being called from the fourth floor, Xira rushed to the opposite end to bide some time as it descended to the chasm. Still sporting the gas mask, she took the Yaraks on a carousel-like trip around the area, as they followed in menacing shouts and with the dodging on each gliding rotation, she ran at the opening to reach the exit. The dinging chimed with a Yarak's appearance from the way in attempt to corner her down, but as he and his men charged their routes, the two doors opened to the empty cube and with seconds away from their grasp, Xira dived inside and slammed the buttons to a narrow escape. Gulping in breaths, she slumped down the side, took off the mask and dumped it beside her — exhaling in relief of it all. The ascension grazed the gears below, with only the small window above the cab showing view of the cables throughout the hoistway sparking up to the LED lighting wavering from its position. As it'd paused at the third level, she pushed back up to prepare for leave. A broad, resonant area greeted in its faintly lit halls, with almost the entirety of the dividers being polyvinyl architectural glass, directing to either way of the floor. Unknown to what resided inside the mirroring rooms, the kiosk desks of the lobby appeared to be not in use, as Xira walked up to find a notice placed next to the rolled down gate. '*Be back soon!*'

"*Hzzt... hzzt... t-ss... t-ss... h-zzt...* "

She walked towards the sound coming from the edge of the path ahead, unable to witness its presence but the aura that came with it, for it evoked an unusual essence, of that of a machine, though something closer and more personal, a touch beneath the surface. *Where is everybody?* she wondered, venturing through. Trying to peek inside the windows, she could only spot a few of the members standing by with their backs turned to a layout of pages spread across the various modernised equipment. Facing a pearly, rubber wall that split the path into two ways, a holographic message blinked along the front of the electroplate. It'd read as a welcome sign to the third-floor personnel, listing the key components of what was located in the surrounding sector. The noise became more evident, luring Xira to its point of origin as she overheard a number of voices colliding to the reinforced passage doors down the left side. With a murky glance through its casement leading to a high-tech lab consisting of the Yard's equipment, she could decipher bodies upon bodies attached to an array of angled beddings, supposedly for observance, though the group of overcoats and Yaraks seen roaming about, spoke something aversive. Although it echoed a muffled exchange, she could just make out the words that uttered off their tongues.

"*Subject Nota… chaplet of Notum…*"

"*Proved a success. We have progress, sir. Should I look into it?*"

"*Retrieve me our data cartridges, align the needle to the base… test to amplify the growth.*"

"*Uh, right away, good sir.*"

Xira sprung beside the door as a Yarak left the laboratory, skimming fast past the smooth tiles. Going back to spy within, one of the patients they were examining wriggled in the seat, restrained of fluid movement with their wrists and ankles attached to the leather as their vexed grumbling rocked the pad by the feet and the tray table next to a member clutching on the PDA in-hand. In the sudden alarm, a voiceover blared through a static speaker.

"*Immediate round-up dispatch! Code red! Intruder on the premises! Code red!*"

Everyone inside turned at the announcement, just when Xira hauled over towards the opposing way. Checking around her, the formerly quiet area now became a mad house, like an avalanche snowballing during a storm. Running down an empty corridor, she could hear all the distant and near commotion that had arised. In the midst of it, the impacting footsteps looming on her trail, a half-knocked door was sighted on a sharp, left turn. As Xira slid on a drift with a banging entrance of a couple of Yaraks down the narrow end, one caught a whiff right at the swift disappearance seconds later, then made an alert call to his allies just as she barged in a storage compartment packed with commodities. The scent from it grasped at the mid-way of her nose and throat, refraining to emit a cough while she hunkered down the space. After the crossing of the Yarak's boots elapsed, she used this moment to peer out the side, to see wandering members casually girding the area and no sign of the herd of hunters. She walked on forth to find the closest exit, when she dropped down a flight of stairs and witnessed two well-armed Yaraks getting a hold of Willow, who looked like a deer in the streetlights, carrying an old Yard uniform and getting escorted out of the second-floor lobby. *What? What h-*, her thoughts raced just as she chased them down to a tight passage. Hearing her voice, Xira bounced between the coarse interior, hands gliding the sides, then arrived at a two-door entry — locked, and which required an OCRs activation gadget. Before she could muster a way through, a pair of Yaraks shouted angrily behind her, joined by four more armed, who were standing at the other edge. *Shhhit! GO!* her mind jumped high as she sprinted to a door in her reach, barging in and followed close by the security group, hot on the dark, dim trail. Speeding through and far ahead, Xira navigated around the newfound area, unclear as to what it contained, nonetheless, getting away from the ricocheting flashlights spotting over the room. Out the next exit, she was met with a maze-like warehouse, with only the ceiling fluorescence to guide on the maze's twists. She darted left and right, feeling along the hedges that had tiny sharp spikes sticking out its brims. *There's a contraption... and... some dice?* she wondered, rolling it in a palm. After many tries and turns throughout the maze, she realised upon reaching the middle, that the remainder half consisted of deceptive routes for the solution. No matter which one was selected, it'd taken her right back to the centre. The centre, which placed at a miniature set of buttons shaped like petals of a flower and a dent on its anther. The Yaraks could be heard skidding about the forefront, exclaiming in aggression for their impatience led them astray and pointing fingers between themselves. Xira pressed the dice in the anther, resulting in the petals coming to life in the electric light that resembled a breathing pattern. In the first attempt, the maze shifted clockwise, altering the platform in its orbit. A sound effect rang out from a corner speaker, indicating the sequence of the flower puzzle. Another glow emitted from around the dice, displaying the direction it'd been facing. *Three.* As soon as she'd attempted at the opposing button, the speaker came on again. '*Roll the die, roll the dice...* 'The maze's perimeter angled to a cross, tipping over some of the guards.

"Forsaken, are we?" Shouted a voice.

"If we don't get out, we are grinded meat to this chomper!" Yelled out another.

Xira shifted the maze once more, when the answer begun to surface, as it faced on a new light. *Four.*

"Three? Four? The last one is..." She muttered, "Three, four and..."

'*Roll the die, roll the dice...* 'the speaker played again in between the furious voices of the Yaraks who seemed to have scattered close and far. Just when the idea came to her mind, a lone guard rushed from behind in full swing, stumbling off route as she dodged in time to spot him. He charged forth in another attempt to seize, but the maze then shifted and tripped his footing — Xira kicked up his other leg and slammed his front to the selected button, activating the final turn of the dice. *Three.* In the sudden opening of the mechanism, the maze had positioned itself in its correct angle, before ascending a particular key for the exit door — illuminating a hologram within the anther that revolved below. '*3... 4... 3... D... I... E* '

Switching her glance to the guard, he had started to regain himself in a grumble to his arm on the floor. Xira took the key and headed to find the way out. '*Refreshing systems in five rotations, evacuate the area, repeat...* ' declared the recorded tape. As she ran to the sides, enough distance had been formed before the same guard had caught on the trail and meanwhile, few of the others were heard screaming in the back and some calling out emergency alerts, seemingly unaware of the design made by their own devoted organisation. Their cries indicated so, as it did not portray even a hint of a trick but a pure, soulful plead for mercy and redemption. Fear could be felt through their tones, reverberating among the effects of the clanging spikes, snapping at each turn. Although she did not know how badly they'd been wounded, she continued to remind herself in clear conscience… they would've left her for dead. Nearing the last curve, the few of the Yaraks still on the chase, uttered their chants but in gruesome volumes, unlike she'd heard before, that gave off a prickling chill right beneath her shoulder blades. Watching the shifts occur, a noise buzzed as a red beam aligned down the path. A camera faced in her view, located a metre's length by the door.

Quickly launching a star-shooter to break the reception, she whispered under her settling breath, "That's seven."

After approaching the door, a rectangular case protruded from the concrete structure. She applied the key and as it unlocked, it'd swung open with a green gleam zipping above the sill. The door closed behind, as Xira walked on out, leaving the group of Yaraks to their karma. Past a couple of corridors, another two-way hall between lobbies greeted her again and was occupied with the Yard's personnel, ranging from lab coats to base and Yarak uniforms. In search of guidance, a lab member confronted by a remote post.

"Why hello, are you lost?" The woman asked, holding a binder, "I don't recognise that uniform as an official, can I take you aside?"

"Take me to a computer, I need to navigate something," She replied tactfully.

Without a word, the woman in the overcoat escorted her along the way, before gesturing to enter one of the glass-cased rooms filled with desks, tech and the like.

"I'll be back in a quick minute, you should find what you seek in there," the lab member stated then roamed off beside the windows.

In a sigh, Xira spun in a metal seat by one of the operating computers closest to the back. While the screen loaded to a main page, she observed the surroundings and the equipment they'd installed within the space, unusual and modern looking — like it was of a particular purpose inside the organisation. Not a second too stretched, the display screen provided connections to a different set of categories, organised alphabetically and in a layout that divided the sectors of the Yard and beyond, into their aligned provinces. Clicking to the third-floor icon, the index branch revealed a search engine for her to use. The list of examples to read didn't dwell in the deep of the source within the Yard, so she turned to type in manually. Blueprints, maps, layouts and all of the relative aspects she'd inserted to uncover more information about, lit up like candles in an evening blackout. Dropping the tabs to the extended files that represented the Yard's model, she found a new image elaborating on the depths of the building and its hidden locations entirely. Tracing the path she had covered until reaching that OCR operated hatch, she zoomed in on the outlines with the blue shading on the shape and read on its heading with the description. *Interrogation Wing, Supplies Facility, level three access and high-end personnel only.*

"Interrogation…?" She exuded, scanning the rest of the map layers.

Just then the lab member returned to stand aside as she spoke, "I assume that you've achieved the task. May I ask of your business here?"

Before there came an answer, two of the third floor Yaraks glanced with eyes widened towards the very room. Barging in and knocking the woman to a desk, one of them declared into a transmitter that they'd *located the intruder.* Within the sudden upheaval, they interlocked a chain gadget to capture her as she balanced the stance in defence.

"Hnn! The hell, m — Get away from me!" Xira shouted by the chains, as the lab woman brushed aside — not a blink, but a quivering lip on the abrupt leave.

Struggling to form a divide among the guards, they pushed against her while arriving at a reinforced metallic door. Throwing her inside, a room of jet-black paint on the walls and a glass-like white floor met her view as she landed by the far back side. On the high alert she was breathing short, watching as they locked her in and abandoning by the thin window panes. Empty, isolated, confined — mirroring the space itself. Just four edges and a door. Haunting silence. A line of water traced the bottom eye lids, the questions that ran through her mind, in wonder, in decomposition, sunk down the air ways into a vexed exhale and brought her to a bend, fiddling the spiky chains over her knees. For a long while there'd been nothing else to occupy the raving thoughts that crashed like waves over the calmness. What could be seen of the opposing hallway was merely the bleak, unventilated shelter that aided in concealing just about anything involved. The two guards later returned, assuming position by the frame of the door. She squinted her eyes in a hunched gaze, breathing out of the mouth as their heads turned in unison at the arrival of one of the wing commanders. Entering the room, he slowly pushed it to a close in his fresh sight of her, a low smirk wrinkling at the flesh, with a tip of the hat, the high personnel placed both arms against the uniform.

"To what do I owe the pleasure?" The wing commander began, "Are you from a certain division? I hear my people don't find you familiar."

No reply was returned to the man, as he stifled a chuckle in a crouching pose.

"Ruzak. Wing Commander Hunter Ruzak. Humbled to meet you," he went on, "Would you care to tell me who you are?"

Xira sat up to the wall, yanking the chains as she answered faintly, "Your men put me in these bonds... I *don't* care..."

Standing tall before her, Ruzak twirled the hat about in his hands while he said, "I can offer you a grand exception. Maybe even a complimentary drink, on me... or on your friend, poor girl, who on the contrary seems to be having a lovely time. I could turn this place into an art room, if you'd like that."

"What have you done to her?" She snarled, holding to the chains as she sharpened her focus, "The same treatment that you've done to all those people...? Your endless string of puppets..."

Ruzak glanced down in his reply, "Now, now...your little assumption upsets me quite — actually, I'm interested to hear how that theory came around in that darling head of yours."

Another group of Yaraks joined the pair outside in the hall, as the wing commander idled by, his grin contracting.

She saw the men slide in a line and answered in a blunt overtone, "I *know* what's going on here... a town doesn't just disappear... and weather? There has been a snowstorm and nobody has been evacuated like that... and so much for that... they're all sitting ducks in a dry pond now!"

The man glared through as he gripped on the centre of the metal, an ominous motion seething between the close quarters, "So a solitary invasion on the Yard and you claw out the confidential intelligence that had been safeguarded, rather oblivious to the devoted army we feed here... how docile they are to my command. You want to play with the hounds? Do you want a turn, young lady? Seeing as I am the one that—"

Hindering his vulnerable position, Xira ironed the chains together, tightening it over his wrists as she spun to pull him down with her feet, but once one leg had wrapped around an arm, the guards immediately flooded the room — dividing the matter apart. The wing commander adjusted the collar in his stance, massaging the bones before they escorted him away from the containment area. When he stepped out, a smug tilt of the head was gestured to her and as a Yarak assisted in fixing the hat, he then vanished off with the personnel. The five Yaraks remained inside, all surrounding the perimeter in a watchful eye of their captive. Xira huffed on the floor, staring them down while they stood there motionless with folded arms and an empty mien. Shortly after, a woman donning a long juniper coat with her bright hair in a pin waltzed in to greet. Being excused by the Yarak at the door, she clutched a board close and brought a devious demeanour.

"I'm the Yard's specialist, also known as The Dissector. First question, presently, how many years of age are you?" In the midst of her uttering the sentence, the imagery before Xira's eyes came to a blur, sending her in a dizzy state as she attempted to gather herself to concentrate — no doubt, however, the spinning resumed and what she could see manifested a wave of voices coming from the woman who still was posing these questions, disregarding the change in behaviour and attention. She sat half eyed and baffled, swaying aside the duplicating silhouettes of the specialist before she was slapped out of it a sharp moment later. Regaining her focus, Xira slid back, her brows furrowed and the eyes' surface clear as cold crystal.

"Tell me, where did you come from? Who is within your family?" Right back in the double state, the waving of a hand fused with the walls, for the tones reflected the cream shades in the black hue — completely distorting the facial recognition from each member inside the room. Another swing across awakened her once more, this time, Xira's hand was being held by the woman in close inspection.

"Don't touch me... what are you doing?" She said sweltering, like she'd been in a rest, just as the specialist returned the hand down.

"Entity. 23. Glacial Mist. Sereni...? Serena? I couldn't comprehend the muttered words... and finally, your name?" The Dissector spoke softly, peering into her silver glowing eyes.

"Xi... X... Xira..." she mumbled quietly, while going back and forth her clear consciousness, "Wait, w — I need to f — find... "

A guard walked over to set her down in a gentle lay, but something had ripped in the hollow of Xira's gut, a signal, piercing... as she knocked him away and went straight to the side — repeated breaths scraping the throat and a fiery target lock at the specialist who retracted to a distant pose. Witnessing the aura, she ordered the Yaraks to maintain surveillance and then walked out without a second glance, leaving the disrupted space to the six inside. Through the perspective of the thin windows, they had formed a ring around Xira, one foot on the floor and a harsh grip on the locked chains — with nothing else but the flaming silver light in her irises.

The hallway was a lengthy and narrow path walk with few cubicles apart from the other neighbouring doors, as the muffled noise of The Dissector and the Wing Commander Ruzak's footsteps tapped along the tiled rows. Nearing the containment room, they overheard a low shout echoing from within the walls. Walking to the entrance, they prepared themselves to go in when the specialist stuck out an arm to stop Ruzak from turning the knob as she looked inside the windows, her eyes widening at what she'd just witnessed — a smear along the glass obscured majority of the interior but by the parallel wall Xira's hair liberated over the shoulders in a heavy focus to her surroundings, eyes completely filled with the silver as she put both arms beside her, with one in the tangle of the chain, bloodied and trailing along the river of the sullied floor. On the tips of the toes, The Dissector could count all five bodies sprawled in their own ichor, parts of it subtly marked along the black paint and dribbling on the vinyl board, snailing over the boots facing the frontier. Xira whipped the chain across the glass and inked a maroon zigzag line on impact. As the specialist turned to confront Ruzak, another crack at the window was heard, causing them to jump in their skin by the frightful unexpectation, cautiously viewing the indentations and then seeing her stare directly at them, the birthmark on her wrist pulsing in a metallic silver while she played with the darkened irons.

"Bring in Willow," announced The Dissector, before the wing commander spun in haste of the sudden matter.

"They're not finished wi—" Ruzak begun but was intercepted.

"Bring her in," she said once more.

Meanwhile, Xira turned her gaze down to both gloved palms, one entangled in the metal and two in the blood of her foes. Folding the fingers inside a hand, she could sense the heat that exuded between the tips and the centre, for the other felt to have been making the iron burn the longer it was held — a gentle steam orbiting its form. She watched the birthmark settle its intensity, then towards the four walls, observed a lashed carving down each one, with the fragments scattered over the fallen Yaraks. Their uniforms torn and weary, much as everything within the room. She brushed the liquid against the knee sides and kept her steel gaze to the entrance. As droplets dripped from her bottom lip, the keys that jangled in the knob had twisted to an opening and when the frames revealed the specialist folding arms by the opposing wall, a grim look crossed the surface at the sight of her just before it disappeared into a mellow tone. A frightened and reserved exterior, Willow stepped in the arch and after The Dissector shut the door behind her, she heedfully walked towards Xira, who's face had begun to dampen once again. This time, through her eyes, a wounding emanation flooded over the silver iris, tracing the lashes to the marks along the cheeks. They stood in an outstretch, with the chain unravelling down by a spill, as Xira embraced her companion in a despondent sense of her surroundings. Pouring the weight from the profound breaths, she clutched wrists as Willow perceived the battles that had scarred the inner depths and brewed a fierce impetus. Although she'd known this, it'd only grown in magnitude and augmented the multifaceted mien thoroughly. Xira took back a step, wiping off with a glove.

"Hmn, am I glad... oh am I glad," she uttered curiously, "What happened to you?"

Willow cleared her throat quietly, then replied, "... I found out about my father. The reality they'd manipulated for mother and I... led to *believe* he was doing mighty work. I think I heard more than I wanted to, because it hurts now. All over again. Reliving a new past... mother was... murdered. Mother was double-crossed. It's all because of him! He fell under their hand and was played, then, he played us."

Unsure of what to tell her, Xira raised her arm to inspect, "New bracelet too... were you...?"

"I'm sorry, I'm so, so, sorry..." Willow pleaded, retracting the arm in grief. "They told me I could meet him. To... join him as family. That, that if I were to tell them about you, they could grant me my escape — you were right, this place is not safe and I have another chance. A chance at overcoming my past. I don't want this to be of a burden, but shouldn't I take it? If this means to get my father back, to make amends, to get his redemption."

"He murdered your mother. You want to forgive him? No matter that he was under the guise of the Yard, he didn't stop to think what he was sacrificing, *who* he sacrificed."

Puzzled, she glanced by the window, "How would you feel? Finding out what occurred to yours? I know what he did was vile, though I feel like I need to hear the whole portion of this... it will really help, a single session with who he has become... will reveal to me than leave me in agony."

The specialist then unlocked the door to greet them together, slipping the keys inside the front coat pocket. Xira eyed a sharp glance before stepping on the curled iron.

"Settle down. Your friend here has been given an offer. She has yet to make a decision," The Dissector announced with indifference, "Miss Willow, what do you say?"

The girls exchanged looks between themselves and around the area, noticing the empty halls and the exit standing right before the two. There was a pause just when Willow turned, forging a composed counter.

"Would you mind taking this off? I already pledged my Yard alliance. Please," she asked.

"I'm afraid Wing Commander Ruzak holds the activation apparatus. By the by, have you made your decision? I will need to escort you back to the holding sector and await his arrival, then meet with Wing Commander Jason."

In the loitering dismay, Xira intervened, vexed, "Unbelievable. Do you realise what is happening? It's one disaster after another."

"You. Do you really want me to report this incident and get you terminated?" The woman asked with a fixated complacency, "I leave you for one second and I dare to witness a bloodbath — not that we don't have spares, after all — to what rapture do I tell of this? The fact that your *friend* here doesn't appear to be bothered in the slightest... despite wearing an electro-snare on her flesh."

Ruzak sauntered by the window, his uniform seen among the tainted glass. Before he tried to enter, Xira went forward to meet The Dissector's height, an unsparing look cast towards her.

"See, that's the thing. You let my face fool you," she spoke in a low hush, "The difference is, you've got her walking a plank and wanted me to tip the boat. Easy, except, that's exactly how you want it. I'm playing this *my* way."

Barging in at the slide of the wing commander's boot, he stood in awe and beckoned to his associate for an immediate evacuation. A blank impression coated The Dissector as she spun to calm the situation. Explaining to him a fable of an explosion that occurred in the room, forming the mess, she shrugged in the coincidence that one of the lost guards had been carrying a lethal gadget with him and happened to accidentally lure enough mileage between the Yarak group, impacting the guards' radius.

"Get the first-floor sector to handle this. I need to meet with the Commander to arrange the masquerade event he wanted us to hold at the outer town square," Ruzak announced, "Let them out of your sight, and it's final days for your position. Heard me well, Nathara?"

Suppressing a gulp of air, The Dissector answered, "Transparent. After me, *you two*."

Among the dim passageways and a spiral of stairs, nothing but their tapping could be discerned from the lowest base of the floors. Taking them to separate cubicles further apart that opposed each other with a blockade in the middle of the encircling four halls and only two that contained the stairways, they were left with a mere rectangular window to peer through — the view, simply a grey wall and the reflective blue light from the nearby chambers. As there was but a bedding and a Yard magazine rack, Xira took to rest herself, aching to get away from the place. A loud knocking hammered beside her, before she sprung to look around — empty. Hollow. *Hello?* She called out but her voice seemed to be lost in the echo. Xira felt for the walls as they collapsed to a dirt filled layer, twirling through the fingers in the midst of a storm that brewed in the vast area. *Hello?* She called out again, louder, though the winds carried it through the wreckage of the weather. Again, nobody was near. The whirlwind zipped past, sweeping her out from below and to a red glowing underground cave. A silhouette graced the meters ahead of her, its tall, wavery figure lending out a hand. Right as she gazed down at hers, radiating by the terrain, she reached out to make sense of the environment, the warmth within, before it flashed away to a hard blink and awakening to the white, metal door. *Aghh... another dream...* her thoughts wandered. Checking outside the space, there was a flicker coming from a corner, its brightness shining on the glass when a grumble accompanied after the couple of blinks, stretching to an alarm that had been then set off. Skimming the sides for anything of use, the door unlatched in a sway, as Xira stood up at the draught that seeped in. She headed out to see some of the far end chambers had been broken out of, where the flashes were, in its intense blue and green emphasis illuminating the dark zones. Making her way to the left, upon cutting a corner to locate Willow's point of place, the two-way door ahead flung open heavily when a sable mech brute emerged like a loose cannon, obstructing the path.

"What the hell?" Her exclaim prompted the brute to a dive, as she quickly raced in the other direction.

Searching for the second stairway, it had already reached up too close to even get to slam out of the two doors — turning to the next narrow hall, she spotted a lone entrance by the same blockade. As she leaped inside, the brute rushed to stalk in her tracks, pausing when it'd stomped in — unknowing that she hid behind a bulky generator. Xira watched the corner while it revolved around the aisles of the Yard's ground enhanced machinery. Using her sling to attract its attention to a side panel, she snuck by a dual tube contraption connecting to the upper pipes that suspended from the ceiling poles. *Right. Six.* she counted. The brute growled in its walk towards the back, giving a much-needed spare moment — attaching it back on, she sprung for the exit. Though the mech brute overheard the door close, she had managed to put a few feet away from it, sufficing for an escape. *Where to now?* She darted between one area to the next, while the blaring alarm was pounding down and swallowing the pit to a static reflection. Seeing a shaft lining to a dented vent, usually used for transporting goods, Xira marched right in at a timely dodge of a calamitous swing, as the brute knocked the shaft to the side, partly closing that very opening. Hearing the mad, raspy voice, she went on to go further away as she possibly could — arriving at the other end, which led to the adjacent portion of the lower sector, she walked along the perforated steel floor. The fluorescence shone through the boxspan vault, as Xira found herself in a rum, dispensary room. A smell rather unpleasant, weaved with the near smoke of an operating diffuser — its wall tiles mirroring the dim green aura. Exploring the room, there'd been trays left on trays on the benches where the personnel were working, now unoccupied and a mess slathering the floor to the main door ahead. Outside, the metallic edges of the lobby interior suggested that anybody that was here had already left, whether just the level or the building itself. Xira saw an elevator by a plant and went straight to try its function. Still working, she waited by the side for the bell. When it had begun to close, she heard a shrilling shout from the lower sector. Immediately switching gears, the elevator then descended to the previous floor where the chambers resided. After storming the halls to locate the familiar voice, she spotted a partially opened cubicle and peered inside.

"Willow!" Xira called out, seeing her knock her foot on a shattered machine.

"Oh, there you are, I've been trying to get away from these *things*," explained Willow, closing the door, "They're like drones, scanners, catch a scent and they go nuts. We can't leave, not yet… I think it's — it's still here."

Glancing out the small window, Xira remarked privately, "That tall mechanical beast? Yeah, had the pleasure of meeting it. While we're here, do you care to tell me what you both were going on about? Turn heads, did ya?"

"No, Xi, I would never. It's complicated… just, hear me out," Willow went on, picking apart the pieces, "It's here and there, but here goes. They took me inside this… secured area, no other member below level three could enter. First, I was navigating a washing room, it was where I had landed. Then, I was about to go to the receptionist when they found and hassled me about my business there. So… back in that *area,* they realised I was the daughter of a wing commander. Jason. My father's name. Things altered like I hadn't even thought… they offered a visit with him personally, if I were to tell them everything. Of course, I didn't say too much, though, I guess… I said enough. The specialist came in too, sitting beside the other wing commander, Ruzak… so… I just discovered their track of lies, disguised as supposed righteousness. They tried to excuse the fact that it was all a matter of crime and not duty. Saying that it was for the better, when they took the one other person I was closest with. I think I can mend things if I have a conversation with father, maybe, he will see the outside. Then there's the other thing… oh…"

Xira noticed the sudden change of expression on her companion's face, a grim sadness that replaced the neutrality, as she spoke up, "What is it?"

Looking up, Willow paused before her tone grew quiet, "Your parents. You don't even remember them. They didn't abandon you, they... lived close to Glacial Mist... a whole separate town but your mother worked in a cafe and your father was an officer, in the while of trying to recruit their troops, he was involved in an offer that went horribly wrong. After he denied to the schemes and noticed the uncouth methods of the Yard, it is then that your parents were divided and asked to give you away. You were only three. They asked to hand you over to the care facility where you would be placed for adoption. However, there was a woman by the name Andromeda, who was a close friend of your mother for years. She devoted herself to provide a home for you, seeing what your family had been going through. That's when you were introduced to Serenitatem, who under his civilian file, called himself Odion — that's who they know him as. His brother was Odion the Second and I'm guessing that's why he used that name... to hide... pretending like they were actually given the same mark at infancy. From there, uh, that's where you stayed, with the, formerly, new family. As for mother and father... shortly between the recruitment and the establishment, my father had already been a rookie in their army, not even a wing commander. To prove his oath and loyalty, they'd placed him under the task of termination — throughout the hometown and elsewhere, riding with his four-man crew... and... they'd been targeted just the same, anybody affiliated with and by the Yard's *enemies.* If I could, I would go back, if I had known him... Xi... — Xi?"

"Why did they tell you all this?" Xira asked rather wearily, lost in the thoughts.

"I agreed to perform as an associate... to meet him, to figure all of this out."

Xira turned to face the door, as she leaned on its cold frame, eyeing the corridor.

"They must've found our old stuff," she uttered bluntly, in disbelief, "Bastards figured we used a tracker's truck... well, okay. With that time bomb on your wrist, how will you execute this exactly?"

Willow placed a hand over her shoulder, showcasing the bracelet, "I know Ruzak holds the detonator, therefore I am a threat to their threat. It seems one sided but they don't know that tilting a see-saw can only mean one thing — what happens when the other retaliates differently. Please believe me, Xi. We've got it under our hands and with you around, the truth will rise and it will shine on all the realms' doom. You know the way, Xira. Trust me, once he clears his past, I will come right back."

"Huh," Xira scoffed, opening the door, "Oh, yeah?"

She ran through the blaring halls, as the mech brute spotted to chase — booming around the corner.

"Xira!" Willow shouted from inside, sticking her hands to close in on the foggy glass.

During the escapade, Xira cut sides and vaulted towards routes in a tactic to rid of the vicious brute. By a sharp turn at an intersection, another tall figure showed up on the opposite side.

"Argh! There are two of you?" She yelled, before gliding within a shortcut to a laser activated lobby. Swiftly gliding beneath and over the beams, the duo bruto brutes marched together right through the pointers, with only a graze on their metallic exterior. Seeing this, she mustered sonic speed to leap towards a bench and kicked up to a back flip, thrusting both feet on each of their heads, taking them for a stumble into the laser beams as she rushed the corner to the other passageway. Their grumbles resonated within the narrow cuts, after arriving inside one of the Yard's security quarters, adorned with the high-tech equipment and Yowndrift's speciality gear. On impulse, she noticed a brown hexagonal button that'd said '*Launch*' in gold imprint — hung by the side wall, slammed a fist on it and pressed to discover it was a hidden kinetic platform ascending from the tiled floor where she was standing. Heading down, the last thing she'd seen was the two mech brutes scowling over the closing panels before being lowered into an old office. The lights came on in a sequence, the boards and desks illuminated by the protruding lamps, as Xira inspected the area that'd appeared to be a safe room for the wing commanders. From intel to blueprints, everything they'd been hiding was uncovered in the pile, most of which had already been known to her, along with certain things that were confidential to the specified members. Using the main table in the middle, she flipped through the Yard's files, reading about their general schemes and visualisation maps. A computer by the side lit up its screen as its machine played a recording;

"Welcome back, children of Yowndrift Yard. How may I help you?"

Children... of? she muttered silently. A long pause filled the space, when the virtual assistant spoke again.

"How may I help you? Who is operating the YWM device?"

She walked up to try out the keys that displayed on the desk, opening a barrel log upon the trigger. The screen turned a piercing green, dropping columns of all the data and notes that were applied by the wing commanders. With every row containing contents of the Yard, she searched using their engine to find out the truth of the people she knew and wanted to know.

"Odion... there you are. Huh. Family man. Sure, *Odion*, family." Xira remarked while reading on, "Last seen two weeks ago. Location... Outskirts of Lunaris Town? *Seen talking to our current associate Erma and another man with her. He what? Resides in a lodge room and tends the local smoothie bar. Roommate... unknown. Very private person, was part of a family of lost children and mentors.* For the love of — *Research on what he has declared to a Yard's own Yarak, to see what he had meant when he preached unto the Yarak... 'I've been under and I've been out, once I've been there, I know what it's about. The belly of the beast, rumbles in the red mist. Guide to the ground and dwell for the below...'* — *p.s. they had known each other previously.*"

The log then glitched to a quivering presentation of the various intel that tapped along the screen, its green letters revealing some familiar and others odd, names of which all held clues and leads to the particular people on their servers. She pushed back as a blue wave covered the glass, rapidly switching the frequency and layout of the contents, right before the assistant blared out a new signal — shutting down the machine's access.

"Unknown personnel. Detected. Activating defences. Backup initiated. Unknown personnel. Detected."

All the light around the space blacked out in a moment's haste, with just the machines' emission in the view. Xira began to scout the way through when the panel from above opened to a halfway point. While she slid by the table to hide, two spheric flashlights could be seen entering the quarters, as the silhouettes walked forth to pause in their tracks.

"Sir Jason, perhaps they left already? Want to analyse the equipment?" The Yarak next to him asked.

"On your feet, not on your head. Search the area, I'll reboot the network," The wing commander stated, "And bring them to me."

As Xira held the edge, the Yarak circled to a route on the other side, flashing the area through. She rolled underneath and glided to her knees, backing away as much as she could. The guard's footsteps trailed alongside the beam and paused by the front.

"Hmm, that's quite grimy," he remarked, before lowering to inspect the floor.

Her silver iris glow focused on the Yarak, noting his movements. The beam redirected to a shift under the table, following the gap onward in view.

"Nothing here," he said, then crouched back in position to stand right before a gasp clutched the throat.

Holding him around the neck, Xira pressed the guard to the ground and cupped his mouth.

"Keep this covert and you're a free man," she whispered to his ear as he winced in the muffled wriggling, "Some of your *friends* can't say the same…"

The Yarak booted the leg of the table, causing to distract the wing commander.

"What's going on over there? Find something?" He called out in a turn, "Soldier?"

Walking over to see for himself, he was met with the unconscious body of the personnel, dumped directly beneath. Xira idled quietly in the back, remaining by the unused machinery.

"Hydro sector, restore safe power," Jason voiced into his communicator, "Shut down all terminals for these machines and reactivate."

Among the altering of brightness within the room and the opening of the floor once again, the wing commander personally scanned the lair in the search. To find nothing, he returned to the area above and leaned on the panel board. Xira silently left through the door and made a turn towards the right hall facing another exit, far from the compact circuit by the laser lobby. Entering through, she arrived at a base lounge room where a crowd of members huddled in the middle, engaged in a ring conversation on attached plush seats. She dove to the side of a pillar, creeping around the bare parts, with only a couch and a plant placed amidst — as the words by the chattery members ricocheted in their utterance. A lab woman stood up to face the ring.

"Pairing up sounds like a great idea," she said while her hands waved about, "The theme is a hybrid of Midnight Dancer and Jungle. This is going to be so much fun! I've already picked out my dress and the mask to go with it. As it is a masquerade ball, I'm hunting for a partner for the night. Any chips? Any… dancers?"

Another raised their hand in response, calibrating their glasses, "Martha, I heard the lieutenants will be present with another special guest. Do you know who that'll be?"

"They mentioned a mouthful of guests that could attend," Martha explained, "Although mainly saying one of their new associates will accommodate the ball presentation, therefore, going as the special guest. The decorators are stamped right in, as well as the performers! Oh, a blast it shall be."

Xira ran off to the far end wall where she spotted a flight of stairs, curling up to the first and second floor in fluency. The reception desk had been closed and beside the closed bar sign, flyers and pamphlets had replaced the mint bowls. *The Renascence Masquerade Ball,* she read its front. Taking one of each with her, she hurried down to a path and found a main supply room, the boxes placed just outside indicating of the recent restock of the items. Inside, a decorative layout of Yard supplies was displayed on the fixed furniture, along with lavish goods including the crate shipments for the ingredients and the ball. Looking through the things, she uncovered a bubble wrapped load of masks and clothing gear folded underneath. *Perfect...* she thought, slipping the selection into a pull-up bag dangling beside a cabinet. Thoroughly examining the room, a few of the taped gear boxes had been placed among the rest, inked accordingly. Her mouth raised with a curve, as she went on to gather a handful of items and swivelled inside the closet behind the counter. A brief while after walking out, carrying the bands over the back, Xira had used a palette to cover up the scratches and marks from the encounters. With an exhale, she threw on a docker's apparel that was mounted by the second door and hooked a denim blue hat on her hip, before leaving through the main entryway. Going past some of the roamers in the building, they'd either greeted or shot a puzzling glance as she pretended to be heading towards the unloading base, laying low while descending the levels and marching out the back exit. Xira snuck around the perimeter, searching for a good vantage point to escort Willow. Near a distribution board there was a conduit fascia connected to a sealed aperture which loosened on its edges. Beyond the space inside, the hollow noise of the Yard's machinery could be deciphered and a thin zap of electricity scaling the innards of the margins, fizzling out to the underground layer. Along the board's rows of switches, they had been colour coded to coincide with the assigned terms with keywords. The red tabs on the top row read as *main power, f2* and *f3*. The second went on as *CHQ, HQ,* and *HR,* lined with yellow tape and then the third with the green read for *base 1, base 2* and *f1*. Xira visualised where the chambers were and where the two were kept, calculating the way on through each of the switches and forming its layout to reach the outside. From there, she flicked the main power to cause a blackout over the entirety of the building. Immediately, the clamour of the people blared out as the high roof speaker crackled on with silence following a mere few seconds, before a lethargic voice rinsed through the device.

"Calm yourselves, this is your Commander speaking. There has been a power outage. The backup power will resume shortly, as will you. Keep hands and feet inside. Commander out."

Xira scrunched her brows, piercing the mouth to an angle as she snaked a finger along the acrylic surface. Remembering the time that the Family visited a getaway lodge for the winter and bringing with them Willow, who hitched on the certain activity that Xira had proposed — where the nearby theme park area contained a ride and a team versus game, she replayed the events that were of the two going against another pair in the elusive enigma that was called Wayward Wonder of the World — an escort and escape strategy game that would go on for hours at a time, to the point where the Family had thought they had gone missing, to then find them sneaking back in at night and awaited by none other than the league of mentors. She flicked the base switches back and forth, attempting a blinking signal for the floor. With hopes that her friend would catch on to the method, she tapped onto the base 2 and f1 switches in synchronicity, alternating between the speed and direction while deactivating one or two others to dupe personnel into diversion. Looking around in case of Yard roamers, the ear that she'd pressed beside the aperture hovered in the attentiveness, her hands playing on the board and re-enacting the merry-go-round effect — a patient and ghostly stance by the wall as the people from inside resonated throughout the space. By the movement and closing of doors, she could assume that the Yard was not only on high alert but thinking that an error in their machinery was the reason for the glitches — seeing them rush around about the premises and calling out various work terms. A while later of the dishevelment, the back exit door pushed to a swing, as Willow ran across, leaving the garage to use the first corner and catch her weary breath. Xira waited near the wall, bending the hat down to hide most of the face when her companion cut a turn, scraping the gravel to join beside her. Relieved, they went over the furthest to the back of the building with the Yard's vehicles positioned in a lot. A construction beam lit up behind a barrier that cast towards them.

"We need to see if Serenitatem has been hiding anything or even left much since he's moved," Xira begun to say, "That'll help clear my mind and find him out for good. All of it. Get this fog right off… are you with me?"

Willow stepped forward, looked around, then replied, "Forever, without question. I'm just dwelling about my father, these piling thoughts inside of me… I don't know *what* to think. It's like the side I knew about him vanished and a shadow replaced the memory I have of him. I knew my father as a smiling, caring human being. Now? He should tell me. See what he has to say about mother."

"If you want my advice, I say you talk to him. For the sake of your mother. It'll save another knife from being put in your back, knowing who he has become and what his motivations are — he'll see you in a new light as you'll see him."

"Okay, well, what are we using?" Willow wondered.

"A bike, oh… and these, but these are for later, I'll fill you in," said Xira, walking to the compact lot.

Arriving at the house, it had appeared to remain the same as she had left it, as Xira hopped onto the porch, eyeing the trees behind her while Willow followed closely — a gentle approach to the entryway, the sweet aroma of the old home embracing her senses. She turned to spot the owl token still perched there. A blend of emotions whirled in her gut, while they walked onward to the couches. The table had ring marks from the last time the Family had seated for a drink, its slightly faded outline rubbing off the thick glass.

"Hmm," uttered Xira, circling atop the table with a gloved hand, then said, "I can vividly imagine Yiya swaying on the hand rest with a bottle in his palm, shouting a song in an on and off key… Menkos didn't like it, but those nights were the ones filled with laughter, great music and the lighter air. Another family night with the whole of us, I would talk them dry. Not even the TV has any signal…"

At the creak of a cupboard, a portal pool emerged in form by the couch, when Xira got up to inspect. Edging to discover the occurrence, Willow shot back abruptly and from her view, she could see nothing but a little whirlwind spinning upwards. In the midst, like the motion of a vacuum, Xira was swallowed within and disappearing into thin, cold air. Roughly blinking her eyes, Willow jumped forth to witness what she found it hard to believe. From a moment ago, simply engaged in a conversation to her being gone right before she could even comprehend.

"No way, what just happened… where are you? Xira? Hey, Xira?" She yelled from the top of her lungs, with no response but a feeling of despair settling down inside. Like something had snapped from deep down, Willow swung in a frantic flow and tipped the side dresser to the ground. Struggling to control the breathing, she paced about for a second before noticing a decorative bowl that she'd seen one too many times ago and flung it away — breaking at the collision with the stone tiles below the dining table. Letting out a frustrated cry, the plinth and dangling lights wobbled as the reflection flickered in tune — Willow barged in the other rooms, yelling loud her sorrow, a weeping stretch along the throat with every escalation of her voice. Turning the place upside down, she fell to the knees, palms dampened with the tears that painted the skin… in bewilderment and the gloom that weighed upon.

Meanwhile, Xira awoke to a crawl, pulling the body along a bumpy cavern floor. Adjusting her focus on a hand that was holding on a protruding rock, a distant voice began to speak and emanating a red mist which sanded the whole of the interior. She scanned around, seeing the path elongate past the stalagmites and towards the bowels of this mysterious, peculiar location. Whispers ricocheted off the walls as Xira walked forth, watching the passageways roar to a gape and trudging on to a vast area where a spheric indentation met her line of sight — its carving illuminating before her with an ancient design. Just then, a hole formed in the middle of it, ascending a platform bearing an adorned throne raised on the top. Keeping a close eye, a figure emerged from the back of the throne, slipping between the grips to stand in front and put out an arm in a welcoming gesture, as if a little too familiar with this action.

"Ah, so you have been summoned by a fellow dynast. A moment while I alert him so," the man spoke, beckoning to his right, "Menkos, if you will. *Visitor...*"

She turned in an awe look of realisation, as he went over to meet with her. The exchange of fervour when they opposed one another brought whatever was idle in their gut to the rims. Xira had entered a state of déjà vu, riveted by the atmosphere's familiarity, alternating among facing an old resident and unravelling all its cores.

"Come this way, let me show you a certain place," Menkos said in the piloting manner.

"Menkos? You left home for the Rove Dynasty?" asked Xira once they'd ventured through.

He paused, bringing a vessel to offer a refreshment, then turned. Walking to the below, an area that exhibited four thrones and one larger throne in between each two adjacent, Menkos sat on the first seat on the left.

Lifting a leg over, he replied, "Precious as ever. Only if you knew, the foolish mesmerism fed to you had you all hoodwinked on his little finger. Did he tell you? I was warped into this hell of a home, a different silver spoon this round, and deserted proper disasters for a resting place. But no, *I* was the fault in his performance. I derailed his stratagem, cut the strings where nobody could see them… leaving that filth with nothing other than the waste of a long, long ago known potential."

Xira hopped the way down, wandering around the thrones in thought.

"Why would he rival with our own family? After all I've heard about who he truly is… I'm finding to be torn at the roots, questioning if anything he ever said or did was for *us*. The true motivations to which made what the Family was, then shattered to a figment of an image," she expressed, walking to the side, "The man I confided with, trusted to guide me, altered without regard — was from the inside. It was untouchable, a sanctum for your spirit and where my own peace was not at war. He didn't have to go and ruin that, because messing something so cherished, doesn't sit well with me… rocking the very aircraft that was operated *for him*."

The deep voice she'd heard mere moments ago, returned in the disposition of an echo in the walls.

"Xira? Have you finally returned, lady?"

Wondering with her gaze above the scent, then back to Menkos, she replied, "Where am I? I want to know why you summoned me here. Who I'm really talking to?"

A crow riddled through the stalagmites as the area darkened in its hues, the path behind the row of thrones clearing in an extended capacity with the lowering of the chairs bringing a flight of pyramidal stairs.

"By confidence of that, you don't remember. They know me by no name but a hinted crypto, they honour me with loyalty, undertaking missions that are destined and with triumph, the kernels that are dispersed hit the heights we have targeted. One with the kin, one with me, shall be revealed the naam that I am found to be. Your truth lies with me, Xira, the beginnings and by all means, the ends. Memorialise where you were, hold on to your way and embrace where you want to venture. You will see the forthcoming light, leading by the nature of yourself and for the energy within, it will create the fate of new day. Ever eternal, impassioned Xira, you have arrived in my world again. A relation also to you. This is my family, we are the Rove Dynasty. With no vessel, my eyes cannot be seen, it is why they believe. They hear me and here they remain…"

The rumble from beneath the cracks of the rocks tipped them aside, setting a new platform to emerge. Menkos disappeared into the depths, leaving her to the cascading spectral voice.

"With the order to my Menkos, you were summoned to my hands that you need to see," he continued to say, *"Haven't you heard of the true father that crossed with an outsider and thus, landed you right there?"*

Xira looked around to find the platform she was standing on, marked with an ancient symbol and once lifting to observe her wrist, the birthmark had begun to pulsate then again.

"What charming silver orbs you have," the low tone settled by the ears, as he uttered, *"How I have missed you, young lady. Your mother didn't keep her distance for nothing. From your father and this place, we haven't met her since — she lived in the Spirit Realm, which I'm sure*

you know all about. Although their relationship was undoubtedly special, they figured it was best for them to part ways... as you did. The decision made by your father, was to hand you over to the civilisation known to you as Glacial Mist, your hometown. However, the pair that resided just ahead of the fringes were served a cursed calamity done by the hands of those people. The rest, piecing, brought you to Serenitatem. Joining his family, you were raised and watched by **them***. It was a golden sunset until things began to storm a locomotion, entwining our kind with all the others. We all wanted different strands, yet divulged to be the same. I couldn't bear the tragedies that shouldn't have happened at my leisure, as you now understand, child, they have submerged to a blitz on all tides. Should there be a rip at the seams, well then, it's not only a cause for a rebirth, but ah, a feat over the terra firma... and that's where you gracefully stand."*

"What...?" she bluntly shot a reply, turning to a slant.

"They fed you lies, did they not? Made you put your faith in empty vessels under manipulation, knowing they could never be filled. What they were missing is what they wanted from you. Something you cannot give, except... exhibit. Even then, a haunting mirage meets the eyes of a beholder. Nothing to which a being can place a finger on, let alone leave a mark." The low voice explained, *"Let fly the energy within you, Xira. Never give the mercy to ones that aim to hurt, when they are incapable of change. Misdeeds often breed punishments and that is our control, for they want to hurt and we want to punish. Don't mistaken our craft for cruelty, when you have* **that** *plague on the grounds. A new world will only ever be done by us truly. To that, I tell you this... between the Spirit Realm and the Rove Dynasty of the underworld, you are the fusion of the realms, into one free spirit, your own wild being... anyone should know to abandon, lest they witness you... Xira. I wish you had heard this sooner... but I guess it's never too late. Welcome home. Do make yourself comfortable."*

Bringing a cushioned Windsor seat to a floating leaf carpet, Menkos gestured for her to sit by as he went to fetch a surprise while she would wait. Not long after, he had returned with somebody that had accompanied alongside, hidden underneath a draping cloak and holding in their grasp, a golden, four-sided orchid stained glass off of a curled metallic quarterstaff. A part of his profile was revealed as the man stood with the gear, quietly placing down the secured glass on a hovering platform from which he had cast. The two stood side by side, while Menkos reached out in regard and the other shuffled his feet to turn.

"Ophintom. A metamorphosing mage, ritualist, and of course, a loyal dynast," he addressed, glancing towards him, "The one of three in their domicile, wielding beguiling flair and each complimenting the different parts to themselves, making them just as good alone as they are a flock. Never often are they working together, but you can tell, that miles isolated, the tie is there… simply magical."

"Greetings… I am indeed Ophintom… Mage the Third," Ophintom had said, "I knew your parents, they were here awhile, though I was not informed that the mother bore a child, since personally, I was away for the time being and discovered of their departure when I returned. Feriklef… it is why when she brought back that piece… she was very distraught… upon her encounter with *you*. She knows. I assumed it was us alone."

Menkos threw a wary squint before replying, "That means Syphon has this knowledge just as well. This can't be right, I understood that it was to be kept private, for *her* sake."

"We were imparted different things, my good man. Albeit, it could merely be an odd misunderstanding, there are many mysteries beyond magic… *that* I shall avow," spoke Ophintom, concealing the quarterstaff, "Hence, unearthing. *Xira*, correct? Lady Silhouette and Lady Solar— making Lady Solarouette; is what we pinned for a sobriquet, and so, she mentioned you as a hazard during a temperamental breakdown. Besides the evident radiation, my, I'm afraid first mage has overlooked that of which is not visible… I can unravel… grant me the inner key…"

"Erma?" Xira voiced briefly. Menkos darted between the faces, like minding a kettle and an old microwave.

Pushing him back a notch, the two opposed one another as the mage drew to a leave. Mutating into a wraith form, he slithered off and vanished through the crannies. As she looked to the reflecting object, Menkos removed the lid to fish out a sphere of galactic turquoise stone then placing it in front of her, with its illumination crossing paths, he bounced a step to the platform — folding the arms with a nod.

"Would you explain this, dynast?" Questioned Xira, eyeing the core.

He slipped along the walls, where Menkos seated himself in an idle position.

"Go ahead, try it," he told her. "Say, *'the duality of I, fuel to me, cut like a blade, full moon I see'*. Hold it in both and repeat this."

Doing so, she watched as the stone's brightness increased and bringing a swift orbit of its pure essence, revolving around her while the outline of his face came through.

"A phantasmagoria has presented itself," the man remarked, retracting into the space.

Xira kept her attention on the visuals with the background voice narrating by the vapour. The same song that Serenitatem would sing at night, began to play throughout the way. Things she'd heard of before, whether it was from the conversations or special moments in the past, surfaced like a time capsule, giving an incentive to well up the corners of her eyes as she'd seen herself at a younger age, playing blissfully in the grass — gentle and accompanied with what had appeared to be Willow and a few of the former residents sharing a good laugh in a good time. Something which she'd cherished, now felt like a weight that'd sat upon the chest cage, glissading the fine memories of a once upon a great paradise. An image fluttered above the outdoor scene, showing Serenitatem and a dynast disputing in an old, downtown library.

"Silence! Don't tempt my fiend, I have warned of your ridiculous warbles," the stranger frowned.

"Calm down, Syphon. We were just analysing our matter of family. Please, understand my reasons for this…" Serenitatem replied, "If I go through and resolve the interference, I could maintain the gates so that none of the realms fall hostage to the tempestuous reckoning. It's havoc on all doors should you and Erma Merideth attempt those devious plans, which quite frankly, achieve a bare morsel and throws away the balance… there is no ownership of any terrain, of any species, no matter how much contrast the others negate — it is always an open land and that it shall be. Work with me, not against, Syphon. Otherwise, what is now known as our home, becomes that home nevermore."

The dynast huffed, turning his back in the profundity, "I suppose I'll let you know. Erma will definitely have a word to object. Wouldn't hold your breath though, old man, there's but a choice in a burning flame, in its amicable range."

As it fizzled out, the moisture dampening the eye lids dried up into icicles, a thin layer of it breaking off into smithereens along the sides like little snowflakes.

"This is usually in the hands of Syphon, a tool that's proved viable over centuries of descendants," Menkos commented while closing the lid, "An heirloom, in fact."

Standing to compose herself, Xira went down to the other direction, hoping to find an archway.

"Ahem, with the method that you were brought here, you are to be returned the same," he chimed in, "I just want to share with you a token of origins before I send you off."

"Or what?" She asked.

Hooking the glass on the wall, Menkos chuckled, "Let's say… you use the main door, skip through the hedges and on a walk of your dreams. Verbatim. Any nightmare lurking about comes to fruition. With only learning one line… you don't want a bite out of that, now, do you?"

She stood quietly, then walked back towards the opposite cavern. Guided to a stairwell, it'd led to a room below, filled with an old workshop while he tended to a wooden bench.

"Here, take a look at these," said Menkos, cleaning the shelves, "Quite the antique, it helped me out of my darkness, showed a fresh beginning."

The scripts strewn in front of her were of the identical style of the ones in the cottage basement. A theme of wisdom, chaos and zenith. After discovering the details in between, Xira responded.

"Too quick to trust, Menkos. Too quick to abandon the home. You're telling me… *this* is something you go by? No wonder, you're all just nesting dolls. A stranger is no problem to be attached to, whereas the people residing with you have already displayed their deck of cards. I guess I can't blame you. Forgetting your niece in exchange for yourself, for this, was an offer too tempting in order to evade your own pursuers. Choosing a stranger at this point, seemed like your grand escape. Only… I would've been pickier."

Menkos latched onto the bench before he shoved the scripts inside the wooden drawers. A disgusted look graced his presence, teething at his lip among the low tip-tap of a shoe.

"Ever experienced an epiphany?" He then voiced while he chronicled on a blank sheet, "Between every fragment in air, there is a

fine difference of a subjective perspective as well as the clashing...
there's white... there's black... and then the grey interlude. Grey? Can
be any colour. Need I iterate? Point here is, everyone wants to think the
grey is the default. That nothing can come of its opposing ends, be it
either angle... well, it is why the bleakness is where they stay. Without
colour, it stands to wither. Desire the complexity and that's where
evolution begins. Everything becomes what you want it to be and it
couldn't be more raw, than that. Those that falter under the lacklustre,
disappointingly enough are sometimes people that are known to you and
people you have met. It is their choice, however, you can also fray unless
you walk the other way. Suit yourself, make the best for you. Be what
they fear."

As an elevating portal appeared on the charred floor, he stepped to
bow in valediction. Xira's focused and gelid venture to the spot met with
a calm manner as it swept. A voice could be heard clamouring above the
area, when they'd realised Erma was here from her announced entrance.
Not wanting to lure her down, they kept to themselves whilst the portal
operated.

"Be it a solitary run, I will do mine," Xira remarked as she vanished
through.

In the wake of the uproot, a couch cushion fell atop her back as she
saw what had become of the home. Seeing her companion step to a
confrontational impression which rather mirrored her own, softened with
a heavy relief upon reaffirmation.

"Willow... what is this mess?" She asked, getting the couch back
up.

"Mess? What mess?" Willow fired in response, "The only thing I
see is you disappearing! Thin air, like... what even happened? God...
this time 'round it wasn't even a visible structure. It's like the air itself
devoured you whole, then spat you right out — I didn't know *what* to
do... if only I-*no, no. Never mind.*"

Xira circled to sit, giving an empathetic, gentle look towards her, "I
could see it. Here... I'll tell you about it."

With the post meridian sun aiming its rays at their feet, Willow
shifted an inch when discovering the shared details. Inspecting the room
by the makeover she'd bestowed it, an uneasy feeling settled in the
stomach, repentant of her impulsivity.

Revolving in a recoiling manner, Willow sincerely said, "I'm — I'm sorry, this, I shouldn't have done this to your house. Never would I have clearly thought you'd be inside the... their *lair*. Oh, and you're part of that realm? Through your father? It just seems... well... uh—"

"Helical?" Mused Xira, "I understand if you want to take some time apart. After all, getting you involved is not something I think you need. It's better if I'm on this alone."

Willow replied, quite bewildered at that, "Overwhelming... scary... sure. We don't need to separate though, I think we can sail regardless of all of the wild facets... our friendship is not built on the belief of division, because it has never been cut, you and I would leap off the highest mountain before allowing an action like that to be done. Sticking by each other's side, *that's* what makes it worth it. Worth all of the hardships... even if the cost is absolutely everything else. You don't find something like this in an excavation point... the depths are immeasurable, Xi. Please."

As she walked to the front door, kicking aside an old hay basket, Xira then answered, "It's not that we need to. Maybe it'll be a good thing. Go, see your father. Talk some sense to the old man. While you're at it, take these costume pieces too. I'll make sure you know when the ball drops. En garde, my friend."

Willow ran to sway on the door frame while shouting out, "Wait! The keys?"

"You take it. I'm going on a quick visit along the way. See you there soon!" She told her while racing down the littered path walk.

Later that night, the construction lights of the Yard lit up in its sequence, leading to the adjacent speakers that blared through the hissing announcement.

"*Assemble at The Garden, all Yard personnel. The colloquy will take place in time for preparations regarding tonight's event. Do come with your desired sunny-day best. Lieutenant Gyrfalcon, over and out.*"

Pushing through the doors, the entirety of the base floor seemed to barge out of either side, leading the way to the point as Xira merged in the herd with the themed costume overlay covering her. Crowded as it was, it'd been an advantage for such a highly maintained establishment — for everyone that wore a costume carried along their accessories, including the masks being worn. They'd arrived at The Garden, when two representatives waltzed to an elevated podium by a sprinkling fountain. She watched them share a hushed laugh, before lining to the front's edge.

"Evening to our people. This is your Lieutenant Gyrfalcon and with me, is Wing Commander Ruzak — looking relatively dapper, may I remark. A night awaits your groove, in the name of Midnight Dancer in the Jungle, as we've officially stated to name. You probably have heard that the event will take place inside the oldest library on our homeland — the antiquity that we've cordially cherished... and to that, I welcome to declare, Wing Commander Ruzak — if you should so, please..."

"Thank you, ever honourable man. Yes, indeed, the library we know as Greaper Nestle stays to always be our knowledgeable, historical landmark and the respected foundation that helped shape the towns and neighbourhoods within." He resumed to say, "While we gather here for our rides, I would like for you all to remember the holy grail that the Yard has placed to serve and deliver. With that... I sure hope you enjoy these festivities and dance the night away to the moon. We ask for your patience as the transport will arrive shortly — that of course, we will be present at the masquerade ball along with a few of our very own high personnel and a special guest in an alliance. That is all."

The gusts took to glide below the dressings as the misty dusk turned to a dark, frosty atmosphere — with the others in a chatty endeavour and peering out for any oncoming vehicles. Xira walked to the far side, glancing over to spot Willow in the packed area. Although it made for a rather difficult task with everyone wearing individual garments, she kept a close eye for distinct manoeuvres and approaches in the midst of the scarcity of Yard beacons. It wasn't long before a row of grey hybrids pulled around the cobblestone corner, with their black tops reflecting the moon's rays and the underglow from the chassis emphasising the ground beneath. Out stepped the chauffeurs, adjusting the uniforms at the brief salutations. The Lieutenants walked to the first car, then shifted to the crowd behind, motioning towards the other revving engines down the avenue. Each chauffeur stood by the passenger seat in a polite stance while the dispersion began. Ruzak tapped the car's hood when crossing over to the opposite side.

"Ah, I should mention — this row is for the third level personnel at the moment, the second level, first and base will receive the following escorts in the next route of drivers. Catch you all at the ball… *ha, ha,*" The Wing Commander informed right before entering the vehicle.

A fuss sparked throughout the dazzled crowd in their watch on the rest of the four doors being slammed with every drift around the fountain. The splashing of the water fused to the sound of tires scraping along the path, catching a honk of the horn to signal the conga line and made off on their merry way. As the next night hour went by, more and more were sent to a chaperone. Until the last of the last sat waiting, it was only the base floor sector keeping hands out in front for the rides. When they came to, the personnel hurried in grasp of their ensembles while Xira joined in between the mild havoc that was the dive inside. To wishing that Willow had entered one of the few, the whole journey through to the library involved a loud prattle and nothing but a window in view of the outskirts. While it trailed on upon reaching Lunaris Town, it became a snail drive as the cars tackled the streets curling in direction to the open road. A tavern brightened up its carnival glass windows while a shimmering effect waved among the ground to its neighbouring restaurants, neon hotel and parlour signs and a funky, tropical smoothie bar. Xira watched the buildings roll by, the town's gaiety gracing the frost of the car's side, then contrasting the alley ways that were spotted between every mere gap, a tangible yen painting her with the area inside and out — people that wandered were engaged in the friendly aura and in the midst of their car driving around, the town's reflection warped into the far edge of the door and gently shifted to the main exit, as the scenery became more distant on the drive forth. It'd seemed like a ship's voyage until they'd arrived at the old Greaper Nestle library. Once they'd stepped foot onto the gravel scattered towards the entrance, the tall structure loomed over the herd of vehicles parked on both sides — a tiny bit of moonlight bouncing off of the surface. Within the opening, the balladic music roared to the groups of people walking along the carpet that then led to the main hall. The way through had already been propped to two cubes adorned with accessory gifts.

"Welcome to tonight's grand event," the speaker on the microphone began to say.

"With honour," chimed in the other beside them.

"The Midnight Dancer in the Jungle, Yowndrift Yard's own Masquerade Ball!" He announced, followed by a cheering applause from the guests, "Therefore, I would like to now present to you, our prime party organisers... Wing Commander Ruzak, Lieutenant Gyrfalcon and their particular associate, Miss Erma! Please give them your warm gratitude!"

A flurry of hands clapping across the ball room resonated with the background music that played symphonically, for the height of the skylight beamed down the elegant chandelier as its ornate gems created a stellar effect through the atmosphere. Ruzak stepped to the microphone stand, his mask resembling that of an emerald peacock and a dressing to match — its outer layer dragging on the stage rug. The lighting quickly turned to a spotlight sequence, where it radiated what graced the surroundings, as the wing commander's suit design shone with all others.

"Enjoy your celebrations, hear, hear. There will be exquisite food and drinks, accompanied by various performers that will attend later on, music oh plenty that will also fill the theme," his voice soothed lowly, "To that, dance to the rhythm and make the floor your partner in crime tonight. Here's to the Yard's horizons and say I to thee... dwell in the question and it shall mirror inception..."

"Hurrah!" Gyrfalcon added in before the three waved down the steps and into the shadows of the library's back end. Xira saw them seat themselves at an assigned refectory table, who were then joined by some of the personnel, huddling the sides.

"Care for a shrimp, miss?" A waiter asked her, holding a tray of cupped treats whipped with icing and a lime piece placed atop. She refused the offer and walked towards the staircase that led to the second-floor balcony, before leaning on the bar to observe the area. Noticing the twin staircase on the opposition, there were a lot of the members wandering about, almost as if aimlessly if not on for dancing alone or with another. Every few compositions, the style of the floor would alter in the theme's colours, forming layout patterns to best suit and provide a meticulous jungle experience. With the way that this had appeared as a celebratory wonder in an illusion of unity, embracing a belief with another meaning each time like it was implied for something peculiar residing beneath the camouflage, no number of sly wares could wager a capsize. It was entirely conspicuous to Xira, who didn't need to gaze any further to scent an ominosity was afoot.

"A cherry for your thoughts?" Said a person carrying the rims of a victorian-esque costume, then joined next to her.

Xira shifted a quick glance before replying, "Not enough trees for that."

The member chuckled, plucking a cherry with their mouth, "My name's Maxwell. Figured myself the loner type, until I averred, my, *that* person knows the best spots. Tell me, what sector did you find yourself in?"

She observed the dancers below, then answered, "New recruit, in the labs — I, uh, work the forensics department."

"Oh, goody! Fresh meat… *ha, ha, hah*, pardon my folly, I personally am in the chemical labs," said Maxwell, finishing the cherries, "I may've, mm, had a drink or two, but I vow it was mostly fruity. Okay. Joining the dance floor or what? I could use a cool swing of the hips."

"Go on, I'll come by later," Xira told them, "Know where the tables are being arranged for the base personnel?"

Maxwell then flung aside playfully, "Suit yourself! The tables will be announced, as for the cha-cha down there? It awaits me! Pleasure meetin' ya!"

Watching them descend the velveteen carpet, a conga line began to form around the tiled floor, its design and effects vividly seen from above. Like a pirouette that of a crystallice, the crowd immersed themselves in the music, engaging the main floor as a flare of green and orange spheres graced the dancers. The tapping of a microphone etched through its nearby speakers as a host took to the stage right under her position.

"Yes! Yes! Free yourselves in the rhythm, let the songs take you to the jungle," the man uttered with joy, "You hear that? The night is singing to you and you will do a daring duet under the light of the moon, between the rustling of the monstera leaves and the soil beneath the tip-tapping feet…"

The performers took to the stage, frolicking in their positions before vocals weaved in the air.

"A one… a two… Listen to the music in the air…
Settle down, they say, find somebody, make a pair
Always in question, hair oh so fair,
Humble as they turn, not wanting to care…" As if the towns were as one, all present, in freedom and the groove, the people whirled about

many forms of dance moves on a floor of costumes and flailing fragments of garments along a mesmerising, colourful sequence.

"They desire the dance, all fancy in trance,
Hand in hand, what is seen, they don't understand,
The light they like to see shine, but the ground they forget
Where the shadows come in place, oh a graceful silhouette… "

A place of no trouble, where all the chaos was forgotten, now placed a sweet moment of bliss. By their cheers of utter joy, the old library flourished this night of dance and music… creating a vibrancy so comfortably invariant and yet so delicate.

One of the singers approached the front microphone, tapping when they declared, "Our next song will ask of *foot-on-foot* frenzy. Get ready for Funky Jungle! Enjoy…"

"Put a hand on ya' hip and the other blow a kiss,
Do a, do a, do a twist, in the funky jungle…
Smell that green leaf right between ya' teeth,
In the jungle we play, by night, by day
The spotlight is on me,
Careful of snakes and rats slithering your feet…
By the grass on the dirt, grows the seed
That was planted for a tall, funky tree!"

With the song booming in the area, all members across the dance floor jumped to the rhythm and expressed an enthusiastic connection to its design, like the ball room oozed as the sole place they knew. Like it was the only place that *was.*

"And now," said another vocalist, merrily, "Bring forth… *The Belle of The Ball!* Hear! Hear!"

"The swing of the doors,
Aim forth, forevermore…
A sound of a whisper,
Creeps down the very hall…
Music then plays, in the distance,
Where gowns and shadows come to dance,
It leaves everyone entranced,
Like the masks and gloves on their hands… "

Xira watched the bustling crowd in the midst of chewing a lime and then tossed its remainders inside an empty cup, once filled with fruit juice.

"Do you hear that step of a hidden grace?

Feel the lure of the wild, here comes her soul…"

They twirled and leaped, by the feeling of the music, in an elegant poise and with its gliding guise made every member be as entranced as the dedicated next.

"The Belle of the Ball…

Hmm…

The Belle of the Ball…

Oh, a sweet rhythm she sings…"

While the delighted vocalists cruised around the stage, their instrumentalists were shone a spotlight among them and with each turn of a singer down the stairway, other twinkling lights followed.

"There's a ring, don't forget, you're the guest

What's lost can always be forgiven,

In the dark the dance, of magic and trance,

A bird has left their nest this season…

The Belle of the Ball,

Hmm, the elegance of a twirl,

Oh… the dancing feet brace the world."

A moment of an instrumental intermission was then introduced, highlighting the individual layers and elements of the song, to its musical fusion that which then returned to be sung again.

The Belle of the Ball,

Hmm…

Oh, shines through the light of the

Darkest night,

The… Belle… of the Ball…"

Loud as it played, she eyed each point of the room throughout the embrace that filled all floors. Although the groove shifted to an allied waltz, its brimming footsteps and sound made for a shimmy exit towards the opened halls. The dancers tried to lure her in for a round but were rushed past in a waved hurry on out. *As if,* she thought, *excuse me.*

As they continued to sway back and forth, Xira went on to explore, covering all details of the area. Notably, the high personnel and their associates were also on a roam, with a distinct Yard badge identifying each one. To the drinks table, she fetched herself a lemonade before another member approached from behind.

"A chalice of prune wine, with ice?" A woman's voice emitted through.

Within the drinking motion, the lemonade spritzed into the glass as Xira perceived this member's tone — uncanny coincidence.

"I think you've mistaken me for somebody else," she responded, pointing to the jug machine, "The selection is all there."

In a quiet chuckling demeanour, the member then added, "Uha... so I see. I'd suggest you meet with the Lieutenants for a brief sermon they're holding. It's in regards to the seat allocations. You shall find them in the Constellation Room."

After Xira walked towards an arch ahead, she had entered the next hall that led to a various number of refurbished rooms. *There it is,* she thought, finding the Constellation Room in the far end of a right turn through. Inside, quite in fact the Lieutenants had gathered themselves around an antique desk filled with what she assumed were their devoted allies. Politely announcing herself to question the rattled beings, they hovered at the front, taking to a bow in respectful concord.

"I heard this is where a sermon was being held?" she asked.

Instead of a quick apprising, the members exchanged looks before one of them stepped forward.

"Come with me," he gestured, going behind a concealed door, "Right this way, now."

In the nook of the four-walled space was a placement of wooden chairs beside a chalkboard marked with citations, presumably by a member. Some of those chairs had people miming to each other, before she was given a seat to use herself. The personnel proceeded to the exit, leaving them with a vague reply.

"An operator will tend to you all shortly, your patience is very much requested."

The person beside her nudged an elbow, in means for a private discussion.

"Psst... doesn't this seem fishy or what," he whispered, eyeing the only door out, "I was pulled out of a laugh fest, simply for I don't even know... my partner was left with an entree, I only hope it'll suffice to comfort."

Another dressed member leaned to add, "Hey, I thought the same.

Something just doesn't quite make sense to me here. A sermon? For just the group of us? Even if they bring in more, where will we all fit? Unless this *isn't* the room where it takes place."

"Come on, you don't honestly think our own high personnel would mess us around like that?" Asked the guy beside them.

The puzzled man next to her answered promptly, "Whatever it is that they are planning, I'm not staying for it. If you're with me, we can figure a way out. This is a party. *Everyone* should be involved in such a thing. As a matter of theory, I overheard two guys talking amongst themselves not too long ago, while I was waiting for a bathroom stall. They claimed that a weird discussion happened between the *high hounds*. It didn't sound pretty. A job is a job, yes, but it is *not* worth walking the hawser for."

The slam of the other door cut in the seconds of silence, then they knew the room was in the clear. A man stood up to check while the rest stayed close by. All seven of them creeped down the carpet lane and towards the golden knob.

"Okay, tail end — watch the back, front — watch the right," the man leaving first whispered the plan, "Spot anybody with a badge and you whistle — wait."

A member was making their way through the hall, wheeling a cart with them to the room. The group hid behind separate plant vase pillars along the path, just evading their line of view.

"That must be the operator," said one of the others, "I talked to someone carrying that type of thing earlier. Let's hurry, hey."

While navigating the entirety of the main floor, the doorways to many of the places had been a mystery to the group as they jogged forth towards the end of the building. Apart from the dent in the wall, there was no indication of an outdoor exit when Xira ran to take a closer look at some cracks in the interior. Sliding her hand on the wallpaper, it had sunk into a mechanism within, activating a hidden passage with an odd wooden ring.

"I wonder where this goes. Look, you can spin it," she told the members, feeling its rims, "It may be a puzzle. No doubt there is a secret room right behind."

The person keeping look-out introduced herself as Rosetta, then joined forward to explain, "Can I help? If I recall correctly, these five portions are the library's historical relics. Each holds a significant period where a commemoration occurred and I think its order could be that — from the old beginning to the end."

Upon doing so, they'd revealed an opening to what consisted of cupboards and couches stacked by the side. A staircase was seen past an arch in the narrow way, before a member called out in a thrill, "We can go down here, it's dark but uh, it might be a—"

"Ohoho! What is this?" Another man chimed in, as he took to yank down a lever he'd had his grip on nearby, launching everyone on a slide ride to the bottom floor — rolling in an obscured area. The muffled complaints suggested their different methods barely intertwining halfway.

A slightly disgruntled member didn't resist the urge to speak up, "Good going Sam, we just got ourselves in a deeper mess. Now where?"

After wandering through to find anything that could help the team escape, the man who called himself Ilari had luckily located and turned on the fuse box, illuminating the grounds. Now they could come to uncover just exactly what was being kept here all along. Besides the general library equipment and gear, Rosetta fished out rusty documents encompassing detailed layers of the building's blueprints. Adding to that, Ilari immediately brought up a weary box to the same table where she had been — clearing its lid before exclaiming a dulcet reaction.

"Remarkable," he said, rummaging the particles, "These look like things a wizard would use. Check it out, here's a wand... a cipher wheel, some kind of metal tube, a pouch of — ooh — beads? Then there's a bottle... and this... locket."

As Xira walked up to him, she inspected the objects and recognised the locket from time ago, "Does it say who it belongs to? The locket?"

The man shrugged, handing it over to her for he had claimed to be clueless about it. Inside the left metal frame, a creased image of the grand launch day of the library was firmly placed and next to it, the information of its construction and design in print. She noticed the right piece to be a little loose, unlike its predecessor. Removing the tiny fragment, a message was carved on the metallic base with the works of a lapidarist.

"To my wonderful baby daughter," Xira read, "... — *Love, Mother.*"

Just when the occasional snaps of the ceiling bulbs cut out to a backup power engine, the floor remained the only source of direction —

outlining the edges to the opposing way out, which was through a webbed corridor. They hurried to evacuate and taking the items with them too, they'd agreed to share who would carry what, as it'd led the team to a completely different hall of the library's first floor. *Good,* Xira thought.

Sam spun to add in quietly, "No way they can find us now! I'll use my brother's name if I have to!"

Peering over the path's balustrade, Ilari remarked in revelation, "Lo and behold… they sure are not sparing any moment. Let's just get to the main ball room and fuse in from there. Best bet is we lose their pursuit. Advice: don't care about the latter factor. Peace of mind."

Underneath the byzantium mask, Xira looked at her new-found ally before walking onward the hall's carpet. Trailing close behind, the team then nodded at one another as they signal bumped to break the routes with each bearing a personally chosen item — the pearly locket being clutched in her gloved hands. Soon after arriving back at the ball, the dancers were twirling to and fro in immaculate rhythm with the wild instrumentals that played. Noticing a vacant seat by a water cooler, Xira took to a sip and sat by, watching the astir crowd intently…

The song came to a finish and on the stage, appeared a badged personnel, tapping the microphone, "Attention, this is your Wing Commander Ruzak delivering news. We will escort you to the library's theatre where you will be provided luxurious dinner and *ha, ha, ha,* a movie made by us truly. Once two more tracks embrace your ears, Sir Gyrfalcon should lead the way — off with the dancing then, *do* enjoy yourselves."

The plenty amount of people that idled about in their snacks, beverages and loud chattering, didn't appear to take into account that without question, such a glamorous event was held in a desperate time of today's occurrences. Xira pondered on the possibility that it could've certainly just been a fulfilled desire, however, due to her burning instinct, it was most definitely a lean towards the deep end. Hungry sharks only yet to be fed. She walked on through the tall pillars, curling around the structures and to the far end where the high members resided. With only two still in their seats, she slid over to a confectionery cascade in an attempt to listen among their conversations. Besides the simple exchange of event topics, not much slipped through the teeth apart from then knowing who the two sitting together were — the Lieutenant Forest and another Lieutenant by the name Paris. It sounded like they knew each other well, by the assumption of using their first names rather frequently. The next song blared off the speakers as the others returned to their seats, rather flushed and in annoyance. Xira stayed close to the snacks, her ears recoiling to their grumbles. Ruzak bickered on about how *the scoundrels* could just leave and mentioned briefly the appointed operator that was to interfere. While Gyrfalcon attempted to settle down the situation, suggesting that there were to be *backup plans,* a host had stood to speak — rounding the crowd to a unified dance.

"Didn't I tell you to visit the high personnel?" A woman standing at the backside said to her.

Xira greeted the inquisitor, marshmallows in hand, "I went — they dismissed me after we had a talk, that it was just a matter of misunderstanding. How did you know that was me?"

In a scoffing grunt, she tended to the stand and picked a ladle as Xira began to walk off, "Well, I recognise that bedazzled purple mask from a world away. Do me a favour and send my regards, the table over there — Erma wishes to be of assistance and that *she* simply means the best."

A plump marshmallow in Xira's hand came to burn at the tips. She then uttered a composed reply beside the brief silence, "You're Erma? Guess I could lend a hand... ma'am."

With a pleased smile, she turned to the bowl, hearing the dimming footsteps leave the area.

Once the announcer declared for the guests to waltz to the theatre, Xira quickly jumped the stairs in reach of the balcony through a pair of beige doors. The emptiness of the hall to the adjacent room made for a nice, quiet vantage point. As everyone was guided to sit on the given tables, all of the badged personnel walked the grand stage with the spotlights focusing on their presence. Although it was still difficult to spot Willow, she kept as concealed as possible while the event carried on. Among the rounds of applause following each person's speech, there was no doubt that many if not most of these members were easily enticed, without even a try in the hands of a mage and to think what would happen so then. The screen stretched to the curtains that pulled in a pinch, as the room's power adjusted to the theatrical mode on which a lens' flicker played a film reel. All the recording displayed was, in her eyes, a sifter to everything that was going on behind the scenes, secrets to which camouflaged as a plan for a better world and walls of haunting mirrors for a means of getting every being on the claws of the handlers. Thinking that that had sufficed to maintain a distraction, the portière was flung out by Xira as she headed towards the Constellation Room — figuring it may contain the final key to full dismantlement. To her fortune, the knob had been left unlocked. Inside, the empty cocoon oozed of a particular odour that was detected in the facility's underground. *Hmm, they must've wiped out clean,* she thought, *wait — what's this?* Sticking out of a drawer beyond the centrepiece desk, a loose folded piece crumpled in the partially opened component.

"A nightmare that is realised," she remarked, "…"

INDENTATION OF THE CAPRICE — CONSORT DISCUSSION

ATTENDEES: WING COMMANDER RUZAK, LIEUTENANT GYRFALCON,

ASSOCIATE MRS ERMA, LEVEL 2 AND 3 MEMBERS; IN TOTAL 5.

SUBJECT AND CONCLUSION: UNKNOWN MECHANISM TO ADOPT,

DATA FROM MRS ERMA TO BE ANALYSED. TRIALS OF THE CONVERGENCE.

DECODE THE UNEARTHED CYPHER WHEEL. LAUNCH THE PITCH: PROJECT.

A NEW WORLD MANOEUVRED AND DESIGNED BY THE YARD. END. -

OBSTACLES: MAINTAINED — OTHER? UNKNOWN. SURVEILLANCE. HIGH

SECURITY IN POSITION. LOCKDOWN TO INITIATE. THIRD DEGREE MEASURES

PLACED. BACKUP SYSTEMS ARE GO. OUTSIDE FORCES IN CHECK. SUB STATIONS

ARE MANAGED. INTEL TO UPDATE — PERSONNEL IN MAIN OFFICE.

NOTES: BACKUP KEY FOR CIPHER MOLDED. ADMINISTERED BY MEMBERS. MAIN

KEY WITH WC-RUZAK. LOW PROFILE: SUCCESS.

"I don't think they understand the consequences," Xira muttered under breath, "This puts everyone in a hellzone. A snowballing pitfall. For what?"

Searching through, indeed there was a sun-shaped key wedged into the wood, beneath scrumples of papers clipped on the points. Overhearing the thriving swarm returning to the main hall, she snatched the key and slipped out the exit. Minding the sides, a clear route through the library's second floor led to an open space where majority of the bookcases and shelves were kept. Between a horde of tables, couches and ladders, resided an emblematic structure within its antique curtain wall design, resembling a serrated gear ring in the frame's shape of an eye. Since it was the time of night, the outdoor light could be seen bouncing off the metallic glaze, shimmering through the old parquet floor. In wonder, Xira watched as the glow outlined the rail and all across the sandstorm window panels. She walked on quietly and examined the surroundings — rows and rows of untouched books abandoned along the cases. The smell hinted of no visitors having tended to the furniture in a rather long while. The main front desk still had its shell lamp on the top end — scuffed and moderately dusty. As the oncoming footsteps averted the current tracks, she dashed around the closest bookcase and peered its corner to witness a group of members scaling their way to the upper floor. Once they halted at the open section, they formed a ring between the furnished sides, opposing one another.

"Then Sir, what do *you* propose we tackle next? Since, apparently, my concept of fundamental eradication deviated from your radar," said a man's voice, whose identity soon later was caught on.

The other shot out a laugh before replying, "My... certainly you know the operator was sent for business. Of course, he doesn't accomplish the task. The room was tampered with — alas, it's irresponsible to narrow down to *that* group of members when there is a hall of them! Ha! Stepped right into that one, now, didn't we my good man? Madam? Eh?"

That's when Ruzak cut in hoarsely, "It doesn't matter, Lieutenant Gyrfalcon, we shall tend to these actions by control. Not allow some pesky illusions wither the plans that are made. The cipher wheel is missing and without it is Plan B. So what if they're rascals, they're *missing* rascals and that is double the trouble, Lieutenant. We need to find that cipher! Commander reasserted that it will work. Long as we work together, nothing and no one will stand in the path, lest they fall to their fate… it is just another anthropoid case, no?"

"Heed, gentlemen," Erma's tone shattered the air particles, feeling like sparking sand, "We need a clear conscience in order for this to be triumphant. With a clear conscience… comes the devastating abrasion. It will be triumphant, but we cannot sympathise for those who do not stand with us. A pure sacrifice is yet a treat for our lor — I mean, the Yard's evolution. To be done, men, be done for always."

Xira's disgust lingered by, in her efforts of keeping quiet while they finished up the discussion. When she thought they were to leave, the two men provoked a dual argument whereas Erma began to tread off the way as if to look about and avoid involvement. Although she was ready at the feet to change spots, Xira noticed something odd about her movements, how she wreathed by the old tables and switched the corner glance to the other point, edging a bit closer each time she reappeared. *Not taking this sly chance,* Xira's thought barged as she jumped the next desk to the farthest aisle. The Wing Commander's voice resonated in the space.

"A trivial hindrance, Mrs Erma?" He questioned.

There was a pause, before she spun their way and said, "It must've been a mouse. It is known for them to lurk in forsaken buildings. Never mind…"

The ambience returned to its hushed quality, as Xira spied again to find the trio descending the staircase. She went on to explore the main desk when she found a key card dropped at her feet.

"*Mrs Erma… Access Yard Card,*" she muttered, "Hmm, finders' keepers."

Throughout the extravaganza of the ball, many members were still lighting up the dance floor and many more had retracted to their assigned tables, feasting on the chef's gourmet delicacy. Xira marched towards the exit just as a waiter hurried to meet her.

"Apologies, I'm afraid orders are that members are to be inside the building at all times. Please, go enjoy the evening," they had said.

"I need some fresh air," she answered, seeing the tray of alcohol, "One too many drinks."

The waiter halted with the available arm, "That's not my decision, I can advise to take this up with the Wing Commander — he's in charge of the departures."

In an exhaling manner, Xira walked back to the jaunty ball room. Focusing on the different routes, she clashed with another wandering guest and both tipped in each other's grip.

"Oh, I'm so sorry! That's on me, I was watching the chandelier," they told her, fixing up their yellow bow.

"No, no, it's — I too was—"

"**Wait**—" They exclaimed simultaneously.

The two stood by in their masquerade ensembles, like the surroundings had all grown quiet.

"Xixi?"

"It is you… is it? Well damn," Xira responded.

"Oh goodness, you are all right!" With a spring in her step, Willow fell into a hug and held her for a little while.

Xira grabbed by the companion's arm and lead on to a rococo bench in the hall.

"You were right. I feel terrible for leaving you like that," she explained, clutching the locket within the sleeve, "If it kept you safe… then I've done my faithful part."

Patting down the cushion, Willow uttered endearingly, "Being alone, I don't prefer it. Despite all that, I don't blame you though. Yes, I met with my father. I found out a lot of things, but at what cost… I knew you were coming here and I still felt inside of me, that, that feeling… of being torn apart because of what has become of this place and where it is going."

Some of the guests tramped along the way, seeming to be lining for the rest room on the opposite end — their loud chatters booming through the air space. Xira slouched downward to maintain the private conversation and motioned ahead to the route pointing out the high personnel's table.

"That's where the five dumbbells are seated," she said, "Nice and convenient by the snack stands. Perfect position to spill your guts to your delight… or keep them hidden if that's the choice."

Willow squinted at the guests as something stirred a recent memory, "I sure am glad they provided a bus. Oh — get this, that specialist Nathara, comes in just as I worked up the confidence to approach him — so I had to improvise and I thought, what would you do? Then—"

"Wait a minute," Xira intervened, "You got in trouble? You *were* in trouble?"

"Not really, believe me," she added, "My father handles a uniform compartment for the higher levels in the facility — so I, kind of, uh... *borrowed* a Yarak's uniform..."

A grin painted the surface as Xira marvelled proudly, "That's my rocking girl."

Her companion chuckled, then resumed to say, "And in honest thought, it was actually comfortable. Anyway, once she left, he kicked out the remainder of his support squad that he had called up then... which made him be on his own, until I introduced myself and that's when it went in a completely other way than I had anticipated."

As they shared everything that had happened while they were apart, the night became of a soothing time with the gratifying background music as the masquerade was reaching its concluding period and the high members were already taking to the stage for the wrap-up announcement. Like ducks in a row, they spoke in turns and how the transport would already be waiting outside.

"And so," continued the wing commander, "You should eat as much as you can fit, drink as much as you can spill and we will sound the Yard Alarm when we are to leave. Treat this as a buffet, if you will. Be my guest."

The personnel walked off the stage and disappeared into a door on the right, including both Lieutenant Forest and Paris. The members rallied up again on the floor, working the dance moves to the playlist that blared out the tall speakers. Xira thought it was best to navigate more of the place while they were preoccupied, in hopes of uncovering things that could help. The pair set on towards the curve, calculating the different rooms on each side and roughly checking for potential access. Landing the door down a few after, they were met with a clamouring screech as a huddle on the carpet spun in angst, their masks no longer on the members' faces.

"My name is Sam! Not Sam!" Said one person sitting up.

"Shh! Don't you say it!" Whispered another loudly.

"They're not badged, Ilari. Look," Sam motioned towards them.

Xira entered inside as she then knew they were the members from before, "I was with you when we found that hidden room. I carried the locket."

A surprising relief waved across the group and Rosetta stood to bring them in and barricade the door with a chair.

"We were *not* ready if that were to be the high personnel," Rosetta remarked, introducing the two to their brief scheming, "There is a piece of evidence that suggests we all were right, that it was an odd assembly of just... us. Definitely proves right here, on these blueprints. If it wasn't for their marking over the areas, we wouldn't have known for sure. Then again, I'm sure we wouldn't have followed in like some sheep."

Along the pages were simply the outlines of the library's layout and layers of its three elaborate floors. In red ink, a particular location written as *"Cellar"* was now replaced with *"Restoration"* and underlined beside it was a tiny notation; *"For any strays — WCR"*. Ilari traced a frame drawn to an exit.

"This is our spontaneous exit should things go off plan," he went on to say, "It seems easy so far. Get in, checkmark the highlights and get out. From the sound of it, there could very well be more of us in there. No way did we ever think they would do us wrong like this, but with the way the organisation has been operating lately... I wouldn't put it past them, quite frankly, they don't really seem to care about *unifying*. It's all for the top man. An error if I consider muttering his name."

Xira pulled the front sheet and eyed the group, then said, "Let's go down there now. The ball is ending soon and we don't have a spare to take that luck."

One of the other members declared their name as Saffron, who asked, "May we know what to call you both? In case we need to... I do respect your privacy, mind you, albeit I think it would be a solemn favour."

"That's all right, Saffron. You can call me... wait, one second," Xira voiced in a quiet tone, grabbing the marker atop the items, "Here. *That's* hers and that's mine. I don't know if these walls are exactly too secure."

Rotating to read the writing, Sam added in, "So... is that... as in *Ex..x... ee...?* Or..."

"*Zee*. That's fine on its own too, though in full — *Zi* — yeah," she explained momentarily, "Good to go?"

Before they left, the remainder of the team wrote down their name below theirs, stating that at first, they weren't quite decisive if it was needed but the others reassured the confidence of the member known to be Fiske.

"It's nice to know we're on the same page," he told them.

Rosetta opened the front and gestured to the hall, "Okay, everybody has everything? Yes? Right this way."

After following the directions on the map and finding a vault-like door on the library's ground floor, they paused to inspect its mechanism. Even though Sam claimed it was just a wheel, Ilari had another notion to turn the points. As a result, it activated its gears for it to be rotated to meet with the carved arrow symbol above it. Clicking in the steel, the door granted their access and revealed a path through an area that split in two alternate destinations — Rosetta suggested they part in half and cover all sections in what she claimed it to be the Restoration area. There were voices heard as Xira walked through with Willow and Ilari, who tried to figure out where it had originated from — then in fact, they discovered little wooden doors used for storing the recycled paper after it was all made, attached with padlocks that could only open with whoever had the keys. They crouched in a low manner to discern if there were hostages inside, when the bellow of a betrayed man and woman banged by the side.

"Hello? Can you tell us what happened?" Ilari called in, waiting for an answer.

It was a moment before the muffled cries became clear as they each replied, "Cuffed to this bar, we are. Please, help us, get us out of here, we don't know why they would do this sort of thing—"

"The cuffs are quite short, you hear! There's no means of reaching over this door... oh for Pete's sake! What a—"

"I'm sorry," Xira spoke up, feeling along the wooden surface, "They've placed padlocks on the entire row. Did you see who they were?"

The pair of members cried out in sorrow and the man next door to them said, "A few of 'em, wearing their masks. Don't know much else... sure as hell were high personnel. I've named it a betrayal. Go figure..."

The three went on to examine the back before letting all the hostages know that they were to do something about it, even if it simply meant as an attempt — they wouldn't allow this on their watch. While Willow stayed to question every member and find out any new intel, Xira had located another room revamped as a work station for the wing commander and the lieutenants. With minimal equipment brought in to suffice for their hidden plans, it came to look just like a smaller version of one of their laboratories. She sent Ilari to keep lookout as she searched throughout the clues involving what the Yard was up to here. The buzz of the electricity zapped along planted cables and flashed a spark near a low granary that surrounded the chained members in the coops. Ilari swung around from time to time, startled by distant noises of inebriated people. He fiddled with the cipher he kept beneath the garment.

"Anything?" He called out.

Xira tapped on the machinery keys and answered, "It looks like a device for altering subjects. Says it was made for Yard objects but… man… this is unbelievable. They really went the extra mile… desperate bastards…"

Running back, Ilari joined to check out the equipment himself for he admitted to a sick feeling in his gut and that this wasn't the Yard he knew.

"I've worked with them for years," Ilari began, "All that time spent giving and giving, to then be working *for* them. You know… there is a difference. Now that I see it — now, it's like the oddity makes sense. It wasn't a dream job or a place of purpose. An illusion, it was. The magic trick was there, we were just fooled — rabbits out of a hat."

The opening of a door cut their focus abruptly when they felt a draught rush past the dust. A single glance they exchanged was then pulled back again once hearing Rosetta ringing out a shout. The two rushed to their location to discover two of the lieutenants confronting the others who stood feet away. Willow quickly followed after catching on the commotion.

"Hey! Leave them alone!" Said Ilari ardently.

Lieutenant Forest revolved to greet him, a slim smile gracing his face, "More of you? Splendid. If you should just tell me upfront, what is your agenda prying down in the cellar?"

"We can ask you the same thing," Xira urged.

"What's up with that station? Why do you have us under tabs?" Ilari grew impatient, watching the lieutenants feast on his boiling disappointment.

With the motion of Forest's hand, he insisted on a civil concord for the sake of the event, "Gentlemen… ladies… I may not know who you all exactly are beneath those suit and ties. I can surely state that you must be lost, therefore, put your faith in my palms. Let me show you the right choice to make — like you've done when you first joined us."

Saffron shot up from behind as Rosetta placed herself to maintain distance, "Choice, sir? You kind of ripped that out from us already!"

Rather bewildered at what to do then, the lieutenants held their position like a game of keep away. Although it was quiet and the team waited on their next move, a scraping against timber wood captured everyone's attention and the malodour which reinstated full focus. Seeing the floor succumbing to a roaring flame, the team jumped at the thought of the hostages in the path. The fire was extending to all the halls before they could lend a rescue. As Xira jogged over to look at the waves of sinopia red, she perceived the loud weeping of the last row of members banging the chains to the walls. Her breaths sunk into the vapour and she could just barely make out the fore of the locked coops — the heat creeping along to the banging on metal bars.

Faintly, a member's words pierced through towards the team, "Help! Here! — Third stall! Olivia Jane! — *Pleeease!*"

They stood back in evasion of the fire when Rosetta then hurled in, "Olivia! Shit! Oh, shit! OLIVIA! No-ooh!"

The lieutenants had reached the exit, the slamming of the door indicating so, with little regard of what will be the remains of the cellar and ones within. Sam and Fiske both held on Rosetta to keep her from going in the smoke, as the view was becoming more obscured and torn. Her tears and cries almost synchronising with the effects of the disaster, muffling to the sparking tone of crackling fragments throughout. It soon arrived at their feet, when Willow headed for the vault door — found locked over by the personnel. She could feel the oncoming heat, as Xira ran up to find an alternate escape. An added hindrance that was the case of the door, was that it did not contain an indoor niche to activate its gears and no other objects beside it. Feeling a nudge in her leg, Willow noticed a darting reflex pushing the knee upward, tickling underneath the ensemble. A swift, uncontrolled kick caused a dent in the bottom end of the surface.

"Ah?" She uttered in her surprise.

Twice it had left a larger bend in the steel and she figured there to be a single chance in this to actually work. Kicking in each time, the door begun to curve at the height of her boot print. As the fire arched closer with the rest of the team stumbling backwards in a heavy haul, Willow stayed persistent to slam it open when her companion came through behind her.

"What are you doing? Holy—" Xira exclaimed. "It's about to come off!"

With a few booming kicks, the wreathing effusion of the fumes pushed through like a cannon with the door launching against a break room wall in the hallway and along tumbled the team over the floor — the last of the flames flushing out the craggy gape in the entrance. They laid across the carpet, bruised and battered from the fall. Clearing her throat, Xira watched Willow's foot of the dress turn to ashes, its particles then vanishing on the fabric and then towards the way, Rosetta, in the arms of Ilari — wailing among her pleadings to Olivia, the grieving weight turning the voice to pure soul-pouring. In the background, she could discern the gentle words of Sam and Fiske — as they huddled around her in a weary crawl.

Saffron pulled at Xira's sleeve, then asked in a gruff tone, "That, what just happened? How did we — even…"

Getting up then to stand, Xira answered calmly, "Let's get out of here. We can't help those inside… left there, ugh… will you help me bring us outside? Make sure they don't stay behind. Nobody."

Over to the main hall, an empty room awaited them as the two waiters standing between each side hurried along in tendance. Willow sat down by the cushioned chairs with the others while Xira talked to a host that was cleaning up.

"Did they leave?" She asked, eyeing towards the main exit.

The host let out a laugh, then told her, "I believe the cavalry is right outside. They're just arranging the transportations. Go on, hopefully you were in the fun house tonight."

She went on to the entrance and there they were, the rows of cars lined up once again and all the members crowding the vicinity. Xira turned to the view of the hosts helping the team with a refreshment, before meeting up with her by the gates — together, they were escorted to their given cars without question. The old library soon appeared like a smoking chimney painting when the driver set off in the miles, its marine colour sifting through the darkened landscape and with only the headlights bouncing off the road. A quiet drive it was, for the most part, besides the telecoms on the dashboard. Ilari leaned by the window, fidgeting with the cipher.

"Was Olivia a close friend?" Asked Xira, looking back.

Saffron turned around on the passenger seat and replied, "She was her sister. They signed to the Yard a long time ago. I remember meeting them both the day they arrived. It's such a shame."

Lifting the device to gain some light, Ilari then added, "Who knows… they could still be down there, waiting on a rescue. If I figure this thing out, maybe I could go there to help them — that is, unless, the others find us out."

"Did you not see it? Were you not there?" Slightly irritated, Saffron voiced, "At least a faction of us were held against their own will. Probably failed their experiments and were marked as disposable. Oh, it is nauseating… it's been my workplace for years."

"From the looks of it, I wouldn't second guess it," remarked Xira, sitting back.

The car's wheels swerved on the road's glazed surface, a momentary plunge on the gravel as the three shot up towards the windscreen. A radio call dialled to the chauffeur. Next to her, Willow rotated from a brief nap, who also was now listening in to the transmission.

"Contact. This is Lieutenant Forest. There's been reports of a turbulent road ahead. Watch your lanes and call if you—"

In the attention to the lieutenant's intel, a sudden collision between the vehicles occurred along the two-way route as they were overturned mid-air, a fiery eruption hurling from underneath — then crash landing across the grasslands into an aura of the amber filled night. On the soil, Xira coughed up the parched air, seeing the impacted surroundings be encrusted with the large fragments — a vague view of the nearby destruction rippling in the flames. She could discern other voices attempting to catch their breaths amidst crawling to a safe area. Although many of the members appeared to be leaving at a steady pace, the engulfment had them overwhelmed, making for a difficult navigation between the heavy lines of the current circumstance and the greener side of the field. A foggy embrace circled her position, while looking out to the distance where a mere few were limping out and holding onto other injured members.

"Willow!" shouted Xira, her throat hoarse and torn.

Another explosion blew up a car's hood far behind her, prompting shrilling screams of the disturbed personnel. She continued on until reaching one of the chauffeurs clutching on their cap, their knee dislocated from the fall. He called to her in his anguish and pointed to the area beyond.

"Terribly-sorry, you must go over there, the fire hasn't touched down quite so," the man said tiredly, "Go! These fumes are not your helper!"

Xira rushed to lift the man and bring him along when he insisted, "Linger here and your poor lungs won't like that! It's okay, I'll go there myself! Go!"

"No, no way. I can help you! Please," She huffed, carrying the chauffeur carefully along the way. In a metre's distance, a tall, patchy figure emerged before them, an angled disgust for an impression. Paying no mind, she cut the difference between when Erma stood over the path, recognising the identity now that their masquerade masks were off. Xira gave one good look at the enchantress, before being drastically warped to an open site in proximity, as if she'd flipped the ground up from under. Watching her hover over with a seething gaze, Erma flung the burnt bottom of the garment and cleared the mud by her feet.

"You — nuisance — again? What are *you* doing here?" She questioned, "I thought I handled you."

The flurry of ashen clouds above covered the night sky as the temperature dropped to a wintry point, filtering the aerosphere and returning the land's essence as it were.

"I don't know what *you* want with me," Xira answered forthrightly, "Your search does not tangle with mine. You've caused enough trouble to feed the both of us."

Erma swayed, her sleeve waving over, "I think you know why my foot's on your tail. Cutting to the chase, child, we are very much entwined. The key you're missing has been beside you all along. Your visit to Rove Dynasty proved so, did it not? If you thought I'd miss *that,* then you were incorrect. Twice. That's a foul in my book. Unfortunately, for you, that stands to beckon a consequence."

A spectral entity glissaded down beside her, with a pewter grey mantle and a hair of white, carrying with them a golden four-sided orchid stained glass. Dangling it by its chain, the margins began to emit a radiant glow and the spheric stone placed on petals within reflected its colours on its front window.

"Syphon, would you be a dear and introduce yourself?" She said derisively.

"I already have," the mage replied with a sinistrous gaze, "Remember me? The old man adores to prattle about you. A little too much when it comes to sparing your family. I suppose I taught him well — sautoir! An elegance oh, very precious. The Lady Solar—Silhouette-— Solarouette, correct?"

Unaware of the link between, Erma darted obliquely, "Say again? Why utter that name?"

"My name's Xira. Get it right," she stated, focusing on them.

Noticing the stone flash at the sound of her name, the enchantress scoffed under a breath, knowing now what had been puzzling her this entire time. A gratified smile replaced the despondency that was prior, raising a hand to point at the tip of Xira's chin. They marked each other with a single look, a downward silence from the angle of Erma's stance and a resolute spirit opposing her height when she arched lower and closer.

"Those little silver eyes... ambitious things... shall I do you a favour?" Erma's voice veered through as Syphon elevated himself with the summoning of a cyclonic bluster, pushing the others back in the midst of a thunderous clap in the sky. The enchantress slid far off the way, distancing herself in the echoing laughter that was vaguely heard, followed by chanting.

Growing more distinct to the enunciated words, she attempted to cast a spell of projectiles and scoria, "Pour in gallops, show the water to-—"

An interfering shout blared over, as Syphon warned, "Sweet Erma Merideth, do not spend all that might... without your staff, you know it's only a vanquish wish!"

The enchantress stepped backwards and said, "Then vanquish her! The pair of traitors still carry my belonging. I'll wield what I've got... regardless of the scarcity."

Thrust down, Xira pushed a hand against the imbalance of the ground as the mage continued to throw everything her way. Like inside of a spinning ride, all but their position was a hazy setting — the natural light of the moon had disappeared in the clouds. The next wave knocked her aside and although she dug a boot into the soil, the graze was enough to provide him an interval for ruinous gambits. Tackling the encounters with the terrain at every turn, a force encompassing her exterior set off a vibration that knocked against the sides, returning the wind rotation towards the mage.

"Garrrgh!" He exclaimed, his sleeves tearing, "Erma, you hear! Plant the obstacle, I'll keep this intact..."

The enchantress stomped through in the direction with caution to the weather encompassing the area. Wrapping the garment's fabric over the elbow portion, she pounded Xira's shoulder, launching her to fall on her back as an energy spark zapped beneath the masquerade costume. Scorning over her as she was laying with the dirt that bowled beside the hands, she saw an aim for the sling and punted at it, turning to her in a grimacing posture — a floating motion of a base spell started to form ring curves. Before another attempt was made, Xira flung the upper body in an uproar, hurling Erma now to further down the landscape. Syphon hailed an array of lightning bolts to pin her, while Erma regained footing. The momentary foil allowed her to give a heavy kick by the side, turning her harshly over on the stomach. Another chain of bolts headed down but bounced off the gear and slashed straight across the soil. The thunder rumbled over as more were fired, when Xira sprung up in defence, aptly rebounding the lightning to batter on the mage — watching him whirl with the winds that merged alongside the knockout. It took him some time before getting back up, realising the countermeasures that met the dynasts. With what was left of his power, he tried yet more of the bolts but to their dismay, Xira returned her very own summoning of lightning and the wild gusts to both Syphon and Erma, resulting in a full halt to their wicked agenda. Her eyes lit up like the sparks itself as the area settled to a less hazardous climate. She walked towards the dishevelled pair, seeing them crawl among the grass to reach one another. Like the wafting of her ultra-radiant cosmic hair and the chilling glare directly into their own void, the sky dispersed to an ombré starry ether.

"A thorn in the torn flesh... wait — the Lord. The Lord is calling for us, Erma," Syphon muttered roughly to an inch, "The portal will emerge in a second... says to retreat to... argh..."

An oval pool awaited the pair a few feet yonder, as Erma gloated, "Saved by the bell..."

Xira watched them vanish inside with the pool transforming to a blow of dust in the airspace, trickling in tiny, withering particles.

"Cowards! Finish what you've begun!" She snarled, rotating towards an incoming ripple that swept her.

Awakening from a hasty shift, the ignited area was felt once again as Xira opened her eyes to the view ahead — people limping on, pursuing members' whereabouts. Some even escaping its mephitic grasp and others moseying in debris. She felt a tug behind her arm of a man displaying a raw umber trench coat, lapels pointed, a seaweed green bycocket hat outlined in black, a pearl bow embroidery along the belt of the velvet pants that he wore and a pair of spider jolly roger boots. His emphatic manner ranged to and fro the scene, focusing on her as if he was entranced, the sentimentality which imparted through the brims layered with his warm embrace.

"It's me, good little sunflower, it's Jasper," he expressed, then stepped back, "My lady, Xira, it's been so long. I apologise, terribly... there is much I've to tell you, uhm. That, that crash, was my doing — I — had I known, you were in there, too many were... all right... all right... come with, to settle this. Impromptu error... yet again."

Xira retracted to then say, "Gotta' find Willow. T-the others, they could be in trouble!"

Jasper answered in reassurance, "We will. You have my word, Xira. Okay? I just need to pick something up — I left it over there."

They hurried on to an ornate carriage parked off the path, where a bug vehicle shone its lights to the area. Jasper opened up a stack of containers, fishing out various items he'd stowed. He noticed her bending at the hip in a tiresome manner in between the unpacking.

"Long walk?" He asked, stretching a knapsack, "I could give you a cane, if you'd like one."

Xira propped against the bug in a sigh, "Sure, that would make a solid weapon for me, actually. A little crafting and maybe I'll fly off on my *own* broomstick."

"Matter of fact," Jasper added, a shy grin edging his lip, "Merlot told me of your encounter. The man's been on about you the whole time — it is why we've done a bit of our special meddling. Didn't think it'd backfire like this however..."

A shot cannoned from afar, as the two sorted themselves and the items. Running, Xira turned over to ask him, "Do you know? Has he told you?"

Panting quietly alongside the gravel, Jasper confessed, "Ever since we were married. I care very much for you, like he does — it's why he trusted me with your secret, Xira. The love is always yours, no matter what."

Upon reaching the location, they halted to the view. Watching more people leave a smouldering point, Xira then said, "You are married? A late congratulations to my favourite couple. If I haven't shown you it, well, I'd like you to know I appreciate all that you both have done and continue to do for me. After all the, the chaos... it's nice to be reminded of your support. Although I don't deserve it."

Jasper shook his head, grabbing the bag to go forth, "There's darkness in all of us, Xira. The way you choose to deal your hand, doesn't change that nature but enhances the balance. Very few are fortunate to find that level... let alone apply it to their decisions. Embrace your truth, sweet sunflower."

The shouts of the members lured others in guiding them towards a safe plane, in the while of huddling the people as much as they could without dividing too many. The pair called out for Willow and added on to the names of the team before — searching among the wreckage, a low cry caught her guard as she noticed a waving hand below.

"Xi... ah — help, please, the car's on-," Sam winced, pushing the metal.

She knelt in tendance, responding to Jasper's area concerns, "I'll help him out! Go, find Willow and the others!"

"But—"

"I'm handling this!" She added again, seeing him leave with a nod.

Lifting the frame off from under, a pipe by the wheel lodged down Sam's waist as he exclaimed the weight above. Heavy as it was, she pushed against the side in aim to tilt the vehicle. At a turn, it'd been moved over, though the density of the hood forged a bothersome setback. Taking breaths, she gradually shifted that portion on her shoulder and with another push, placed it on an angle when Sam called out.

"On my legs, the legs, ugh!"

Immediately, Xira force slammed into the car's hood and knocked it away in a tumble on the grass ahead — remaining in position, she carried him up beside the debris that surrounded and sat him to rest.

Sam curled in relief, crossing the arms over himself, "Th-thank you... thank you, so much. Rosetta... she... she was picked up by someone... Fiske... Fiske is with her."

"Were there any exchanges that you heard?" She questioned him, looking around.

"No... at least I think I heard her crying but... it was all a haze," he explained, coughing, "a man... maybe... said he'll take her over, mm... I don't know... I'm... I'm sorry."

As Jasper returned, helping Willow to her feet, the three encircled the patched ground before them.

Hurling the bag, he then announced, "Poor thing, tried to rescue the two named Saffron and Ilari. They're missing thus far. We assumed the members were gathered altogether. There isn't much left here, which is why we should leave. Ready?"

Sometime later, a group of helicopters and buses arrived by the open road for assistance. The Yard's logo could be seen alongside the transportation, with personnel in their uniforms surrounding the field and taking on their needs. Standing behind a high shrub, they kept an eye on their corners while the buses began to fill.

"Better trek on to my ladybug," Jasper told them while hiding, "We'll know where to find you, with that compass of his, makes him a compass alone. Aw... it's quite upsetting to meet you like this, given the circumstances... my apologies. All my apologies. I vow I will make up for it... for ones unintended to target."

Merging towards the crowd, Sam nudged beside her, "That was your *friend*? He's responsible for this? Is that what I heard?"

Xira covered the conversation and replied, "Not what you think. He was going for the Yard. He was a mentor. Found about them long before you came to a clear conscience."

"But my point is, either of us could be in peril and we wouldn't have a darn clue!" He whispered in grief.

"We'll find the others," Willow comforted and looked warmly to Xira, "... That's a promise."

On the bus ride back, the two sat beside each other with Sam a seat only behind. It was a relieving moment for the girls as the calming quiet throughout the way provided a much-needed break. The early dawn's glow began to rise on the horizon, a sweet blend in the sea of blue, among the array of trees that went by with the fluttering birds that flew high.

Looking out the window, Xira pondered as Willow then whispered, "Isn't it odd? I didn't pity most of the members much... am I bad to not care? To be selective?"

She answered to her, "If that somewhat brings you *solace,* I wouldn't pit it against you. Being in that kind of place, it alters shit. In ways you are not familiar with and that rough impact is a stranger to anyone. It pays off, either way."

Down the road, a pack of guards manned a barricaded intersection as they signalled for the driver to go through the desolate route to Lunaris Town. The soft patter of rain sprinkled against the glass, the misty aura among the unveiling of the sage green leaves drew with the travelling of the bus and upon entering a shortcut to the area, a tall neon welcoming lit up the side as Sam jumped in between the seats' gap.

"Uh, what are we going to do about going undercover?" He asked, seeing a roadwork sign ahead of the other exit.

Willow leaned in to say, "Up to her. The fabric is mostly ruined... I don't see an easy way out."

"Not easy — sneaky," Xira added on, "Looks like we're hopping off here for the meantime. Find ourselves a decent trinket, we'll figure the rest from there and as a backup... some more improv."

Her companion chuckled quietly and remarked, "Or as I like to call it... plan Z."

Lieutenant Gyrfalcon stood at the front to declare, "We've arrived at the destination. There appears to be a minor maintenance involving certain construction work that may take a while. Now, per orders, we shall take to this town's offers and delights — whether you want to sing with the alley cats or plant your nose in hot porridge, it is entirely to your liking. Once everything is done here, the voyage to Yowndrift Yard shall resume. There is a pond of ducks somewhere around if you want a little quiet."

Avoiding to be spotted by the high personnel, the team of three set off to the interior of the smoothie bar — overhearing a couple of the lieutenants' discussion as they circled a tangerine shaped table, adorned with a bamboo centrepiece that unfurled like a palm tree's crown. Xira covered with a gloved hand while the companions pretended to read the bar menu.

"Do you think she is lost? Perhaps during the evacuation?" Lieutenant Forest's muffled voice was detected, "I assumed everyone met up at the point."

The wing commander chipped in, adjusting his wrist gadget, "We made it clear to wait on the outside of the crash — the fool of an associate must've went in to aid the others."

"Without those fragments, especially the cypher wheel, the key is useless," said Lieutenant Paris, "It's not like we can initiate a replacement, that is frankly the old library's heirloom. Like somebody had intentionally hidden the artefact there to preserve it."

A bartender walked up to the table holding a pad and fished out a pen from behind the ear, ready to write their orders down. Xira looked to the garland made of lilacs that laid atop their wavy pixie-do, picking up on the resonating scent. The badge on the apron claimed their name to be Peri M, tender at the Groovy Fruity Carousel smoothie bar.

"Hi! May I note what you'd like?" Peri asked, pinning the ink on the paper.

Willow tapped on the resting companions before replying on a whim, "A round of the Tropical Typhoon, please."

The frost glazed window behind them obscured the view of the members as the low chatter mixed along the whirring of the blenders. A brief while later, the bartender returned with a tray of drinks, reminding them to leave change at the counter. The three exchanged a wondering glance, when another bartender walked through the storeroom door, bringing a cart of fresh fruit. At a swing, he reassured the employee that everything was being taken care of but beginning to waltz back towards the bar's staff room, he had caught sight of Xira who'd then also recognised the familiar face — although bearded and with altered hair, she knew by the eyes and manner, who it had been behind it all. The man cleared his throat, approached the front counter and declared for their drinks to be on the house. Looking over to Xira, he gestured for her to accompany him in the back space. A shining look in her eye, she hurried up behind and through the staff's door, arriving to a staircase's landing.

"Do you really work here?" asked Xira in a disbelieving whisper, the former emotions of the bond coming out of its reinforced shell, "Why was I left to watch that damn house?"

Hopping up the steps, the man sighed by an oak door, then plucked a key to enter inside. As she stood mid-way, the same look she once gave the mentor when residing at the family house forged on the grieving, wistful front.

"Serenitatem…" Xira uttered going forth.

With a gentle turn, holding a pearly charm, he then expressed, "My darling child, it is of great elation that we are reunited. You found the doghouse. It has been a sombre, daring era by that very window… all the things I wanted to confide to you… everything."

Observing the room on a flannel rug, she replied, "I am *not* your child! After the abandoning of about everyone under that cursed roof, you don't get to act like your late epiphany to give a damn is now redeemable!"

The mentor drew to a quiet rocking seat, fiddling with the circular charm in hand, a repentant tilt down his knitted scarf.

"Playing the silence game, are we?" Xira prodded, shifting towards the nearby table, "Or as you liked to call it, *reflection time*. That night and every other night, I believed you to be an honest man alone. I was set on your arcane bullshit to be *like my mentor* in every bloody endeavour. By that manner, it would've made me a lying, deceiving coward. Don't expect forgiveness. It's lucky you're at mercy."

As he got up to place the charm by the window sill, Serenitatem took to stand and say, "If my solemn apologies do not suffice, albeit I don't suggest that they do, then please… please. Accept the mistakes done by my hands and the promise of my mending the aftermath. I *will* tell you , everything, Xira."

She let out a hefty breath, answering, "Hmm, yeah, what do promises mean to you anyway? But whatever, I learnt who you truly were and it wasn't even through yourself — you know how hard it is, knowing someone who meant the world to you, for them to turn out and be a mirage in a dream? If it wasn't for… I lost everybody. Thinking you all were going to return, that maybe… you just went over to the markets. Not a soul by that door, I was left in the dark."

"Oh, Xira, I'm-I'm very-," He added, bringing her in for an embrace, "The one fragment I didn't lie to you about is the favourite truth of mine. You, dear. It was always, always you."

Leaning against the quilted vest, surfacing tears in a warm

downpour, she sniffled an answer, "For a long time I've wondered why you wouldn't tell me what I should've known… why you kept that from me… then… then doing things I've never wished on anyone. The sacrifices… alterations… strangers from a strange land becoming my friends… but I guess… that feeling is a homely resemblance — meeting my own shadow, now, I find you… starting anew, way out here—"

She pulled away and continued in a low calmness, "I can't confess that I know my old mentor… I'll say this though. I wasn't the one that lost. I left home and all for good reason. Despite all of it, I found the answers, everything I ever needed. A different path. *My* true path. And finally, an escape… hmm. Seems that you weren't in the equation — which never, ever made more sense to me."

"You shouldn't have done that… the dangers—"

"I shouldn't have done many things but I don't regret *any* of them," said Xira.

On the pile of cushions by the wall beneath the window, she sat down in comfort, looking out into the morning mist. Serenitatem began to head for the door, picking up another crate near a shelf when he turned around towards the window, the sun's rays projecting onto the parquet.

"Do enlighten me," he stated inquisitively, "Were you involved with the Yowndrift facility at a point?"

Rotating the charm against the mellow glow on the sill, Xira responded, "It makes no difference if you even knew. I'd ask you the same, but that applies to me too. You should go mind the bar, I need some quiet time."

"Shall I give your friends a clue?"

"Sure," she muttered back.

"If you insist," Serenitatem added on his way, "We'll talk again a little later…"

Down along the main section, more of the members had arrived to order their drinks — a frail few which wandered out the front and on the bar seats as well. He wiggled past the crowd and to the occupied pair indulging in their tropical treats. Taking the chair beside an untouched glass, the mentor introduced himself, recognising Willow in the midst of the conversation.

"Magnificent…" he had uttered, displaying a delicate look, "As I recall, you'd been friends ever since. It is a sight that harbours a third eye. Considering your diligence, *thank you*, for being there for her. Something I couldn't have done. I'm glad you two didn't step on my own mistakes."

Willow dunked an orange peel on the glass rim and answered, "We make our own mistakes, sir. I — I don't think that even *your* help could sway my girl off the course. She would've jumped ship the second she had the chance and quite frankly, returned the demon's horn in your own home."

Meanwhile, the bartender operating at the register took for a break as she walked out of the lobby and up the stairs. Noticing the door to the mentor's place creaked open, the curiosity got the better of her need for a toilet break. A peek inside, Peri entered quietly in watch of Xira — from that perspective, wondering why a new customer was fondly settling in an employee's room. The absence of members' chatter became a rhythmic clatter of the glassware, with the bar's wall radio playing funky tunes in the bamboo background. Peri carefully approached beside her and tapped a shoulder.

"Sorry to disturb, it's within my work policy to fulfill a guest's needs," the bartender expressed, "May I ask what is your business here? Do you know Odion?"

"I heard you come in. I'm visiting… *Odion*, so I thought to relax for the while," Xira said in return, "Guess I owe you an apology myself, for leaving my drink down there."

With a lean of the eyelids on the arched dimples, Peri reassured, "No matter! I can bring that up for you, if your thirst *ought be quenched*. Pardon. I'm Peri, and I'm on a break. Nice view, ah?"

From above, the scope of the hills, town square and construction crew could be observed in the bright new day, a sense of a civil town life fused with the melding escapades chipping underneath its frontier. The etchings on the charm reflected an outline of a sun pairing with a moon, the tint being a dark layer over the silver plating. Xira aimed it at the window, its elements being detailed with every marking as it spun in her gloved hands.

Joining to sit by, Peri slid the drink across with a remark, "Bottoms up. Hope you like the company, or if you disagree, I can take my garlicky self out of here. Pronto."

"It's cool," Xira told her, grabbing the tankard glass, "Thanks…

also, for this particular barware. The tall cylinder did its job already."

"It's on the house. Words of Odion," she replied.

As the drink's lush colours streamed the fruit, the rear actor on the road clawed into the dirt, piling a heap beside the workers that were conversing with a few of the distraught members. The buses were being parked off-road, the drivers which then hopped down the front while the little bustling town presented its affable welcome. Adjusting the cushions, the bartender wiped off bits of peels from the apron and stifled a rather hushed giggle.

"Compost." Peri jested, propping an elbow, "Coincidence, isn't it? That I meet a charming fellow out in these parts, because a loud bang obstructed the travels and brought you right here. To me. Say, *perhaps*, you tell me your name?"

"Xira. Yeah, it's funny that the land orbits to one's own desires and of course not by these turns of events, yet still to them it's a coincidence."

Miming a burning candle's wick, Peri averred, "Oh, I. Chilly apple of the eye. I mean, this town is lucky to gain such mesmerising beings to wander. Now you wouldn't blame a certain someone for relishing these moments, would you? *'Tis like a forbidden fruit.* Pun *so* intended. Bonus, I do circus stunts in my free time."

Although Xira appreciated the gesture, she returned to examine the charm that emitted tiny flares.

"Anything that is a secret can be solved," Xira mused with poise, "Even a small town like this, inhabiting friendly faces and hitchhikers, has its tales of wonder, I am sure."

Returning inside with a surprising glance towards his colleague, Serenitatem shut the door, then waltzed to the table with an antique chest.

"Look what the cat dragged in," said Peri, standing up, "Pardon, again. I'll be juggling the drinks up until lunch break — see you then? Or not, up to you."

The mentor smiled and said, "I see you've done your rounds. Might I add, it is splendid that you have thus bonded in my abode."

As the bartender left to resume the shift, Serenitatem turned to sit with the chest in arms. Once he'd placed it down between them, she looked at him with a reticent glare.

"What is that?"

He replied, "Hear me out, firstly. It is rather momentous that I explain this to you. That charm that you are holding is the key to the chest. It is the symbol of Antumbra, depicting the portion of the combination — light and dark, quite per se. A guise, if you will, for what it truly expresses. It is yours, I've kept it safe for when you were to retrieve it by choice. In here, is the result of the Penumbra. Everything else beside that is included and there is more to be found, because that's how a mystery dawns. Much of which is within self. Everything that is of you, Xira. Open it and find for yourself."

"But I—"

The charm begun to glow brighter, its blinking pattern warming the surface of her glove.

"What's it doing?"

"It is calling out," The mentor announced, "Look at your wrist there."

Doing so, she'd seen the birthmark signalling with the charm together as they both revealed the light within, coming to a meeting point with the antique. Xira planted the charm into the lock gap and it'd activated the tab mechanism. Upon lifting the chest's lid, the contents inside sprung to the brims while she searched through it. On the top was a folded sheet inked by the ghosts of the mighty ancients. A sable hue that emanated along the script that read in the motherland's language, which he helped to decipher and translated to;

"The Spirit Liberty, Realm o' Liberty,
Wander a Wolf, Light of Silver,
Night of Fire, Rhythm o' Wind,
Xira o' Rise, Xira Spirit return,
Shield on those that burn,
Speed o' Lightning by moon,
Sun's fiery glow on a bright day,
Truth of the Light in the Universe,
Beauty, that of all of the self,
A passion of path penumbra,
Path cosmic, path infinitum,
Xira, Spirit, Xira, Purity,
Nature of the Spirit,
Eternal o' thee, Xira."

A green nonagon beneath displayed an image of dual blades

overlapping a pastel figure of a mountain and its water surroundings. Inspecting the box, she picked out a crystal sphere which whirled the hues of purple and red — the mentor mentioned to use it with the box itself. As she hovered it over, the interior outlined a hidden astronomical map indicating different points of mysterious lands that coexist in the one galactic expanse.

"Watcher of all that wander," he recited, "That gives you the height of observing everything within and around the paradise. Don't be overwhelmed, it's part of — a fragment, if you will, of yourself. You bear multiple facets involving the — the spiritual methods. It remains in that box, however, as it is your private belonging. Barely a scratch off the build, that is a mere gift of courtesy, where you can absorb its knowledge. Put your hand over the opening and witness — go on, then."

Hand atop, Xira could sense the pulsating of the wrist's symbol resonating with the markings as it consumed in the form of thermal energy advancing to the birthmark. After its completion, the crystal sphere returned in its pad and automatically shifted the lid over.

Serenitatem noted, "There, you now carry that information along with the visualisation of the map. You won't always need it, of course, though you should indeed know… future endeavours only may provide its particular *handiness*."

Next to it was an oval mirror adorned with yellow petals on the opaque border. Seeing her reflection, the colours in her hair being emphasised, the scars of her encounters and the metamorphosis of the iris — she then asked for the mirror's purpose. The mentor looked at her with a sheepish grin, nodding towards the frames when he continued to explain.

"Oh, dear. To contact your mother, that is," he said, "you can use it to reach her own spirit from wherever you are, no matter where she is. The chorus is kept in a sealed envelope in this very chest. When you are ready, but I suggest that you do *after* the clearance of peril."

She glanced down in wonder, "… My mother? From the Spirit Realm?"

Nodding, he took out three other items from underneath it all, arranging them beside her as he then added, "These are the last few special treasures inside of this — now, the first which is; a metallic gearwheel. Used for aligning the constellations during a clear night sky, full moon specifically. It will grant you the connection with the ancients of the realm, thus giving certain intel or wisdom for what you ever need. Secondly... ah, the tiger's eye ring. Once wearing this, it will light up and reveal to you guidance, alongside providing you *meditative nourishment* — and this is a great factor, considering what you know. It was your mother's — she wore it all the time. Then so, comes the third item; pearl arrow-dagger earpiece. If you recall — my attempt at applying the old script that you've read — a little sonnet I would usually sing to you at nights, it was relative to its detail that's part of you. Representing the birthmark itself, this piece is something you can wear to your desire. A sonic length of deciphering what exactly your *targets* are saying, which is ironic enough, since you already bear that ability to great lengths — however, this expands it further. Besides that, it marks focus through structures where the targets are obscured, therefore receiving their discussions even through walls. I think I've shared everything there is to discover of the three treasures. The chest belongs to you, though if you'd like, it can be kept here safely. That is assured. For as long as this current circumstance is handled. I'm sorry I couldn't give this to you sooner, I was... afraid. You were under my care and I didn't want anybody else finding out. Especially... well. The waves are tall enough."

Xira packed the items inside, apart from the earpiece to which she then wrapped it around an earlobe and its helix, admiring its vibe. The bottom of it had been attached to the black rose stud with a velvet shimmer she'd already been wearing. She shut the chest and returned it to the mentor.

"Hmm, I can't deny that it was wonderful," she began, "It means a lot to me that you've kept it. It doesn't excuse everything else though, I do appreciate that you haven't forgotten value, at least. At the thought of losing the other items, I would like to leave them in there, all right? As I find treasures, they are to be placed here. Treasures that are not an *item* to be *placed*, are to be kept as a secret. This is the only connection to my mother, so I think it's best that way."

"Certainly," he replied, putting it aside, "Okay. Oh. Let me bring you a substitute overlay for when you decide to run off. I'll be right back!"

After seeing him leave, she turned to the window to see the

lieutenants talking to the construction workers that appeared to be taking a snack break. Curious to wander the room of her former mentor, Xira walked to the near table where a mess of contents were scattered atop the wooden furniture as a plate of cupcakes had been left out among them. She looked closer to inhale their scent when a loose document caught a side glance — employee files that were generally held by the owner. *What is he doing with these?* she thought, pulling apart the pile. Peri's page appeared under the second employee where it displayed her full name as Peri Meri — in brackets it stated *her preferred work sobriquet* for the surname. Below the lines was an implication of the residency of the bartender that also had been in Lunaris Town. Xira shuffled the pages as she heard footsteps in the hall and spun in time to the door's opening.

Serenitatem flaunted a grey raincoat painted with a spiral of berries on the back while he delivered the item over.

"The gift shop next door brings in *pleeenty* of bar merchandise for us to use accordingly," the man told her, "This one is yours to keep. Like a gift from me — a little souvenir of the town. I'll take the rather worn rags off of you, if you don't mind."

Immediately, she removed the ravaged masquerade costume and handed it to him. His reaction to her garment underneath prompted an astonished question.

"Dare I ask?" The mentor uttered, "Quite unusual wear for a backpacking traveller."

After buttoning on the raincoat, she answered, "Unusual is pretty much the norm for me these days. Got to have a shell of a kind to deflect any knife being put in my back. Hazard 101."

He paused, walking towards her with a puzzled side view, "Have you been in trouble? Am I right?"

Xira eyed the window in a contemplative manner. Rolling to his gaze, she said, "You can't help here."

"I doubt that I can do nothing. Let me, please, let me in."

"It's moulded for me. I can take care of it, don't worry, I'm grasping it so far. It's—"

"It's dangerous is what it is!" The mentor raised his voice, "You've been to the Spirit Realm. By the looks of those materials, they cannot be found elsewhere. You know more and you've applied it. Correct? Just how much *did* you find out? I must know, Xira. Everything there is to know of your energy, is inside my knowledge. If they find you…"

"Well, they already have!" She fired in return, knocking back the table, "No thanks to your little friends at the Yard. Driving me and my best friend out in nowhere land and eventually colliding with that *witch* and must you know everything went to what I can now only assume is beneath hell."

Serenitatem cupped his hand over in distress, going towards the window, "So, so, you're with them? Did they hurt you? Did you—"

In a sigh, she sat down by the sill to explain, figuring it was the wise choice, "Can you keep another secret? They were still hunting for us after we found the entrance to the Spirit Realm. Unfortunately, a pack of operatives had slithered their way in — although they were more like some bandits — after their encounter, we discovered the Yard's facility and involvement. We needed to search further, which led us to the base. On from there, I'll spare you the details, but yes, I uncovered a lot of information that they *really* didn't want me to find. Afterwards, well, there was a visit to the old Greaper Nestle library and now we're here."

"Heavens to the sun… dear, dear child. Spare me of the chance that you exerted—"

"It's still new to me but I managed to get rid of them — for the most part that is… until they ran away, as soon as I overwhelmed the two," she went on, "Anyway. It's only harsh under the wild incidents. Again, I am handling it. I know what I'm doing. Heavy, sure, but worth it. Worth every scar, every bruise, *every* damn fall. Once I'm in, only *I* can be the way out — thing is, it's a gamble for anybody else, as I have witnessed. Though if it means punching for peace, then so be it."

The mentor glanced outside with a saddened expression and then replied, "Be careful, Xira. There is such a thing as too much power. Unsheathe it in moments of mercy, but do not let them take you."

"I won't, Serenitatem."

He answered, "They are formed of multiple branches and seedlings, the Rove Dynasty are *never* alone. You must be vigilant at all times, I've seen it first-hand, with or without their weapons they are just as a threat — I just want you to be here in one piece. I can't bear to lose another."

Xira got up to leave, heading for the door when she turned with ruth, "You should've thought of that way back. If anything, having no idea what I've done to get here may somewhat bring you solace. I would worry about your infatuation with the breach I heard about — it sounds calamitous. Goodbye."

"Wait!" He called out once more, "The Yard. Dear. Once you go back there, that is regarding the facility, do consider leaving as soon as you can. The awful uncovering of what they truly want to achieve is not for anybody to involve themselves in, as I'd suggest manoeuvring from the outside — quiet, careful and most importantly, safe. I hope we meet again — it was ever so grand."

With a fervent glance, she swooped out the door and down the stairs to rendezvous with the others. Covering her mouth with the coat's collar, she returned to the seat, its backrest ornamented with an antimacassar. The lines went around the bar's front window as the members all waited for their drinks. While many scattered to and fro the town and the high personnel huddled near the maintenance area, some others even taking to the cushioned comfort of the buses — in and out the doors — the three sat by in subtle conversation and had been offered complimentary candy treats. Peri waved towards the table when Sam awkwardly mimicked the motion.

"We *are* leaving today, right?" He asked, contemplating.

"Hope so, it wouldn't be right to spend the night in muggy drunk buses," Willow remarked, "Although it would be good for you to catch up s'more with him, Xi."

Rolling her eyes as she refused the treats, Xira added, "I think I've caught up as much as I've wanted to… besides, he'll probably ask me to bunk in that room. *No* thanks."

She noticed Peri waving towards them once again, realising the bartender was focusing on her as the nodding response indicated that. Shifting out of the chair and to the counter, another worker came in place to serve the customers. Peri took her aside, excited to show her the backyard garden that the employees have nurtured together. From beds, to pots, to overlays and fenced plants, the place was filled with aromatic vegetation. Along the perimetral fence, the appearance of its exterior would lead one to believe it to be made of the vines that blossomed its delicate ivory and yellow petals, a curly wave of peachy hue with its leaves in an array atop the barbed wood and the outstretched wire of rosary that attached to rouge perianths of a little pine — surrounded by wooden logs.

"Isn't it gorgeous?" The bartender asked, dancing through the soil in the midst of looking back.

Xira walked by a bed of wine and maroon flora, inhaled the scent and said, "As anything like it is. Good thing you all are sharing. Why did you bring me here?"

Peri sat on a log and looked at the greenery, closing the eyes to absorb its natural essence. A gentle wind circled the garden as the leaves behind her fluttered to its rhythm, then the sway of the vines on the fence, rustling the nearby plantation throughout. Humming a tune while holding a handful of dirt, the mounted particles began to float above.

"*It is rare to be in the presence of beauty, let alone of it to ever exist,*" she intoned, "My great grandmother's wise reminder. *If it is all around us, then it is a blessing. A paradise, lest a curse taint its ground. The crossed thorns shall exterminate all.* You hear? Can you feel it? It embraces the flesh, down the gut and the air particles over you. Sit. Enjoy. A friendly favour to me."

Through the path to join her, Xira rested against the rouge plant and remained to herself in a chary manner. She looked at the cupped hands of the bartender, who revealed the flowing components and turned to meet — a dark ember beneath the nails was seen as Peri smiled, a longing glance with a vague orchid powder padded under the bottom row of lashes. She blew the dirt to ascend, its twirling dispersion circling around them and out into the garden. A joyous laugh cut among the air waves where Peri spread her arms like wings, almost in a flowing motion towards a recently planted flower bundle.

"Then I said," she stated, "Since beauty is in the soil from where it all arrives, does that mean there is still beauty behind lying eyes? Gee Gee loved the idea of somebody challenging her. I took that chance of being open with her. It only brought me despair, see, she didn't like it when I shed a tear or became upset — it *ruined* the display of elegant etiquette. Her words, not mine. Sorry, eh, I'm digging up old times again. Let me just ground it. It was tragic for a while, yes, but I learned to find the *funny* in the flaw of judgment. Then I said, so what? Who cares that she thinks of emotions as an empty vase? That if it breaks, its pieces fall into nothingness. I couldn't tolerate that type of treatment... then I said. Gee Gee, we are two different people, we view things very differently. I'll take this door, you take that one — make my leave for people that actually care. I went to the deeper end and never turned to her once again. It has been magical ever since."

The creaking of the back door followed with a clang to the wall as Serenitatem took a step outside the frame. Going down the path, he raised both arms as if to divert the events.

"Ahem! Excuse me, Peri, you must return to your shift," he announced with a high voice, "And Xira? Your friends are looking for you. They're waiting under the bar's outdoor cover. Come along."

As the two marched to the front, Peri hurried past them while the mentor paused by the dangling light. Xira stood beside him in waiting of why he'd done so — noticing a more sincere expression paint the man's exterior.

"Listen," he muttered, "There's something else you should know. I think it's better that I tell you myself, than you somehow finding out later in a way that won't be as simple. Here, take this key card and make your way into the alley beside the bar. Look for file 9 and 13 and play them. Down the narrow there will be a door that reads *'Staff Toilet, key card access',* use it there and no, it is not really a toilet but... you'll see. Everything else I may've not mentioned will reside there, indeed. Okay, before anybody eavesdrops in, go, go. I'll take care of Peri, don't you worry. It is not my first ritual."

Heading out the front, she was greeted by her companions as they walked off to the side wall.

"Where did you go?" Willow asked her, "Sam and I overheard a tell-tale discussion that the road will be ready by tonight and whatever they discovered there was *not* of this land. Familiar?"

Xira looked both ways before replying, "We'll get to that. Toilet first, meet you two back here soon."

They watched her rush the alley and turn the corner. The concrete was less narrow the further she went — Xira reached the *Staff Toilet* with the key card in hand. *There it is,* she thought. Before she could enter, a dashing figure scraped the high walls and bounced off a railing to the opposite wall. Angling above, the being was holding onto a steel balcony, almost camouflaging with the tellurian materials on their dusky acrobatic garment.

"Going somewhere? My, you're a new face," they suspended to the overgrown area below, "You *know* that's not a real toilet, right? Allow me to show you a better place. Going up?"

On a whim, the stranger latched on her arm and leaped to the roof of the town, as Xira staggered to her feet upon landing. Despite being slightly surprised, the view over the region gravitated the disruption to a pleasant hideaway.

"I like to welcome those who want to wander about my home," they spoke again, hopping to sit on an arched vent, "You can address me by, mwa, Neo. Are you with the lords of the mire down there?"

Xira observed the furnished camp as she answered, "For now. This is your *home?*"

They jumped to the various elevated parts of the roof, with a smile that curved along each cartwheel and performed a back flip on the brick edges before settling in a crouching position. Their hands gripping on the bare, mossy sides, she rearranged a shiny ring chained to a wristlet.

Standing to gesture, Neo declared, "Since forever. I hear, I see and I know everything that lurks around here. The walls have ears, the roof has eyes and the air has a voice. And I, I harbour it all. Trusting you can keep a secret, why don't I tell you a little *hush hush* about the bus packers? *I* heard they keep their mess under a rug and pardon the poor, poor cleaners."

Nearing her, the stranger put a finger in the air and claimed, "In exchange for a lemon treat. You can find one in the gift shop."

As Xira turned to walk away and leap over the steel barrage, the landing on the stone path echoed a tremble beneath the cracks. She focused on the *Staff* door right behind, then glanced towards the gift shop at the next corner. *Key first,* she thought. Entering the room, a screen on the wall captured the attention while the spotlights begun to lit up in a sequence, surrounding the interior. *'Welcome, ODION. How may I help you?'* the screen displayed in its green text overlaying the black background.

"Open file 9," she spoke in a protruding wired microphone.

"Access denied. Voice not recognised. Try again or enter with keys."

She let out a sigh, "Of course."

Tapping in the line using the keyboard on the desk, a file emerged with a question prompt.

"Yes, I'm *sure,*" was her remark, before beginning to skim through the contents.

The file read as *FILE 9 — INVESTIGATION — PERI MERI — EMPLOYEE AT GROOVY FRUITY CAROUSEL BAR — COMPLETED WITH NOTES.*

Below it stated;

Entry 1 — New person arrives for bartender job, calls herself Peri.

Entry 2 — Promising qualities and effort for the position.

Entry 3 — Decision with the owner concluded the same night, Peri's chart is now official.

Entry 4 — Trainee appears to be reserved yet fixated on the shifts.

Entry 5 — Meltdown upstairs by Peri, look into this further and tend an analysis.

NOTES: After a thorough discussion with the employee, she has stated that it was a personal reason for her outlet in the bathroom and an overwhelming chill of emotions that swayed the composure of the person. Analyse further.

After the analysis, it has come to my attention that there is more to the layers this Peri is attempting to hide. I distanced myself intentionally to work from afar and come to a definite conclusion to the intentions and motivations of the trainee.

PERI MERI — FULL PROFILE — CONFIRMED

Upon many day and night shifts and my work of prying, I have discovered the utmost surprising details of our new bartender. She's no ordinary employee, that is for certain. Quite in fact, I've seen and *heard* it for myself when I say this... her sister. Her sister was none other than the foolish, wretched woman, Erma Merideth. I should've suspected why this particular person would not care to share her own last name for the staff chart. By all means, I cannot trust entirely in this woman, however... overtime she has proven to be less of a caution and more so a being with a troubled home. From my perspective, it appears as though she snuck out for an unknown reason to start a new life on this side, in Lunaris Town.

We have a solid alliance that I can now say, a friendship that has really grown on me. It's truly a turn for the better with Peri, as I have also become more protective of her, quite like restoring my past as a mentor. It's not easy, albeit... knowing who her connections lie with — in any case, I'm certainly keeping my doors and windows locked. By my guard, no harm or foul by an underworld lurker should pollute here. At least I hope, I can stay true to that declaration.

A wave of realisation made Xira think back, "The garden. She was trying to give me a hint. Probably not entirely about her sister… but it was there. The feeling, I only thought of it to be an infatuation. Of all people… immortals… hmm."

Then typing in for the following file, its title popped up on the front in bold writing; *FILE 13 — JAY'EO — FORMER IN FAMILY HOME — ROOMMATE QUALIFICATION AND ADMITTANCE — COMPLETED WITH NOTES*

ERROR TO DISPLAY CERTAIN KEYWORDS.

Entry 1 — Hooded person enters bar, hands in pockets and asks for a strawberry swirl.

Entry 2 — The customer stays for long hours in the same seat, drink in hand — quiet.

Entry 3 — One of our employees asks if he needs anything else, he replies a short: no.

Entry 4 — Closing hours are near and we politely remind the customer that we will be locking the doors soon and for them to be prepared.

Entry 5 — Reluctant to do so, the man takes off the cover and gives us a cold, desperate stare. I was taken aback, knowing those same eyes. He then says with a heavy tone, *I need a place to stay.*

JAY'EO — FULL PROFILE — CONFIRMED

To my absolute astonishment, this man, after many years later… comes back and finds me himself. Alone and broken, he seems. Jay'eo. The young boy I once took in my home, I gave him as much as I could offer and showed him the ways of our Family. The smile he carried warmed my soul and I knew I had done right by him to provide the comfort and joy he deserved. From that time, he was a bright boy that I loved to call my son. My child. Jay'eo never ceased to enkindle the *Jay* love to any of us. It was a great era, a time of the past that pierced through me when I saw him again. Such devastating nostalgia that brought the harsh end of that fork. To me, he never strayed from being my own child. I saw today, this grown man with a saddened soul look to me like he did the ol' day I brought him home. For all we've weathered, I will give him another home, without doubt. He was the lost boy then, yet again that boy today.

Jay'eo remains inside the room during the night, where he either sings or sleeps — at this point, I don't really mind. As long as he is under the roof and fed, it is not a scent for me to chase. I'll mention the day routine in a different manner, as he is never inside for the entirety of it until evening. To question him, I was hesitant to barge in private matters — given how most of those encounters go… therefore, I found the route to allowing him to open up as he pleased. It worked! Though to say it was what I presumed, would be a right lie, for what he shared with me that one evening… I'll never forget the weight it bestowed on the both of us upon the exchange — it was difficult to bear. No, he is still my child. I will not judge where he chooses to work, I will not turn him away because of a manipulated decision. If my beliefs stand clean, he is to be utterly cared for by me, by all means. A change for a cost.

"Oh man," Xira muttered as she finished reading, "Jay'eo… he's here? What work exactly is this?"

Shutting down the operator, Xira walked out to the alley and ran off to the gift shop. The sign read; '*Flavour Funk — Gift Shop*' — A friendly staff took to greet her with a warm gesture to the store's naturalesque display. As she detected the nearby citrus incense while walking to the counter, she pointed towards a jar on a high shelf.

"Hi, are those the lemon treats?" Xira asked.

The employee nodded with a smile, "Sure are. We sell a variety of flavours if you're interested in a mix — I can bag them up and at no extra cost, mhm!"

"That's all right, thanks. Just a handful of the lemon," she added, "Uh, how much do they cost?"

They gestured politely, "Well, from what I can tell, you are here with the visitors from Yowndrift Yard. I heard about what happened when two of their employees came to visit before, it would be rude of me not to offer *something* on my behalf. Besides, the lemon treats are usually the ones that sell the least around here. Only one other that I know absolutely *loves* these… hmm… any chance it is related to the alley cat named Neo that wanders about town?"

Xira looked in wonder, "The alley cat?"

"Oh yes! We know them as the alley cats because of the way they go about things and the ensemble they always wear — the name practically originated from the first that settled in and after that, more began to show up and spot a homely location. They're all across town, although, most often hiding up high. I can split the quantity among two?"

"Ah," she continued, "That would be great, then. If you don't mind, I have another question for you."

The employee introduced herself as Magda before answering, "Certainly. I adore meeting new folk. Fire on!"

The herd of members outside scattered along the corner and the stone path between the walls in the midst of a downpour that began to splatter over the area.

"That bar across from you," Xira explained, "You might know a, an *Odion* that works there?"

"Why, yes, he's very friendly! Visits every day on his breaks."

"Right," she went on, "About him… has he shared anything personal or unusual with you?"

Magda chuckled lightly, "Well… plenty, I suppose. He comes from Glacial Mist, the neighbouring town yonder. Moved here the same day I started working in this store. My… come to think of it, it's years of getting to know everybody here. There should be a ceremony to celebrate."

In thought, Xira picked up the bag from the counter, "I appreciate it. Have a good day, Magda."

"Oh, you too young lady! Enjoy the treats! Come again sometime!"

Off to the alley again, she wedged through the people to reach the corner by the stairs. A head swung over the roof's edge in a whimsical manner.

"I smell the lemon!" Neo voiced down, "Need a lift?"

They seated by the cosy campfire that had been prepared around a placement of rugs and many metal cans. Over them, a crafted canopy was arranged with four hooks at the points, as they both indulged in the lemon treats. Using the warmth of the fire, Neo added some of the treats to an empty can and melted it into a honey-like dew, forming an alternative."

"So you're an alley cat, huh?" remarked Xira, chewing on a piece.

Placing the cans aside, Neo swung up, "Aw, someone snitched. *Teehee.* Kidding… yeah, I am. Is that an inconvenience?"

"Mm, no. It just makes more sense now."

The companion then lit up, "Okay! Want me to run through the details now? Need to scout for food later — either way works for me."

With agreement, Neo and Xira closed in on the camp, rubbing their hands to the few cask pieces.

"Listen. I gotta' do this quietly. Cool? I may encapsulate the town's structure as a form of *spy couture,* hah, boy, do these places carry more outside its *perimeter.* To me, the edge of the realm is barely the edge. Nothing is off limits and no matter how many barricades they want to divide us with, it doesn't put our hands down and feet apart. About those people… they claim to be righteous in their schemes… you ever seen a *folk's* tale? Me neither. The stench has oozed my friend, *their* stench. Heard they got people locked up. Keeping them like a bunch of experimental subjects. From the sound of it though… not for long. There are double agents in there that are doing wild favours, for me at least — and now, you. Can't trust them, girl… They're planning to eradicate anyone that won't stand with them. They want to take over whatever we all once shared and change it. For the worst, I believe… Unfortunately, they've already started to clean the streets. Already plaguing most of these regions and I'm afraid I'll need to jump town when they come here again. It's lucky we're far enough, but our luck runs out with us the moment they step foot — I'd rather keep my luck. It's bad enough I make it myself, then again, not so bad in fact."

"I'm not *with* them," Xira told her, looking over the area," I already know what they're up to, but I'm glad you cleared up one thing for me that I have been dwelling on. They would go to the lengths of going against their own townspeople *and* workers if it meant achieving their end."

Neo turned, "Yes. Exactly the point. Now hold on… if you're not *with* them, then *who* are you and with?"

"In a brief sense, I came from Glacial Mist with my best friend. We got involved with them during a search of ours and now we're along for an infiltration and to ultimately burn it down from within," she stated in a casual, diverting manner, the campfire's flames sparking up on the fingertips, "That needs to stay between us. We're already down in the deep."

The companion placed two hands over hers and whispered, "Cross my arms and forth I leap. My sincerity is yours."

After some time of munching on the treats, Xira decided it was time to go back to the others as she waved Neo farewell, approaching the side as the town resident whistled on.

"Thanks for the lemon!" She exclaimed, "Maybe I'll see you around again."

"Back at you — goodbye!"

The rain poured heavily on the stone ground while Xira entered the bar to be greeted by the two seated companions in a corner booth. Relieved to see her again, they vouched to head on to the mentor's room where the quiet was more to their liking. Inside, Serenitatem was not to be found as they had assumed that he joined to ease the overwhelming load of work downstairs. The three sat at the now empty table, with only a candle lit in the mahogany's centre. In the soothing sound of the patter, they huddled together as Willow went on to share the overheard intel.

"At that point, we'd consumed like a bowl of ice-cream that Timothy, the bartender, made from fresh fruit," she said, mimicking the bowl's shape with her hands, "So we went outside for some air and a little walk-about, when a couple of personnel stated that they saw a dispute between Ruzak and somebody he was holding — not clearly detecting the identity but he was then seen throwing the person inside a Yard truck he had called over. I'm beginning to think discretion went over his head, because if this happened not too far from here, then he must have been desperate and there can't have been a reasonable explanation. *Then,* another mentioned that they were going to be *initiating* and *evacuating* tonight. As soon as everybody returns to the facility. Odd, no? Goodness…"

The birthmark's glow thumped on the table surface. No one else seemed to notice with their focus on the current topic. Xira rolled down the glove to see its emphasised outline emit the traces of light that reflected within the accessory. At a bend, she concealed the forearm and leaned towards the little ornaments, arranged in a style of a seasonal carousel.

Xira mused, "There is no question that the Yard is one abominable pit, which is why we should cut to the chase or otherwise everybody pays their price. Why do you think they arranged such a ball when all these towns have been under the Yard's control and evacuation protocol? It's a disguise, *everything* is a disguise. Nobody cares to explain what fell through the ground's layers while they were lining up at the bridge. We know the sliver amount of a collision between realms but not how *they* are operating around it and why they want to override the entirety of this realm. Of course, power is in hand, although… why now? Why not several years back? It makes me think they've made a discovery and *we* need to find it before they do something none of us can turn back — I know it's a lot… you'll need to trust me, all right?"

Sliding the chair to the side, Sam lowered himself with a reply, "There are… you mean… other worlds here? Where?"

An abrupt clearing of the throats, the girls looked to either way in reluctancy when the two came forth to further elaborate.

"That's all you can know and that's if you swear to keep it," Willow told him.

Raising a hand, Sam moved to motion a zip across his lip and sat back up.

He shook his head, adding, "My gut knew you weren't from the *labs*. I mean, *first* of all—"

"Careful," Xira remarked bluntly.

"No, no, I'm just saying. We would get along, since we know what the Yard is all about now. If only the rest of us knew, heck, all the people they've trapped — imagine, how we could overwhelm them. Right? Outnumbered by miles!"

She tapped her hand forward and then said, "Even the vilest person has contacts, probably more so than anybody else. You fall in their trap and it's a field day for the bastards. It's not about outnumbering, it's about strategy. Do it right, you won't have time for a crowd. Our best bet… we get in and get it all out. After we actually agree, that is."

The friends gathered round to a quiet form and discussed the details of figuring out the facility.

"The Commander is the top dog in the workplace," Sam went on, visualising with hand gestures and old memories, "Sits high up in the bird nest, looking down on the second highest in the building — the Wing Commanders. Then I'm sure you know the rest… ahem, assuming you've been up and about. Anywho, there are a lot of employees that are hypnotised by their illusions and won't hesitate to become sacrifices for the boss. If there's any way around them, I'm sure it'll be easier to pull the plug and intercept."

Footsteps running up the floor could be heard becoming clear-cut and closer to their location.

Xira whispered to conclude, "Break the spell, capture the caster. Spins, the key."

Entering the space, Serenitatem called to the group as he brought in a steel, steaming pot and hurried to the table with the mittens that displayed acorns and leaves, its corners slightly burnt.

"Ha! I was just on my way to call you all for a special dinner by me," he said, placing it down, "Perfect — perfect, perfect. You're all here and yes, it will be a delight — oh, let me set up the table now. Lend a hand?"

As the four sat around in an evening's feast, with the travelling aroma of vegetables that'd been picked from the garden, a jug of fresh water and a hand-made helping of a loaf of bread, the mentor wore a large grin on his smug complexion while chewing on a slice of carrot. The team ate through without much of a peep as the soft clattering of the silverware slid along the bowls, between the faint tune that played from a golden gramophone and the raindrops on the rooftop.

"Ah, just like old times," Serenitatem remarked, turning a glass to sip, "To think this would never have been done again, how silly of me."

Xira bit down on the bread, rolling her eyes as a vexed sigh muffled through the raised spoon.

Apart from the chatter by the mentor and occasionally the others, it was a rather dulcet evening with the four seated around the table. After a few drinks, Serenitatem insisted that they *settle the reins down* for a cordial conversation before they were to leave. He cleaned up the plates and glasses, arranging a board game in place of the pot, then distributed the standees and cards along their positions. Fiddling with the ship's helm piece, Sam appeared to be more driven than the pair, for a round of *Marooner Roulette — The Board Game.*

"Really, thank you for this great dinner, sir," Willow began to say, "I do think we should move on now, as it is late and we may miss the one bus that we technically hitch-hiked."

"Nonsense," he replied, "It's on me. Besides, you will both leave and how can I cope if not without another moment to cherish?"

Picking up her piece, Xira placed the shiny sabre above the row of cards. She chimed in, "Why don't you tell me why Jay'eo has been hiding out here with you? No way is he not running away from something, or someone."

Serenitatem paused, then answered as he dropped in his adorned treasure chest piece, "I'm afraid the confidentiality of my beloved boy is to be respected and kept with me. Ahem… shall we?"

Before anyone took a turn, she slammed a fist against the rim and slid the chair, "Yeah, because you care. It shows, clearly. Once you leave him again, without question, you would take him in and repeat the insanity. I'm done here."

The mentor shot up to a grab and pleaded for her to cooperate for this one time, tears in eyes, "Just this once? Let me. It is completely old man's wish."

She looked at Willow and sat back down. Looking to the board, cards in hand, the piece was shifted to the starting location. Her companion smiled as she did the same, then Sam followed with an endearing chuckle as they began a game of Marooner Roulette that long, rainy night.

"Between each turn, we will participate in a selected topic by the player who has rolled," he explained to the three, "These translucent components will be rotated clockwise, at my starting point. Everyone clear on the rules? Need I explain them again?"

Sam called out, "It's good! I'm caught up."

"Then let's!"

The dice spun to midway of the board as the mentor drew a card from his pile and moved it to a space on his *asphalt row* — where all players use the base for their turn. He nudged the handle to a land on Sam's area before selecting a card from the *captain's deck,* resulting in a *triple question reward* — arranging the pick to his side, Serenitatem tapped the chest standee.

"Ball in court," he announced, then asked, "Firstly, do you still work with Yowndrift Yard?"

The member stifled a cough when he answered, "I guess I do. Although, it was par for the course… I am actually considering to resign. Think I've found something more suiting."

Serenitatem nodded once, then continued, "Is it true that most, if not all, of the townspeople are held captive in your facility in means of discordance and propaganda, instead of legitimate transference?"

The girls exchanged a wary look, before the formerly mild expression on Sam switched to an earnest demeanour.

He replied, fidgeting the helm piece, "From what the Commander said, we are to take them elsewhere when preparations are complete. Other than that, he wouldn't tell us much more. Next question?"

It was a moment of quiet and hesitation on the table as the close focus kept on him by the relentless mentor cut any partial subtlety. The treasure chest standee was taken to the centre of the board, where they called it *the island*.

For the third question, he uttered to Sam, "You say you want to leave, but I know that the Yard provides you with a sealed contract that states a full devotion to the job, once it is signed. A close fellow of mine told me all about it — see, maybe you are reluctant to share that information, and I do so comprehend, however, I don't appreciate being lied to at the price of others' freedom. Be honest boy, how do you plan on executing that mighty escape?"

"Okay, that is enough," Xira cut in, returning his piece to the start position, "This is supposed to be a fun game. How I remember it. You want to ruin that, too?"

Sam looked at her thankfully and both retracted to their seats, along with the standees.

A while after it had been Willow's turn to roll, as she tossed the pair towards the *captain's deck*. She'd chosen a card from the stack that the handle's point was aimed at and the given activity for that round was for someone to guess a re-enacted segment done by the player. Standing to begin, the motions of a mime and a ballerina came to play, coinciding with what she'd attempted to present.

Within a single moment's haste, Xira fired an answer, "The Plum-Mallow River tree!"

Her companion jumped with the excitement upon the correct given reply, then turned to introduce a quick topic to cover on.

"The world we know is round, an endless terrain for an endless travel curiosity," Willow added on, "It is with effort to find something that you deem valuable, just like a solid good friendship. If I were, hypothetically speaking, to reach to an edge and you were the only promising exit, would you take it against all of the odds?"

Xira shifted in the seat, a kind glance to her direction when she told her, "As ever, by any means. I wouldn't let you go, you know that. *On my watch, you undoubtedly remain...* I am always there."

Hands together by the chin, Willow evinced, "Awh... you... you just quoted my mother. That is really, *really* sweet of you."

The two overlapped their forearms in an embrace, then resumed with the next dice roll.

"It's your turn, Xira," Serenitatem said in a reminder.

Landing on a card for a truth or dare round, she looked to Sam as he had selected *dare*.

"Okay, I dare you to tell me where I can get access to the Commander's lair?" she asked.

"Errh, between you and me…" he began, lowering down to the table, "the Wing Commanders are your best option… but you'll need to get through the security and panels. They hold the key access. Otherwise, no clue."

With a glance, the dice was handed over to the member who cupped the components in a palm whirl. *Figures, guess this dog will need to go for a bite,* she thought.

Later that night, the table had been cleared and they'd been standing out the door while the mentor was preparing a cupcake for each person. At the front, all personnel and members could be seen lining up beside the road as the buses were being driven over to the set-up, where the construction workers bid their leave. Serenitatem went in for a group hug, even Sam, who was still in his mixed feelings about the man. Once they'd drawn back by the bar's window, it was all on for the Yard's given alert to be escorted.

"Well… I'd just like to say I'm sorry for how I treated you beforehand," the mentor began and continued, "It comes from a place of concern and I wouldn't be honest if I didn't say that the overwhelming portion was simply because of this little reunion. I want all of you to play it safe. Whatever it is you decide to do, do it from yourself alone — never from a puppeteer's mitt. Nothing good can come of a second-hand choice, make it and bake it yourselves, understand? Oh and a few more things, hoo, do not underestimate the ferocity of that place… or any place. For what is well covered, is well layered with what truth lies beneath, for consistency in good intention will almost always baffle the witness. Mark your way and it will be seen, though do by your own terms and not in an outstretch to others at very different angles, because that truth is yours to shine — all right, Xira, when you're done with the strawberry cupcake, please don't throw the wrapper, hmm? About the trip, I'd suggest taking the farthest seats to the back — I've heard there's a rear door if you should need an alternate outlet. See you soon, yes? It was grand, oh truly. Be safe, young sprouts, do be careful."

In that moment, Peri stormed out of the bar and into the alleyway where Xira observed her lighting a cigar. With a farewell hug, tears below eyes and sentimental glance, Serenitatem returned to the building — looking back with a heartfelt smile as he waved, then went on to mind the business.

"I'll be back in a bit, need a quick bathroom break," she told the others and rushed to the alley.

Confronted with a poignant exterior, the bartender chipped at the binding and uttered, "What are you doing here? They're about to blast off. Miss me?"

Xira replied in comfort and gently, "I know about you... *of* you. You've dealt with a rough past and then an escape presented itself, you took—"

"No, it didn't present itself, I moulded that shit," Peri cut in, then retracted, "As hard as it was... I remind myself every day that it was worth it. I'd still be in that hole, looking up."

"Believe me... it is so worth it," she told her with a quietening voice, "I hope you understand that me being distracted or distant wasn't because of you. That was a beautiful garden, I hope it's ever as blooming. Your heart's in the right place. All right... I can hear the buses. See you around."

The bartender clutched on their damp, slanted cigar, before responding cordially, "Lightning speed, stranger."

On the rear end of the bus sat the three companions, whilst the row recoiled during the travels. Rain continued to spatter across rimy windows and in between the skidding wheels, myriads of chattering people and a long, outstretched road behind them, the cupcakes in hand were promptly consumed like the grand night air. Xira folded beneath the crumbs as she noticed a taped fragment on the wrapper. *A micro device, huh,* was her thought. Hearing the static effects on its exterior, a receiver had been sending through someone's transmission when she came to know the identity of the caller. By her instincts, Xira attached the part to the earpiece, assuming it would synchronise, then caught on the clanging noise in the background of kitchen appliances.

"Hello? Can you — are you hearing this? Am I — is that — hello?" The crackling call began to clear up.

"Wait a minute — how did you? Never mind, what is it now?" she asked.

On the other line, Serenitatem explained, *"And about that, for every time we contact, do address me as Raptor. Code, dear. For safety purposes — the person did tell me it should be secure, albeit... can't be too careful, ahem. Anywho, I better return to the bar — that's all for now and please do call me once you are in a safe area. Ta-ta!"*

With a sigh, Xira leaned against the seat and adjusted the raincoat to conceal herself. Willow propped on her shoulder for a brief nap while Sam gazed out the back, the rear lights illuminating a portion of the gravel — soon after, the ride on became a moment of utter repose. As the driver swerved to the next route, the chemical ooze could be seen over the tall trees encompassing the facility's grounds, a soft mixture of tones highlighted by the electrical properties and the looming high tower intercepting the trajectory of the full moon. The bus was parked by the grass before the personnel announced their arrival — instead of entering the driveway, they'd given specific instructions for the members to walk their way inside. Hopping off from the rear door to a far side area, the three stood behind the others crowding ahead of them and waited on the cue to leave. Xira's throat had begun to feel torn as she gasped to a clearing within the raincoat and fell down to the shrubs.

A cloud of befouled air wafted before her as Xira eagerly walked through the confusion of the people that roamed forward and backward, ragged, the strings in the seams coming apart in their bleak selves and surroundings — holding out like a desperation for something to fill their void after what had been left was absorbed and then spat over again. Knocking into one another, she pushed around the horde with them attempting to grab her as humming, skulking whispers pattered down the ears and drained the clarity of the air. It had become more like a haunt, the burden of theirs being visualized, with the birthing of a nightmare.

"A hand on my hand, set me free! Here! Here!" a distant voice cried out.

"Why did you leave me alone? Do not leave me here, no!" Shouted another.

Xira slid among unfamiliar faces, evading each clawing hand

stretching over her. The bellows reverberated beneath the feet and a shrill sound waved on about the voices.

"You left me... you turned your back this time... didn't bring me..."

"Fool! Fool! Fool! You little miscreant... a rascal... monster..."

A tumbling child emerged from the side, a despondent look between the frilly hair buns when a ghostly aura circled the contrasted form.

"I want my precious... I want you to bring it to me... please, a sliver... vowed..."

In the distance, she could discern the path, with only being a spring apart...

Another being muttered, *"Look at you... the ravaging you have brought... didn't want to get us out... you left us all here..."*

"You've made me a scar by our ink, our sacrifice... you've made a choice... lone lady... lone... lone... lone lady..."

In the midst of the pushing, the shoving, the knocking, Xira continued to slither through and although casting the towering haunts aside, she could feel the unloaded weight sit itself onto her. Heavy push to the outer portion, the crowd magnetised on both sides. As she grunted to push out an opening, she exclaimed in a harsh undertone for them to leave her be, then propelled right above to a landing flip across the scraping ground. Forging metres between, still they dragged on forth in the famished mannerisms — glaring down to a barge, in hopes to consume, to rend such an existence. She saw a vague outline of an evergreen nearby and crawled towards it. Eventually regaining a stance, Xira crossed to the edge of the way, reaching its extending, projected roots. Her hand placed atop its surface while turning back to notice the crowd beginning to disappear each step they arched on, dissolving the imagery to a blend and then a cascading whirl among the atmosphere. Xira gazed to the tree as it returned her to a field of grass looking on to a cobblestone path, the Yard's lamp post flickering softly with the creaking back entrance behind the fountain.

Whistles of the wind gave her insight as to where the people had gone — seemingly already in the base floor sector and muffled by an ominous whirring, she turned round in search of her companions. *How did I get here?* she wondered.

A tumble of footsteps rushed to her location, when a huffing voice enounced, "Oh, hey! There you are!"

"Willow. Sam. What happened?"

Pointing to the outer land, Willow answered, "Well, first of all... we were waiting to come here together, but once I'd peered to find the lieutenants, you just disappeared. How, why, I don't know."

"Yeah, you kind of freaked us out. What gives?" Sam added in.

Xira shrugged in wonder towards the way as she said, "Last thing I remember is landing in a shrubbery. Then... uh... there was a mirage, I think, it's not the first one though."

"Why didn't you tell me this?" Willow asked her, "*I* thought it was merely bad dreams. I can help you — simply with old recipes from my mother."

The sound of a horn blared throughout the building in an echo between the walls. The three looked on in avidity, seeing the perimeter's lights flash in a sequence to the adjacent poles.

"Okay, while we're all in the same boat and confessing," feebly, Sam divulged, "About the crash — at the site, I — I *did* recognise the voice of who helped Rosetta. Or, helped might be a stretch. I was too afraid..."

They pinned their focus on him as he continued to say, "Oh man... ah, it was Ruzak. I *heard* him practically forcing Rosetta to follow and the somewhat subtle outcry was enough to make me presume that she could be in trouble."

Xira then expressed, "You tell me that now? She could *very well* be held as a captive by that shallow shell of a man. In that case... the others may be nearby, or with our odds, anywhere in that cursed place."

Walking to the door, the three exchanged a wary look upon entering a dim, wrecked hall. Empty as the omen of what had been going on within the premises, there were the few bulbs reflecting from the opposing rooms, their sparks swaying to and fro the static emission of the speakers. A camera revolved to the exit with its blinking red lens, followed by a multitude of hurrying footsteps in the vicinity.

"All right, I'm going after the Commander," Xira told them outright, "Find the others and whatever else you can, keep out for distractions — we'll meet outside the front."

One foot by a double-swing panelled doorway, Willow called to her again, "Xira, go get him. Do not let them near you! Catch you later, partner..."

Xira affirmed before jumping to the staircase, "I'll be right by... partner."

Going up to the second floor, she breezed her way to a working elevator and repeatedly slammed on the keys. While standing beside the indicator, a pair of Yaraks patrolled along the side as Xira hugged the corner wall in patience. After they left, she returned to the chime of the machine and aimed for the third sector. She arrived to a scattering mess involving the frightened personnel, seen scrambling around the area and carrying things in hand as if it meant business. Although certainly busy on something, they were clear for their impressions, that an unpleasant circumstance troubled the Yard facility. Xira went on to locate the offices of the wing commanders and ran off from the noise, to a silent turning direction. Spotting a slightly opened panel with the title *FOREST* on the plaque, she slid inside and shut the door. *Wait, if Erma's card only works for an associate's second floor access... then... no. Keep it just in case,* her thoughts raced on while searching the office. A rather tidy layout made for an easy clearance. Apart from the locked drawers and cabinets, all that was found lying around was a letter to one of the other lieutenants, Paris. Xira was certain to leave when a few keywords caught her eye.

PARIS —

Is it love? Is it a lure? —

Dispense this immediately if you figure yourself to be uncomfortable. This may appear to be unprofessional, given where we work — but this is a private matter as I believe so. You may ask why I don't just send you an email... if it were that simple. It isn't, in case you were wondering. The WM would get a whiff out of this and I'd end up in the sack. Too much of a toss if I let them trace the contents back to the sender — me. Back to the point, you and I can agree that our relationship has grown over these years and you've become quite a patch on me, in a good way, of course. If I were to find something better, I'd consider leaving only if you were to come with me. Would you run away with me? It seems silly but our recess times are something I personally cherish. If you would kindly accept, my proposal for you to become my favourite ally, confidant, my darling?

Put this in a good hiding place should you choose to contemplate the question.

Otherwise, I apologise in advance.

With love,

Dylan

Throwing the letter on Forest's desk, Xira walked out in haste to resume the scavenging. Down the far end were the overturned halls with the opposing rooms belonging to the lab specialists and the OCR Yaraks. Manoeuvring further by the side with roaming Yaraks approaching the lane of dispersed documents, a scanner's beam tracked the way before them as she snuck inside a vacant room and yanked the shutter. She overheard the chatter among the two with the new earpiece, while they turned to stand by the railing — leaning to the other direction.

"To ask what you think, would I even want to know?" One of the Yaraks asked.

"Look, you say you're happy, you're in a family, a newborn is arriving," the other replied, *"the way I see it and the way it does appear... are quite similar — except, I'm the supportive role and well, the appearance is deceiving. After we complete this mission... they already have more things lined up... I am not sure of their generosity."*

A tap of the shutter against the window brought the discussion to a pause, before a Yarak remarked, *"You hear that?"*

Shining through the gaps was an azure light as Xira eyed the scanner rotating the interior. After a brief second, they scraped back to their patrol when she picked up on another reply.

"They have us in shackles, man," the Yarak muttered on, *"Code this, code that. Pursuing by code. It makes me feel like a machine and less of a human. I want to be a better father and this place isn't giving me my way home."*

Xira quickly left the room and ran off to the next turning point; the office belonging to *JACAN* was arranged at the hall's end. In the moment, a disruptive alert ripped through the ceiling's speakers: '*ATTENTION YARD PERSONNEL. WE HAVE DATA OF A RECOGNISED ENTITY TRESPASSING THROUGH THE BUILDING. IT IS KNOWN THAT THEY HAD ESCAPED FROM THEIR CELL AND IS POSSIBLY ARMED — ADJUSTING INFRARED SETTINGS. — FULL IMAGE TO DISPLAY. — FIND THEM."*

On a built-in monitor screen below the equipment, revealed a camera's footage of a crossing along the second floor. Her berry raincoat was captured briefly with the profiling achieved by its hood shifting in a flutter. *Damn it,* she brooded. Off in a sprint towards the lieutenant's office and without any hesitation, she barricaded the door to a portion of the small window panel. Xira looked around for any means of escape. There was a bookcase with an oddly assorted row of identical layering and materials when she went over but was interrupted by a loud thud against the entrance. A grumbly voice uttered from the outside, jangling the handle. She hurried behind the main desk, its elaborate design providing enough cover with the high shelf atop it — waiting in a stance as her focus darted from the door to the weighty bookcase. Hand at the sling, the slamming noise deemed them unceasing. The person booted the items down, stepping over them as the hinges creaked the detaching panel. The member carrying a long rifle glared at her in their padding with the tech armour.

"Answer for yourself. Tell me what you are doing here!" He yelled out in aim, "Identify... first."

"Hmm?" Xira, in disbelief, looked to the man with wonder, "*You're* Jacan? No — it can't b — Not you..."

The badge on the lieutenant reflected in the round fluorescence, when he said, "Tell me. Tell me now!"

She stood at a tilt, watching him and uttered, "Jay'eo... please. It's me... don't you remember? It can't have been that long... what have they done to you...? Jay'eo..."

The man raised the grip and a disturbed hesitance overshadowed his conduct, when Xira used this chance to move closer, except the fallacy turned shattered as she did — ringing a single bullet to her chest. Seeing the shell bounce to the floor, she swung to disarm in a scuffling bend down the barrel and smashed the gun through the glass aside a coffee table. Xira went in to wrap herself in an ardent hug, hoping to sway him over. In a moment of catching their breath, Jay'eo's lips puttered before sinking on her shoulder in a muffled whimper, changing his posture like that of a burdened man; no longer in possession. The speakers could be heard blaring out in the hall, announcing a full Yard search to all the employees on the grounds. He backed away to examine the impact, though to his witnessing eyes, a restoring dent came to be — the special suit that was worn guarded off the charge. Jay'eo looked to her then moved towards the side.

"They're all looking for you," he gruffed, picking the gun, "Many armed to their gums. The Yaraks are well proficient to land a couple of hits when commanded. If it counts, it's fire in the hole."

"It wasn't my intention to blaze past an open season," viewing the case, she went on, "I've made another route. Question is, how are *you* going to believably explain to your superiors?"

Jay'eo turned to face the door, replying, "By doing just that. Listen, hide in here until I whistle for the clear. What you do plan to do next, I can only advise for it to be far apart from any employee. I'll hold the others off."

"Don't put yourself in their line of sight. Even if you do see me… I've come this way. I don't plan on letting some fool with a toy trip a trigger gimmick. They really don't want any trespassers coming back twice… anyway… it was a heavy relief to see you, after all this time…" She replied.

"Years, Xira. I just received a sector call, there's trouble in the upper east quarter. I hope to see you again," the lieutenant whispered, walking out to be greeted by Forest. Rolling behind the desk, she kept hidden until his signal.

The lieutenant's tone resonated through the raucous, "Jacan, a pleasure. Where are you off to, sir? Do see to these matters immediately, then help us locate any non-personnel that taint our foundation. What's with the rifle?"

Jay'eo coughed through the dust as he notified, "I'm going to see a man about a dog. Never mind the broken gun. Meet you on the upper sector. Eyes peeled, Forest."

Minutes later, the whistle that echoed among the floor alerted Xira to the bookcase in means of an escape. Trying each cover on the shelf, she muttered to herself, *I've seen these mechanisms before, it should work… c'mon…* — with each attempt, the walnut wood began to shift, then following another crank turn, the case rotated by the form of a pivot door; leading into a hollow, private chamber and a stairwell on its end. Inside, it'd appeared as a quiet space that he would use when the need to be alone rang true — upon was known, the correspondence of an old friend. *Hmm, guess being alone sits well, for what it's worth…* was her thought. Along the stairs and across a perforated floor hall, she was met with a slider door — activated once solving its five disks on the round imprint. With ease, Xira hurried forward and to the fourth level area. As she reached the entrance that required particular granting, an arm yanked her aside a rest drop and hushed while an assemblage of Yaraks stormed the high grounds by the spiral.

"You're still in here? You're free to go, you know," whispered Fiske, the kind man who was also divided from the team.

She angled to answer him, "Hey, they're holding Rosetta. She has information that could be used against their corruption. Ilari is missing too and he has a cypher that from what I know so far, is vital and they're looking for it as well. We can't let them take anything."

Inspecting the corner to continue, he added, "Oh! — Right… sheesh, I'm glad you told me. It has been terrifying trying to be undercover at a real position I've worked in for a while. I keep to myself as it is, but it just feels like I'm supposed to tell someone something… that it's part of my job tasks, that they're always listening… or waiting… lurking… hunting."

"It's part of *their* bullshit," Xira reminded him, walking along, "To get inside your mind, take off the vessel and use it to entertain an element. Let's go find a Wing Commander's office, will you help? Either is fine, as long as I retrieve a key."

They worked together to sneak through and approach the nearest office that the humble companion could reroute to — evading patrols on the way, barely dodging detection at some points, where it'd been more vast, with every member's eye on the tail. At a hill to the scarce doors that opposed the two, a shiny plaque to the right read as; *WM-RUZAK OFFICE* and on the left, surely it was the engraved lettering of the *WM-JASON OFFICE,* also realised as Willow's father. Off to the right, Fiske assumed it to be the safe option now to first inspect this personnel's room, for he was not on this floor when previously overheard.

"I sort of have a way about lock-picking… with these utensils," Fiske spoke quietly, "It's an advantage I suppose, with the type of tech lying around this place… how can you not take matters in your own hands?"

The office door pushed open once he'd tampered with the lock device, bearing no alarm at all. This time, the companions were met with yet another form of security placement — lasers. Although it came to as no surprise, they knew they had to come up with a secure plan to execute this correctly, leaving traces only to the mice. He grabbed an air freshener beside a workbench and used it below the crossing rays. Its structure made fit for those who could apply a moment's grace, when it meant to decide for vanishment. The buzzing of the machines right behind the last row flickered its computer screens in indication that the office was in lockdown; with just the wing commander's password needed to neutralise its configuration. Xira slunk to the tiles, meeting the red laser's beam as it reflected against the silver glow within her eyes. She formed a path in theory and for what would achieve a landing on the other side. While observing the button systems along the office board, there was one that stood out when she declared it to be a fair starting point — activating this button would alter some of the lasers' positions to maximise the spacing for her to go through. She reached for her sling and a star-shooter, readying her aim before Fiske intercepted by a tap on the shoulder blade.

"What if we send off a full alert?" He asked, looking onward, "Maybe it redirects to its neighbouring clickers and who knows what is unleashed… Play it safe…"

She focused on its trajectory, before muttering, "Fivefold."

Launching the fragment through the gaps of the still air, its manoeuvring had aligned to a smooth course and then it'd impacted the yellow button, before instantly switching gears for the new layout.

Fiske jumped in his anticipation, whispering, "Ho-ho, dang! Bullseye!"

Xira handed him the raincoat, slid below and orbited her way across — patient as she was, the slight rotation of the beams forced the action in moving fast. Balancing between the two forms and with an arching land, she stood to dust herself off as Fiske cheered her on silently. Searching the office stations for any keys, she warned the companion to keep an eye on the halls — luckily, curtains were a preference to the high personnel.

Meanwhile, Willow and Sam had tracked down a receptionist who took time out of their night shift to fill up on a staff luncheon, despite the ongoing chaos. According to most of the second-floor employees, they felt without reason to intervene in the matters that weren't handed to them — emphasising on the fact that while at work, meant to accomplish nothing but *it* — completely ignoring previous announcements cutting out the speakers. Willow walked up to the crowded table and tapped on the receptionist's back, standing beside her together.

"Please excuse us, we have a single question that you could possibly help us with," she stated, laying low, "Wing Commander Jason. He's my father, you see. I came to visit — although, looks like I need a key to reach his floor. May I borrow one?"

The receptionist gagged on their spoonful, not expecting such a request. She answered in a droning manner, "Good grief... as you can see, I'm trying to indulge myself in a chef-made soup and croquettes. Leave me be? Perhaps there is somebody *else* on a step stool that can offer you the satisfaction."

Sam leaned to be in view and added, "Hello, hi. I work here. I'm supposed to take her up to meet Sir Jason. But my, I don't carry the access myself — in exchange, I will bring you a bowl of ice-cream from the front counter. Deal, ma'am... Barbara?"

Barbara turned to take a quick gander, when she said, "It's strange that you haven't already been given that access, young man. Even so, I remain whelmed and would actually appreciate a nice refreshment — for once, when somebody *else* gifts me the delight."

The pair thanked her and arranged to meet by the dining room's water station once the staff dinner had been concluded. While they waited on the cue, the receptionist soon walked over to their position and gestured to follow. Above the level, they were taken to where she'd been working and within the next few minutes, were given a third-floor key card.

"Return it once you're done, I've marked your names on the clipboard," Barbara informed them, opening the shutter to a secure length, "They will ask why one is missing. Normally, these are distributed to third level employees — just don't lose it."

On their way towards the next sector, Sam remarked under his breath, "This area, we will need to be extra cautious. If it wasn't for her... wham, we'd be in another jam. Well... there it is."

Locating the entrance with the key card panel, the two waltzed to the disordered hall and continued further along the rumpus. Muddy footprints were briefly discerned on the marble ground as more pages were seen scattered around the area. Willow looked on down the way, as Sam stayed beside her in a quiet, inspecting manner.

"Just over there," he mentioned, pointing the view, "From the map, it displays each room to all the other cubicles. Jason's office is right around that corner. I've never been, which is rather thrilling... I've heard it is as peculiar."

With a pondering motion amidst the hall, Willow responded, "I used to care, really. He's already out of my family, already off my own radar. Whatever we can use in there, everything there is, is why we're going in. I'm doing this for Xira and I. He is just another stranger to me now."

Back in Ruzak's office, the drawers and cabinets had been rummaged through and an easier solution to the security was yet to be found. Fiske's eyes peered by the side, reporting the various members which roamed about — keeping a low profile behind cover. Among the adjacent desks within the office, piles and piles of Yard documents that the wing commander had been working on were left in a mess as Xira filtered between the layers to gather what she could apply against them. Of all the intel that was already known regarding the Yard's schemes, there was but another that caught the slightest attention — its title reading; *Back Door*. Perusing on, she could tell the disgust and shame the wing commander had subdued for the associates that did and still work with him. A lining even she thought wouldn't be crossed in an environment where the higher personnel typically stood together. Now knowing just about anyone would go to any length, to achieve their goal and outdo a once straightforward task. The file, typed and underlined, went on as;

Back Door

Sire Shepherd. Where do I begin? Where is the structure*?*

I presume you've received my fax on the recent reports*.*

My position is mimicked by those who do not tend accordingly.

I cannot *idle by while these miserable excuses for* affiliates *attempt to deconstruct the* official objective of the Yard*. I hereby solicit what I like to call a* "Back Door"*. This would consist of additional* measures

in countering these riling minions and anybody polluting *the way.*

My tolerance has been tried. Thus, I present to you, again, *with utter courtesy;*

Experiments *— All to be issued wherever necessary. Note: Max Chem.*

Machinery *— To be managed by LTNTS and WCS only. Note: LVL*

Security.

Transport — *Typically for all employees, except for the private A.V.*
Surveillance — *ENHANCED. Again.*

Personally, wouldn't refuse a separate bean grinding machine,
thank you.

With the hall noise rebounding off the windows when a series of
flashing screens lit up the mirroring walls, Fiske flailed an extending arm
in an alert for noticing both Forest and Ruzak approaching their direction.

"Hide!" Xira whispered, gathering all the items.

Taking no chance, they set to improvise the best they could to
conceal themselves, as Fiske wriggled underneath the corner placed sink
nearby the front entrance. Sorting the parts inside the gloves, she emptied
out a double door cabinet and shut herself in — in time when the two
personnel opened the door. It was quiet for a brief moment, before a
vexed exhaling by one of the men was followed with a command to the
computer.

"Get off my lawn," Ruzak's voice grated, then chimed the loading
effect of the system.

A tapping on the keys was heard when footsteps creeped alongside
the floor, opposite of Xira. The shuffling of items on desks and below
many containers also met with a low muttering in front.

"Eyes peeled, right," said Forest, sitting by the cabinet window, "He
can hide it all he wants, but no gun I've seen has ever been handled like
that. You find it, yet?"

The wing commander tardily replied, "Foolish woman wouldn't say
a word. I am supposed to guess where the cypher went. Can you believe
what the Commander would do? Sinking her feet deeper makes us sink
ours. We need a plan. First, locking this in the safe. To the upper floor it
is."

The minutes later felt like hours, where the room fell to a quiet office
once more as Xira peered outside the door frame — empty.

"Psst," Fiske called to her, "Use this."

Sliding under the reactivated lasers was a PDA device belonging to
him and once she booted it at a halt as it reached her, the companion
informed that he had used it to record their conversation. That it would
suit for storing evidence.

Xira whispered back, "Thanks, it could maybe help us turn these off.

You could do your little lockpicking on this safe and snatch that key of his. I bet it's for the cypher."

She pulled up the device to the computer and played the recording at loud volume to use the command line. After a few attempts and adjustments, the system approved of the vocal identity, switching the beams to face the ceiling in a roof form with the click of a button prompt on-screen. Hurrying over, Fiske went to the unusual lock on the compartment and stood at an angle to figure out the mechanism. While they waited, Xira arranged the items stashed within the gloves, ensuring they won't fall out. Through trial and error, he figured it to be rather a complex process and that it would take him a little bit longer. The announcements continued to blare among the halls and occasional roaming personnel would be spotted rushing back and forth the way. On the last few hatches, the cover had somewhat begun to project.

"Is that supposed to happen?" Xira leaned close, "If we can make it quick…"

Sticking a wire between the teeth, Fiske replied, "Oh, sure. Almost there… yea — wait. Wait. Give me those scissors, please? On the table."

She handed them over before they were lodged right beside the shell, cracking it open by the metal — its casing tearing down with its added layers. Inside the safe was a propped cushion and the key, welded on it. He fished it out and they examined it together.

"*Another* duplicate? Dude, does he ever walk anywhere without it?" she asked, baffled.

Fiske eyed it near to its side, then said, "Nah, on the contrary — this is something I've seen them do. See, this little engraving here depicts the authenticity of the key itself. If it were a backup, it would contain a registered code that would be clearly seen upon closer inspection. Ah… yeah, this is the real deal. You keep it."

Xira stashed it away without hesitation and marched towards the exit. Checking both lanes, she presumed it to be the right time for them to leave. She lifted a hand to signal and waited for the hall to clear of the roaming members. Once outside, they hurried to the longer route back to Wing Commander Jason's office — out of sight, momentarily out of mind.

"What's going on? Why are the lights out?" Fiske spoke in a hushed concern.

As they approached the door, a clatter rang on behind the windows when the electricity zapped in a blinking sequence and revealed somebody already in the room. Within the second's haste of the power returning to its space, it'd become clear of the inside of this office — to her slight surprise, Xira squinted on the view where she saw Willow standing by the wing commander.

Transparent as the unveiled windows, she called out in a mouthing expression, "Huh?"

Her companion not only was beside her father, but looking rather furious by the grappling around the collar. Seeing him in pure fright, Xira called to her louder this time, questioning the situation. Sam was soon realised minding the door, while he stood with arms crossed and merely witnessing all before him.

It didn't take much before she caught her ally watching the two in their distressed form.

"Oh, God... Xira! Father is a mess, what do I do?" Willow pleaded around her weighing quandary.

Xira arched to the window in a bartering disposition.

"Willow, it's up to you. The shit he's caused, taking a loved one right from your hands. I wouldn't advise doing the same, despite it..." She ruminated, then went on, "Then again... what does he have to lose? Maybe leave him to embrace the light of day and to regret it. It's useless... but... what's the use deciding his fate?"

Her companion grimaced in the frustration, "I don't know. I came here for one thing! Didn't think he would sit here like the coward that he is. Say that you are sorry! Say that you will turn yourself in! That you will make better choices..."

"Willow... he's too far off, virtue is not within him any more."

"I got more than I asked for and it didn't do me any good! He's just *pathetic*! Father, couldn't even provide what I truly needed... you just couldn't leave mother and I alone. My *grandmother* is someone you should thank... ask *her* to forgive your mistakes, until then... argh, why! I'll leave this guilt to you — may the burden be light."

A slam across his collar as he exclaimed with ferocity, resulted in a thudding land on the tiled floor — knocked out, amidst the zapping voltage in the office. Gathering the breaths, Willow tacitly looked out the window and uttered in a doleful tone.

"Go on, Xira... I need some time here, we'll meet outside later like we promised."

Off to the access panel, the two awaited the lift to descend as soon as the card had been authenticated. Fiske looked to his ally, a thoughtful yet fairly silent impression that they then both shared. The sympathetic return of Xira's glance altered to a hopeful, better slant, when the doors reeled back and there, was an empty cage. The way up quickly turned to a downward trip because of a demanding request for a pickup. Walking in were a pair of lab specialists and their packed hands with embossed confidential folders. A nonchalant but suspecting demeanour, they stood before them, minding their task without so much as a third peer. Xira nudged her friend over to check the files wedged in Yard binders — he extracted the farthest one finely, placing it by his side until they left. The way up provided them a chance to take a scan at what was kept quite near and dear. On its front page stood out in cursive lettering on a project under their sleeves, that of which involved multiple subjects and cases of a transformation for an inhuman. By the time they'd flipped to the last sheet, the chime had already rung. Fiske shoved the folder beneath his clothing in hopes to conceal it and they walked out to a barren lobby, seemingly part of a larger one ahead. Xira listened intently as she examined the environment, a modern but delicate design with the glossy mirroring walls, the grey colouring among its sable overlay in fusion to the illumination extending down from its plafond. It'd reeked of a profound ominousness. Towards the obscured layer of the floor, she could make out a figure or two standing by as if they were guarding the area. By the corner the companions waited — with thought of what to do next, as she continued to listen in on a potential conversation. That was when the bang of a door resonated out in a rather sensitive wobble to the earpiece. The clunking sound of footsteps being emphasised on the flooring and accompanied by a few gravelly voices, came to play. Xira picked up on their communication in a hollow effect.

"*In there. Man this area. Do not let anybody in or out, that understood?*"

"*Mmh, ma-ha.*"

"*Forest. Go to the West Zone, watch the TYG Generator. You. Stay here and listen for commands.*"

"*Ga. We-ha. Tu.*"

As the pair spotted Ruzak disappearing to another room and something dimming the area, the two friends crouched by their positions, looking to one another. The cold facet of the tiles drifted along as if the temperature was altered. It had been quiet, *too* quiet.

"What *was* that?" Fiske asked as he leaned over.

She focused towards the way and responded, "Not sure. I'm going in to check this out. You mind my back."

"Hu — wait!"

Moving to the centre, Xira stood at the opening and was met with two brutes that turned at the steps, for they perceived the approach. Displeased, they slowly reached to seize her when she knew there was no way around it. She slid down the sliver of a gap, barely missing the swings and gaining more ground. She knew she had to move fast. With the high personnel practically surrounding the upper level and Fiske laying low in the back, there was no way out except through. The brutes instantly thudded to follow wherever a turn was taken and pursued their target relentlessly. Although with a hushed demeanour — apart from the grumbles — the menacing methods were enough to deflect even the most proficient adversary. A towering build that obstructed a fair amount of space with an odd increase of speed each time a certain action had been performed. Xira bounced off a side wall to execute a kick across the nearest brute while knocking it towards the other in a tackling stumble. As they swiftly regained their footing, she lodged both knees to one's back and swung the head to and fro, grabbing around their neck in a yanking attempt. They fell to the floor and while she rolled out to evade the collapse, the second brute rushed to pick up and launch her across the opposing hall which led to the West Zone. A slide among the tiles, Xira raised to see it helping the brute get back to stand while reaching for her sling. They began their chase again, when Ruzak stepped out in view of the situation he'd somewhat overheard. With the cold way behind and the draught that seeped along her sides, the two brutes stood at a commanded halt before her — then the wing commander's slow walk to meet her.

"I know you," he remarked, motioning down then continued, "Absolute, resisting, nuisance. Escaping that cell merely brought you closer to our motivations. Clever, you've chosen freedom — at what cost? All you who want to defy us, end up with us. It was never that easy.

You stepping foot on our grounds, tsk — welcome, I'd say. Albeit, it is not quite as tempting."

Xira shuffled to lift up and respond, "We heard what you are up to. Let them go."

"Settle down, the eyes in the walls will hear you. I have a better idea," Ruzak proclaimed, "Get through me and you may enter. I can only guess you are familiar with what or who you will find inside. No weapons, now."

Leaping right on her feet, she then uttered, "Easy was never a choice for either of us."

The wing commander positioned himself to face and hurled forward like a charging rhinoceros, clashing at direct impact. Immediately, she dragged a foot to trip him out from under as he tumbled in a grip to take her down with him. Hindering the punches, Xira pushed against his shoulder, pulling the arm to the left and taking the wing commander over on the backside, gaining leverage with both legs. Placing one atop his abdomen and the other bracing the ground, she crossed the arms over with hers pressing down and against the collar. The man tried to knee from below but hardly budged her stance.

"Give it in, Ruzak. Why do you want to be part of a destructive regime?" She grated the words while holding down.

In a clenching struggle to gasp for air, Ruzak hoarsely stated, "I am one with honour. Carry it through. Made a pact, with people I do not intend — to — abandon. Perhaps — you could see, standing against me means they will — do the same. I gave you a chance."

With a hauling pound, a brute suddenly sent her off to the nearby door as she crashed on its unforeseen opening. A voice called out from inside, shouting, in their startled encounter.

"Rosetta…" Xira slowly crawled to kneel, "Stay there… I can handle this."

Ruzak's looming footsteps came to a thudding halt by the fired wrist on his own at the chokehold attempt. Both glaring each other down as they forced themselves forth, their shoving soon changed when a heating element awakened in the gloved hands — the material which resisted its warmth, instead burnt the wing commander and resulted in a release. His face in disbelief, the man returned with the brutes to rally, as they were prepared to evacuate.

Xira stood on her feet, then revolved to say, "Honour, right? You and your entourage. If I were to guess — you're on your way to the guns and gears with your... bodyguards. Sheep... sheep... sheep."

Beginning to walk off, Ruzak pulled out a hidden pistol and pointed it straight to her. He added, "Mind your accusations, girl. This bears a round that will soon be carved with your name."

"Try me."

An unfurling chuckle echoed from the man as he removed the weapon and gestured to the brutes to stay behind. Off the way, Fiske remained close to the wall as low as he could, watching him take the exit and terminating the access. Xira went over to Rosetta, who jumped at the fresh sight and was liberated from the cuffs to a steel bar. She threw over all the furniture around her against the door, long enough for a plan.

Beaten and wary, Rosetta confessed to her, "Don't worry, I, I'm fine. I never wanted to tell them anything and I didn't. They, uh, kept the blueprints... they can't seem to figure them out entirely. That's not to say they don't know about members being against them... ugh. To find all of us is what I fear, being inside this... this dump."

Xira rinsed out the components from her glove, noticing the burns on the fragments, altering its form. She sighed, tossing them on a nearby desk.

"Fiske and I found what is, left of these items from Ruzak's office. Key — some old badges and I think this was a... a tool of some kind. Honestly, it's the key I'm mostly wondering about. Its bow is slightly melted, but it can still be used."

The member retrieved the other items and held them in her palms in scrutiny of their form.

"These were the badges of the previous possessors that stayed here," Rosetta explained, getting up, "This was never built by Yowndrift Yard. It was taken. An army that lied their way in, manipulated the inhabitants into a new world and convinced all that it was for a better, brighter future. What kind of a world takes but doesn't give? The equilibrium has been breached."

Going for the door, Xira questioned, "Why did you continue working for these people? You say you've been here a long time. The Yard didn't have these plans then and now, it's ripe for the picking."

As she walked out to be met with the pair of brutes manning the front, Rosetta followed, swinging the cuffs to distract, then ran to gain distance and soon realised the maddened reactions of the two charging towards them. Fiske called for a dodge, as he propelled a metal pipe right in a brute's nose, causing him to retract from the steps.

"They oughta' hire a plumber," he remarked in a crouch.

Xira slipped through towards the west zone and turned. Eyeing them directly, she asserted, "Give me the cuffs, Rosetta. I've thought of something that could work."

After they'd been handed over, she gripped the chain between both fists and an oozing steam rose off the rims — rolling open her eyes as she twirled its material in a hovering position. With a quick start, Xira jumped to a run along a side wall, extending an arm out with the chain and whipped it in a wraparound both of the brutes' collars — while she flung in a spin and back, resulting in a burning fizzle on their neck. An electrical effect was noticed sparking from their flesh, before tumbling down and finally being neutralised. The companions rushed to check it out for themselves, when Xira approached to return the cuffs.

"Oh, this really burns," Rosetta exclaimed in awe, "I — I don't need these, but how?"

Walking away to the opposite hall, she told her, "A girl's got to keep some secrets, right?"

Figuring out what to do with the other rooms, the three huddled round in planning as the space fell to a moment of quiet. The members explained to her about the generator that resided inside the west zone and how she could use it to dismantle the Yard's corruption. They kept their glance to the hall, knowing of the threats that await the team.

"The catch is… if we overcome the machinery in that high sector, it could catastrophically burn down the premises," Fiske went on, "What I mean, is, there will hardly be enough time to evacuate anybody because of its power. The Yard wasn't playing around when it came to configuring that thing. Neither of us knew what we were in for. It's too bad we didn't see it before others were involved."

"All blaming aside, it's not just a web of machines and boards, however…" Stating the intel, Rosetta hesitated in the discomfort, "It carries every single data that we've worked for all this time, everything we know about multiple towns. We could use that to help rebuild and restore. Otherwise… it could take longer and with our resource limitations… but look, I know we need to put the matter of this place first — it's, it's priority. Also, to honour the founders of the buildings in town that they've tarnished. We are all the natives of the motherland, so we can find their family and connections to their history. Perhaps there's a declaration, somewhere this Y.Y. doesn't want us to find. It belongs to the children, not these particular groups — based on that theory of connection, like us with Galaxaeria. The thing is, about the Yard, unless they were wanting to refresh the aim—there's information to discover anyway—let's go. I don't even know if it's the safest option, I mean, there is sacrifice here."

Xira wandered towards the west wing as she examined the division ahead. Protected by more of the Yard's experiments and oddities, she could make out the various door frames that they were standing beside, almost in fusion with the metallic walls. She looked back, certain in her own decision.

"I'll go, I'll rid of everything in there and get out as soon as I can," Xira stated reposefully, then continued, "Keep the key. Make sure people are leaving the building, do whatever gets them to move out — including the containment chasm. *Leap!*"

"Are you serious? No way are we letting you put yourself in our predicament," components in hand, Rosetta cut in, "Not alone, especially since there's probably heavy security in there. We're doing this for everyone's liberation. That counts us, that is, if we make it out."

Ignoring the offer, Xira walked on and said, "Trust me. Out of my soul, out of my mouth. I'll be seeing you."

Watching her run off, the companions shouted out in their distressed manner and hopes to inspire reflection, although knowing she was set in her way and already far in, they could only wish for the ultimately better outcome. On to the area and the many eyes that darted in her direction, Xira concentrated on a quick method to reach the other end. With each charging threat stomping in a looming guise, it was realised how the high personnel went to the extremities when transmuting the unfortunate subjects. The long-gone humanity behind it all, replaced with an instructed obsession, a one-way street going down a place void of virtue. It was a hollow gaze to the fire, recklessly and aimlessly, throwing themselves towards their target. Instinctively shifting ways, Xira leaped in a kicking boost off of a myrmidon and atop another brute which shuffled in position as she knocked him over to the others, ending up in a pile on the floor. The incoming troops towered over her before she furiously slammed herself in the frontman's guts, taking them aback with high speed when one on the sidelines intercepted once they'd been knocked and picked her up in a hold. Suspended feet above, Xira wriggled to place the feet on the opponent's shoulders and lug them down amidst few others that were approaching. She rolled to the side in the evade of a launching mitt and found herself being surrounded with the remaining, unyielding foes. Picking and sliding her weight up, she looked at them in turns, eyes rising in its silver and hurled her body to the right, taking a brute many metres down the way — crash landing on the tiles and creating a rip in the floor, her energy and the might that graced their sight, set them afar in their perplexion. Once again, they rushed towards her — in remembrance of their marked code.

In the while, Willow had come up with another plan when she'd left Jason behind, in his secured office. Off with Sam who was carrying her father's key, they marched towards the flight of stairs at the exact time Ruzak rushed by, colliding in their tracks. Startled, she stepped aside to manoeuvre through but was abruptly cut by the wing commander.

"I believe the ball already finished," Ruzak began to say, "We do provide those commodities, my associates."

She turned to the floor, avoiding the contact and replied, "Excuse us."

As they descended, there'd be no further remark but a heedful regard from the wing commander before both then disappeared out of sight. Telling the companion of her idea and that starting from the containment chasm meant covering all areas that they've intended to, Willow entered in a room of mirrors, somewhere neither of them have heard about — surely it led to the containment sector, however a cold and unclear portion on the base made for a narrow crossing for the companions.

"I would've known about this," Sam gently whispered, "It doesn't seem like a thing the Yard would hide. And all these tall mirrors? Man of dimension."

The way forward in figuring out the routes separated the two to different areas nearby. Puzzling as it was, they could still hear each other talk — despite the mirror panels obscuring them apart. Willow continued in her improvisation alongside the analytical chatter of her ally behind the divide. Occasional tapping to test the trail would wobble the mirrors on their way around, revealing subtle corner turns.

"You know what? Next time you ask for a position, maybe take a good look of where you were lured," she told him, inching through a slight gap.

Sam averred among his footsteps, "As you can probably tell, it wouldn't have mattered if I found every toilet and cellar when a place like this keeps many secrets, even they can forget about."

A brick wall lined with attached wires to a heavy frame that shaped like a door was found at the end of that floor. Inspecting it closely, Willow assumed it to be a hidden exit, but what had diverted her from proceeding in confidence was a loose trip wire hanging down by the edges and over to the left hall of mirrors. The will to risk this chance overcame the concerns of what laid beyond this wall. Sliding it to the side, she looked into a dim blue opening to the sector with lofty empty cages.

"Uh, Sam?"

Before he uttered out an answer, the door slammed back in place, leaving her inside the containment chasm. Cautiously checking the path amidst the lattice array of transmitted light coming from a high window, Willow looked to the outdoor lamp post that flickered in its surrounding glow of insects. She tried to call for her companion once again, but no answer. Turning away to the centre, it'd seemed like it was the single way through and out.

Facing the storm, her glare meeting their hostility, Xira's guttural exclamation sent her in a brisk propulsion over the stampede of member variety and upon a grazed landing, the floor was then left with an imprint. A heavy breath to settle as they began to approach, it was the choice of the west zone entrance or a direct clash. With her eyes on the scattered fragments, she noticed the surface give way after every step they took. It'd felt like a second to nothing when a collapse of that portion from the upper floor sunk them to a gritty pit below. Not too long post impact that the ground began to rumble, causing the tanky members to apply their weight atop the sand hill — the soft, low outcries of the brutes was the next thing heard as another submersion occurred, into yet another dark pit underneath. All were strewn across the dust, lost in an abandoned two-floor section that the Yard had undoubtedly concealed. Scraping her hand against the side pile, she rose once regaining momentum and quickly inspected the surroundings. Dark, desolate and dusty. She searched for an escape when soon discovering the one opening waiting above was the same way entered. Without the interest to let them catch on, Xira took off in a grip to the former pit's edge as she pulled over to stand again. The next step was rather higher and it'd meant for her to put her faith to a trial — a trial of gravity versus a bend in its laws. With a leap to the splintered tiles, the emptiness of the area had drawn quite a relief as Xira crawled atop to safety, knowing they were down there now. On towards where she could step besides the floor that was formerly smooth, a door plate caught the attention for it'd mentioned the generator in the west zone and along its adjacent, relative rooms. *Huh, good thing I found this,* was her thought. Walking inside, nothing but a glass case of a preserved titanium shard was placed at the back wall where on both its sides contained an elaborate steam machinery — used for opening the case properly.

"Raptor, can you hear me?" She spoke into the earpiece, eyeing the design before her.

A brief few moments went by, before a transmission was received with fairly clear signal.

The mentor then added in, "Sweet child, are you all right? Did you arrive there in one piece?"

"I think I left something on the bus," was the grimly sarcastic response. She then said, "There is this setup that's installed on the upper floor. Do you know anything by it? It's by the West Zone hall."

The quiet pause which ushered his reply after the busy background noise, crackled the communications before he announced, "May... have heard of a thing, or two. Ah, dear, I really shouldn't be telling you this — well, listen up. A little squirrel came to my window sill and told me this; it is a prize, a piece of solution for the cauldron of gold. Like the petals of a flower, I'll surmise a count of five, to find all the delicates and ever so apply. They should all be nearby... nearby... keep an eye. Once it comes to bloom, you'll see for yourself. Watch all your sides, sunflower."

Thanking Serenitatem for the information, Xira spun the gears as the handles rotated the spindle and removed the casing with ease. After she picked up the shard, the structure returned to its place and position.

Outside, the neighbouring room contained the same components, although it being a different colour of shards — followed its identical design, a resembling match. On to the next and tracing a pattern across all the rooms throughout this level, she came to bear the five shards in the palm of her hands. Each placed beside the other while treading by the direction screens, a dwelling enigma came over her, for the next part of the plan was to approach and settle this.

In the meantime, the containment chasm was nothing short of eerie as Willow slowly scouted the area with a stench quite harsh, the need of a mask was an understatement. Although there were empty cages and it was left without a patrol, it'd still given off the feeling that a lurker was amidst, that it wasn't as empty like a guest would think. Seeing an abandoned doll down by a set of bars, she knelt to inspect the cage and the dust beneath the placed sheets. Hearing a distant yell of her name, she turned in its point of origin and then recognised the particular voice — repeating again with a synchronous bang against the walls.

"Hey! Sam! I'm over here, wait up!" Willow said in response, before rushing to reach him.

The noise stopped once she'd arrived at the door, where Sam attempted another shout, "I don't want to be by myself! Please, help! This room is making me uncomfortable… hello! Willow! Is that you?"

She replied reassuringly, "It's all right, Sam. I'm here. We need to keep it a bit quieter though, okay?"

Back at the west zone hall, Xira walked towards an old, regal gateway with an attached device beside it. Grabbing the device, its label indicated that it was primarily used for the voice operated access. With the speakers that would on and off announce new orders for the members, she figured it wouldn't be an odd attempt to retrieve a sample by that method. Extending the wired equipment as far as it'd go, as a cable reeled out of its built panel, the device was aimed high to the blaring personnel while Xira remained focused on the door. Eventually gathering enough to analyse for confirmation, an unlocking sound that then opened the entrance, retracted its operator and played an automated message; *granted, welcome.*

Once inside, a bedimmed sector awaited as Xira exclaimed, mystified, "Well this is j—"

Before the entirety of the room exhibited itself, a hovering platform zipped above in the way to arrange itself within — idling by the grazing generator. Behind the amber frosted glass stood a slender figure draped with a distinctive sash along their uniform, who then waltzed around to obtain the platform. Coming to encounter an unaccompanied visitor, the lieutenant barely masked a sneering impression towards her.

"My word. The sinner barges in the fumigator's cocoon," Forest uttered in a honeyed manner.

Xira slipped behind the nearest divider in hopes to be steps ahead. A pattern of footprints followed as she continued further along the glass, watching the high personnel's outline track the path. With a turn inside the space of multiple connectors leading to the generator's base, Xira knew this was bound to stray further from simplicity. She eyed the formatted flooring to each corner and technical barriers that separated the single rows of electronically and chemically powered panels, all directed towards the Yard machinery.

"This TYG Generator is my responsibility now," he said, gliding by walls, "Since you clearly do not respect Yowndrift Yard and their work, I will, with pleasure, show you the splendour myself."

With a quick sprint forward, she placed one of the shards in their coloured compartment and upon observing it, it'd then activated a single connector above. Crouching low beneath the dividers, she could discern the frustration that the lieutenant displayed by his fuming chase.

"What do you think you're doing?" The lieutenant asked, searching for her again, "You're not a Yarak. Not with the high table. Hell, not even a brute! Who *are* you? Leave that alone."

"You want to know something, Forest? I don't care even if you do find me out." Xira said aloud, "What I do care for is to rid of this mess you and your fraudulent army have dumped on us all. Rethink your priorities, old man. That's *my* word for you."

Dashing down the path to plan the next placement, she encountered another platform before her as its lasers skimmed in a scanning rotation. She dodged underneath and ran for the generator along its narrow flooring and slammed in the corresponding shard.

Forest shouted madly once again, "Enough! Off with your inanity! Command fro I, detour exit!"

As Xira hugged the wall in realisation of a partition obscuring the way through, she raced towards the sliding door when the lieutenant's desperate attempt to knock her down was shattered by the launched handgun that chipped the glass and carved the board in the new hall. A knife which protruded from below the grip like an attachment, a formidable design to enhance its lethality, was scraping along the wall's edge. She picked up the weapon as the carved initials on the leather read; *L.D.F.* Turning it over, the blade was sharp enough to even cut the beholder. Inside the magazine contained a lone bullet. With never having held a gun, let alone use it, Xira switched to the pointing blade and continued on up the stairs to an ascension taking her to steel door and its remotely controlled window. *This must be the last floor, it's got to be…* she thought, before knocking a few more times. Dropping the raincoat down, she listened in by the frame. The door swung open and seated in an executive chair, was the revolving commander who then introduced himself as he greeted her.

"What a sight, come in. — Do tell me about yourself and of your intentions for being granted the visit."

Xira entered the elaborate, cybernated lair as she cautiously addressed, "It's a pleasure to meet you, Commander. I'm sure your hands are full, so I'll be brief. I've heard about your interests… you want to bring a new ideal."

"Please, my, you are certainly correct," the Commander expressed, hands overlapped, "I'll be honest, it is a fine harmony to be understood by your pursuit. Despite taking almost everything within the grasp to witness a victory so… refined, with such delivery… wouldn't you agree? The environment ultimately becoming… ethereal. I'm not the chief of this corp for nothing. Therefore, how else do I owe the delight? Would you like a personalised documentary? A pamphlet? Or perhaps your very own position?"

A vexed sigh uttered from her watchful self, then offhandedly Xira launched the handgun against the padded wallpaper behind him, pinning it right with the grip's blade. She remarked, "I said I'll be brief. I'm not here to be swayed. Finish whatever machinations you've placed around here and do something far wise with all these resources. Give yourself the chance to be better. I promise you, no one will benefit from this. Nothing good comes from a war-torn agenda, fuelling the eradication that leaves a home to not one soul."

The commander fetched a tool from a drawer, arranged it on the desk and composedly sat by the confrontation. After a moment, he answered in a guttural means, "Perspective, young lady. You may see it as a wipeout of sorts, however… sometimes to see and believe, lures one in the need to delve deeper. It goes without saying, to find the answer, no? Well, I say…"

Xira marched forward in hopes for him to reconsider, vividly from an opposing being to the matter at their hands.

"**Shepherd**," she muttered, glaring him down, "Taking only proves the giving for yourself. Will you still be satisfied? You don't own these people, you don't own this land, nobody does. This need to *own,* to act above your kind. Foolishly, you're filling a void's appetite… and what then? If your capacity to love, to simply exist within… hmm… or are you lost? Look… no wall or window will help you hide from or see… the truth is out there. Step outside, *Commander.* Take it all… and leave it be. A home is something great, something people like you take for granted. It's an open land — a world — for everyone, together. Why destroy that paradise? To what end?"

Curving a hand beside the desk, the commander walked to the window panels and stood by the screens adorned above and along. A footage that emerged, zoomed in on particular scenes via the siding display. As they watched, he pointed near the screen's corner and folded his hands behind facing at a turn. On the recording was various imagery of the grey berry raincoat being captured by the few hidden cameras throughout the way. Then after, an altering layered video where all the levels were seen in a montage that showcased the fourth floor, played and with its most recent security footage; the mess of the brutes around that sector.

"It is *foolish* to assume I'd not borne witness… Xira," he declared with a sinister undertone, "Perhaps vindication is something left behind, although… if I were to make an excuse for every outsider that dares to invite themselves… well… you best be joining the rightful habitation. You've dwelled here enough."

In the abrupt upheaval by the floor, the surface panel beneath her feet had retracted to a gaping duct which as she began to skid, the commander slowly rotated and looked over from his position — towards her drop into descension. Below, she recalled on the map layout and instinctively thrust her legs against both rims to make a rough dent, continuing to do so while cutting the harsh somersaulting in the means of switching its implemented direction.

"Shit!" she yelled out.

A heavy thud on the lower level's ground, Xira sat up to examine the muffled space with a soft light shimmering through the nearby door. Pushing herself back on foot, she walked out to see the mirroring narrow pathways which would lead to the generator room, as the board by the wall's curve had indicated. Onto the barred access was the dusty aperture that revealed Forest seeking for a route to recover the inserted pieces. Although it would require him to use the lever in the deactivation process, setting for a trial against perseverance, he was seen in the light of chagrin and the long-time guise of the lieutenant had been coming undone. She slammed against the door until it'd opened, swinging to the side as she rushed after him to then knock the man down in diversion from pulling on the switch. After getting back up, Xira formed a planned track around the place to secure the shard placements upon each entrance to the generator's location. With success and a mere remainder of one shard, she catapulted with the incoming charge of the lieutenant, towards sticking in the fragment just as they landed — sliding across in the tackle she'd gambled for the sake of the task. By the dismay of events not pertaining to his liking, Forest unsheathed a pocket knife to her neck and channelled some platforms to surround her. The machinery began a rumbling echo, with the panels overriding the personnel's controls and tracing the charge to initiate detonation.

"You're forcing my hand," Forest muttered through his teeth, "Step away while you can."

"And you, mine," replied Xira in the hassle, before slamming down the generator's fuel button — taking to the unfurling of the Yard's downfall.

Like a thunderous, volcanic avalanche, the upper sector gave way to the flaring cracks which soon ravaged the hold of the structure, as a swift miss by his blade tumbled the lieutenant off one of the remainders of the tiles. Dangling with a single hand to weigh, the debris below ranged to a daunting distance. Xira knelt on a shuddering tile with a foot to the closest one available and lent down a hand to a disrupted Forest.

"Grab on, quick!" She told him in the midst of the whirling flames that crawled the walls and the collapsing ceiling.

"What? I can't jump out myself?" Forest said miserly, angling down then back up, "Let me go…"

Alongside a grunting effort, Xira lowered herself, insisting on a voluntary rescue.

"Whose smart idea was it to ventilate this room with gaps to below? Hurry, Forest!"

The lieutenant's fingers scraped down the breaking surface and uttered a genuine, sorrowful declaration, "Please… tell Lieutenant Paris that I… do."

Watching the man succumb to the depths as all else crumbled around her, Xira spun beside the closest panel to catch her breath, with a weighing sigh to push on towards the exit. As the fire began to rise and overwhelm the room, she glanced once more down to the debris, before running off in a ram through the door — racing against the looming destruction to the way out. By the time she'd reached the third floor, occupants were already desperately scavenging their belongings and covering the corridors once they'd been alerted of an evacuation hazard. Despite her brooding over the wagering of escapees and ones still inside, she stormed on to now locate the companions and intending to support them in their endeavours. Arriving at the base floor, either exits were packed with members itching to leave. She noticed townspeople going up the stairway, knowing by their ragged clothes that they were coming from the lower sector and walked right towards them. Down the steps, she'd run into her companions at half point and going up alongside the crowd.

"H-Hey! Oh, w — we got out as many as we could," Willow explained by the handrail, "The containment chasm is empty, I-I — we checked all the areas, but I think people were still kept somewhere down there."

"Its surveillance arrangement may be in use around their position," added Sam, "If we were t—"

Xira looked to the lower perimeter, hopped down beside them and stated, "I'll go look for them. Make sure you're all out of the building as soon as you set foot. The upper floor is already in shambles."

Grabbing her in the sense of bewilderment, Willow replied earnestly, "What about you? You'll be inside with who knows what else… I want to see you out, we've done enough."

Swerving past the panicking people, Xira glanced at her companions as they returned the impression, knowing no matter who'd have told her otherwise, it wouldn't change the mark made.

"You will. So go on, get out! If there's anybody else left, I'll do what I can — watch the doors!" she said, running off.

Once reaching the base level following the chasm and zipping through the double doors, she could hear the nearby clamour coming from another area ahead. The alarm that blared over the speakers grew louder with every hall crossed and even through the announcers that would alternate, their alerts were quelled with the ongoing effect that grazed the facility. On to a row of cubicles within the far sector, both Wing Commander Jason and Lieutenant Gyrfalcon were spotted in their fleeting inspection of the people residing in there. Figuring by the way of their hesitant behaviour, as if they were planning to abandon everything else among this floor, she took to approach them — standing by as well, a group of well-armed and instructed Yaraks.

"No! Let them out!" Xira shouted, observing the area, "How many more are down here?"

Turning to meet, Gyrfalcon held out a device and declared, "This will pick up the signals we need. Otherwise, to whomever luck is within the pillaging. Or was that… a sword? For a parley?"

"Luck? Listen — get the people to safety, not the damn experiments!" she returned.

"Party or parley? Your choice," he went on, walking forth, "Gentlemen…"

Before they even considered to reflect on their decisions, the Yaraks charged towards her with a Yard weapon. Etched on the steel spinners was their emblem and attached to the edges were electronic pins — that with a swing, could burn the opponent if the pointers were to be renewed by voltage power from its mechanism. Focused on dodging the personnel as two of them attempted to land an assault, she slid under in aim of the high members and dashed to the side just missing the next Yarak and paused by a concrete pillar. They went after her once again, with an order to be taken down while a sweeping was being done in that sector. She drew in the cold air and targeted the oncoming Yarak with a star-shooter, using her sling to knock out the other opposing the side as well. *Guagh, damn it...* she thought, *okay. Three. Three left.* As the remainder of the group rushed by in aggressive action, they tossed their weapons, hitting her against the shoulders when she braced to evade. Seeing them surround her in the corner of the area, it was notably less obvious as to which path led to where from that unilluminated position — however, a courageous stance led her to believe one thing that was then abundantly clear.

"Enough!" She spoke in a low, irked manner.

Breaking off a bolted pole from the structure on the wall, she steadied to an angle as they each threw their hands in conflict. Xira deflected the Yaraks one after another before carving her way out of that space and through the next hall that would take her to the high personnel within the sector. Although still being followed during the approaching flames tumbling the floors down to the base, she continued to pursue them and soon found herself at an encounter by a covert entrance to two adjoined rooms. Inside, the Lieutenant and Wing Commander were treading on about with some baggage, while she secured the door.

"You're all leaving with me," Xira told the startled pair, "Or it's no one. Don't even think about a second exit."

Gyrfalcon cut off Jason's attempt at raising his rifle to her as he warningly informed, "Stop it, do you understand if we stay here and fight, everything will be ignited in a blasting disaster? This room is where the Yard's propellant systems are placed and if that — we — yes, everyone is leaving! Now!"

She immediately spun to unlatch, eyeing the two just as the ceiling's corner came to fall atop an old machine. Leaping out, Xira was thrust against the barren floor and was met with a collapsing plank shortly after getting up. The fiery debris weighed heavy on the waist as she pushed to oppose, tipping it over when its remaining embers blew out of the material. Seeing the personnel rush past, accompanied with another crowd from both the neighbouring towns and the facility, she soon joined right by before checking the base once more for any case of a person still inside the blaze. As Xira went for the battered door, a member rushed from the side at that time in their sense of scouting.

"No one left behind! Go!" They shouted, gesturing to hurry along before exiting out the front.

Xira tugged at her stomach, for it'd been sorely grazed amid the tender portion of the suit in the events prior, causing a limping delay down the hallway path. Persistently stepping on during the destruction which caught up at the heel, fragments of both walls chipped by the minute as she slid across to hold the weight. She could feel the heat clouding beside her when evading its crackling deformation that snapped down each way. As Xira harshly walked out, the force of the flaming building erupted to an explosive calamity, originating from the upper floor sector. This had catapulted her over on the gravelly terrain, sensing its damp texture with the fire right behind and the arrant conquering of Yowndrift Yard's headquarters. Laying among the relief of her escape and the hazardous, elaborate plan, she remained in a rest before subtly hearing distant voices call to her and arrive — muffling upon every blink and there, entering an induced slumber.

"Mmh," she mumbled as they carried her to a safe point, far from the sunken ashes.

Awakening to her friends sitting by, the grass beneath had cooled off her exterior in the midst of spotting a jogging, bewildered Fiske approaching their location.

Willow was inspecting a wound on the side when she said, "There were a few screws underneath this fabric — I looked into it but it probably, somehow wedged between — I don't understand. It's such a tiny fraction where it is attached — see, this fabric is tougher than all I've seen. Must've been a hell of a fall, Xi..."

The noise from the gathering people at the hills beyond, gradually eased to a hushed discussion among the personnel. As further down they were, the companions kept themselves at a low profile, hindering the Yard's chance in finding the escapees.

"Ruzak took her again... I tried... I couldn't," Friske began as he crouched, "There was no way of me taking on him — he said that Ilari had run away with the cypher wheel and he went after him, along with Lieutenant Paris and Wing Commander Jason... they intend to get it back. I saw Saffron being threatened into helping them, he had the two women at gunpoint. Said he wouldn't think twice..."

"Bastards..." Xira remarked under a breath, holding Willow's hand over the waist, "I need to find Ilari before they do. If that cypher really is the one I've heard about... we can't let it fall into their hands..."

Patting along the shoulder frame, Willow urged and beseeched,

"They are armed. It's too dangerous to put yourself in their light of Yard methods, he's not the same man like those gone, old days when I was shorter than mother's little lemon tree. He won't dust you off from the sandpit this time…"

Taking to an observant stance, they lowered in a huddle when Sam pulled out a pair of binoculars to cover the landscape. Her companion slouched beside her, giving a reassuring hug around the arm. In the moment where the high personnel began to escort the members down the road and rallying everyone in multiple rows, the team crept behind a floral hedgerow, under a street post with its fluttering illumination on the night's coarse air.

Friske whispered in a glance, "You truly brought binoculars, Sam?"

The former member replied, fidgeting with a shrug, "The first thing I grabbed when I heard the building coming down like that."

"Really? Nothing else seemed more appealing?"

"A-po-lo-gi-es if this makes for an aversion rather than a tool in *your* view. It's a weapon in its own right."

Meanwhile, the crowd began to reduce to the vaporous backdrop tailing them as they were led to various transportations that'd emerged. So did the fire and flames, within the remainders of the accursed tower, known as a service refuge but discovered to be a fool's playground.

"You did it, Xi," whispered Willow before standing again, "The Yard is backing down and no longer do they hold such a station. Home is ours once again."

"For now," she returned, "We still need to figure out what brought on the mess outside as well… now that I think about it more… it is starting to connect. All the realms… hearing Ruzak going after some wheel — the library. Of course… *somebody* knows and assumed for it to be displayed like an artefact, unaware of the residing truth."

Quietly, the team wandered off towards a crossing where its split directions would take to the desired waypoint. Regardless of the region's deserted grounds, they searched for the nearest signpost in aid to their travels. The tumbled debris along the road's edge appeared to have formed a barrier from the cleansing of the hilltops and each particle that has descended throughout, an unrefined display of the plight among the neighbourhoods.

Taking her aside for a private exchange, Willow asked, "Jasper mentioned it to us in an evening tale — long ago, yeah? We need to bring it to him."

"A metamorphosing token. Meaning what exactly, he should know. Ugh," lowering her voice, Xira added, "The residual Yard personnel are not the only ones onto us… let's go. I'll handle Ruzak, you guys find a vantage point to surround them. Keep our secrets safe, Will."

In honest agreement, they set off down the path with the others, on a hunt through the dark and wintry — sundering at a steep climb extending across a valley in the shimmer of the moon. Running down the vast lands, she felt the wind along her hair, as she breathed in the chilling air with her special suit keeping the warmth. A sky full of stars, each their own glow, among violet shades that painted the view — adorned its infinite universe and the towns that were further below, in their peaceful, uninhabited display. Merging with nature.

I can almost hear the songs again… the tales and the old wisdom, were her thoughts.

Looking over to a view of the lush woods that beckoned to be a quicker route to Ruzak, Xira observed its lush greenery as a gust blew forth among the leaves. Going by her gut feeling, she saw the overgrown post marking it as The Deep Forest and entered. Untangling the muricate grass from below in the walk to the murky shortcut, delicate vines drooped above and a low whistle pierced the gaps between the boughs, swaying her attention to the rustling lavender ahead. Arriving at a small sunken pond, she dipped a gloved hand inside its shimmering verglas, noting a change in the floating hues. Bizarrely, the grounds had become scaly with a protrusion of magmic stones trailing until a standing shadow, or so it seemed, a quiet yet humming visitation of an estranged entity — fathoming her buoyant footsteps in the ensnarement that surrounded once near.

"Ah… wild comes to the scent," they emitted, facing to counter, "Of all the wayfarers… here you are now again."

Xira discovered the identity behind their long, lavishly designed garment, the voice which bequeathed a shiver beyond the acre. In the moments of the atmosphere turning to gloom and its twinkling haze drifting through the greenscape, a lurid flash was cast upon the woman's hand when she set to run away.

"My locket… Erma!!! That's *not* yours!" Xira shouted out,

immediately bolting after her.

Among the chase, many of nature's high and low terrains made for a rather erratic traversing with Xira leaping over mossy logs, adamantly pushing between hanging creeper vines and well-hidden plantation that often flourished as a floral, oval nest. Listening to her uttering which haunted around the compass, like an ever-morphing matter on its own accord, she stormed on in pursuit of the enchantress — always within distance but about a tail just out of touch.

"If only you'll learn," Erma echoed through the forest, "Friends they're not, never one with the likes of us... did you really believe? Everyone comes with a purpose, they stay for the taking. What for... in lies... aha... yours is a beacon to their *humble* melody."

Xira cut by a mire in aim to divert, barging among the dispersed fronds and bellowed, "Give that back! What the *hell* do you want? Are you not done!?"

By the leaves, the water and the dirt, a second of a shaded umber hemline zipped by just under her fingertips — with Erma's eerie cackle disappearing into the mist, leaving behind a muddy trail as Xira hovered her hand across the tracks. A thrilling shriek soared through the clouded woods, resonating with Willow's voice, making her worry that the companion was in peril by the hands of the enchantress. This prompted a boost in her spring, sprinting faster with each harsh leap.

Continuing a rumbling, chortling voice, Erma's cavalier reply, soon pealed, "Dynast reap, dynast do... hit the wrong string? Make no mistake... stand by, lady..."

As her boots covered with haste, Xira then hopped out of an elaborate herbage but was suddenly tripped down in the dirt filled ground, stretching to three different paths leading further into the woods. Coughing and picking herself up, she paused. Around the patches she could discern a faint apparition emerging to a threading murk.

"An oath, drawn from kin to kin, fusing elements from alike perspectives..." a chant was heard from behind a trunk.

Coming forth, Erma as herself held the locket by its hanging chain, glaring beneath her hood as she approached Xira resting on the knees. The enchantress placed one hand under her chin and teased the item above in view, before shattering it into pieces — sprinkling down the locket's dust, still fixed on the glare as its remaining particles fell like snowflakes.

Xira's gasp sunk to her gut when she desired to knock Erma back, however the dynast's deceiving capture had her in an apple's grip, chanting lines from a spell and slowly stepped aside. The enchantress focused on her as she rose in a stance, following her move towards the front. Erma looked down once again, right at Xira's mahogany gaze.

"*Love, mother,*" she recited the locket's message.

Examining her garment during the orbiting walk, she realised it to be a personalised craft within The Spirit Realm — from the rare materials to its thorough design, a style that was a first sight to the woman and curiosity bit and marked again. Whispers in ear and telling of what beliefs and things Rove Dynasty had truly ever applied, Erma went on and on about all sorts, attempting to insert a plan in tendance to the underworld. Xira in that moment tried to break free from the trance, to create distance between the two, but unfortunately; the spell had been sung.

"Now you know, your little pack of anomalies are simply devoid of what is right in front of them," the enchantress began to say, "They need you when the current is calm… and the *moment* turns a wave, no longer do they linger. The weather is anew, an empyrean descent right onto your palms… blissful… treasure for you."

A shuffling within the foliage was overheard upon trees and their dancing greens, going from one area to the next, then right by their location as Erma expressed to reveal them. At first, the silence muffled about the terrain, hiding in the low fog and altering positions. Soon after jumping over to a greeting, there, was Willow, Sam and Fiske — standing by side as they watched intently. A smile drew along the delighted Erma's face, before straightening up.

She spoke in a soft, complacent form, "Here to witness? Oh, marvellous it is, this, without even a scratch. Would you like a treat or a fruity offering? Or to the point, as the crow flies… hmm?"

They idled like deer in the headlights as Xira turned around with her flaring iris opposing in a cold exchange towards the companions. A breeze snuck right under and past the icing floor, with the dirt becoming a rink within the woodlands. The particles flowing in air revolved like spiral wind chimes amidst the rising vines of thorns that enwreathed throughout the area, shuddering them in their stance, unsettled by such an encounter. Although it'd obscured most of the routes, there'd been a hint of moonlight beaming across the lush, deep green.

Willow stepped forward, as cautious as ambivalent — then opined, "Pardon our intrusion… I think you know why we're here."

Before the woman could admit, Sam chimed in on a suspicion, "Wait, uh — you look kind of familiar… haven't I seen you somewhere around?"

From the misty depths stretching far beyond and behind, a low sound resonated through its grounds.

A chiselling smirk emerged along Erma's pitying answer, "I must confess, I come bearing gifts… this one is not for you… for you shall see. A confidante of mine, but never yours to be."

The steering soil tripped the three a few steps back, watching as Xira's clement walk towards their way ruffled the surface in all its verdure. Down on both grazed elbows, Willow angled up to witness what met her eyes, a peculiar and haunting glare by the spirit of her childhood friend approaching in a manner which ignited out the rims — crawling away for the fear of an unwanted encounter against someone she'd known for a very long time. Someone who she could never imagine to be the sharp end of a blade that would point her way. An aura was noticed swathing Xira with a growling impression below the nose, swaying a hand down in the frost, a reluctant miss as the team dispersed into the nearby foliage. Her tempestuous lens scanned the vicinity, scenting through each epidermis amid the undergrowth and glided in the ominous hunt. Rustling through the leaves was a scurrying pair of feet as Xira split a way to her target, locking on once in sight. She tried to overturn Willow but briskly resisted, who'd merely been within arm's reach and hiding beneath whatever could provide enough cover from the ghastly encounter. Between the path to a great tree and further on into the mist lay a grounded log, festooned in creeping flora as Willow pulled herself over in desperation to lose the seeding trail. Behind the tree ahead, hid Sam with a harrowing glance by the fallen nests around him — some of the eggs which were left to hatch, still cooped inside a feathery base. He tugged at a loose branch and as it cracked, Xira darted her attention to the origin of the sound. For a moment, the quiet forest emanated Erma's flailing garment before it returned to a mage's offhand venture, when Xira refocused on the scent of the targets and rushed across to find their position.

The enchantress drew her distance, motioning forth as she denounced, "She was never with you. Who you thought was beneath that exterior is nor your ally or benign. Would it surprise you if you knew that underneath her fingertips resided the design of your relationship?"

Throwing herself atop Sam in an abrupt transition from the unruly plantation, where he did not foresee the movement, a landing against the nests caused for a diffusion of ripe leaves as Xira met the terrified reflection in his eyes — bringing on a sense of qualms while both hands placed for a swing, though in their tangle, Willow intervened between the two and with all that was mustered, rolled her down to a defensive position — led by a sinking sorrow within herself.

In aim to control weary breaths, Willow pinned a leg to the folded arms and with all, held her amid the brittle tone wavering in her imploration, "It is not *you* who is doing this — Xira... I cannot bear to handle someone ever *losing* somebody, *not* like this! — You must know that you are loved, that I am beside you... see? Here — remember these? These bracelets? I made them, back in that shrine... yours... and mine. Believe in the love around you, Xi. They mean something. — *Y—*"

Even with the struggle inside and of the wicked spell, it had vastly overwhelmed Xira when a brutal slam against her companion sent Willow at vaulting speed. Soon followed by the sudden urge to his stomping steps towards them as Sam charged, she backhanded his arrival just after getting up and knocked him down by a tree's aerial roots. Looking at a moving bush in the distant view ahead, she could see an arched figure sifting through when the pair of wounded companions rushed forth once again — only to be met with a double cross punch to the jaw, viciously taking them back afar and hard on the ground. She kept track of the scent and set off to find the target's point only to discover a meagre footpath, brimming with shrubbery on both sides and proceeded by its raking to a river's shore. Standing on the opposing granite rocks was a dishevelled Fiske, carrying a weighty stick through the mud when she approached the cold, untamed waters. A detection of drenched clothing oozed along the crevices as it'd enhanced the pungency of his scent.

"You're not crossing this river, are you?" Fiske queried, a composed posture shrouding his intent.

One foot slowly crept under a lurching current as Xira continued to glare onward, countering the tides that entwined throughout her resolute walk to reach him. While she was about to land the boots on an elevated portion, Fiske extended an arm out to keep the distance with the stick pointing against her shoulder cap — which was then quickly grabbed from its way and because of his wrench for a chance at a proper escape, it'd resulted in her toppling within the path and taking him down not far behind. Down a sluing passage amid bristling surroundings, the two spun about their attempts to swim across to shore. However, due to her amplified power, Xira shattered any obstacles that may've rendered a beneficial method to accomplish that. A flutter of imagery coincided with the occasional wave bringing her underneath, where she could discern Fiske's cries of despair and come to her own senses in moments of intercepting realisations of what havoc was unshackled — although it'd held them in a busy ride towards a nearby lake, the spell remained in prime possession. As she rose from the gritty submersion, she eyed its perimeter leading a sand route back into the forest. The leaves of various flora and plants covered its altering grounds after a shoreline crossing. Arriving on land, Xira fought against the corrupt disruptions but once catching sight of Fiske washed ashore and clearing any swallowed water, she locked on towards him without a regard for reason or judgment. A kneeling pounce to the waist, he let out a wailing bellow when she rammed down the jawbone and exclaimed after pushing her to back away, barely stumbling to hide in the foliage ahead. This took to another second of overlapping senses to which was an added effort in breaking free herself — from one battle to another, yet to be spared of the hexing spell. Marching on to find the way of return, Xira observed each zone of the double tracks that she'd come across. A mild pile of sand sifted between her fingers — she could tell in the distance, a guiding gust unveiling the path. From the series of bushes outlining every edge and adjoining with the next, she pushed on in the search, beneath tall and embellished woodland evergreens. Walking to an arch made of thistle and umber vines of thorn, there's a wary voice which echoed by the hollows.

"Stay away from me!" Cried the young man, who soon then was figured to be Fiske.

Following to locate, Xira slunk through the density, occasionally catching petals and leaves in her hair as she arrived at a frosted garden broadening to an open area ahead — with its mist, ice and particles coating the land. It appeared like she'd been nearing Erma again, wandering along a surface of wintry sense and aura, where Fiske was then spotted ambling towards that same direction. Through the fog, a set of silhouettes were recognised in their idle positions, almost like a motion painting settling in a three-dimensional scene.

"Now that you've seen her true light," Erma began, holding the companions at the chin, "Perhaps there's a point to reconsider giving your faithful ally to me."

Xira hurried towards her when a heap of flashbacks and visions played like a retro film in an old, overgrown theatre. Nobody caught on the approach, for their mutual focus belonged to each other's defiance. On their knees, they appeared to be threatened under Erma's formidable capability.

"Leave them out of this," she called out, walking over.

Alongside the greenscape, a shifting Fiske was weaving his way around in subtle discretion.

The enchantress took a deep breath in a rattled turn, before uttering a dubious reply, "Were you not taking care of the matter yourself? I sense an alternate thought… a faulty decision at that."

They came at a meeting point, halfway across the grounds within the arctic essence — standing by mere feet apart. Erma examined her shimmery silver iris return as its mahogany flakes vanished into the layer, whirling upon the retrieved, true aura. The two exchanged an undaunted front as Willow peered in the relief of knowing her friend was in her own shoes once again. Coming forth, the dynast set a grip on Xira's right bracer and a malign demeanour that disassembled any of the former facades.

"Do you understand, girl…? These will not protect you, come the fires of Armageddon," she averred, lifting the other.

Pushing to break off from her, Xira responded in the engaged hassle, "You don't know what I've seen, what I've heard — I wouldn't try that luck."

Taking her with both arms to the neck, Erma pressed down in aim to strangle using Xira's own pair. The companions heaved to be of aid. Despite of their amicable attempt, they were sent across by force — on to a hard land beside a stump. Xira wriggled against the weighing, brutal arms and raised to knock the enchantress away in her vexation. She angled the boots for a defensive kick before being levitated by the dynast herself, a compelling disparity to their current combative means.

"I know everything about you," Erma taunted, then launched her over the ice, "So much to learn, sweet sunshine. I'm certain that little home of yours shared a notion or two, be it with a tale around the table... or a sacrifice by someone near and... well, here."

In a defiant transformation while in air, Xira dived to a swinging punch and hurled the enchantress between a rift below its crisp surface. A desire to make her surrender, she kept her down and with a grim feeling that took over, suppressed Erma's onslaught during the particles that swam along the woman's lips — twinkling by the weather alteration that was cast inside the forest.

Xira grunted in the hold, "I'm far ahead of the cover-ups, what you and anyone else hid from me, *took* from me! It ends, it all ends... nothing escapes from my detection — this is one too many mistakes that is about to cost us the *whole* of Galaxaeria, *because* of all of you! Couldn't — just — *be* — *peaceful*!"

The companions crawled towards the fight and came to discover the upheaval between them as Willow rushed by, weary and torn, yet with all that was gathered she ran up behind to grab her friend to safety. A selfless effort in accomplishing what she thought to be right, for the better of Xira's spirit — saving from a wager too great of a barter. Although she'd distanced her from the enchantress, it was far known that it wouldn't be that simple to bear that kind of unparalleled force but instead, mending the weight bestowed upon Xira. With a careful hug around her waist in a trying lug that prompted full body appliance, Willow stood near and tackled her friend's counters amid Sam's shared assistance, who took a place right behind her as well. After some time of dividing her from Erma, a flurry of frosty clouds emerged before Xira's eyes in the sequence of the obscurity and her lowering to a sitting stance, before the two allies beside her comforted her as she searched the distance. With the way being unclear, she burst into tears like a bellow through a gorge... a sense of seeming lost in a faraway, deserted passage. The friends sat beside her, watching her focus into the ground and then to the dark forest ahead.

"So this is how it goes, huh?" Xira expressed in a choppy manner, looking forth, "It was never... my intention to *hurt* them like that..."

Another set of visions emerged in a flicker and brought on like a form of guide showing her what was to be known — the enkindled events of the past, whether she'd been there or not, regardless, by the harrowing moment as Erma had already disappeared in the greenscape.

"That control she used over me. *Hmh*, I'm still at unease looking at these stains... let alone, ugh — this is what I've gone and done. Ruined... hurting an innocent, hitting a defenceless, *shit*... my own damn best friend... — you all should go now."

Willow came closer to the side and uttered a solemn reply, "That's not something I can do. That will hurt me more. These guys may not know about you, but it didn't take long for me to figure out what was going on here and why that wretch deserves to be brought to light."

The sound of a hollow, guttural voice echoed among the whistling trees, giving a chilling shiver by their collars and down below, "You frolic in that pool of water, I'm off to capture what belongs to *me*... with or with*out* my beloved staff!"

A cackle which followed the enchantress' flee sent a haunted reaction by his afterthought, as Sam muttered in a cautious turn, "What — *Who* is that referring to?"

Out from the bushes came a startled Fiske, quiet and calm in one, yet minding each of his steps towards them. The moonlight finally cut through the smog and circled around the area, beaming atop the restoring grounds as to how they were formerly. The two sides looked to one another in their dishevelment while frost with its fragments settled on the damp soil.

"We'll tell you later..." remarked Willow in a hushed tone when they were soon approached by wounded Fiske.

"That wasn't their only building," he began to say, slouching to handle his hip, "I can share with you that the Yard owns and operates from many sites across various other towns. The catch is, they're hidden well to blend in with the neighbourhoods. Argh — uhm, it was their HQ that burnt down, that's for sure, but that doesn't suggest that they won't set place elsewhere. Others will take helm and there are plenty that are terribly loyal to those people. At least you saved the rest of us... though they are still out there, picking at crumbs and clawing trouble — and that wheel... cypher wheel?"

Xira then asked him intently, "What can you tell me about it?"

The companion went on to explain his discoveries upon working for the organisation and how often times he would find himself in uninviting situations where it would be a case of mistaken positions — leading him to unwillingly pry in personnel's conversations and private meetings about what went on behind the scenes. This at first, appeared to the former member as a mere, odd coincidence and that surely a place like Yowndrift Yard wouldn't be a mask on a mask kind of territory. A workplace in which he dedicated much of his time, provided a new outlook on how he perceived everybody and everything within that one building. As somebody who had been indoors for the majority of his shifts, Fiske affirmed that the absolute naivety that he'd borne about the outdoors was an upsetting realisation — due to a confined foundation, he knew he couldn't keep up with their vile schemes, once uncovering what indeed the Yard was actually implementing.

"I don't know what exactly all of that meant, what they were thinking of doing with it," taking another step, Fiske added, "Something about alterations... realm refreshment? For a fact, the wheel is with Ruzak. I saw Ilari go after him but I'm not so sure where they went after that. This key... we found... uh — not so sure it is still intact, after all... worth a try, though."

Standing up beside the two, Sam replied, disturbed, "You knew all this and left for us to handle it? I — I — From what I just *saw,* that — that wasn't anything like us... it was — it — very strange."

"No, don't blame him, Sam," Xira cut in, "I understand why he would do that. I know enough about that wheel now and I'm going to continue in finding them again. For good."

The companions circled within the grounds, wandering by the three divides. Xira began to cross the path between with plants growing towards it and almost concealing its way forth. She looked back at her friends and then nodded in motion to Willow.

"They deserve to know. Don't wait for me," she told them, her hair twining alongside, "I figured it all out — it's why they kept it hidden from me. For fear of me knowing. They really thought the truth can be sealed and lost — that I wouldn't come across what I discovered about myself. About everything. Towns are bound to be within proximity if things go south and it won't be safe to stick around. Do what is best, Will. I know I can count on you… and yeah, it wasn't just sweat and tears that you all put in. That will be honoured in return. I'll do what I always do."

Her earpiece emitted a static noise as its frequency cleared up for the receiver. In contact, the mentor blared out over the signals, like a man who'd been waiting outside a door in pouring rain.

Xira responded to the transmission, "Raptor. Good to hear from you."

"Where've you been, child? I've tried to reach you, but it only ever crashed each time — are you out? Outside? Is the — the fac — with the other people?" He spoke amid clanging plates.

"We're safe. For now, handling it — look, there's something that needs to be done… would you mind staying with Willow in the meantime?" Upon asking, she then added, "This is also what should be safe. It's the one item that hasn't been destroyed, taken or misused — it's better for her to hold it for me. I'm going after Erma, again. You take care of my belongings there. Deal?"

The mentor grew quiet in a pondering mutter and soon replied, *"If you think that's best. I can't imagine I can convince you otherwise. Mind your steps, my sunflower. Take it from someone who's seen and attempted all sides. Please, let it not consume you. Your light shall persevere above the might and flourish among all the realms."*

"I'll be careful."

Taking off the device, she handed it to her companion who watched it drop into the cupped hands, before learning about its placement and initial purposes.

Willow sighed, looking on ahead, "Where is our new rendezvous point? I'm not going anywhere if you're thinking of staying by yourself."

"Hmm… remember that high obelisk? It was where we visited for a picnic and there was the view of the region below… yeah," Xira explained, "That seems further from anywhere else… a great and far position within that area. Steep walk up, but so worth it."

Her companion adjusted the piece, then answered, "Okay. Good… I better see you running there, unless I beat you to it. Winner earns a *piggyback*."

"Sprinting. I promise you," aiming towards the forest depths, Xira expressed, "All right… always watchful."

As she dove on into the dark, green and misty landscape, the rustling of the leaves swayed with the cold breeze that wafted around the three companions, who stood by after a while in thought of what to do next. Savouring every ounce of the once again tranquil environment, they sat by on a log to rest and forge a few new plans. Fiske tinkered with Yard tools from the pockets when Sam gave him a disgusted glance. Shuffling forth, he scoffed and retracted to sit.

"You in for a reconsideration?" He teased in earnest, arms over his knees.

"Give me a break," Fiske said in a low tone, "What happened back there was the sort of thing of nightmares… aren't you the least bit concerned that she'll do it again?"

Dusting off particles from the garment, Willow reaffirmed, "I've already told you, guys. It's much more complicated than *good* and *bad.*"

"… evil," muttered Fiske, tending to his jaw.

"Fiske! For the *love* of—" Sam scolded, furious.

The dust that kicked off between them rose within the night's atmosphere, before settling down along the grass sprouts leading towards ochre shrubs nearing the log.

Willow went on to say, "Uh, goodness… like I said… I myself had no idea of what was inside my own best friend — and I've known her ever since the family introduced us shortly after mother and I moved in to Glacial Mist. It was horrifying at first, being in a new town and knowing just about nobody at that age — everybody seemed like giants instead of typical strangers. When I got to know Xi quite thoroughly, I just knew we'd be in it for the long run. She was never like my other, older friends, you see… she stuck by me. Even when I told her the reason why we'd left home before. That was just the surface scratched… she showed me what love in a friendship truly meant. Mother could tell… I was finally not alone. Even when she would speak of the future and how one day when I'd leave, I'd do just fine all by myself — but now, with somebody like her, huh… she made me forget what being alone was — that's not to say I don't remember the harsh times, but she's my… you could say, protector. An angel of sorts. She says she's the lucky one to have found me, oh… that's not even *slightly* the case. Xira was the one that told me, that with a past like mine, it was okay to be okay with it.

Like the water, she'd say. So I did. I believed her. After getting to know others around her, I finally understood what they were about. What kind of family they were. They were very warm and welcoming, gave me a place to stay should things go awry, or heck, even for some camping. Yeah, I made sure mother felt the same way. When people started to take her for granted, advantage of her selflessness and kindness, it was terrible for me to know that these people claiming to know each other would treat her like that. It was awful, I felt the disappointment myself. I've always tried returning the gesture, but Lord knows, it is hard to ever apply the same for all she's done for mother and I. I'm forever thanking her for that, and ever since, Glacial Mist has been our home and it's where I continue to stay, by choice. Although, knowing all of these other places, I wouldn't mind going wherever is truly right, and with her, I'd go anywhere. With being beside Xi, everything she's endured has not always been courteous. I don't expect you to see it from my point of view, though I hope... you can understand better. She's never with intention to bring harm. Not to those who've proven to mean well and no... that woman... Erma. She's not who you think she was. Much like your former colleagues, a seething destruction resides beneath the exterior. Look deeper... you'll find what we also found. As I learned, truth is almost never on the surface. With a hint of searching, you can be surprised by what you see... what you hear... — try to trust me, like I've done by confiding in you with our personal things. It's easy to point your fingers and accuse, but it's pointless when it is baseless. I don't blame you for thinking that after what happened before — you gave us a chance, gave me a chance to explain it to you without arguing. To feel what I feel. We're dealing with arcane energies here, we need to work as one. That's the spirit of a team."

The two young men glanced over as they cleaned themselves with what could be scavenged. Sam drew a leaf across his hand when he said, "I'm glad you shared that with us, Willow. Gotta' say, it's better that we were informed of these things. I would've bailed first if I heard about some *abracadabra* do going on outside of the HQ, but then that wouldn't be the wisest idea."

Fiske grazed off the last of his wounds' residue, turned and replied, "*We*. It'll be some time until I come to terms with this... do know that I'm trying. It's not easy, although, we wouldn't be out here without you

344

both."

Willow shuffled a foot about the soil, ruminating on the events as she went on, "Okay, but just so it is known… she didn't desert us because of being careless. She was going after Erma, the one responsible for the actions that bent our odds. That woman's set of advantages means we need to distance ourselves and that's what is being made sure of — Xira knows her way around and the idea of her teaming up alongside Erma would've left us with absolutely nothing at all… Erma is dangerous enough on her own… let's — let's just get going."

The three set to a long walk by a less obscured path as the night grew even colder, with the moon's rays blinking among the tree tops, the forest exuding its refreshing and wreathing environment. They could almost taste the green that reflected by the beams and all its colours throughout the ventured depths. It was like the air that soared between each sprung branch and leaf, rid of their excess dirt from both on the shoulders and the burden of which was carried. Later that mellow walk, Willow hummed a song that her mother would sing to and beside her, one that would give a soothing mood by the tone alone. Sam turned at the sight and chirping of birds fluttering by, fusing with the swaying leaves and the moments of glowing moonlight in the lacunae. Arriving at a muddy margin, she informed the companions of a ride down to the next area, hinting at the action of a slide. The three glissaded side to side, descending the terrain by its stony texture and upon a swift landing below, they shared a relieving chuckle amidst the colder grounds.

Entering a boggy slime trench, encased by walls of old moss and dappled soil, Willow paused at her sinking feet. In search of the way out, she couldn't seem to pinpoint another route opposing the long and narrow view. The team stood together with their hands beside the wall's edge, contemplating the decision.

Sam remarked, "Are you sure this is right? It would take some good cleaning for all of *that* to come off."

"From what I know…" She recalled on earlier memories, "The quickest route to reach the open area, is in fact through here. If it proves to be as accurate…"

"So that's a no?" Startled, he retreated his steps.

Willow pushed on, before stating, "Aren't you ever kept on your toes? After me, then."

One after another, they delved in a foot at a time, through the substance which left a muddy imprint on their gear. Keeping a close distance between themselves, the team arched forward until it had reached above their knees. It had been more of a challenge the further they went, grabbing what they could on either side of the walls. Fairly soon, they had arrived by a sturdy surface that required a decent climb. She stood beside the two and unleashed the chain by her belt, Attaching it to an entwined branch on the high edge.

"Think that'll hold?" asked Fiske, looking up.

"It'll do," Willow replied, "Besides everything being handcrafted, the materials are unmatched. You won't find anything alike here."

Using a boost atop her leg to ascend the chain, the companions rolled over the ground once reaching its height. Taking a turn to pull herself up, she dug into the soil and joined alongside them. Ahead of the three was a makeshift tent and supplies by a recently distinguished campfire. Its embers still in bright hues and the smoke which soared to the treetops, was then met with a clanging noise, somewhere near. Followed by a series of footsteps, somebody rushed towards them in a maddened swing with a weighty axe.

Meanwhile, along a crumbling street covered in a variety of debris, Xira leaped over a fence and climbed the roof of an abandoned residence — overlooking the town which was known as Sunset Cove, a neighbouring place to Glacial Mist. There were no shortages of delightful experiences when one would enter the area but that was before the weather destruction had occurred, leaving many towns in shambles — much like this one, a mystery that befell its usually warm, pleasant and relaxing ambience, to then be replaced by a ghostly presence with a hanging town board. On to the next roof with a springing vault, she arrived to a two-storey building with a torn entrance sign that read; "*Art Galore*".

"That's quite a jump," she muttered, examining the gap to its second roof, "Come on, tricks are playing me."

Tipping a boot towards the margin, Xira launched forth with a gust of wind on her back and landed in a roll by a window. She glanced at the former canopy and was thrilled at her fresh discovery, like the wind was the voice of flight and speed, taking her to great new lengths. *Lightning, wind… I imagine there's details I've yet to find*, she thought. Once inside, a plethora of canvases were piled across the room's carpet and by the wall was a shelf filled with paint buckets, some even knocked on the floor. She walked to search through the mess, noticing shabby posters which advertised the night craft events that celebrated prehistoric periods of encounters with intergalactic visitors, ones which landed by untold methods — a secret very honourably kept, to that, was uncovered the wisdom shared and imparted. The archway leading to the following room was cut off by its broken staircase and with only a ledge towards its adjacent side door, she used the brief platform to balance upon the wooden structure and continue to an old office. As Xira's attention was captured by the things decorating around in a frugal yet saccharine design, a framed form of gratitude was displayed on a wall casing, presenting a '*Fiona Hardy*' in green inked letters. Below, bearing an inscription; '*Sunset Cove Hall grants a thank you gift to our very own Art Galore owner and compassionate civilian. We are glad to show the support that is truly deserved, for such a dedicated and generous person.*'

Hm, Xira reflected, *if that's the same Fiona... you've done well. Hope you forgive me.* Taking a look at the owner's desk, a collection of pictures and notepads were left beside a dusty, blue computer. Inside the drawers, a stamped envelope caught her glance as she picked it out to examine. The front sketch of a sun and lemon bore an inked title, a handwritten '*Epistles*'. Within the envelope was a pack of pages, folded in triangles when she pulled them out one by one and took a little break by the room's window sill — skimming through the crinkled letters while the rain poured down right outside.

"*Jewellery Design Services*," Xira read, coming across one of the printed pages, "Huh...? That's the locket."

The following displayed;

'*Thank you for your submission. The images for the locket are attached as file_Q. Per your selection, the message was inserted accordingly — please let us know if we shall try alternate palettes or if you are pleased as it is.*

Ever welcome,

Fiona H.'

Flipping it to its array of locket prints, the text shown brought on suspicion as she noted its font and an additional quote underneath, coming from the client directly.

"*For my darling sunshine, Xira*," the text read.

An audible gasp turned to a cough when Xira realised just who their receiver was — with her gut rolling to inversion, she searched for any indication for the registered name of her adoptive mother. Only a reply that was given to the owner directed to a nearby arcade, a place of which the mother had been visiting while in town — referring to a contact in any case she needed to be reached.

"Damn it," she emitted with tears on the verge, "*Frenzy Zone Arcade...* hm, yeah okay..."

Stowing the envelope in the drawer, she immediately climbed out the window, minding the wet ceramics under her boots. She set off to a building's back entrance but to no avail, the door was supposedly jammed from its opposite side as she figured it to be barricaded with stacked furniture. Looking around, a sign above resonated the sound of wind chimes, when she soon noticed it to be the arcade building. Along rusty windows, Xira scaled until accessing the second-floor balcony, an entrance that appeared promising. Inside, a quiet and arranged space cast a forward route to its other rooms ahead. Beside a railing were stairs, leading to the first floor, although dark and uninhabited — or so she thought — when she heard a tumbling noise echoing from below. After descending the ragged stairs, an illumination of a torch light was seen between a few arcade machines. Onwards, she followed its beam, finding herself in a spherical area with a singular suspended lamp. A carpet that surrounded the floor was a shade of maroon, green and black, with an imprinted symbol of *Frenzy Zone* and its vivid, rainbow curve to an ocean's wave. Behind two *Cave Mountain* machines hid a lone figure bearing the torch in a huddled position. Xira approached silently to confront the person, crouching to meet their line of sight.

"Is there anybody else staying here?" Xira asked.

"Please, I am content with where I am," the woman replied, shuffling back, "It's my home. Yowndrift Yard is not the place for me. Please."

"What? No, I'm not with them," she explained calmly, "I came to look for some information. Was there a Dagny that used to work in this arcade?"

A brief interval was then cut with the woman's solemn answer,

"Yes… I am Dagny. Who is asking? Why?"

Xira leaned forth to question, "I think you knew my mother. I'm Xira. If you do so remember her…"

Out of the corners appeared the woman's comforting grace as she portrayed a sympathetic expression once greeting her again. Two chairs were retrieved to the carpet, then taking their seats, she offered her a woollen blanket to dry.

Dagny looked to her as she went on to explain, "Oh, excuse my distrust. I wasn't like this before, heck I can safely assume my walls are higher than the ones keeping me relatively secure. Say, you don't know anything about her? We were friends, that's quite correct. She'd visit me every other day. Camilla Dove was her name. A sweet, selfless being at that."

She hugged the blanket down, her thoughts wandering — then uttered, "When was I with her, until? All I know is that… she gave me away shortly after the orders came to — that someone called Andromeda suggested the new home for me. After that, it's all I knew. All I remember. I want to know everything."

"Well, where do I start?" Dagny leaned aside to explain, "You were three—"

"Yeah, so that is right. I heard, just wanted to confirm myself. Continue."

"Right. Yes, she was happily married to an officer who made a mistake that followed him when he entered the Yard's lair. I told her many times, *leave him to start anew*, he was too obsessed with the idea that putting his pair of priers in a business not made for us will only benefit their agenda," she dangled the torch below, "Not even her closest friend could convince her. We both tried. Seeing her ecstatic with a child in arms, I just couldn't leave the matter unresolved. It was after Camilla confided in me that Alexander already left for a confidential meeting — I knew something was peculiar, he didn't return until later that night. She called me in such a way that was upsetting, a shattered tone if I've ever heard one. It was then that I found out they were going to be separated, order of the Yard. No calls for a while, when she finally came to visit once more before packing and told me she was to give you to somebody else. Poor woman, with only the cafe… Andromeda soon offered her the best chance for you — a place in Glacial Mist, by a man known as Odion, who agreed to take you in. I miss her, I always will miss her visits. That cursed Yard carries a karma like flames in a jar. Something else to remember her by… she loved the outdoors, coffee and you. There are some photographs she used to give to me that you could check out, be with a happier note about her. When I first saw you, you were in orange overalls with little flowers and a brown, wilderness jacket. A fine young lady, now. Found yourself the exact place to know about sweet Camilla."

Xira looked to the torch, a sighing feeling sweeping the thoughtful glance to the floor. She replied, "Thank you. I must be going though. I need to meet somebody. If I ever return to Sunset Cove, I'll be sure to visit you again. It was a relief to meet you, Dagny. I'm glad you shared that with me, truly."

"Keep forward, honey. A pleasure to know you a little more. See you around, then!" The woman called to her as Xira approached the stairs and turned at an angle.

"Lunaris Town. If you ever need a new place, I heard they can be quite accommodating. Odion is there. Perhaps you two can make acquaintance."

On her way out the arcade windows, Xira jumped across a fencing gap to an ornate restaurant's roof and scaled the levels to look across into the distance. A vaporous blast filled high in the aerosphere as a low rumble shook the carmine acrylic brims. The water which steamed right above, carried through its moisture towards the way. It'd become warmer with each gust that guided the rain in the storm.

"That's the Springs… The Lilac Springs. They must be there," she remarked quietly, hopping over an old musical store's display and to a dice cube figure, dripping down the cover of a local games market.

Sliding past the building's fence, she walked across to a flooded road of abandoned cars, discarded baggage and a view of barricades supporting the side of the cars. A hill crossing arched above the landscape, with the area beyond barely in sight — the sound itself, however, still rang amid barrels of rainfall. Xira ventured knee-deep through the path when she heard a voice call out by a gutter. She approached a hooded and weary person who rose to meet her. Beside them were a few others, all with hoods alike — almost as if they'd been hiding out here.

"You're not from around these parts," said the young man, pointing out to the area, "'Ave you noticed any… trucks or cars drive by? M-May've heard them, na'h?"

Xira glanced to the slouching peers, then back in response, "It's clear from there. You from this town?"

"All of us, found one 'nother," he explained with few gestures, "Ma' names Evelon. I came from the southern district of my hometown, here with the little sister, Rebecca. That's Tank over by that motor, then Chili beside him — oh and uh, our friendly neighbour Uma here, *haha,* with Olive by her. They are two roads far from us and we only ever saw them at the local diner. What a way to meet… we felt hopeless. Thinking everyone was in that horrible place, that nobody was left to question *them.* Lucky my sister was with me, don't know what I would've done. Scarin' her outright."

Looking to their friends now facing towards her, Xira mused on about the girl who crunched both hands in the cold, if she'd been the niece of Fiona or if that was a mere, odd coincidence. Uma inspected from head to toe and fidgeted within the pockets of a smeared, malachite jacket, standing to meet her visage. Olive soon stood to join, although stayed a little further apart out of general tact.

"What's with the suit? Care to spare me some?" She asked candidly, still eyeing the elaborate garment.

Xira noticed something being carried in one of the pockets when she replied, "It was a gift. Why aren't any of you looking for a safe hideout? Most areas around are practically empty."

"Well, didn't you hear that explosion? We thought the water here could shield us should a fire break out," Evelon stated, gazing to the nearby hill, "I'm afraid nowhere *is* safe. If we go far out, I could put my sister in further peril. Can't afford that when — you know…"

"Our families are with them. No chance to even lock the doors," annoyed, Uma cut in, pointing a waving hand to the town, "They corrupt them, I heard. Yeah, sit them nice and cosy in a sewer dweller's basement and rod 'em up, without an inch of food crumbs and left to scrimmage with the rest when people start to become hungry. You ever hear of their loyal subjects? The ones that go right up to your face, a tower where no mercy is known and the door is on the highest *darn* floor. Hot rod… hot metal…"

With a wrapped pocket knife sticking low between their space, Xira intercepted Uma's sly slant, "Do you want to keep that…? I'm *not* with the Yard."

"Uma, please," Olive implored, pulling back by her shoulder, "Her parents, brother and my aunt are missing. We're all looking for somebody. It's hard, as you can see, we're not exactly well equipped… I honestly hoped that there were more people hiding out in our town but… as far as hopes go… we held each other's backs. For what it was worth."

Xira faced the young woman with a consoling curiosity, then elaborately noted, "Fiona Hardy? Is that her name?"

"Yes. Uh that's right(?)"

"I crossed through her building. Found her car some time ago," she went on to say, "It was deserted. At first, I was in a position where I myself was trying to figure out what was going on. This was in my town, Glacial Mist. I went through her things… took a recipe she'd chosen for your liking, thought I'd run into either of you — *then* it was with good intention, assuming that I'd done the right thing. Look, Olive, if it still means that much to you, I can try and retrieve those fragments and the pocket necklace. It may be a fluke, but I've done such attempts. They could still be in that car, at least you could hold on to that."

A flush of emotion carried to her lashes as Olive soon answered, "Mhm, it doesn't matter. Really, it's fine, you don't need to regret that. I'd rather you did search the car… maybe there could've been a clue to where she'd disappeared. Anyway… I'm thankful. I don't need them any more… not when she's missing. Uma's been with me, my special kinda' rock. Guess I'll always be hopeful that she's out there, somewhere."

Another gust of explosive water launched up in the sky, covering like a fountain wave, before splashing down in its heated effects. Crowding around the edges, they watched for a path around it. Evelon climbed one of the cars and surveyed the neighbourhood with binoculars. The friends stood alongside on high alert among their surroundings. Xira continued on towards the hill.

"I'm going this way. There's somebody I'm looking to meet," she announced to the others.

They turned, as Evelon kindly responded, "Be watchful over yonder. If you need anyone, we'll be around."

Uma added, "And sure to find some paraphernalia lost about places.

I *will* keep this knife. Good to know you ain't a Yard-douche, g'al."

With a nod, Olive chimed in a smile, "Thank you, friend. Sure brought us relief, I'll tell ya'. I'd love to know your name, if that's all right. You've been good to us… all things considering."

"It's Xira. I'm glad to've done good, *all things considering.* Hope you all find who you're looking for, too. If you need a new place, go far across the bridge to find Lunaris Town. The Yard haven't touched down there quite yet and I don't think that they will."

As the crew waved a friendly goodbye to her, she ascended over the dampened grounds and marched up to the point of the hill with white roses embellishing each side, a dirt path which continued down to a slope that then led through a crossing and overlooked The Lilac Springs. Xira ran along until the path curved upward once again, into almost a rocky climb to reach her set location. The row of trees surrounding its route dangled themselves atop every grasp for progress as she nudged off occasional particles that slipped between. She lowered her position with a buttressing kick in elevation, soon before approaching the next site where an exchange could be heard, fusing with the boiling water.

Somewhere in the Rove Dynasty's lair… some time ago…

"Menkos, fetch me the records," ordered Syphon, sitting upright by a desk, "This calls for an analysis. Is there anything left from the household or its perimeter?"

Upon delivering a handful of locked cases, the man arranged the items across a fair, antique table.

"There really is no need to lodge in the past," Erma asserted, her sideward pose turning the corner, "Rather certain we know all there is to know… question, to what benefit…"

Joining the dynasts around the table, Menkos tossed a heedful query, "Excuse me, madam, was it *not* in your diligent interest to involve oneself in undertaken matters apart from yours? Do correct if that current pursuit of Xira is but further off in the haze."

She placed a tiny box beside the files and replied, "I admire your attention out of the general zone. See all, know all, nevertheless no fiddle. You're excused."

Situated around the table were the remaining two as Syphon continued his thorough search in the lost pieces of home. Upon finding secrets untold that belonged to Xira's family, the other contents proved to be the likes of his time spent with the mentors and what they all shared. A pile of old records surfaced the table when Menkos jumped at the sight of it, leaving his chair to disappear into the next room. Unfolding page by page, the dynast sunk his regard to the fresh information revealed before them. Syphon motioned for a proper consultation within the space.

"They were protecting her," he declared, dispersing each document, "It seems Serenitatem holds a key for Xira. Merlot, another mentor, keeps... keeps — ugh, it doesn't say. The faded writing is unclear. Then there's this... if we locate what every mentor is still hiding, we could gain leverage, access to something beyond even us... truly."

"An uncaged terror by means of error, is disaster," approaching them with his mage rod Ophintom added, "Take it as advice, Syphon. Utilise what is at hand and you will benefit. As a dynast."

The pondering eased into quietude, three seats filled, with the inspected pages circling the golden case on the midway portion of the table. A low echo emerged from far into the room.

"*Remember; it's only if she wants to be found, only desires to reveal it, that you will be granted the honour in bearing witness.*"

Erma, bemused, held a letter in hand, then uttered, "*Bare hands, bare soul. The wildest of them all.* About that... symbol, wasn't that mentioned by you in our previous declaration? You shared that it was the form of The Spirit Realm... watched by a... an entity... unfurling across the entirety of Galaxaeria. A spirit, to which shone their self thus frankly — Lord, do understand this... I believe she is our opponent. One that stands little chance against the likes of us. Despite the matter of herself containing a sliver of our world, we are underneath for a reason. She cannot afford to give it all away. Let alone... to me."

A muffled sound wafted between the chambers, ruffling every page along the carved veneer. They contained the contents within their grasp, arranging its former layout.

"*Insolence brings you no further. The task for this particular alliance was to achieve what marked the stone long before. To do that, I will remind you once again; break your oath and we become a labyrinth. She will not co-operate if you push her off. Understood? This can easily be transferred to a new set of dynasts that would gladly fill my objectives, Merideth. As I recall, you were once doing so — besides, there's another thing you should know now. You may be difficult to vanquish,*" *undoubtedly a harsh dynast… yet are expendable. Whereas she meets the ground like air meets everything… though as much as you like to bring her there, she can never simply be eradicated. Her energy is one of a kind. It would be wise to play it right, don't you all agree? Take into consideration, you've been here awhile. I've known her since the father was around. A pity if such an entity didn't grace this world like we've all done as dynasts. That will be all. Continue your tasks, do not induce my hand in this."*

Upon his alert, a draught left the table with the voice, as the dynasts sat around their researched papers which scattered among the surface. A soft glow emitted through the glass, creating a warmth on its base.

"For our next move, we need to pay some people a visit," Syphon stated, pinpointing spots on a map, "Divide and utilise. Ophintom, be our hidden eyes. Settled."

Off towards the archways, Erma stayed behind as they cleared the room with Menkos. She viewed each document once more, for a cycling afterthought itched at the nose tip. All that afternoon, it'd been a private haunt between her and the scripts.

Back at the odd, marshy campsite, the swinging man barely missed when Willow dodged with a roll to her side, exclaiming in fear of their charge. Quickly on her feet, she scurried in a stumble to the nearby bushes and trees. As for the two companions, they turned towards the other side where three more people rushed to overwhelm them. One bore a rake, the second a pair of gardening scissors and a wrench for the third. The man carrying the axe stood to survey her steps, sporting a ripped jacket with a patched *Sea Ferris Ave* logo on its charcoal back. Willow kept hidden behind various plants while trying to find a way around the green and this crew.

Calling himself 'The Hound', he then stated, "You whiskers were sent to find us, eh? To dare and come in here, bold and brave… get out and face me then! I'll let you meet my partner in crime, *Cruelle the Axe*. That'll sharpen your judgement."

The crew that searched among every curled leaf dispersed within the area to cover more ground as Sam and Fiske followed their noise away to an opposite direction. Circling the perimeter, they soon found themselves at a midway point which faced the tent and the hunters on both sides. Afraid they'll be caught and maintaining a crawling stance, an arm bump caused Sam to jump in his spot when they realised Willow arriving at the same area as the two, which startled her briefly before the three let out a breath of relief in the moment. She told the friends to ready a back-to-back position and look for any means of escaping this unrelenting hunt. Seemingly trapped between a rock and a hard place, they shifted to a crawl beneath the lush foliage and cautiously made their way to the tent's fold. With eyes to either side, the crew arched closer by each second a foot tapped forward, alarming the three, right before Fiske entered the tent last, in time when two of the crew's hunters met once again. Inside, there'd been some camping equipment beside other commodities, a set of portable appliances but nothing that could quite outweigh the level of menace that opposed the team.

"A pan?" Whispered Sam in a crawl.

"Mind lending a better idea?" Fiske fired back, gripping the handle.

Quickly rummaging through an unzipped bag, an extendable wire tool and a carving fork was retrieved when Fiske shot the two a taunting glance. Willow watched out by the front opening, testing the wire tool from one side to the other. Hearing the Hound approach this way, she remained hidden until he tread on, then signalled for Sam to join her position.

She uttered in a hushed crouch, "Hold this bit — on my alert, hurry over by that shrub and pull as far as you can. Okay?"

"Yeah, but — that one's all *prickly* and what if a rash… oh-lright, uh, I'm on it," he replied.

Soon as the coast looked clear, Sam rushed on to stretch out the wire, reaching its capacity when Willow felt a tug and returned the motion to inform him. They waited patiently for the crew to waltz over, hoping to at the very least trip them into an improvised trap. Laying low, she spun the device to dip into the soil while keeping it at a reasonable height. A sound of faint footsteps creeped by, before phasing in a muffled guise of mud. Ashen brown waders could be seen below the fold, shuffling and leaving their trace, as the two companions yanked the bars to result in a stumbling fall of one of the hunters. Approaching the man with a rake, Willow wrapped the wire around his feet while Sam inserted the carving fork in the rake's gaps and attempted to take it from him. Although it being not as simple, he stayed focused and Willow with him — just when she was to turn her focus to the others, a tall crew member carrying yellow gardening scissors crept right behind. Fiske jumped out at the sight and swung the pan in a backward swing, knocking their stars out along with the pan. He hurried to grab it when The Hound approached in a glowering confrontation, holding the axe below his waistband. Grabbing Fiske by the throat, he raised him above the ground and tossed him next to the rake man. He walked over with a grunting expression, shortly joined on the other side by the ally spinning a wrench in one hand.

"Looks like my skewer row is complete," The Hound voiced in a sneer, "No point in hiding out here, with a claw like mine... nothing to ponder little ones, merely relish this score about prey that fell to the hunt."

Imposing the wielded axe high above her, Willow instinctively kicked up in return, hurling aside the weapon — right out of the man's grasp. Furious, he moved forth and charged but was denied with yet another vicious kick which sent him far off on the grounds. The wrench ally then grabbed Sam in a double armlock, disarming him from the fork and retaliated against the trio with a cunning undertone.

"Never underestimate even the fellow with a pocket-sized weapon."

Fiske, in a bound towards the pan, was immediately stopped in his tracks — with a threat to Sam once again. As The Hound returned with a harsh regard, the three were then being surrounded by a daunting, confined portion of the terrain. Watching their desperation meet his, Sam took a chance to hammer down on the man's foot at the fore. With a nudge to his abdomen, pushed him to back off and flee towards the companions. Just when The Hound attempted to a charge on Willow and Fiske, Sam thrust the rake forth, setting him off a few steps. To another unfortunate grab by the wrench man, the companions were left to fend against their ever furious, stomping opposition. As they tried to figure out their following move, the one man who'd been knocked out was seen on the side, coming towards their way with the axe itself. With a targeting swing, he joined beside The Hound who was sneering amidst hassling them while she kicked in a flurry and before it'd even landed, Willow used the body leering above in a shielding deflection against the axe, watching it savagely slash down one of the latched arms and tear its layers of flesh right off. Leaving a hanging forearm below, they fumbled back to stand when The Hound's exclamation turned to his ally. A loud crash was then heard after he'd hurled himself towards the man and vanished out of their view. Not wanting to linger around here, Willow went for the axe as Fiske tackled for the rake and faced the last of the Sea Ferris Ave crew. Against their defences, Sam was in the mix of fending off his opponent, before Willow kicked down on the guy before them and threatened wrench man to release their friend while lifting *Cruelle the Axe* in the air. Without much hesitation, they'd begun to dart off the tracks and clear themselves into the forest. Sam reunited with the team and thanked them for their efforts. The three stood around with their backs turned, catching heavy, weary breaths to an attentive glare for any more retaliation. In a pensive drop of the axe, Willow settled to adapt after coming to terms with the campsite ambush. She turned to a refined realisation of the company kept and any discomfort then changed into faith.

"Can we keep her?" he asked eagerly.

Walking on to their route, Willow answered her friends, "Why not? There's a fine lotus lake near here."

At the lake, Willow kneeled by the cold water as she scrubbed along the blade. Approaching, Sam revolved in the sand.

"You sure about…?"

"Yeah, I'm handling it," she replied with a brief sigh, washing the stains thoroughly.

After vacating the area, they ventured on to the roads ahead until arriving to a split field leading a path over its calm terrain. Onwards, a tall sign caught their glimpse in its display of the town's name; *Sunset Cove*. Sam pointed to an old, spinning post of a dragon diner with its ice-cream scoops display. A quiet, blissful turnaround when a subtle clang was heard near one of the buildings, scattering objects atop others, leading the team to move forth in their suspicion and enter the town's quarters. Inspecting its showery grounds, they were greeted with another group coming from around a corner. The two groups were at a halt within the junction as one of their own stepped forward to break into clarity.

"Who are you and what do you want?" They announced, standing behind makeshift barriers.

Willow sat beside sundry debris and was joined by her companions who were made aware of keeping their guards up. She kept a close ear to the others, using Xira's earpiece beneath her aviator trapper hat.

"We were just going through here," she told them, "We're not trouble."

Another chimed in with stridence, "You all could be armed! Noticed the uniforms, ya' know!"

The two friends peeped at each other's torn layers but remained quiet behind cover. The rain poured along a sullen landscape, drenching the dirt by their resting hands.

"So could you!" Willow fired back, catching onto their muffled breaths, "They no longer work with them — neither of us are with The Yard! There's no reason for any conflict... they are with me. They wanted to escape, *just* like you!"

It was quiet before too long, when a young man rose from the spot and announced rather composed, "If you say so. First, show yourselves and we'll do the same. Arms out — eyes here."

Upon every person's careful stand, the groups met with their gaze's locked like a clash of the wilderness. As they walked over, all eventually growing to feel more reassured, they carried on towards the front of the diner — seating at its rufous and garnet structure models placed next to the footpath. A dragon structure overlooked the surroundings, perched high on one of the diner's flamboyant welcoming displays.

The young man attaching his binoculars on a denim strap began to say, "Don't assume you bunch need my directions? I'm... it's a pleasure to meet ya'. Evelon. These are my pals and little sister over there. Sure enough, I speak for myself when I say it's quite a weight off, coming 'round more people after all commotion. Lucky to say the least..."

"Likewise... and we're good. That's Sam and that's Fiske," she replied, adjusting in her scaly seat, "I'm Willow. We've seen first-hand what Yowndrift Yard has been up to — if any of us knew before everything what that place was actually arranging, people could've found freedom elsewhere."

Kicking a pebble over where she crouched to draw in the soil, Uma muttered, "Yeah... what a shame. No one could tell me about the shrilling screams... the night the house burnt down. A miserable shame, to be witness to a crime you couldn't erase."

Olive sat up in question, "What? *Your* house? But you—"

In unison, they turned themselves to her downcast appearance.

"As if you didn't have other things to worry about. Don't look at me. Let me be," she went on, distancing even further about the area, "Word of advice to you three; don't desert your loved ones, being present benefits much more."

"Wait... wait up, hun!" Olive called in her hurried run.

The others watched as they left, before returning to their conversation after a silent moment. Rebecca sat in the grass beside Tank and Chili, who'd been keeping her occupied while matters were being sorted out among them.

"Okay, okay... none of us were with any clue or idea what she'd been going through," Evelon began, scratching against the polished surface, "You'd think you know somebody well enough to tell when they're hiding a secret. Sam — Fiske — I don't mean to be rude about this, but... why on any level would you want to join with the Yard? I'm sure their red flags would flare up the second you step foot into that gate."

Sam paused, twirling down the axe before answering, "It's not like there were signs put up on their walls that would make you turn back. I needed someplace to settle after moving so many times. It kept me distracted, until I landed my preferred position. By then, everything else didn't matter, I was in an encouraging job."

"Of course, when you're their puppet," Tank remarked, playing with a few sticks.

Chili quickly added as they tapped beside his shoulder, "Oh-ho-h, I believe they were just as innocent as the rest of our people in that facility. Let's not point to blame, instead, understand and maybe relate all the aspects."

Stretching to stand and face the group altogether, Willow nodded, "I second that notion. It's not that easy, especially when there are people like that trying to manipulate and control absolutely everything. It can sit right under your skin, wear and tear until you realise what their actions really meant."

Another loud explosion flew up over the hills of the town, soaring within the ashen clouds and sprinkling its residue back down. They all swung their attention to the disturbance, fearing of what was occurring beyond this region. A ghastly expression waved over Evelon, who slid to the side.

"I hope she's safe out there..."

"Who?" Willow asked.

"Uh, this girl who came across here, we met in the other part of this town," he continued to explain. "Said her name, was Xira. She was looking for somebody and went over that hill. Don't know what's up there but... it doesn't sound like a festival, exactly."

At hearing the information, she jumped to the path's edge and tried to figure what resided in the view. Seeing all the smoke and fire only led a grim feeling to sit within herself, convincing her to reroute once again. The reverberation rolling beneath the grounds were reaching even to the points of Sunset Cove's roads, dwindling towards the next turn and leaving few crevices in the asphalt. She began to walk the other way, working out a fair direction to cross each curve and hill.

"All right, thanks. I think we need to be going now," Willow declared through the downpour, "Keep it safe, okay?"

Evelon and the others said their goodbyes, before he added, "We will!"

Upward a steep road, curling to a high corner, the companions embarked on the motion to go over the land in aim of finding the bustling location. As Willow ran to a broken post which showed few directions, she angled to read it by the view of the land.

Fiske walked up, shaking his hair when he asked, "I thought we were getting out of here... why the change? She even suggested it — how are we even going to help out?"

"It's not far, but we are going to do what we can," Willow assured, looking over, "See that...? If we perch on that overlook, it can give us a good perspective of whatever is happening there — The Lilac Springs. My grandmother has mentioned it before. Let's go, it's our best plan."

Earlier on...

A tunnel paved the way through and out a curvy wooden hatch. Among a meadow, stood tall the enchantress as she examined the nearby huts — fenceless and emitting a glow by means of kerosene lanterns hung from their birch canopy. With the whistling of the birds charming to the flutter of shrubs and other planted varieties, the open path directed her towards a nailed post; "*Food and Drink is provided — nightly campfires.*"

"Since you earnestly offered," Erma voiced under a sly tone, "A reward if this is the place... now... where to begin?"

Off to the side was one of the huts left opened and seemingly vacant, for an empty basket lay placed on its carpeted porch. No shuffling of feet nor furniture.

"That'll suffice," she whispered, seeing its wind-chime, "Knock, knock... a wandering friend comes to visit."

Within the main room was a tea table and a cosy kitchen opposing it. Next to a bench, decorated two corner seats with padded edges and a vase by a drink stand. On towards their second area, displayed a set of bedding items and a hand-made stool beside an old sewing tool, still with placed fabric beneath it. The clothing basket left nearby was filled to the brim. Erma scoffed at the opacity she'd felt from the place, eagerly trying to locate the antiquity. Leaving to search every other hut, she came to a locked door after only uncovering old cans of food and building material. On the door was a pinned notice, handwritten by the inhabitant;

"Off to pick berry-pods and fruit leaves.
See Taran for spare keys!
Niko"

The dynast swerved around the huts again, in aim to find the one that belonged to Taran. It took but a few moments before overhearing a vicinal shout from a local villager. She approached a young girl who'd slipped along the mud and was tending to a scraped knee. With a single look behind a shoulder, the girl's audible gasp turned her attention to the enchantress.

"Here, up on your feet," said Erma, bending a grin, "Bring me to Taran."

Meanwhile in a muggy and cold front of a tavern that evening, eyed a disguised Syphon in his partially sleeved trench coat. Fixated on the illuminated entrance, he pushed open the door and walked in to a musical performance by a wall. Although the tune marched with the decorative lights and entertainment machines, the sound of the poured beverages and mellow chatter, Syphon approached the bar, remaining on the set objective. A bar-keeper slid to offer a drink when a hand tapped on the wooden surface.

"Where can I find an... *Odion*?" The dynast asked, leaning forward.

Looking around, the man replied, "May I ask who and why?"

"An old pal, you see. A favour to me, good man."

"Sure. Just fulfilling this matter of form," the bar-keeper noted, "Out the door, on to your left; there's a smoothie bar two buildings down. He should be in there."

Syphon, pleased, then added, "Good. — I'll accept a hosed down icy water when I'm done with that pit-stop."

As he left the bar, the town's high neon display flickered through the frost. There appeared to be some customers near the door. Going inside, he spotted two workers bringing in a set of bags to distribute. After the area cleared, with a few people left waiting on their orders, Syphon was approached by a man donning a walnut coat.

"Order up!" Was heard from the counter.

A ghostly look painted his fore, while the man couldn't bring himself to utter the name before the locals around them. A low, nasal breath came out in a huff. Making way to the hall, Syphon soon followed in his unmediated mien. Inside the apartment, Serenitatem poured fresh tea into a mug, its steam rising along the moisture on the pot.

The dynast, seated on the side began to say, "You appear as if though a day hardly went by — I'll care to venture a guess, it's been forever and a day. Do correct me if I'm wrong."

"What is your intention of coming here, Syphon?" The mentor questioned.

Ruminating, he then mentioned, "I see Peri is settling in well... how is she doing?"

Not indulging in the small talk, Serenitatem brought in a chair and drank some tea quietly.

The dynast went on, "I certainly hope the feud of family is not remaining a burden to a bright being like her. After we figured she went missing, it wasn't a surprise to me as to why, but still... I kept that to myself. Although, you already know about her sister... perhaps the abandonment as an infant, in such a place like ours, well, it would take to her behaviour and mirror the hardships. I'll say, she's far more capable now... maybe they both share that bonding resilience. It's admirable that y—"

"Enough. Why are you here?" The mentor urged sensibly, placing down an empty mug.

It was a quiet while within the conversation as the moon set to rise, unveiling the cold roads encircling Lunaris Town.

Swirling the tea, Syphon cleared his throat before clarifying, "That dear girl of yours. There is something you'll need to give me in order to complete an old heirloom arrangement. Everything you know about her, from the former and current, would you do the honours?"

"I'll first hit the ground running and with all rags on my back, to make sure *neither* of you hold anything from her." He said in a push of the seat.

"You don't seem to recollect what we previously discussed — the wheel, or uh, should I say in translation of the ancient mother language; *The Formula*. Everybody knows it as the *cipher wheel*, but of course, only we, connected, know that. If it were to fall in Xira's hands, wouldn't you fear of what she would do? From what I hear, she's been on a rampage of sorts, on a plan of her own. All I need is a *source* of enticement... then she can willingly comply."

"There was never a plan. Once she'd left home, home went with her. I know her too well by now. She was kept safe from everyone, with pure intention to bring righteousness," the mentor continued, "I can only imagine all she's witnessed, the mistakes of fools upon fools, pulverising the lands."

Syphon stifled a discontented sigh. He broached, "The reason why these presumptions are misguided, is because you left her all alone. For what, look after a house so that she's distracted from herself? To lie that you will keep in touch? She understood that the house was handed over to her. People change around, old man. Can you truly say what she is thinking... now?"

A knock against the frame disrupted their exchange, when Peri pushed in a carton and immediately shut the door again. There was a sticker labelling the side as '*Goods*' — decorated with a golden-brown apple patch.

"That's up to her," Serenitatem answered, unpacking a worn shirt from the box, "Memories count for something. I'm sure the past can help replenish what's at the horizon. People *can* change, yes. Learn what the better choices are, to know what actions will benefit."

Placing several items on a quilted sofa, he took a moment in viewing of the bits and pieces that were sent. The shirt lay unfurled atop the cushion with a scarf below. A weary wrist-light, packets of gum, a black bear pen, two harmonicas and a note.

Sir —

Found these in the old luggage. They mixed with my uniforms like they knew I'd need them someday. I'm grateful. Something believed I would come back. Take care of these while I'm out, would ya'?

J.

P.S. Not part of them any more. I'll be home soon.

The mentor returned to his seat, then poured another mug before looking to the guest. A clang to the plates and a turn to each other's way, they sat a good metre apart beside the lamp on the table.

His nose scrunched above the beverage as he went on, "There's nothing you could possibly offer me that would sway my decision, Syphon. I stand by my word... whatever you orchestrate, only ever means to more mischief."

"With all due respect..." The dynast answered, "I came for the chest. While you opened merry gifts over there, it caught my eye enough to know that's what you were keeping. We need that. For Xira. Rove Dynasty can show us the way."

Serenitatem scoffed upon his remark, "Xira doesn't need you. I've told you long ago, your ties with her are but a fraction left, whatever else stayed with her true father... not that I need to tell *you* that. You certainly earned a front seat."

Walking off to the exit, Syphon paused along the way and turned, "There's still Rove Dynasty in her. Whether you can accept that or not. As long as we are on opposing sides, this is our matter too. Galaxaeria needs the wise one for redemption."

As the mentor saw him out, he was left with a contemplative responsibility within. Later on, the mage's figure was spotted in the tracks and all that Serenitatem could dwell on was the fact that they would always be watching. Just like him. A matter of what one would do for family and an ally potential.

Wriggling the key in, Erma scanned her area before entering the empty hut. With the room now available and windows covered in slim drapes, she began to search throughout every corner and gap, yearning to find it. As she walked the boards to a dining room, a heeled foot slipped on a loose plank and emitted a clicking noise below. Revealing from the bottom corner of that interior was a secret entrance to a cellar in construction, still enwreathed in fabric and wood from its building materials. The dynast stepped to the floor, its congested surroundings bringing up the dust along her footprints towards the next part. She stumbled into a recently polished portion where placed was a low cabinet filled with basins and pleated sheets. Atop, lay a collection of buckets with a violet extract in each one. Behind it all, hid a blanketed display of something which caught her eye in its glow sifting through the fabric. Erma took off its cover to discover a mounted staff by that plastered wall. It's as if the twinkle radiated within her gaze as she approached it in a clement manner, then prised it off and back it settled into the hands of the enchantress.

"The ducklings always find their way to the mother duck," she muttered, holding it delicately in her retreat to the cellar exit, "Never a doubt."

Off with the staff, Erma threw their key over to a flourishing garden patch after vacating the hut and tread on, leaving the village in its tranquillity and with not even a mere glimpse behind a shoulder.

On a crouch, Xira focused on Ruzak's disagreement towards Erma, who'd been standing opposite of him, Wing Commander Jason, Rosetta and Lieutenant Paris. Ilari was soon spotted at a further distance from the rest, seemingly trying to figure out some object in his hands. With the springs rising around them, it'd become a warmer and vaporised environment. Even more so that the enchantress' presence was charging the potency of the water — elevating it at heights which prompted the splashing that brought around some steaming puddles. Once deciding to move on, a cold hand crept on her shoulder as Xira spun to be greeted by a green liquid oozing, chemical effect in bronze, tattered uniform wearing Lieutenant Forest. At first sight, she couldn't believe it to be the same man, but as soon as his voice was heard, it'd been too distinct to doubt. A blade in one hand, mirroring his other that'd been rumpled to a thorny, buff aspect. He looked at her with a glaring front and a slanted pose, as if he'd been undertaking a marathon. Forest's torn hat hanged off of his hair in the while of the leaking substance painting the skin. Xira returned an odd perusal at his demeanour, not knowing of what to say but instead, watch a forgiving alteration of an unforgiving man... formerly under another's hand and now his own, rigorous resolve. Only then noticing a grip on her wrist, Forest hurled Xira over the edge and she rolled hard against the terrain, with his focus quickly shifting in the other direction — disappearing off to the side as someone was capturing his spotting eyes. Xira turned back on her feet, moving on towards the dispute. The dry particles from beneath cut within her throat while evading the springs along each side, their manner mimicking that of Erma and her counter to the Yard personnel. Jason, who'd been standing beside his ally, angled with a concentrated aim of a Yard rifle. Not too far behind, Rosetta was seen in shackles, joined by Lieutenant Paris, holding down an apparatus.

"Listen to me," Ruzak's grating utterance was heard, "The protocol is in motion. To favour humankind, we must enact — this is, of course, involving your compliance, *Erma*. Don't you recollect our meeting? There's no room for betrayal. No man left behind, unless they choose."

The enchantress waved a sleeve to unveil, yet brought it down again when she replied, "If this *were* a room, I'd leave it no windows or doors. It's unfortunate that you find the need to disagree like this, like one minion was not enough, you brought another — with a gun. Give that key to me, Ruzak, I know *exactly* what's to be done."

With the outer spray of the waters sizzling the soil around them, beyond the rocky grounds was a high cliff overlooking below, where Willow and the team idled by in their surveillance of the events. A frightened look mulled over the area as Fiske huddled close to the companions.

"I don't think us being right here is a good idea," he stated quietly, hiding in the clothing material, "Tell me your plan is not about us joining their fight."

Willow fixated down the way, responding in resistance, "This *is* our fight. I'm not abandoning her. Even if we don't do much… what we could do is smooth the odds."

Across the springs, there'd been a rising in the commotion where both ends were shouting at each other in their reluctance to meet at a halfway point — a fragile alliance splintering at the seams. The impatience of the high personnel brought upon a resentment that echoed through the harsh, gesturing demand of Ruzak. The next thing resounding among the hazy aerosphere was an array of bullets flying towards the enchantress, reflecting the promptness of Jason, before Erma hovered an arm in front and redirected them to the Wing Commander himself — the absolute terror reigning over their once firm miens as Jason fell to his knees, then down in a merged pool of the spring water and the clang of the weapon.

Seeing this, Willow exclaimed from atop the cliff, her sorrow tearing the voice, "Father! No…!"

They'd overheard that from the distance, turning to find the three in view when Erma snarled back to Ruzak and raised an arm to cast a spell — suspending him high up from the ground. As Xira saw her friends beginning to descend the side path, she quickly barged by the two in conflict.

"At least play it fair!" She exclaimed towards the enchantress, "Come on… you've already overturned enough!"

Erma's irked demeanour spun to confront her, "What in the Lord's name are *you* doing here? Did you not get the message, was *I* not clear?"

Keeping a close eye on Ilari, Xira remarked, "Nobody deserves to take on such a wager. Nobody is an exception! Let them go… or do it right."

Tossing the wing commander a few metres beyond them, she set a trap to encage everyone else besides Ilari in a circular, rocky pillar form that derived from her sorcery. Not a gap to intervene, not a sliver of mortal escape. She faced her in a complacent pose, with sleeves resting over the garment and a hidden glimmer contouring beneath its hem.

"Now why don't you make yourself scarce?" The enchantress then continued, "I certainly do not need you here, an absolute nuisance."

Xira answered, glancing to the cage of terrified complexions, "You're right. *They* do."

A quiet whimper emitted from within the muttering group as Rosetta cried out, "My sister is gone because of the Yard and your lying habits! She could've been free!"

When he came to, Ruzak sat up and grumbled in the space, "What does it matter? Ergh… The Commander fled, leaving the higher positions to fend for themselves. The only helpful thing was that #%^& cypher wheel. With Gyrfalcon taking everyone to refuge, it was a perfect opportunity… to acquire what's rightfully ours. Bring Yowndrift Yard's design to sweet fruition…"

Using this distraction, Xira rushed to liberate Ilari out of their way but was hurled aside by a chanted word of the unrelenting dynast.

As they chattered inside, banging against the hard surface of the cage, Erma simply walked in disdain and announced once again, "Run along, young lady. Do not linger around too long for me to do that for you…"

"I'll tend to my liking."

"As you wish," replied the enchantress, a sinister tone in her look and voice.

Soon as the ground began to tip the water's angle, another person came running from the far side and shouted atop their lungs. Merlot, flailing something in one hand, arrived by them and paused.

"Wait! Don't you dare," he exclaimed, looking at Erma, "I will not let you take her. Xira, that wheel is of great significance… it's not unlocked with some metal-based key… *Aurora*… remember that name. She shouldn't be *thrown* into this, Erma, and you know it. It's far out of both our hands if that relic is not used righteously. Consider the source… the chaos that'll unfurl… you must retreat. It's absolutely a m—"

With a slam of her staff on the coarse ground, the enchantress revealed a whirling vortex between her and Xira — as the mentor eyed in arrant disbelief, holding a shining charm in his palms. The dirt beneath the two was in a crumbling dishevelment, raising Erma's garment fabric before she took one clean glance at Merlot.

"I believe it's my move. Don't wait up," she averred as the two then warped inside and out of their sight.

The surrounding environment quickly changed to a drier, magmic aspect. In view of the vast sky, reflecting its many components, a wave of light soared across the night. Xira crept up to her knees and saw what resided in the distance — a pair of joined pillars, adorned with a sun and moon, and their different forms. Standing far apart from her was Erma and under a hand, the staff which belonged to the dynast's borne powers.

"How did you-?"

"Never mind how I obtained what's rightfully mine," she spoke, her tone lowering, "Welcome, girl, to the Arch of Galaxaeria."

A calm, fresh wind swayed beneath her nose as Xira looked around, to find the unfamiliarity uncomfortable and only the rocky, crystallic land which they were in, was a hinting answer to her curiosity.

A moment between, where the members of the Yard and Merlot were left in a dilemma of their own, searching for means of opening the cage. The mentor revolved its outline, figuring out the elaborate exterior of this spellbound structure. Ahead of the group was Forest, seen arriving to the springs. Ilari walked to Merlot, standing beside him during the analysis.

"I'm terribly sorry, sir. She took the device," he stated, the eyes darting between the mentor and the cage.

Merlot turned to reply, "Unless you're made of magic, keep your sacrifices for when they count."

There'd been no trace of a crack or indentation to be used for applying a gap. Encountering them soon enough was Lieutenant Forest as he ran to the cage. A bewildered Ruzak shot him a glance, given back a furious one from his former ally — a confrontation that couldn't be cut even with a blade like their own.

"Can't even look at me? You *fool!*" Forest shouted, glaring him down, "What'd'ya think? Leave me in the dust and a phantom would not come back to haunt their traitors? A pity, a cage doesn't even hide your mistakes."

Ruzak replied, approaching the lieutenant by the rough margins, "I assumed you were with Gyrfalcon. Free me and I vow to make it up to you, Dylan. I stand by my duty as a Wing Commander. We can continue on the Yard's legacy — with or without anybody else."

A vexed exhalation hissed from him, as Forest vulgarly remarked, "Partners do not turn their backs besides a defence. Lucky the blade is in my favour now. Forget the reconciliation, my old friend. Yowndrift Yard is no longer the preference."

The pillar was slammed across by his claw of a hand, tearing it down in pieces where the group then scurried on out except for the Wing Commander. Slicing through his uniform, Forest lifted Ruzak high up with a following glare to his old friend's disquietude.

"Let me make something sound," he uttered, displeased, "If you go on and assume that I'm here to do you a favour, you can think again. I meant what I said… it could've been one hell of a partnership — but I must forget about those pretty lies. Instead, *you've* done me a favour. You be my very own pet, in this new world now… we'll call it even."

From behind them, Lieutenant Paris intervened, "Dylan…? Is that what you really want?"

Upon hearing the gentle voice, evoking something within him, he turned, "Paris… uh — hmm? You're safe… what are you — are you still working with him?"

"No," she said, noticing the Wing Commander frown in his wriggling, "Let's leave them, while the transport is still being set up —

I heard they'll be moving to different points. We can find something new."

Forest pondered before answering gloomily, "I think you know where my choice is. However, I can't just leave him without anybody making up for what they've done."

"I know," the Lieutenant told him, "Then let him carry Wing Commander Jason out to a better place than these grounds. Make him face the consequences. After that, we can move on — it's not worth it because it's in the past for *us*, but for him, I cannot say the same. That's not our fight any more, Dylan. He'll already be carrying the weight of it. As will all the others. Let's go."

"Hey! Where is he? Let me see, let me see!" Willow shouted down from the path that she'd crossed in reaching them, as she hurried towards the Springs.

Moving aside, they quietly considered to leave her in mourning, when Forest sighed, throwing Ruzak aside and then joined Paris in a compassionate hug. She knelt down slowly upon seeing the father's body, sobbing while her hands dipped in the pool which surrounded him — the companions comforted alongside her, where she emitted an outcry in the midst of pulling the Wing Commander between a grim embrace, holding him once more with the tears dripping by the garments. Merlot's empathetic nod was then added with a rather ashamed treading of Ruzak, who bent to pick up his faithful ally and the rest merely watched as he went off to fulfill a fair, noble task.

Reaching for her sling, Xira eyed the dynast while she twirled the staff around the cape. Something raised her off the floor and slid the feet a few steps behind. Erma looked towards the area in an attentive manner, cutting the distance and wedged the staff by her boots. Xira, watching its glow, grabbed onto the bottom of it and made her way up to confront the enchantress directly — deflecting by angling it to create a partition between them. A clap of thunder coursed the sky, with the winds whistling on their sides.

"I refuse to be a part of this," Xira declared in the contention, "Take me back."

"You already are," Erma defied against her, "There's still a decision to make, however, that falls more on me. Whether you desire or not..."

She snatched back the staff and brought out the cypher wheel, presenting it in her palms. A vague line traced its shell and shone a reflection of the stars and the ground. Erma held a key beside it and made a blatant offer. Unwavering as they were, the clash of their beliefs came to a blend in the temptation of what was found and orbited beyond this relic. Xira reached for the key, turning it in inspection as it read initials in old inscription… but were not all that clear.

"There's no lock cylinder," she pointed out, descending it below, "It's opened another way. *You* just want me to figure it out — you have no idea. This thing was stolen from one place to another, all by someone with an agenda but very little clue. Why the desperation, if nobody knows anything about the wheel?"

Tossing the forged key beside her, Xira's eyes switched between the relic and the dynast. Not a charmed look graced their response as Erma huffed in an unfurling of her garment, casting out a spell that catapulted Xira far across the grounds and landed her against a crystallic mound. She curled to her knees, with a grunting return to stand again, in the while of Erma's exterior becoming a haunting display among entangled sorcery of a mage.

On the outskirts of Sunset Cove, were the team along with Merlot, gathered by an ascended hill between a valley and the Lilac Springs. Holding on to a fragment of his uniform, Willow's lost train of thought dwelled upon its stains. The mentor looked to her with a sorrowful front, as he sat to rest on the boulder.

"He honoured his duty. Therefore, no futile resolutions," he said in consolation, "It doesn't change what he did, but you can choose to forget or understand."

The material crinkled along the fingers, as her voice eased, "He was the last of my family. If he was that awful, what does that make me? He could barely look at me, all I wanted was an explanation, an answer."

"Loss is loss, no matter where you are — it makes sense for it to feel like the burden is on you," the mentor went on, covering them with his mantle, "Moving on is the way to achieve refreshment. If you sit and ponder about his mistakes, there'll be nothing left to learn."

Willow huddled close to the earpiece as it crackled, then said, "Right… he's just a bad memory then. — Hey… sir? Are you on the receiver?"

With a door slam, Serenitatem blared through the static,

"Remember; Raptor. I'm eager to hear of the current events, are you safe? What's going on?"

Once it was all elaborated to the mentor, a brief silence filled their exchange as a rumble was overheard in the distance, atop the fogged mountains.

"Is there a way to get to her?" he asked in a heedful tone, "If it goes out of her hands, there's no way of extinguishing the fire that is unleashed. Without magic, nobody can reach their location! Unless there's a — a hidden route. Somebody needs to find a method, for I fear disaster awaits these lands... she is the key! She is the arcane spirit! The way... only Xira knows. Within her, although, wild by all means... will reveal Galaxaeria's truth! She's coming — they know — they are upon us! Hurry! — I must go, people need me here. Please, child!"

After the transmission, Willow turned to Merlot to inform, "That was Serenitatem. Once I told him everything, he snowballed like I've never noticed. She is the key. Said something about fire... and the place where magic is guidance. He sounded quite... terrified."

"Yes, well... she is the key," Merlot declared, tracing the mountains, "Long ago, a tale was told where the Arch of Galaxaeria, a place where magic entered and the mighty wandered the very lands, was found only by the very same and those blessed beside them. Aurora, her mother, was among the first inhabitants of the Spirit Realm who discovered what exactly that place was for — albeit, she was a goddess guardian for healing and the realm, she did not possess the power to venture over there. She would say, however; 'Heal yourself to heal your friend. What you give is what is sent.' Her own love that she would sing out; 'Love is me and love is you. Love thee, for love is peace.' Also; 'Glide among the sea, sing yourself a symphony shanty, the magic one believes, blooming high with the leaves. To the universe. To infinity.' Along her dedication, she bestowed upon the womb and declared for her own child to find what she could not, by means of which she did not bear. Little did she know... Xira was already set in blessing, a mystery even the mother was kept in the dark from... only for the ancient folk to know and others to discover themselves — after that night, she not only echoed her voice, but the truth that was to arrive to that very realm. See now, that is why Erma took her there — it's a place for settling arrangements, whether it is for all or for one. That wheel, they do not know what they're toying with. If

Xira gets the opportunity, we can't be certain what she'll decide, because she can. She can alter everything around."

Running down the area, Rosetta called out to the group as Saffron and Ilari followed close behind in a hasty approach. The friends looked to each other in the midst of their tiresome selves, as Merlot gestured for them to join but the offer was dismissed before they announced again.

"You guys go on without us," Rosetta explained, treading about, "I need to honour my sister properly. Seeing what went on up there, it's the least I can do for her. I'm sorry you witnessed that, Willow. If there was anything I could do…"

"It's fine, Rosetta," she told her, dropping the piece of the uniform and twisting it in the mud, "To find ways to move on. I hope we can settle for peace and not allow someone's foul intentions tamper with our essence. My mother told me that and I stand by it every day. I'm glad we were there for each other."

The two thanked the others as Rosetta then added, "When you see Xira again, please thank her as well, from us — for all that she's done. She carved a new way for the *Yard Rebels*, giving us all a fresh start. It's something I've wanted for a very, very long time."

Saffron chimed in, "Yeah, whatever they're up to now, we're cheering on for our friend and the betterment of this darned place. May she soar upon all… and get out of… wherever she is. Anyway, we'll see you around, altogether, right? Every one of us."

"Seconded. Cheers!" Ilari exclaimed in their leave.

Off they went, as the team encircled once more and eyed towards the stormy mountains. Merlot held a charm in his hand, whirling it around in a quiet, brooding moment of his own. The sky lit up in its thunderous outlines across the way, with sparks of purple and scarlet glimmer, weaved beside various dark clouds. In thought of getting themselves to a safer place, they kept close to a pair of trees by the soil of a hill.

Looking down to his hand, Merlot suggested in a notion, "Say… maybe he can help us too. What do you think about visiting Lunaris Town?"

Willow answered, her eyes drawn to the motions in the far distance, "I'm not too comfortable with abandoning her. There's no way of telling… we can't even — we *need* to be there for her."

First on his feet, the mentor adjusted the garment and gestured towards a path, "It's a choice to help, better than simply idling… if you all are ready."

Leaving nothing behind as Sam held to the axe, the group dashed through a path sloping below.

"Onwards, at my heel now!" Merlot shouted in the rain, stepping among pools of mud as the thunder clapped throughout the sky.

Willow followed close by, holding her hat, and said, "I don't think this is really a safe move. What if he's already out of Lunaris Town? We can't just leave her."

An array of trees swooshed in their crossing, then upon the main bridge, he halted with a warning of his unfurled mantle. A group of Yaraks were manning its roads, armed and covered with their equipment alongside PBTU trucks. There'd been a paved dirt road off to the lower grounds that led under the bridge — imprinted with the wheels of a truck.

"Even so, it's the way forth," he added in a concentrated manner, "Through there, we'll take a shortcut. Remain low and stay close to me — we can help her once we get to the town. For now, ears out… keep it hush."

They crouched towards more puddles and together, descended below in a quick shift next to sluicing water. The mentor placed a finger to his mouth as they lined up to a wall, where Willow could overhear the Yaraks' discussion. She whispered to the companions what was discerned and mimicked to a docked rowboat at the turning trail. Following behind, Merlot set to paddle with a night voyage to Lunaris town.

"The Yaraks are still searching for them," Willow told the others, "They're marked to the Yard's main goal. Aside from learning that Xira knows too much about Yowndrift Yard, with all that's happened, it's just added to her hunt. We were somewhat hoping to sneak in and sneak out. — I knew it was rather uncanny when she heard of Erma's whereabouts. She was determined to find her and sort it out… only, you know. Then the Yard… and their horrid actions."

Beyond the settling waters, a vague view of the town emerged with its mellow details while the glow of the moon shone a reflection of an emblem beside the rowboat. She leaned over to identify its mirrored design on the rippled surface.

Sam called to her, "What is it? Rocks?"

"The Yard. This is their equipment too. Does their work include boating transport?" She asked in return.

"Sometimes," added Fiske quietly, "From second to base, we were never informed of their tasks... when it was offshore matter."

Upon arrival at a miniature stone arch bridge, the boat was rowed to the far side when Merlot waved to scale it. The team walked on for some time before seeing the forefront in its dark hues. All but few places were still open, along with local residents that roamed about and the captivating ambience that wafted through with radiating doors and windows.

On to the smoothie bar, Merlot announced, "I'll go on my own, you three ask and look around. Cover all corners. Then we'll meet out by that town bow."

As they entered Groovy Fruity Carousel, the three split up across its interior, going from every wall and corner with sheer hope. The few customers at their stools casually angled a peep before Willow proceeded to the counter.

Tracing the manoeuvres of a flipping glass, she asked, "I'm looking for a man who works the Groovy Fruity Carousel bar. He also resides on the second floor. Have you seen him?"

The tender approached, wiping the wares as he replied, "Y'know what... somebody else came in here earlier and was looking for the same person. Odion, was it? Yeah, first time was odd enough. It's the second whiff that makes me suspect all of this. Look, I don't suppose you're a troublemaker but do tell me why. Was he on the news?"

"Listen, sir, I don't know of anybody that was already here but I do know I'm here to find *Odion*. If you will," she went on, "I just need to know his whereabouts — it's a personal... family thing, it doesn't concern anyone or anything else, only your support."

Raising to pour a drink, he mused. Then said, "Most recently... I saw him out by the road. At first, it looked like he was throwing out some junk but Odion soon vanished and nobody here's seen him after that. Sorry."

"I'll keep searching, thank you," she told the tender as the companions reunited at the door.

Fiske held up a handkerchief that revealed a note wedged in it. The others joined his focus when he elaborated, "Found this in the lavatory. Smudged lipstick and what appears as a pen — it says; *Meet me at Citrus Mill. Midnight. ~ Peri.*"

"That's the tender from the smoothie bar, she works with him," Willow stated in their quiet huddle, "It's a lead, do we agree?"

Sam nodded with a shrug and added, "It's all we've got. Suppose we give it a try."

"We should probably hurry though… it's quarter to when the owls go hoot." Said Fiske.

Outside once again, they recalled their rendezvous with Merlot at the bow as the mentor arrived a little later. They shared their findings between each other, noticing fewer wanderers about the town. It'd been a cold yet peaceful moment, while they all walked on to the road's side. The note in the handkerchief flew far off as Fiske missed a catch in the air.

"It's okay… uh, Merlot? We think we should follow on Peri's message," Willow spoke up, "If we see her there, she could tell us more, if she knows."

The mentor looked to the area beyond the margins and sighed, "Be on guard. There are many Yard folk still on duty, despite being scattered… for now. I'll need to—"

In the midst of their exchange, a woman yelled out from the gift store nearby, "Excuse me, hello! Can you *please* lend me some assistance?"

Going towards her way, the team discovered the open doors and the owner standing by alone.

"There's been a blackout," she informed them, "I cannot figure out where the panel is and my employee for today left long ago, so there's nobody else when all the lights went out."

Willow and Sam offered to help as the other two set off on another task — exploring all further areas. With the woman's guide to her store, she provided them enough to know what they could run into during the panel search. Starting from the windows, they skimmed through gaps and aisles until reaching a locked door. They fidgeted with its knob and surroundings but to no luck, the two paused next to unsteady crates.

"You found the door? Oh good," the owner announced from her spot, "I was afraid the new shipment which arrived this early morning would make a mess before I even unpacked it. Not too sure where my keys went… it's an auto-lock door, you see… maybe put an object there. Surely there's a rather safer approach."

On the opposing side, something zapped along its frame, causing the door to unlock in a strange, dark welcoming. The two carefully shuffled inside and began to feel for the walls, circling its perimeter before uncovering a casing in their colliding steps. Willow opened the flickering panel and guessed between what switch was which.

"This green…? Or this green? The red? Or the second red…?" She muttered, her fingertips hovering each row.

Sam suggested, "For as long as I've known these things… it's almost always somewhere at the top or bottom corner — can't confirm though. Try 'em out, it's not like we'll be setting off rockets."

One after another attempt at scoring the correct sequence, the room lit up in a daisy yellow flicker, showcasing its contents within a cache space. A back door was spotted beside some pot plants on a shelf. Its window made of frosted glass, highlighted the outside in quite a foggy guise — when the second they spun, the front exit shut right before them. Looking down, the trowel they used on its margin was flipped on a side as Willow knocked against the surface.

"Were neither of us watching… or did someone deliberately lock us in?" She questioned towards her friend.

The two shouted for aid, waiting for the owner to respond. As she pressed an ear to the door, keys were already being wriggled into its lock and soon opened at the sight of the woman standing to greet.

"I am forever grateful," she stated, gesturing to her store, "Pick whatever you like and it is yours, a gift."

At the counter, Willow and Sam thanked the friendly owner and made their way out, waving between a respectful exchange. Carrying a fine sash over her shoulders, she turned to Sam putting on a new tropical shirt. The companions walked on down the path.

"This is where the road parts," Willow remarked, "We'll wait here… or go straight to the mill."

"They should come back soon," he said, looking on, "Last resort, we go alone. I don't want everyone going separate ways again."

After waiting a short while, the team met up at a fruit market on the margin. Merlot decided that they were to go there together but split up in pairs upon arrival. Around an open road lay a cobblestone path towards the set location in sight.

"The Citrus Mill," Willow commented as they watched the water wheel revolve.

Merlot turned to them and said, "Fiske and I will go inside. You two stay outside and keep watch. Whistle if you see or hear anything, okay?"

As they walked in between an opening, Sam crossed around the back to explore. Willow chased after to accompany as they looked for clues of old or recent visitors. Besides the general items of buckets, rakes, wood and hay, the mill was a vacant and calm place — perfect to idle.

"Nobody was here recently," she pointed out, hearing a vague droning noise, "Hang on — look, there's a car coming. Hide!"

She alerted the other companions with a kick along the oak wood, breaking through to a hollow space. A car door shut as they crouched inside and the footsteps in the area then turned eerily quiet. Willow focused the earpiece to pick up a muffled sob nearby, before not too long, another voice joined at the same spot.

"It's me, I don't know who would do that — I tried, I can't keep it to myself."

"Listen... Peri, you must leave the town by dawn. Pack your things and leave nothing!"

Sam turned with a puzzled glance while they were eavesdropping. He mouthed something in question to the circumstance.

The other person went on, *"If they find that you would not only desert but rally against them, you would lend yourself at no merciful trade!"*

Peri's saddened voice answered, *"What would you do? There is no place for me there. She doesn't care for me, let alone the rest. Why not show how karma plays solitary? It's all I've known... at least I should make good use of the connection."*

"I must be going, somebody really needs me. I cannot abandon this, Peri. Do what's right. Allow them to make a mess of you, and you lose yourself. Instead, take this chance to refresh. They will learn of their actions and it may take them a long time. You can do this now. Take it from an ol' man with a thousand eyes, secrets are never sheltered!"

It soon quieted down as Willow and Sam left to see Peri walking off across the road. She'd appeared to be carrying a Groovy Fruity Carousel backpack. With the damp clouds pouring below, the team then huddled within the mill entrance to discuss their next plan. The thunder crashes shivered the floor by their feet, while Fiske propped himself to the unlatched door.

"This fellow here is quite a wise man," Merlot averred, eyeing their friend, "There was a machinery of some sort inside and he helped me work it out. I wanted to figure what exactly one can do here, so we went the extra mile. We found some trinkets, looks like somebody has been a collector. Assuming the mill is rarely inhabited, I'd say it's great for coming to visit. Fiske, I admire your composed ways. Now off we go, neither of them can't be far — try not to be spotted. Meet at that orange lighthouse when you're done. Stay safe out there, kiddos."

At the door, Fiske curved a smile as they then left the Citrus Mill and dispersed to trail them across the grasslands. A while later, a couple of Yaraks were heard on duty when Willow hushed at the hilltop and the two knelt to spy. Pointing to some stacked containers, Sam noted all the equipment that'd been stashed by the personnel and how there could be more transport nearby. Over in the distance, Peri was seen crossing by quietly next to a patrolling Yarak who'd just missed her.

"There," Willow whispered, indicating an open path ahead, "Low and steady…"

Around they crouched and remained out of sight, as the two watched the Yaraks tend to their lit campfire. The discussion had been loud enough to muffle their steps and ease the suspense of being seen or caught. A fair gap stood between their point and the other side of that area — requiring a jump to traverse it. As Willow landed, Sam tossed the axe over before joining beside his companion. One of the Yaraks turned, seemingly picking up on a brief noise but dismissed it once an ally called to their supper. Following Peri, they huddled behind a shrub off the tracks while listening in on any other members. It was a brief tread later when the two came upon a spot beyond their tailing where Peri appeared to be kneeling in front of a chipped monolith. Moving in, Willow angled to listen on the voice picked up by the device.

"What do I do? I haven't felt this lost since I left," she said in a low voice, distressed, *"Then again… why would I think that anyone would be considerate? I see how things go about with everyone I meet… how is this, one wise man, any different?"*

A pond's water around the monolith rippled amidst the soft sway of a tree, soothing Peri's breaching sorrow as she sat there rather silently. The view from the top gave the two companions a hint that they should leave her alone when movement was noticed. They focused on what was occurring before she began to descend well into the pond. Willow's alarm set right off as the two companions stood still — no further action could be discerned from the surface, aside from the few wrinkles on the sapphire reflection.

"She hasn't come back up, Sam, I'm going," she told her friend, rushing down in a hurry.

Her feet skidding to the pool's edge, kicking some rocks off its side, Willow looked among the water to see a vague shadow below. Without dwelling too much on the idea, she dived in and promptly stretched the arms to grab her out — only, to be met with a defying glare on a distorted image of a figure. Attempting to reel Willow in herself, Peri's form took place when a glistening alteration came to, making for a hassling engagement with her as they spun over in the depths. Bubbles were seen popping out of the surface when Sam eagerly awaited for their return, but realised it to be far more peculiar than he thought. Going down there himself, he couldn't tell whether if they were stuck or that still waters ran deep. Underneath the cold aura, Willow twisted in the effort of detaching herself away while Peri, determined, clawed into her suit and peeled out a very subtle layer. A fearful shiver ran down Sam's back once he figured that they were likely in trouble. Using the blade, he dipped it in the water until the axe's handle was submerged, hanging on to his wishful thinking that they would attain it.

"*Rughh*," Willow exclaimed in the grapple as she eventually lifted her foot to kick at the ribs.

Peri tried to latch onto the sash when she was blindsided by another power kick to the gut. Freeing herself to ascend, Willow swam towards the surface like a propeller and reached out a hand after seeing a waving object in the current. Just about to grab on the axe, she felt a grip over an ankle, yanking her down once again. With a swift bend of the knees, she booted the hand off and instead, attached her own in a hopeful aim to rescue Peri as well. Avoiding any countering motions, she managed to pull up around the handle and as soon as Sam felt the harsh tug, he heaved the two back on ground. They coughed and turned over the dirt, where Willow picked her bag to shield herself from an incoming charge that was cut short by Sam — who pushed her off to separate them. Back on her feet, Willow insisted to Peri that they were here for a good reason and that no harm was intended towards her. The bartender got up from the fall, shaking the drenched clothing as she looked to the two companions.

"I — I apologise. Something got the better of me," was her crestfallen reply, "Tell me you didn't really... see that."

"Nothing to apologise for, uh..." Willow paused, checking the area, "I can tell you I won't share this to anybody — but... we — I would like to know what this location is..."

Walking off to the side to rest, Peri explained, "It's a place I come to visit when I feel disconnected. That monolith represents somebody that meant a lot to me — I met them not far from here... that's all I can say about that."

Willow reassuringly added, "It's fine. Honestly. We're just glad you are yourself again."

"Yeah," she answered, a quiet sigh releasing from her, "Thank you... you didn't need to. It's my baggage... a mess of a mess. Why would you? How did you know...?"

Fixing the axe on his new shirt with the old one, Sam glanced to his companion as they sat under the pouring sky. A brief silence filled in the while of the noises that could be heard from the Yarak group beyond their position.

"I understand. It's not ever easy," Willow then began to say, "It doesn't need to be yours alone, of course it's a mess... a friend can be there and *for* you."

Peri frowned, stating, "... but what good would a friend do if they won't do good with you? Not like I can really rely on anybody. There's few left and all hidden so well."

The two companions stood up again when Willow replied, "Consider us your trusty allies. Now... please get yourself inside a better place to stay and to hell with that man if he won't lend you a room."

Puzzled, the bartender turned in response, "What man?"

A Yarak suddenly appeared behind them and shouted an irked alert. Looming with armed uniforms and standing beside him, were a Yard group that rushed down to reach them. Sam raised his hands to try and settle the situation, when one Yarak came forth in a scoff.

"Old Yard employee goes rogue. Didn't think that of you, Sam," he said, pointing their Yard equipment.

Taking a subtle step back, Sam diffused, "Let us go through and we won't be a problem. We were on our way, just leave us be. Sir."

Another armed Yarak aimed an electrifying rod that powered up with each grip rotation. They saw among all of the weapons, a matter of being outnumbered and not only with the count of figures. Startled in their way, Peri kept close by her friends as the group eased forward to the team. With a motion of two electrified rods and a chain-lock dispenser, the front Yaraks marched for a capture when Willow barged in front of Sam. From the forward, outstretched crash of her leg, the ground split in multiple slants — creating an echo within the group. As they tumbled down, letting out efforts of climbing back up, the team used this advantage to escape — narrowly darting by the Yaraks when a clasp circled on Willow's foot that pulled her towards them again. Surrounded, they collectively launched some trap gadgets to attempt a capture when Willow seized her own chain and began to whirl it at high speed, knocking both the items and Yaraks out as she spun in the spot. Whipping the side against an unsteady crack, clearing the way forward, she made a run for it — far from the fallen Yarak group and back to her companions, who then altogether disappeared into the lands far ahead, hearing the exclamations of the personnel.

Pushing back her hands on the crystals, Xira braced herself as Erma towered over with raised palms, ready to charge. She looked around to see what could aid her before the enchantress released a ball of static in fragments of magmic stone and just as it reached, Xira bent forward an arm to defend.

"Shattering these precious little gems? How dare you..." Erma uttered in a leering pose.

Xira hurled herself against the dynast to a grazing takedown across the terrain, where it was quickly countered with slashes along both sleeves, as Erma tried to knee her away. After many swings to break the quarrel, Xira's eyes turned full silver when she deeply shouted among the howling aerosphere.

"Let me go, Erma. Enough... sort this!"

With the two at each other's grip, they whirled to a brutal casting on coarse rims. The enchantress ascended in an altered guise of a fierce flow that surrounded and began to form spheres embedded with occult shards. Steadying herself to flee, Xira let out an effort, watching the spheres revolve in-flight. She sprinted off down the way while avoiding every projectile until a hefty one cut between, leading her off-track. A turn to her pursuer, she slammed a fist to the ground — breaking through its surface.

"Come on…! Try your luck," she said in a gruff manner.

The enchantress continued on, picking up the speed after each frequent attempt, exhibiting a frightening mien as she hovered down to ground level. Chanting an incantation to bring forth a destructive graviton that could tear apart any obstructions, Erma directed its course to capture the target. Xira resisted its bonds, although it was not much of a hassle as her bracers deflected by barriers. A grunt sounded through when she went on to find an escape, but the dynast's seething temper echoed in another daunted shout and an array of piercing beams following like a lock-on trajectory that was desperately aimed towards the young lady. The skies were filled with a horde of elements and forces to which trailed beside the windborne effects of the calamity. She leaped on a side-ward kick-flip in the air, returning a projectile sent by Erma to her, taking her off the levitation. Without much of a moment, the enchantress hurled her with a charm segment, sending her across. Xira uplifts and powers forward to charge the dynast and as she did, the dynast launched a sonic swoop which savagely tore the garment-armour around. She noticed the armour was peeling off and Xira began to take it off bit by bit, yanking its pieces as she then walked toward Erma and continued to peel off more of it — the garment fragments fell to the illumined floor, in her venture forth.

"You can shed off the garment, the armour, my own belongings--," she said, "—but you cannot take pure light."

Cleaning off the remains, the dynast ruffled a defence guise, with Xira eager to leap. She ran forth through the grounded stardust, and noticed the hovering material char about, her fingertips knowing of the winged warmth. Then, as she sprinted up at the ready, a magical voice of a being called out to her like their energy flew down into a song around the young woman's tattered sleeve in her protection.

"Remember yourself," the voice uttered gracefully, harmonising, "Choice and purpose. What you are—be. What you do—choose. What is yours—purpose and all that you are — remember the pure wisdom."

Upon her calm step into balance, Xira exhaled a huff when Erma wildly sent her to the floors again, swinging the dirt to spin her over and toward another chase with flung projectiles.

During the turns, some of the sprung projectiles knocked Xira aside and caused a tumble beyond the area — leaving her among the other crystallic mounds encircling her position. Kicking some rocks to the dynast, the young woman's attempt was deflected before sliding out of her aim. She crawled forward, dragging herself to a higher portion when Erma's duplicating cackle creeped up in the moment. Lifting a foot to a step, Xira clawed into the crystals and retrieved a piece in each hand before the barren land beneath her started to dissolve into an orchid slimy substance. The heels of her boots were caught in the consumption, much like the actions of quick sand — she searched by the sides for any surface to latch on.

"I never need luck," Erma sneered in her stance.

With the crystals, Xira cut down and consistently climbed up and eventually reeled out of the trap in the process. The enchantress pushed her away once more into the barbed fragments. As she cast a new technique, its reaction was of a way that would collect the being themself and banish them out of place and inside the chosen capsule. Although when its use is inspired by sorcery as such, the general results may actually differ, depending on what the subject is marked for. Quick to counter, Xira crossed the crystals over and fought off against its might — holding it high as the dynast began to notice the defiance and between them, was a matter of whether it would cast through or be reoriented. Sending her a rather few metres back with the staff falling beside her, she rose up to rush towards Erma when it was denied by a hurl aloft — taking to a landing on both knees and forearms.

"Ugh!" Xira expressed in an effort, getting up to be graced with a zapping light on the two crystals.

This altered their forms to become identical in hues of violet, black and silver on the right and silver with sun gold on the left. Their design which elongated to measure from a fingertip to the tip of an elbow, rested in her hands as dual crystallic, mystical treasures. A look towards the enchantress, where she attempted another spell was automatically halted by a power surrounding the two. Xira felt the wind descending from the skies and elevate her from where she'd been standing. Few feet off the ground, Erma's maddened shout pierced on to only interlace along the waves of air encircling the body. As she reached for the staff that was nearby, she could only watch now where Xira hovered above in the heated air and stared her down, her iris in rainbow hues and cosmic energy, both hands beside the waistband.

Xira recommended a return to the realm, when she voiced, "You don't need to do this. Bring me back home, we can't sacrifice the greater good."

"My mission urges to be completed, that's not up to anybody but *me*," Erma responded in the struggling grasp of the staff, "I *won't* lose. I'll make sure of that."

Just when she aimed it to her, whispers from beyond fell to Xira's ears while sensing the energy around and slowly was burning the outer layer of the gloves.

"Fire and spirit come to bring, light the wind and spark the dark... rise on the truth. Let it all be known."

A low whirling spiral of green emerged on top of the staff. Erma began to utter words frantically, summoning a spell in the scarce remains of the dynast's hope. It'd seemed like it was bound to interfere in the events before her, so with effort, she went on to give another single serving charge. The light from the night sky stormed down the way, as Xira ignited in flames, her entire body enwreathed in the orbiting energy. Her eyes lit up in silver and then to her rainbow essence with sunny flight, while her multihued hair flared alongside and melting off the gloves, she wielded the dual defences in her aerial bearing. The fire blazed out in a wild flow and fused with all the elements that surrounded. The dynast looked with pure terror, something that which haunted the very own eyes of Erma, when a heavy gust knocked the staff right out of the grip — taking it way far out of arms reach.

"Do I believe... am I deceived... no," a quivering voice emitted from her response.

The ground begun to tremble, creating many angled cracks on its exterior as it all became a tempestuous sight. From the falling skies that carried out the winds, to waves of elemental fury around the coarse area, a blast occurred with Xira's fire and in a moment's haste, blew a bright light that consumed the entirety of the Arch.

Running on to get closer on the trail, Merlot huffed beneath a lightning zap in the sky as he turned with utter fright.

"We must hurry!" He shouted behind him, "I think I see something — is that — an avalanche?"

Fiske remained by the mentor as he asked, "An avalanche? Here? Who's doing that?"

Upon arriving at a field of sprouting fauna, Merlot stood in the enthralling view.

"I believe that is Xira. The might of Xira herself."

The man they tracked wandered in his focus to the mountains, before coming to a halt, holding something in hand. He raised a shining mirror to its direction, before being interrupted by the mentor's call.

"Serenitatem? Is that… what are you doing?" Merlot shouted in the storm.

"Wh — Merlot, why are you here? Go! There's a snow-crystallic avalanche! It's already reached the Springs!" The mentor explained through its commotion.

"The mirror… you're not planning to do what I think you are, it'll attract entities beyond this realm!"

Lowering his aim, Serenitatem turned to inform, "This already has. If I allow them to intercept and bring their old wars to Galaxaeria, then we've already lost home."

From the mountains to the valleys below, the glimmering avalanche filled its lands like a coating over an uneven surface. Covered in the fragments, a thunder bolt plummeted down the way and created a wave around the impact. The three men witnessed its dispersion across the other areas nearby, followed by a reverberating sound.

"Do what you must, then," Merlot went on with caution, "Guide her far from the destruction."

Returning to raise the mirror once again and focus on the trails of light, a translucent beam shot out in a wavering line to the skies. An array of spheric particles followed its trajectory as the mentor stepped forward into the field.

"The ancestors… the ones of them which still bear an eternal quest," he began to explain, "They've made their presence known by entering Galaxaeria once again, lured by *The Formula*. Driven by their immorality… see, betraying every other ancestor that was once alongside them."

Amidst the discussion, Willow and Sam's rushing footsteps were heard shuffling to the team. Just in time to hear about an era of the olden disputes, their eyes were locked on the mirror's channelling of its power.

"Quite right, Serenitatem," Merlot then chimed in, watching the light and sparklings soar across the realm, "Too many attempts at using the wheel resulted in a feud between the ancestors of Galaxaeria — fuelled with tainted intention, the mechanism itself was lost far from them like it contained a renewable design that separated itself to a different location. After that, it was moved to the ol' Greaper Nestle library — we still don't know who moved it, however."

Fiske turned to greet the companions who were standing nearby the mentors.

"What are you planning on doing with that axe, Sam?" He questioned, noticing its wrap.

Fixing his shirt, Sam replied, "I don't want to be going around empty handed, man. Being cooped up can imprint an alarm on you, especially around these parts…"

As she tapped the mentor on his shoulder, Willow went on to mention, "Sir, we were heading towards the lighthouse before when I saw something strange in the sky. We would've stayed there, if it weren't for whatever is occurring over there. Can you please tell us what that is about? You said that's where they were…"

Merlot averred to the point, "That appears to be Xira. Perhaps with or without Erma. In all honesty, it's best for us to keep our distance for now. I know how much you want to be there."

Soon as the team ventured forth, the avalanche arrived down the way and to their feet, crossing through every patch of land that encompassed. They looked around in the combination of fauna and snowy layers, spellbound by its effects. Onward to the mountains with careful footing, their attention shifted to a fire-slash which went under in the breaking of the ground — that sent an echoing rumble from its encounter.

Meanwhile, in the beginning of the aftermath…

The scarred hands twitched in the dirt as Xira coughed over to notice the melted bracers paint along her sleeves. The dual crystals still in her palms, she raised to find the ground beneath in an incurved wreck, scorched to its outer fragments. Seeing her arms transformed into her great cosmic spirit, she observed the hair and then all else that went from flesh to her purity. The shine trailed along the grounds, with her fresh hair flung high and over in a new cosmic-wave flair. The aura, which resonated throughout the Arc, travelled an elegant tranquillity which reflected the bright, vast sky. Emitting a low exhalation not a mere metre apart, Erma was getting up in a turn when she came to — sorting her belongings before Xira saw of the dynast's presence. She jolted up in her seat, eyes focused as they were soon met with a scuffed look in return.

"A way was made for the mage…" Xira voiced between a throaty huff.

"Oh, please… *tuh,* fortune smiled upon me," was Erma's response, sitting up, "Got a second bite at the cherry. It must've fallen from you. Oh-—"

A flurry of clouds wafted above them, as she expressed, "Don't get too comfortable, Erma. We are finished, all right?"

Xira got up from her kneeling position and began to glide forward. Her soothing and charming mien graced the Arc grounds, admiring the true form and glanced over to Erma, the emotions settled with wisdom.

"I suppose we are at a truce. You can choose for your light, Erma."

The dynast remained further off, picking up the staff before she stated, "You look—different. The Dynasty was right—my, my—it is you. You—you are here. Xira. Great, it is a truce. An honest truce. Perhaps for the favour, I'll summon two portals at your disposal and alert you of our new company… up high — go on… get yourself out of here, they are onto us."

Watching the portal emerge as an aquatic oval, a dissonant voice blared down from above while she came to realise what or *who* the enchantress was referring to — she saw, from the effect of the portal, that she'd indeed turned to her homeland form for the moment of honouring her secret, as the flesh arrived from crystallic-scales of energy designing the planetary surface. They exchanged a dear glance at a distance, before venturing to focus. Turning to the path, Xira sprinted forth and launched through the portal amidst a declaration;

"Hear! Surrender The Formula! The Formula of Galaxaeria!"

Finding herself at the mountain's edge, she looked over a coarse way to the far bottom and behind her, more rocky surroundings following the location of the Arch. With all that was left with her; parts of her gear on the shoulder blades, around the thigh material and waist, was along an empyrean armour that graced as a brand-new garment design — which replaced the fabric-made layer, shining a metallic-crystal bliss. Out of the cosmos and her cosmic self, her spirit that bloomed on and in this magnificent gift — arrived the dawn that is. A blend of voices then gave a haunting echo across, forging barbed antlers out of the overhang before duplicating themselves around its form.

"Reveal to us The Formula! Return the relic of olden purpose!"

The ground beneath began quaking to hurling parts of stone that tumbled along the uneven surfaces seen from the highest point. Although some clouds were obscuring a portion of the view to the valleys, it was evident that a fair route was not granted in the hazardous boulder placement. Barefooted with the boots' tint, Xira slid off to descend the mountain as thunder resumed its bellows, weaving the many obstacles along the way. From the skies, they uttered again as a row of spherical objects were flung beside her in a close encounter.

"You do not wish to defy, hear and offer!"

Between the grating ride down craggy angles and clouds which sent an uplifting gust as she swayed along the sides, Xira's fluttering hair met the spinning pebbles that sifted around her fingers in a hold of one of the dual crystals. Once reaching the lower section, avoiding any barriers and particles, a barrage of ice projectiles fell from above like a raging glacier. Upon the plummet, it'd propelled her over the rest of the exterior and right down to a shaded region's valley. In a hefty sigh, Xira raised herself to a curve for a run, pushing forward after fixing the crystals against the belt's side and barely dodging an ice flurry.

"Awakened be our spirits, returning to retrieve what Galaxaeria needs... what we lost long ago..."

She sped up through the path, carving a scorching impression right behind her — from the foot's heel, setting a trail among the vast grasslands. Over a slope, she came to a few hilltops that gave a clear sight of a Yarak pack scouting ahead. In high speed to cross through their camp, Xira was already heard manoeuvring about when a member shouted at full volume;

"Enemy presence! Presumably *Alpha Target*. Capture them!"

After alerting the crew with unloading armoury, the Yaraks bravely charged to catch her as she ran off from both pursuers. Evading left and right, Xira's whirling and somersaults led a swift flight by the sky projectiles that appeared in ice, hail, stone and magma. Leading the wind to her advantage, almost every fragment of munitions ricocheted off of the refined garment as she rushed onward to more Yaraks roaming the region.

"For Galaxaeria...! By the quest, all will be beckoned! Revolve to our plea!" The voices shouted from above.

With the ongoing chase and Xira's quick dodging moves, they'd eventually arrived at a rather round part of this region that stretched off into a hazy distance. The wheel in hand, she figured to turn these odds in her favour. Changing direction to circle the land in a looping stratagem, the projectiles were lured to a specified spot within the grounds, a means of landing each charge at that same point while the Yaraks stood back in their defence from being near and not quite equipped for various sky-fire.

Xira rolled in diagonal cuts as she sprung down the dirt and exclaimed, "This belongs to the realms. To the entirety of Galaxaeria! Never one or other being."

They responded, hurling down hunks which cracked the surface between the patch, *"Eternal cannot be matched... divinity is not only a light source, it resides within highest spheres. Hand in hand, child!"*

"It is not a solution for conflict... it ignites it. A power for one is balance to none! This stays right here!" She fired back, before additional barrages dug holes into the weathered ground.

The Yaraks took a retreating step once realising the events and braced themselves behind their own Yard barriers. As Xira observed the sequencing crevices, standing over its unsteady, chipping surface in a view of the effects reaching to its outer layers, she went for a leap to the skies and raised both grazed hands together. Darting below, she blazed through a vibrant echo into the depths, creating a pit by smashing to a low landing — a dark, dusty area of dismantled rocks and soil, between barren walls surrounding the point.

Removing the rubble from the fist print and smoothing out a soil patch, she formed a hideout for the cypher wheel before fitting it within and covering the top with what she could find around there. Among layers of roots and stones, Xira stacked the radius with boulders, carrying variables to anything in reach and placed them together to secure the wheel's position. Dusting herself off, she drew a breath as the skies lit up in fury over the crumbling exit. *X marks the spot,* she muttered under a huff. The cryptic voices boomed down the storm, where she readied herself before taking another leap outside the pit and using kicking motions, sealed its exterior with a light pile — applying one of the crystals to etch a muddy frame. Wiping her chin, Xira's focus redirected towards the mist ahead, continuing her escape as they followed the chase. Throughout consecutive slides and turns away from the relentless attacks, the path blazed on, leading the Yaraks to split ways before a meteoroid zipped down against her back — where she scraped into the soil a few metres along. Xira let out a guttural outcry, feeling a net trap her in position. The group hurried to surround as they activated its electro-pad and watched the voltage creep on its anchored web. Her hands pushing up to detach it, the sparks recoiled her to lay low before Xira began to gather an energy force that magnetised over every inch of the body. Tearing to the tips of the suit and outer flesh, a surge of arc flash radiated between the net, destroying its components upon the counter. Xira's silver glowing eyes flared out with a high exclamation as she quickly rose on foot and dashed off once again.

"Nowhere to hide, the skies see all," the voices then announced, *"A land so wide, mountains so high, an entity that treads every corner can only find the missing pieces that we keep secured. Wishes made in the dark light are the loudest ones."*

A flurry of cosmic projectiles were sent below, when Xira unsheathed the dual crystals and used them to deflect all oncoming segments. Apart from the adamant Yaraks and their particular gadgets, she knew they were unwilling to just let her flee. Aiming the crystallic blades to slash across each attempt to bring her down, Xira bounced from one foot to the other in the blazing flips and curls, to then spring through the swathing mist. Although slightly losing their trail among its cold obscurity, the land residing ahead was rather a mystery in essence and wonder of what would welcome their barging visit. Without much distraction for her personal stampede, she ran on among the wild valley and upon her approach, Xira could discern a quiet spout of water that became clearer the further she ventured through. All that was thrown landed in a thud beside her, even at the tip of the heel where emerged the blazing path. The juggling dissonance between the Yaraks and the voices from the sky came to a halt when Xira's flaring iris expanded a flaming wing on each side, clearing the way forth — with the glowing crystals by her waist, she sent out a windswept impulse that set the members far back across the grounds and static frequency up high which gave a moment of silent respite as she rushed on out of the mist.

Looking over to a lavish green landscape, she remarked in a breath, "Keep going... forward... doesn't matter... *forward.*"

As Xira ran through the damp, blooming environment, she could finally see the water flowing in hasty yet calming motions. The area next to this valley was connected by a tall barren cliff, followed by more craggy slopes all the way to the opposing tracks over a river. The utterance coming from the gloomy skies merged with the commands of the Yaraks, shouting at each other to reach her point before Xira discovered exactly what was over that verdant edge. Winds waved among a refreshing cataract, surrounded in its natural beauty and much like a hidden paradise, its flora framed the scene above and below this very region.

After they'd chanted something towards her, Xira's focus was already pinned on the new area. She exclaimed above the gusts, "This land deserves its freedom... like we do... everything is its own... that's the beauty of true happiness!"

A wave of wraith figures dove from the clouds and as they whirled down the way with the Yaraks approaching on her tail, carrying their high equipment, it'd presented in the likes of a haunt forged by old curses. Sprinting across the grounds, with melted bracers shining along the burnt glove stains, Xira sprung above and plunged herself into the water. The mist surrounded the top of the cliff, hiding any view beyond it and fractions of frosty flakes swooped along the night air. Where the place of quietude met a mysterious aura that encircled, a daring escape served as an answer, a way to the now protected realms of Galaxaeria and its orbiting truth for a better home. Although no person resided within this landscape, it was known about the whispers of the birds and gentle motions of plantation, that there's more than what is seen on the surface — a view, a secret, a question, a wonder. Through the day and through the night, no light was left unseen and when it was the darkest, one patiently learned to breathe in the hidden beauty and rise over any unsettling ominosity… becoming one with the light in the shadows and welcoming all of it for what is truly symbolised. Balance. The fusion of light and dark, the art of creation. What is all around. The truth, among land and skies, an infinite being in the universe and in the wildness of the spirit, comes to be akin to the wild realms. Be oneself, to be.

In the underworld of Rove Dynasty…

The clanging of cups by a table startled the mage as Menkos poured the tea for the two seated dynasts. Erma stood with both sleeves folded before her, bringing the garment around as an utterance was then heard calling to them.

"Care to enlighten me?" Was echoed through the open cave halls.

The enchantress replied, rolling her fingers along the cuffs, "Thy lordship… I bear my report on the mission, including… her. Once I found Xira, we opposed on the two sides of the wheel, *I* with my — your proposition. It was rather a challenge but I managed, of course. I brought her right before me, except… she vanished. Xira, with the cypher wheel, disappeared off into the mountains. I'm sure being at the very top would in fact be a hassle for the way down. Besides, she doesn't know its use like we do, Lord, for that I would not apologise… sincerely. We can set out on a new mission, I'll gladly perform, for you and the family."

"Assumptions… underestimations… did that end in triumph on your most recent pursuit, Merideth? It's clear that this disagreement is not a preferred cup of tea for either one of the dynasts, however, I think you and I both know the highs and lows of responsibility."

Where the others sat around the adorned table, a hovering capsule appeared before them as a fluorescent inlay traced its outer margins and beside it, a transparent charm revolved on a wand as it's placed — the form itself made of a whirly pearl compound in engraved refinements.

Oriented and at ease, Erma stood tall and broached, "Well, if I must recall, Peri was not in my hands. It *was* her own decision. Lord, my sister did not feel warm here because of beliefs. Again, out of my hands, she set out to figure a fresh vista and place for herself. Rove Dynasty and practically everybody else, did not fit what she personally required. That *is* partly my fault… I am a dynast, after all. Somebody who bears these powers beyond a need for a stranger's moral compass. That's what we've become. Sisters — to a painted apparition. I can't blame her for starting anew. Quite the contrary… out of that derail, we learned the unknown.

Therefore, you see? Darling… we both earned victory. How we use that in such endeavours, is entirely up to us. I like to imagine responsibility as a swing… to and fro… the winds will still blow, so long as you know the swing."

The low, booming voice then answered, *"You are correct… Erma. You are a dynast. Your sister, Peri, is not. Knowing the difference there, I'd suggest you take action that will benefit your position and the outcomes of the underworld. I'll be sure to inform my loyal dynasts of new objectives each will undertake — together. In concord, you will follow suit and do right, to present — while Rove Dynasty seeks out any discoveries, all that which is left. Should you defy, there is a warm alternative in place. Now, go on and find leisure with a fresh chalice at the table. Drink the tea while it is hot, Merideth."*

Around the high chairs resided the other two dynasts and Menkos, who was mesmerised by the capsule. Its emission highlighted a spot on one of the papers arranged alongside the items. As she sat down, reading the inscription, a flush of memories came back to the mage — as she folded her hands in front, dwelling on the floating capsule's evocation.

After a while later…

The river's stream coursed along her feet as Xira walked wearily on the soft terrain, observing the coating avalanche in the distance. With a gentle breeze sweeping through the way, a lift was apparent in the sky, as the stars came to view and a wave of cosmic light weaved itself through. Looking to her reflection, she could see the distorted scars were correlating with each strand of her hair. A palette that fused to the late-night ambience and the far coasting constellations. Amid the onward saunter, the pebbles on the other side of the river began to swerve and roll, joined by a coiling smog as it presented itself in human form. Wearing a draping mantle that dipped down the soil's edge, a man carrying a mage's rod then turned to greet. She inspected him between her forelocks.

"A wise decision, Xira," he said, synchronising his walk to hers, "Who will that satisfy, however? I don't suppose you remember that many are looking for it. Many want change. It is the value that keeps them in check."

"Who the hell are you?" She asked, her voice raspy.

The stranger fixed the collar of his hood and modestly replied,

"Mage the Third. You may refer to me as Ophintom. I mean you no peril but there are a few untold points. Take these fragments of myself for consideration... look at them hover around me. The decision made to alter, for betterment, is not always taken to apply. If it means for what we need and everything in relation, then wouldn't we figure it to be righteous? It's as ancient as the ancients themselves, lady."

Xira continued down the river, eyeing the revolving wraith forms that followed above him. The snowy covering inched to her feet beside the wafting air flakes through the travels.

She shot a dismissive glance when answering, "There's no need for *wheels*. The right to decide that is tainted. Call it what you like, but *nobody really* wants the best for Galaxaeria. They *all* want the best for *themselves*. Be the one in between and you'll find what is rarely discovered. Something old is not always something right."

The two went on towards the glimmering grasslands, where seen was the far rising dawn as the frosty flakes settled around her hair and the mage's garment. Xira walked ahead and dipped into the layers, its pieces kicking up to the knees. She briefly paused at a displaying flower by her side and the light breeze swayed its blooming petals within the greenery.

The mage remarked once again, "Whatever you admire then, Xira. I'm simply the messenger, albeit a dynast, wishing for reflection in a sea of antipathy by not being left behind as a lone exception. To what will these fires bring desire to...? To whom will the embers fall through... in the palms of their hands? Is that not what you claim a power too great for one, lone entity? That kind of leverage can alter the universe and young lady, it is no trial for any morally ambiguous judgement. Even a stone bridge will surrender to a misled wave, leaving its remains to the ones using it as shelter. The ones who were believing to cross it are taken aback on their former land. Such a burden... to sit with the shadows, meaning well to bring your honesty — but as everything is entwined to bear its realm, then I'd suggest a settlement would restore the fair orbit for all that inhabit. Like the sun, it will cover all that it sees... therefore the spirit that arises to the immortal power can take a moment and examine the surroundings. Remember, it's the same with the moon at night. A world of wonderful fusion, Xira, there is only so much to unearth."

Going on ahead, Xira spun in her answer, "It's my fire then, dynast. At least you chose yours and were taught efficiently, I would consider that lucky. Thing is, you don't get to decide about my own, that is where the fine, silver marking is found. Control is not the same as freedom. *That's* clouded for all of you — merely sheep in the crowd. Nobody seems to *really* know what paradise is, so, why should I bear the priceless, abandoned knowledge for all of your sake? Galaxaeria deserves what is good. You've brought us trouble, nothing honest by it and I made my own bag of promises. Fear me, fear me not — you decide, I'll perform. Fair?"

"It's fire among the wandering spirits, brought down by an eclipse from the shadow lights that carve the soil," the retreating mage uttered in a low but crisp tone, "I'll take to where I so belong. These relations are kept protected. Simply ask your own mentors. Ones around these parts. Catch you on a different riverbank, lady…"

Watching the dynast shift into his phantom form, she echoed out a reply, "Many things around here, out there and *many* of *you* are not as content with attuning. Focus on that, maybe… a homely visit can be put on the table. Send them my best regards."

Ophintom then lifted into a coiling vapour and disappeared off into the airspace. Xira, walking along after wiping herself using the river's fresh water, made a turn to the left and towards a crystallic field of snow fragments amidst its blooming flowers that shone in all their colours. As she sauntered through, a hidden force of spiritual energy slanted her to fall faint above the teeming grounds. Gentle rain of the flakes began to drip down soon after, where she lay between the dispersed blanket and the mellow sway of the flora petals. The sun's rays rose up with its beam flaring out and over the land, emphasising on the coat's surface and between the icy droplets, the morning wind coursed through the shadowy gaps.

Making their way towards the mountains after hearing that low rumble, the mirror that Serenitatem had been holding shot out one last guiding light before changing to its opaque exterior. As the mentor faced them with a clutch of the relic, Merlot noted the havoc within the skies that chained along to the right.

"It's up to us now, Aurora has done what she could," he declared, moving past him.

Hiding the mirror, Serenitatem warned, "We don't possess the protection she needs, Merlot. We need to stay vigilant, in her own mother we trust."

Once they walked further into the eclipsed environment, it was then that the quiet had settled again and clear to the eyes it was, as the clouds dissolved to the dawn's first light. Willow used the earpiece to follow an echo that was picked up from nearby and sensed an unusual presence, listening to a luring gut feeling took her to believe in the finding. Where the team trekked forth, amidst the sprinkling flakes and rustling effects, she hurried around the four in an opposite direction.

"I'll go! If Xira is somewhere there, I need to check it out myself," she said, holding onto her aviator hat, "You keep looking. I'll come back right away — it's best we remain close by!"

The two mentors called out in unison, "Be careful, *please*!"

Willow began to run to the sound's origin and although other outside noise intercepted with ones in proximity, she kept her focus to the distinctive channelling when coming to a dishevelled area — seeing her companion's body submerged within the verdant layers.

"Xira!" She shouted in an approach.

Still in a hazy slump, Willow picked up and hugged her as she knelt in front to the warmth. In the moments of calm and silence, Xira returned with an observance of her friend's muffled sobbing on a shoulder. Her eyes altered to their glistening brown and silver when she pulled to face Willow's startled reaction. The sun shone on Xira's relieved glance in discovering Willow by her — a relieved smile curved from the companion's sigh before they went in for another gripping hug, sinking their faces beside each other's arms and expressing in the while of their locked embrace.

Separating the hairs to see her marks, Willow spoke up, "Our guardian… you're home now."

Xira's gaze drew to the coating and its ambient mysticality as unfurling petals flung over the layers.

Willow continued, "With everything that went against, you gave all of yourself."

"A relic so great, just as mysterious. So I hid it. To keep it protected. It belongs to no one," her companion replied, thrilled by the frost.

"And it was the right decision. For all those bruises and scars… led you out, finally… I'm so glad. I was so scared… you knew who you were going after and still, after everything… you went all in. Goodness… for us. For home. Open arms await you, Xira."

The two bent up to stand as Willow raised to prop her beside herself, then began stepping through the meadow.

"I sacrificed what was always promised," expressed Xira rather calmly, "For home, exactly as I intended."

Willow gave a nod, "Galaxaeria is forever grateful, Xi."

The earpiece could pick up static frequencies from all around but their team's distinct voices cleared among splashes of water from other areas.

She slanted to her companion, with flakes that fell by the sash and a fond look towards her — then added, "Let's go find that peace of mind."

Walking forth between the beams and occasional animals that'd come out of hiding, the birds of this region whistled in tune of carefree flight — something that cast a mellow enlacement in the bright sky.

"Did you come alone?" Xira asked.

"I made sure to — the team watched my back though. They're waiting on us. They come bearing gifts," she explained with a wave.

Releasing a low sigh as she crossed the covering by the sunlight, Xira answered, "It almost feels like a festive welcoming…"

"With your mother, I'm sure it will be."

"…my mother?"

"Serenitatem brought this… mirror. Aurora… was with you," said Willow.

"Aurora… *hmm*…"

Following a brief quietude, Willow went on, "I thank her too, she watched your back when we couldn't. Wherever she is, her spirit wanders within Galaxaeria. You know, there's also a watcher for every guardian."

Xira then returned, "As all the spirits. I believe you."

They walked on along the way, where her companion leaned in to a warm, shoulder hug and both gently swayed. With the layers rubbing off by their garments as the two companions shuffled a verdant path to a journey on back, the gentle wind cruised behind them and whirled the floating flakes around the surface.

"*Through lightning and sunshine, we shall remain…*"

A while after they arrived, they discerned a row of figures in sight. Going closer, the man in front approached in clarity — jogging ahead when the girls figured the mentor's obvious relief in reuniting.

"Good gracious, you returned, Xira!" Serenitatem cried out, "My darling dear, it is absolutely wonderful... we were going forth to the mountains, together."

Merlot chimed in, "What went down out there?"

Tucking her hair back, Xira told them, "There's no need now. It's settled."

The former Yard members and their new allies, joined beside the mentors in the greeting. A pleasant look painted both faces upon seeing each other.

Serenitatem answered, "You can tell us about it... at our new home — only if you're willing."

Between a momentary thought and getting lost in the bewilderment of what was in fruition, a sense of solace was felt from within as a glimmering tear tore above her lower eyelid.

"Sure. I'd like that," standing a mere few feet apart, Xira then acknowledged, "Is everybody else safe?"

As he stepped forward to report, Merlot expressed, "They are. Oh, your mother smiles upon us all."

"She certainly is," added Serenitatem, "The mirror is all yours now, dear. I will walk you through on how to use it. You've done the unimaginable, Xira. I could see the ancestors, some of them which were, well, initially summoned to the land and hoping to finish their old war. Not the ones I remember learning from... I think they were wise not to intervene. However, they were never quite a match. No matter their attempts of a hunt, little did they know of the predator. We saw fire, it was like a charge for the ground... was that... you?"

She replied, rotating the mirror, "Hmm... yes. This fiery energy became me. Not sure of its origins. It was kind of... uh, a puzzle. They were ancestors? That sounds about right then... ugh."

"What's great doesn't always make sense," the mentor continued to say, "You channelled a height of your power, your true might as a protector. That's only a layer, but from what I've been told... from your hands, to your soul, you are infinite. Oh, a wonder, come to discover... hm. Shall we? Home is but a walking distance. Someone kindly prepared food for this evening. What do you say, sunflower?"

Curving her focus as Xira looked warmly towards, she walked alongside them and said, "I'm always ready, *Raptor*."

At the house, a lush floral path led the team to its adorned entrance as it read on a wooden display; '*Welcome*'.

Hurrying beside her, Sam reassured, "Honestly, Xira, we agree, we know *you* did not mean to harm us. It is forgiven, heck, it's the least we can give back, really."

Opening the door to a waft of vegetable aroma, someone was stirring a pot on the stove when he turned to the front. Xira, watching the man's expression become the likes of when one is freed from war, realised with a new item of clothing that sat on his shoulders — a déjà vu came to be before her, where her own mirroring awe was observing every outline and feature that hid within the memory. Running up to a clashing wrap of a hug, they exchanged their honesty at the sight of a reunited friendship.

"Old man, older bullet," Jay'eo said with an empathetic mien, "I'm home for good. Under The Yard I was no man, that place is for no man but a coward."

Xira replied, retracting the flared garment portions to her gadget belt, "You left no wound, Jay'eo. Since you came back, I'll ask for an explanation if that is comfortable enough."

"Of course... how I've missed you," he added, "Here, let's set the table for later. We can catch up in the meantime."

Shuffling past them, Jasper was seen hurling over a bag and a pair of binoculars in hand. He waved by the door where he'd begun putting on a pair of hiking shoes.

"It's great to see you all," Jasper announced, "I'm off to tend to a few matters... some vegetable picking and the sorts. Chat later, pumpkins!"

As the others prepared the decor, Serenitatem led Xira to a room where he fished a key to unlock it. Gesturing for her to enter, she turned with a questioning response upon seeing the companions stretch around a corner table by couches that encircled an embellished window.

"Use this room to contact your mother. Take this key and come out when you desire to," the mentor stated, "Lock or not, that is up to you, dear."

Inside, Xira sat on a cushioned sofa that was placed to a lampshade by opened drapes. Holding the mirror in front, she focused on its surface and uttered a chant in the Spirit Realm's olden language, that of which the mentor explained prior — bringing forth a translucent shine, pitched with whispers and effects of a channelled force. A spectre form appeared on its glazed glass, then a voice sung through as she felt it at the grip — every word and every wave that was pictured.

"*Xira...*" a pleased voice echoed, "*My light, my long-lost heart... I see you so vividly. Wonderful... you've warmed this very soul.*"

"Mother...?" She answered, tracing the visuals with her fingertips as her birthmark pulsed in a silver glow, "Quite fortunate you can recognise me, I wouldn't know it's you... not if they didn't tell me. Are you in the Spirit Realm?"

The mother's wistful reply emitted, "*It's a long, long tale my sunshine. There's something I can tell you and something you can solve for yourself. Only then can you really know where I am, for if... they hear a mere whisper, this mirror becomes useless. Write this down, perhaps... or if I recall correctly, my own daughter can memorise ever so effortlessly. I hear of what's been happening, seen the chaos that has taken to the lands... oh if I could lend a hand, although... I saw you, Xira. The one way I could, I offered guidance throughout your path. You did all the rough work, that is evident. There's no way I would not recognise my spirit child, even from beyond the farthest sphere, even if they'd taken you from me and... that will forever be marked within the mother.*"

Admiring in a tearful gaze as Xira huddled close to the mirror, she said, "I will walk any ground, climb any height, run down any land below and through it all, to discover every secret unknown. I swear. On my watch."

"*From your voice to the outer cosmos,*" Aurora told her, "*While I was cast to be inside this mirror, only the rightful might can set me free. I am not just at a location — without escaping the spell, only my spirit will be known there and that simply makes things difficult.*"

"Mother, my word is yours... unmistakably. Someone I can trust will take good care of the mirror. Never mind any mess, through all the dirt is where you find the gold."

Glass shimmered along Aurora's subtle smile as she uttered, "*Your mentors raised you well. I suppose I should share that you may recall a certain crash that occurred in Glacial Mist — well, you encountered that orb across many terrains... that, that was from me. Found a window, ahem... the clouded skies, oh a gift they'll find below surface in delight.*"

Xira reminisced and pondered when her mother continued with ardour. She also revealed more to her about the crystals and few secrets on her daughter that she could express without feeling like somebody was spying or even haunting — keeping it hush like folklore around an open campfire.

"*Everything else you shall find in magnificent travels, 'Solarouette'. Repeat only to yourself. The truth will only ever be in your hands and soul — between you and I, this remains. It was a wish come true to finally see you. Go on, relax in the new day that you've nourished... we will meet again soon, my love. I'll be watching — light with spirit, Xira.*"

Holding the lit mirror by its frames, a mellow laugh emitted of their joyous moment as she then replied, "Peace be with you... mother. We will."

"*As for you, sunshine.*"

Stepping out before closing the door, Xira went off to join them where she took a whiff of a freshly made salad in a wooden bowl. Jay'eo handed out some napkins and forks around.

"Dinner isn't quite done," he said, "If anyone's hungry, please indulge yourselves in these home-grown delicacies. Make room if you intend to eat supper, which follows the gourmet dish that will be devoured later on."

The group leaned about while exchanging tales and memories, each with their own private keepings like a hidden tree house in a forest of a grand maze — out of a stranger's way and means, back into the sincerity rarely shown yet always known. The burdening frowns now turn with joy, bringing on their truth to the surface once again. Soon as the sun had begun to set, they awaited with their noses and hungry bellies as a tray of cards was placed on the table.

"Can't believe you remembered this food hut we used to visit all those years ago," Xira curved a smile as she took a bite, "This lemon bread is still grand as ever — you nailed the recipe, man. Hey, Jay'eo, Here's some lime chips! His favourite."

Sam took a seat beside them and added, "So... this is what it's like, huh..."

"This is what it's like," Willow reaffirmed warmly.

The cards were arranged around the bowls when Xira tossed in an ornate hexagonal token.

"You can keep that, it's for good luck," She said, "A mentor gave it to me... I don't need it."

"Wow, thanks," Sam replied, picking up the piece, "... and please, thank them for me. I'm still getting used to the idea that they accepted me into this new home."

Fiske added beside him, taking a bread slice, "Yeah, a new home. We can start fresh and that's something we've been looking for ourselves for quite a while. Thank you."

With that, the friends sat around together through that rainy sunset, an evening surely to be cherished by them all. Merlot came by to join the round, rubbing his hands above the given cards.

"My patience finally paid off," He remarked, grinning, "Who is starting?"

Walking up from behind, Jasper tapped a hand over his right shoulder. A brief laugh jumped out when he bantered, "Better watch out, a handsome Treasure Hunter is on the loose."

"Why don't you join us, Jasper?" Willow asked.

"There's a supper task to be taken care of," he informed, turning towards the front door, "Enjoy your game, fellows. Guts empty for our delicious vegetable soup, should be ready to serve in a flash. Oh, by the way, *Xira*...? Can I please borrow you for a quick *errand*, outside?"

Getting up to go out, they closed the front entrance and walked on quietly down the pebbles where seen was a wrapped bundle of crates. Beside a hanging orange lantern by the door sat Jay'eo, on an old chair and played a mellow tune on his fine harmonica.

Jasper took in a breath and explained, "Look, I understand if this is not something we should bring into our hands, especially since most of us are inside that house. Truly... but I must tell you of what I've discovered. It's not for no reason, simply because we've already been involved with them."

"What is it, Jasper?"

"The Yard," he mentioned, looking around the atmospheric region, "Boats, ships, convoys... they're unfurling a plan, taking as much of the population as they can to a... far island. Its name, I don't know — I'm hoping to figure that out. Rumours I picked up from a pack of Yaraks earlier today, say that the Commander was seen with other faculty members. Most of the official members are left to scout the lands. Every neighbourhood is being cleared out and very few are wandering these streets. You can tell it's the back of their hand, a plan we would've dug out if — well, that's in the past and I don't think I would've done differently. Anyway, a good thing I found while I was pretty much eavesdropping, were these written notes and a thorough map of the area. Some etchings are rather smudged, yet I'm sure they can be deciphered. So… there's no indirect way to ask you this, but… would you do the honours? Help me shift their sails back to shore and retrieve what they've already taken. Should you accept, I'll be sorting some gears by that shed later tonight… it would really benefit us. No sweat if you walk the other way, I mean that."

Hair drawing with the wind, she aimed to the door, then angled to tell him, "As an offer or as a request… I do believe it's my hand at play. I'll see you inside, Jasper."

The cheerful distraction at the table raised a cosy bliss while they slammed turns, flung about some quips and treated themselves to homely canapés. The obscured sound of the harmonica slithered through the wall cracks, where Xira snuck into a room that was left with a stack of blankets and pillows. Looking around, Serenitatem walked by to inform her of the new room given for Willow and herself. It appeared as though they've decorated this place with a hopeful homecoming in mind — now a gift for use, for it withal satisfied the mentor's lone wish.

"Hang on, sorry… Xira," the mentor reached out, "I hope you know that you deserve all the best. It was never my intention to abandon you — leave you with such a responsibility. I wanted you to be in happiness. Keep you safe. Far from anybody's pollution… all of the befouled things. Our matters involved too many innocents, went in their way without any civil regard. Somebody needed to make things right… guess it runs in the family."

Xira stepped out into the hall and turned to reply, "Were you ever going to visit home?"

"Of course… I just needed to ensure that it would be a good decision before arranging to visit."

"Well… would've appreciated the company. Contact, even," she then added, standing by the door, "If I knew what was right under my nose, I could've used that to benefit. Always preferred not to be kept in the dark, Serenitatem. I'm willing to amend what we both lost, long as your beliefs follow suit. Mother still thinks of you all the same. She shouldn't lose that hope either. I want her to be in this home and as herself, given the chance she deserves. I know everyone will be good here. You will do right by heart. Forward for all, at last. This is what I wanted. You don't need to be afraid, you know. *Use that as fuel...* remember? *Peaceful harmony belongs with the lands and the families of all species. The truth is forever marked.*"

Serenitatem nodded in solemnity, "Good as wise, kid. I'll keep my promise, *do right by heart.* I believe in you, Xira. Ever since I held your little hand and witnessed an ethereal sight, it dawned on me that you were the key. Your birthmark was a cherished memory I kept a hidden secret. Oh, the power you bear. I enjoyed watching you become one with family... learning all about you. You'll always be our sunflower in my eyes dear."

Stepping into the new room, she answered, "You kept a lot of things secret. I don't regret being part of the family. Although, knowing me well, why did you trust in keeping me there? Many of them followed by example... leaving. Like you did."

The mentor expressed, "Dear... I'll be learning to be better from all my mistakes. You became an eternal child of the home, you will always be my answer for improvement. As for the family, the same applies. It was always you. That connection came full circle and you were the key."

"Hmm. There's a personal favour I want to ask for," said Xira, walking off, "Visit the Spirit Realm when you find a free moment. While you're there, greet Valin and Niko at their village, Bloom Core. It would mean a lot to me."

"For you, anything, sunflower."

"For mother as well."

She seated herself by the window sill, inspecting the blossoming garden as her companion's musical unwinding graced the fore. The mentor went off to the main area, by the clanging in the kitchen while the meals were being prepared, alongside its wafting aroma and the quiet down the hall. A moment later, there was a knock by the entrance frame, before Willow sat to oppose.

"Dinner will be out soon," she began to say, "you'll be joining us, right? They've made it from absolute scratch."

Xira mused, "Sure. I'm just enjoying the view."

"Oh... wow, wait — your bracelet. It's still intact, whereas these are welded onto your skin and suit. Huh, how?" She asked, feeling round the forearm.

"It's the crystals, my mother told me about it."

"I should've known, heh," Willow wrapped her palms over in appreciation, "It makes me happy that you two have caught up. You deserve to know the love meant for you. *Super mum*, hey? I bet she's just as great."

Glancing to her companion, Xira then replied, "She's quite a mystery. Few pieces settle in place, few left missing. Hmm. I guess that's the fun. You heard anything about the others?"

"Yeah! Apparently, they were invited to stay with us, fantastic, isn't it? All under a very cosy roof. After all we've been through..."

"After everything. You are still by my side, *through fire and water*," Xira expressed, putting the other hand atop hers.

"*Damn right* through fire and water," answered Willow heartily with a raised dimple beneath an eye, "There's nothing that derails me from walking the ice to the burning coal along my feet if it means going to you. You've been my soul friend since forever and now that we're back home, I know it was worth fighting for, there was light by the love. I would do it all again with you like a promise. I didn't stick my leg out years ago for no reason, you were using a dusty bike — that stays to you and so do I."

"All right, my girl has spoken," she said, "I always believed I'd find something so special and I did — like a sweet soul whisper. My favourite treasure found, you know. Why don't you go to the others now and I'll swing by a bit later? I can smell that cooking here."

Willow remarked in return, hopping back on foot, "Aye, aye. I'll make sure Jay'eo doesn't eat all the bonus treats, if his appetite is all the same though."

A little while later, Xira left to accompany the team back at the table, scoring a pen she'd been holding into a vase before crossing the hall. Seeing Jay'eo pouring the drinks, she offered to disperse them and jumped in for another round of *Caterpillar to Butterfly* — a game told by

Merlot himself, already familiar with the former allies.

Dealing the cards, the mentor announced, "There's room for everyone, so long as you're content with sharing. It seems like you all get along without throwing a swing in."

They played about and drank their beverages, bonding over the game and between their thorough enjoyment and relaxation, the team felt closer together than whenever apart — concurring that no matter their differences, they would elevate one another and stand for what is good, what is right, with courage to be themselves wholeheartedly, united. The cards flew in by each turn, for they scored a particular kind to match a power up — forming a round base which gave a win to all of the players as they cheered on.

"Here comes a batch of fresh goods!" Exclaimed Jasper, rolling crates in, "I can hear the grumbling guts from castle of Fairy Kingdom!"

The mentors placed bowls of hot soup alongside assorted utensils and they all feasted on the delightful dinner, occasionally peering out the window to take in the colours of the sky that soared across the grasslands.

"I'll chip in a *dime o' rose* card if Jay'eo can still fit a crumb down," Willow teased, slanting the fork, "Once I learn all of your appetites, it's game on game for yours truly…"

"Ah, my appetite is all the way into the ocean, but ice-cream would do," he said with a chuckle, "I'll bite — I can eat a marshmallow cup to digest more easily."

Xira's focus diverted to the whirling pot of soup before them as she fiddled the steel spoon and all background chatter mingled with the clattering objects, aside other noise within the vicinity.

"Say, Jasper… did you happen to come across Rosetta, Saffron and Ilari?" asked Willow, "They are coming here, yes? Unless Lunaris Town was the decision."

Jasper, gulping the remainders of his dish, informed, "Quite correct, dear. I made an effort to direct them here when I was gathering things for supper. Speaking of which, is there room left in your button bellies? Strawberry cream cake and cherry layers await."

Slice by slice, each of them received a sweet dessert that was sided with a mug of cocoa milk and mint leaves for the ones of particular taste buds.

As the moon rose along the many stars, the team soon gathered around for a warm and sweet night of supper, drink and conversation. Something that was entirely craved for, a friendly exchange once again, in the midst of the settling in, their much-needed refreshment and reminder of the joy that was missed for so long. All in the hands of the kind beholder, from one to the other, like a ring of truth among the new home. It was a new day, by the dawn's light and the winds of paradise, a fresh reform to a realm of life.

Serenitatem helped clean the table when he then stated, "*Food for one is food for all*. When you sweet children would like to set your rooms up, there are already given supplies that will be well useful and you may do what you please with the rest of this evening — I shall be in the studio if anybody comes looking. For now, I thank you all for today. For everything. Blessings to you all and a great, homely evening. Enjoy yourselves."

The team later took off to sort themselves out and hang around a while before tucking in for the night. A fireplace that was lit by the mentors provided for an easing repose, where Xira and Willow sat on the carpet floor. Two mugs of some chamomile tea placed between them and as the wood crackled, she looked to her companion fixing up the braid then putting on the aviator hat.

"Nice sash, did you make that yourself?" Xira asked in observation.

A hushed, chucking sigh, Willow then replied, "There was a kind shopkeeper we ran into back in Lunaris Town. After we helped her in a power outage, she told us to select what we desired for a thank-you gift. Perfect with the garment design."

"Well, that was generous," she said to her in a sip, "I would've brought back a souvenir if it weren't for others interested in a legendary relic. It was a grand view of things like these crystals. We could camp out sometime… maybe when everything settles down and I grab myself some new shoes."

"Important thing is, *you* came back *and* as yourself," Willow went on, replying, "All I wished was for you to return, Xi, anything else shiny comes second. Besides, camping out there to gather cool finds sounds a lot better than missing out on your expression every time you see a magical element by you. Wouldn't trade that for any world."

A pleased demeanour shone over on Xira as she reached out to hi-five and then wrapped her wrist along the steaming mugs in a lean of their grip.

"I'll always be beside you, Willow," remarked Xira, "Even when apart or together, know I am around. No *thing* comes between us… we are bonded by spirit. *That* is our energy."

In a kind exchange of the two companions, she knelt down to kiss the back of her hand before telling each other goodnight and going towards the room, Xira turned at a call as Willow sat up on the carpet.

"I'll make you some new gloves," she said, grabbing the mug, "Just the way you like them, Xi."

With a glimmering gaze, Xira added warmly, "Great. They're in good hands, then. Sweet dreams, Will."

As the cold of night fogged the moonlit window, she climbed out of the blankets to tidy up and set out to the front entrance. Pitch dark, Xira wrapped her hair in a dangling tail before stepping out into a gust. Over by the shed, Jasper was sorting out some tools in their boxes as he spun at her presence once realising a shadow near a wall.

"Oh, thank you for showing up dear," he stated, carrying a lantern, "Follow me. Way up yonder is where you'll be on the mark."

They arrived at a hilltop that led its tracks to a rocky tunnel in a vague view beyond. A strange hum buzzed by before echoing in a whirl around her. The area in front altered its image, although veiled with a misty web, to then play out a warping scene — soon it vanished to the former surroundings as Xira exhaled upon the light of the moon.

"Jasper, I know where to go," she told him, adjusting the belt rims, "I think I — I just envisioned this cave-like location by a shore… and what looked like a hideaway that was packed with equipment — all sorts of stuff, opening to lots of footprints in the sand. Go back home, you don't need to accompany me."

"Huh—all right, uh, as you say so," Jasper replied, pointing on out, "Be vigilant, as always. I'll keep it hush. Winds forth. Ok, see you soon, Xira."

Kicking up the dirt from behind her, she ran across an elevated ground and halted with a foot atop a cliff-side. On ahead, the seawater could be discerned in its waves, as Xira continued down the way and leaped into a low entrance. Inside the cave, she came across some tables covered in various files, all belonging to the Yard. Sifting through the paper and tools, a well elaborated layout of an unknown scheme appeared

— reading; "*Schema: The Buccaneer's Solitary Island*".

"Nothing but a ploy," Xira remarked quietly, skimming the inked text, "That island will be rid of its sanctity if the Yard set foot on it. What's this…?"

Picking up a map quite similar to the one she'd been given by Jasper, she aligned the two to match the markings placed at every point along the shore's site and to the island. From its perimeter onwards, no land was near besides the opposing, only shore which the boats were situated on.

"No man left behind," she said, placing down the maps again, "They won't cast them out like that. Their hunger is a void, possessive of things made by hand and land… resources which they rely on, without it, it becomes a no man's land."

As Xira rummaged about the belongings, a horn of a vehicle blared from below the cave's floor where the tires gliding in the sand made for a particular discernment. Hearing voices rising to clarity before the slamming of doors was joined with a machine's effect, she located a brisk escape through a narrow climb above her — disappearing soon as the visitors stepped inside.

Up on the far grounds, Xira ventured on towards a rocky cliff, scoping out the region before her. A scattered group of Yaraks and rogue trackers were scavenging the area below, oblivious of the ruins and misjudgements they've crossed. She pulled out the sling and unleashed the four last star-shooters, flinging in a row to crack down the stationed Yard lamps then whispered; *clear,* and re-attached the sling. A flare of cover thorns activated in place of the star-shooter compartments as a protective means to its shell. Taking in a breath of fresh air in the hushed effects of the waves, she emitted out a sigh. Her hair, flailing back, as she unsheathed the dual crystals and walked up to observe the surroundings — Xira crept to a knee and curved a boot on the edge with the other, placing both arms beside her as she eyed down a lone Yarak. The wintry wind drew by, her silver gaze lighting up as she leaped with the raised treasures through the dark sky, while the hues in her hair glowed under the moonlight… flaring with the crystallic blades in her grasp of the soldier.

"Out the shadows, come out the light," she uttered, disarming the Yarak, "Tell your friends I said hello."

She breezed around to the docked boats and observed the Yaraks who then turned towards their odd ally, approaching them with a gold glow between their fingertips. They raised a palm to the armed three, chanting a muffled song by the gentle wriggling of the fingers as their feet cruised over the sandy grounds, enwreathed on the combat shoes a lavender mist.

Meanwhile, in the morning rays through the window...

A soft blanket cuddled around Willow's shoulder as the curtains were noticed to be drawn either way of the glass structure. Raising in her stretch and fixing the bedding, she went off to retrieve a cup of herbal ginger tea. Apart from Merlot's kind greeting at the kitchen counter, the dining table appeared to be arranged with baked goods and a fruit bowl. Walking back, she saw a glimpse of Serenitatem and Jasper working together outside for the garden. Inside the room, Willow set her tea on the nightstand when she realised an envelope with her name written on it was left there. She traced the inked flower on the paper's corner and opened to folded pages of a letter.

Willow...

This is not a letter about me leaving. I want that to be the first thing mentioned. It's hard as it always is to be far from what you find hopeless to be without — guess I should emphasise... I am great alone... good with another... fair with a solid team. Sometimes, something will call, it's beyond a need for company to keep. I must answer, for the sake of what it could bring, what I can do about it. To be completely by myself, I think I need to on this one — I won't tell you where I'm going but believe that I will return. It's just a matter that needs resolving and yeah, I said my shoes are clean but there's an itch beneath my feet that tell me different. My thoughts race about hazards and conflicts that stain opposing walls, whereas my gut lures me to a special feeling of adventure. I'm more than what I started with, or at least, it was with me all along and now only came to be unleashed. For once, I trust the choice I've made for this and it's not something done lightly. It's the loudest thing occupying these thoughts. I wish I could show you just how much I don't want to stray again, though I hope I won't need to... it'll bite me back, that's for sure. You don't need to wait around, Xi Xi's got this by its sailor boots.

The others at home, call them family. I promise they'll be around with you and provide what you need. Truth is, a little birdy told me that more secrets and exploration await this "young lady". It's only right I go tip the scales, don't you agree? I hope you feel what I do, Will, about everything. Peace starts at home, then blooms wherever it can land and I'll make sure flowers grow each step of the way. I believe with who I am, I will only come to learn more, which soothes me that there is an answer to everything kept hidden, like the path that you make among lands, etching your details. From one spirit to another, always remember that neither of us are truly alone and that's about the wisest advice I can give to you right now. Please, if you ever come to a gloomy mood, talk to the skies through day or night — I'll listen.

There's so much more I can say here, but I'll try to keep it clean. Never a doubt goes by that you will do just fine, even on your own. I can be too protective sometimes, you've seen that, it's brought out the darker parts of me that you've willingly accepted and I'll always be grateful that my best friend wants <u>me</u> for all of <u>me</u>. You're as rare as they come — thank you, being beside me was almost never easy and despite it all, you rocked out their windows. Gave them something groovy to sing about.

One of my favourite sea shanties among the sea — you and I shall sing a howling, merry whistling harmony. We are to explore together soon on our adventures, on land and sky. Cosmic infinity! When you feel lost, look into my own treasure box. I hide the key inside the lamp shade, so I'm trusting you with the belongings. You'll find solace in there, even the way to contact mother — if ever desired.

Remember to turn on the light, as it needs warmth before unlocking it. Once it's fired up, all that's inside will grant your soul replenishment. You'll see what I mean. If you need a friend, if nobody is around, it's in there. Also, make sure to retrieve Merlot's old flute from the house when any of you can... it'll be great for him and Jay'eo to play as a duo once again. Before long, I'll see you by an overlook — we'll be running like lightning across the realms, discovering relics of a time ago.

Meanwhile, may the light and dark guide you safely. Look to the sun for clarity and the moon for comfort. Peace be with you, Willow. As always, with us both. Keep true to yourself and on the fun. This guardian watches with and over you, partner.

Love, Xira.

Bonus thing! Keep this bracelet for me, an addition to yours. Two elemental shields for two wrists.

Your grand outfit is complete, fellow birdy!

Gently clutching the pages to herself, Willow picked up the sliding bracelet and in a tearful lean to the front paper, she said, "I know..."

Sitting on the edge of the covers, she mused through as she adjusted the bracelet on the other hand, twirling about the crystals. Willow tucked the envelope beside the saucer, lifting the tea to her grip — holding both the cup and the delicate components of the bracelet.

Later, back at the shore...

"What are you doing, Wyatt?" asked a Yarak.

The soldier placed the hand on his associate as their uniform began to be smeared in the smooth substance. The others caught on immediately as they aimed their rifles to the pair.

One of them exclaimed, bewildered, "Step off! Know your duty and the protocol! You're either in or you're out."

Watcher in the realms, above the valleys far wide and long... Xira cut the ropes off of the pier, setting all of the other boats to float about the sea. She walked across to investigate towards the island, noticing a fair amount of the Yowndrift Yard troops scattered along with more boats, even on its shoreline. With the shimmering light illuminating the gentle waves where Xira looked on, she attached the crystals and relished the fresh, aquatic air, beyond lands that are home... high in adventure, to bring peace and restoration to the realms, by all means. The water splashed onto her feet, where its smear shone an alluring tone. Curious, she bowed to feel the wind which brought a sound from the sea. At the rims of the pier, the sound called to her. Seeing her reflection sway on the aquatic surface, she reached out with a foot when it connected with what she was hearing — a pleasant expression, from the sands to the sky. It sprung her forward, landing to a gliding position as the energies surrounded her and the rollerblading motions that carved waves among the path brightened up with the grace of spiritual ambience. With bliss and purity, Xira revelled upon the discovery throughout the glissade of ballet, a pirouette, the aqua refreshing beneath her feet and the energetic dancing with the wind. Her multihued display emitted forth as the water sprayed over the way, which landed a shimmery veneer on the garment and ethereal effect among the bright fusions. From the sway of the hair — summoned a halo ring around her position, as if flying from the sky and to dance with the aerosphere, hovering with charm and the beauty of her — a mystical ride over the sea, with the radiant halo travelling with the young woman's velocity as it orbited around, creating a vivid trail from her rollerblading effect. The energies sprung out like flying wings from it and over the sides and flaring-like cosmic rays of the magic elevated with her, as she launched onward in her sprint, and elegantly danced among the air and waves that splashed around the surface. Her gaze now toward the island, she charmed forth in the gliding — the spiritual elements with the refreshing spring, the light shining throughout — with an aurora that hinted across the vista, echoing the colourful print cruising underneath her tracks and the wind that sailed, leapt with Xira's cheerful, howling expression of her translucent palm to the sky appearing like crystalline-stars of cosmic energy — elevating to a sunny, spiritual swirling among the blossoming design, which she harmonised toward her planetary return in the air, as she dove underwater and out again, thrilled by the personal discoveries of her pure self. Beyond, Xira dashed over the aquatic scenery, blazing the honeyed path and journeyed to the adventurous mystery. A wonder found in Galaxaeria, and like a great arrow, always flying forward...

An epilogue, a four-leaf clover below a four-point constellation of the clear, encompassing sky...

The flowers fluttered between the grass, going up to a pebble-filled pathway. A recently placed garden post was embellished with two adjoined wreaths on its wooden corner. Sat beside on a low stool, Jay'eo played a mellow tune on his harmonica. In the dusk's cool zephyr, flames of a lit campfire crackled by a chair on the opposite side — where the sound of a flute fused in, from Merlot himself as the two expressed the calming ambience through their music. Alongside an idle barrow, Willow immersed herself in the rhythm, fiddling with a piece of wheat stalk as a smiling fore graced the companion. Soon after, accompanying Merlot on a stack of hay, Rosetta sat down next to the mentor and drank out of a foggy mug, completely warmed up to the family. With the rustling trees of the region and the quiet waters beyond its acre, the tune travelled throughout the blooming lands among an echo to its serene panorama. While Glacial Mist had truly been missed, they grew in the comfort of their new home. Although, this region was one of no name, the family had then decided that there was no better suited gift than the present. In accord with one another, to all cards on the table, they had named the town Aurora. By the harmonious ambience around and after a fresh day of exploring, they gathered as one with the whistling spring of the musical instruments. As family. Unified by a cosmic bond, of a spirit brought to the light.